THE

HARRIS FAMILY

RM JOHNSON

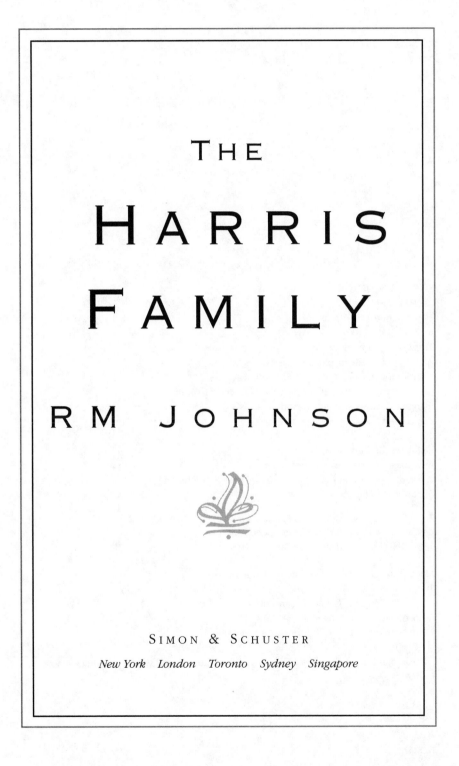

SIMON & SCHUSTER
New York London Toronto Sydney Singapore

SIMON & SCHUSTER
Rockefeller Center
1230 Avenue of the Americas
New York, NY 10020

For information about special discounts for bulk purchases,
please contact Simon & Schuster Special Sales:
1-800-456-6798 or business@simonandschuster.com

Manufactured in the United States of America
10 9 8 7 6 5 4 3 2 1
Library of Congress Cataloging-in-Publication Data
Johnson, R. M. (Rodney Marcus)
  The Harris Family / R.M. Johnson
    p. cm.
  1. Paternal deprivation—Fiction. 2. Fatherless families—Fiction. 3. Brothers—Fiction.
I. Title

  PS3560.O3834 H34 2001
  813'.54—dc21   2001041083
  ISBN 0-7432-1600-8

ACKNOWLEDGMENTS

Thanks to my editor, Geoffrey Kloske, and his assistant, Nicole Graev. You've once again aided me in making another of my novels the best it can be. Thanks to my agent, Warren Frazier. You're the best in the business. And of course, to my family and all my friends, thanks for being by my side. Couldn't have done this without you guys.

For A.G.U.

THE HARRIS FAMILY

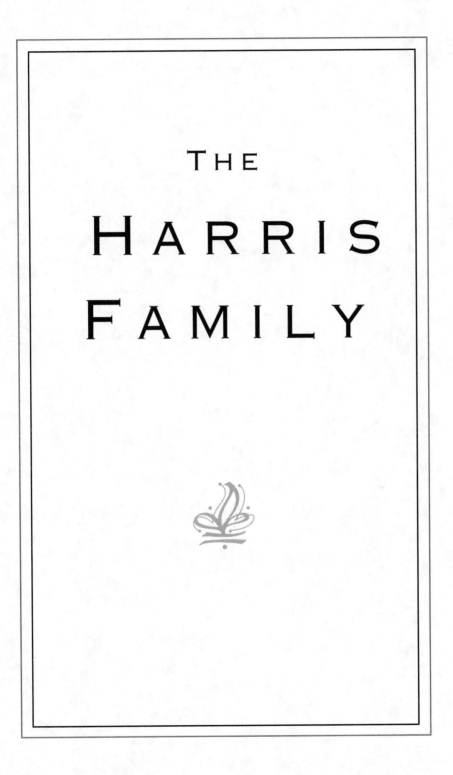

Julius Harris was exhausted as he sat in his car at eight in the morning. He hadn't gotten a full night's rest, and he felt awful. He reached forward, pulled the visor down to take a look at himself in the mirror, to see if he looked as bad as he felt.

What he saw was an unshaven, sixty-year-old man, who looked more like a one-hundred-year-old man. His hair was short and uncombed, dark circles hung under his tired, bloodshot eyes, and as he dropped his face in his hands, rubbing the graying stubble on it, he asked himself, Was he losing weight? Was he shedding pounds without even trying? He sank a thumb into the waist of the wrinkled trousers he'd pulled off the back of his bedroom chair that morning, and gave them a tug. He could've sworn he'd lost weight, but every time he asked his wife about it, she simply smiled and said that he was being ridiculous.

Julius left his pants alone, flipped the visor back into place, then looked toward the window. He smeared a circle in that foggy driver's-side window to reveal a fuzzy image of the small medical center across the street. He had a view of the parking lot, and as he focused his attention there, cars started to roll in.

He wished that he weren't alone at that moment, wished that he could reach across the car and feel his wife, take her hand, and gain strength from her, as he was used to doing. Cathy had wanted to come with him, begged him to let her come, but he wouldn't do that to her again.

He remembered five years ago when they'd last come to see this doctor, she was destroyed sitting there beside him in the doctor's office. He could practically feel the life leave her, her body falling limp in his arms after they had received the news. Julius had decided he couldn't subject her to something like that again, and he knew that would be the kind of news the doctor would have for him.

"The cancer is back, and it is more aggressive than ever before," the doctor would tell Julius. He wouldn't even have to run any tests, because he'd be able to see it seeping out of Julius's pores, his posture weakened by the damage the disease had already done to his bones.

Julius brought his face nearer to the window, his attention caught by a silver Jaguar slowly pulling into the parking lot. He watched it as it took the closest space to the building. The driver's-side door opened, a foot was placed on the pavement, and a man stepped out, a thin, graying man with glasses.

Julius, his eyes narrowing, recognized him immediately. It was the doctor, his doctor. His doctor popped open an umbrella over his head and took casual steps toward the building, as if it weren't raining at all.

With that, Julius reached across the passenger seat, picked up his umbrella, and made his way out into the rain himself. The clouds drenched everything under them, sending down a perpetual sheet of rain on the city. Julius dodged through the cars that skimmed across the rain-slick street, stopping once to avoid getting splashed by a wave of water thrust toward him by a passing car.

Julius saw the doctor disappear behind the tinted, double doors of the building, which made him pick up his pace. He took the stairs as fast as he could, pulled the door to the building open, and ducked inside, his umbrella still open, dripping rain onto the dark carpet. The waiting room was filled with patients, most of them older, their bodies naturally deformed by age, silver sprouting from their heads, sad expressions on their faces. A TV droned on, mounted high in a corner of the room, no doubt there to take the patients' minds away from their illnesses and how long it would be before they could see the doctor, just so he could go about putting their illnesses back on their minds.

Julius looked left, then quickly right, and saw his doctor disappear behind the door of his office. He walked briskly after him, almost running, but was halted by a young, thin receptionist. She got up and leaned over her desk just a bit, as if to reach out and snag Julius by his collar and yank him back if he continued to move in the direction of the doctor's office.

"Sir, can I help you?" she said in a tone that actually said, "You can't go back there."

"Yes, I'm here to see Dr. Phillips," Julius said, not looking at the receptionist, but at the closed office door, as if he was afraid the doctor was slipping out the office window as they spoke.

"Okay, yes, fine," the woman said, pulling a scheduling book in front of her, keeping an eye on Julius.

"And your name, sir?" she said, her finger resting at the top of the page.

"Mr. Harris," Julius said.

It only took her a moment, to say, "I'm sorry, sir, but I don't see your name on the list. Are you sure it wasn't for another day?"

"I don't have an appointment," Julius said, now giving his attention to her, "but I still have to see Dr. Phillips."

"I'm sorry, Mr. Harris, but all these people have to see him, too, and they *do* have appointments."

Julius looked over his shoulder at the half dozen people sitting in the chairs behind him. Their eyes were on him, as if they had been listening to his conversation with this woman since he'd started it. He sympathized with them, but his case was more important than theirs. At least it was to him, and that was all that mattered.

Julius turned, placed both palms on the woman's desk, and leaned into her, speaking softly.

"I understand what you're saying, but I really must see Dr. Phillips today," and Julius even gave her a little smile after his request, thinking it might make some bit of difference.

The dark-haired woman looked up at him from behind her glasses and said, "I'm sorry, Mr. . . . ."

"Your sorrow does nothing for me!" Julius said, pounding the desk angrily, sending a tremor through her Garfield and Odie trinkets, making them do a little dance, then fall to their sides, playing dead. "I have to see him now. Please!" Julius said, softening his tone, trying to appeal to this woman.

The receptionist stared at Julius sympathetically for a moment, then

said, "Hold on. Let me see what I can do." She picked up the phone, dialed the doctor's office.

"Dr. Phillips, there is a Mr. Harris out here to see you. No, he doesn't
have an appointment, but I believe you might want to see him . . .
Okay . . . yes . . . all right," she said, all the while looking at Julius. Then
she hung up the phone.

"He'll be right out to see you, Mr. Harris," the receptionist said,
smiling.

"Thank you," Julius said, softly.

A moment later, the doctor's office door opened, and Julius turned to
face that direction, watched his doctor walk down the short hall toward
him, a phony little smile pasted across his face, which Julius knew was
meant to appease him long enough to get him out of there.

His hand was outstretched, and his demeanor seemed more that of a
car salesman than a man of medicine. "Good morning." He grinned.
"Mr. . . ." and he looked down briefly to his receptionist, who said softly,
"Harris."

"Good morning, Mr. Harris," the doctor said again, keeping his hand
out for Julius to shake. Julius stared down at the man's hand as if he had
just yanked it out of his ass. The doctor lowered his hand, his smile
shrinking a bit with the movement.

"What seems to be the problem?"

Julius stood in front of the man, expecting to see something in his
eyes, a glint of recognition, something. But there was nothing. Julius
was a total stranger to him. But Julius didn't care that it had been five
years since he had last seen this man. He should know me, he
thought.

"I need to speak to you," Julius said, then turned to see that he still
had the attention of every patient in the waiting room. "In private."

"I'm sorry, Mr. Harris, but as Susie told you, you'll have to make an
appointment."

"I don't need an appointment for what I have to say," Julius said, and
now he was speaking loud enough for the oldest and deafest man in the
room to hear him.

"I am a patient of yours, and you misdiagnosed me, filling me with a
lot of pain, anger, and fear, telling me I was going to die a long time
ago, when anyone can see that I'm still living." Julius turned to the waiting room, as if it held a jury, and he was an attorney making a case.

"And considering that, I'm wondering how many other people you've given false information to, causing them to . . ."

Before he could finish, Julius was led quickly by the arm into Dr. Phillips's office. The door was shut behind them.

"Who are you, and what the hell do you think you are doing?" the doctor said angrily.

"You know my name. Susie told it to you, remember," Julius said, sarcastically.

"And?" the doctor said, bewildered.

"You don't know who I am?"

"No."

"I was a patient of yours."

"I have hundreds of patients," the doctor said, on the verge of erupting.

"Look at me, Dr. Phillips. Take a long look," Julius said, and the doctor did that, but Julius saw that the doctor was still clueless.

"Maybe this will help you." Julius took a seat in one of the chairs in front of the desk, the same chair he'd sat in when he was diagnosed with cancer five years ago.

"Now look at me."

"That still doesn't . . ."

"Five years ago, I sat here with a woman. You came in here, pulled open a file, and from that file, you casually told me that . . ." but Julius stopped talking, because he could see the doctor's eyes grow round with recollection.

"I told you that you had terminal cancer, and only one year to live," the doctor said slowly, softly, as if he had made this realization all by himself. "I expected that you would be . . ."

"Dead," Julius said, finishing for him.

After an exhausting battery of all-day testing, including a thorough physical, blood work, and CAT scan, Julius returned the following morning. He was sitting in the exact chair he'd sat in the day before, the exact chair he'd sat in the day he was diagnosed five years before. This thought all of a sudden crept into his head, and he was overcome by a need to get out of that seat. He quickly leapt out of it and sat in the one next to it. Not that he was superstitious, but something told him, had been telling him, that he would need all the help he could get on this one.

Dr. Phillips was not in the office. He had gone out to gather all the test results, so they could find out exactly what was going on. He was a lot more caring than he had been early yesterday morning, Julius noticed. He was a lot more willing to listen, and willing to do whatever it took to get to the bottom of this huge mystery.

The change had happened the day before, just after the doctor realized that he was staring at what he thought should have been a dead man.

"Why didn't you come in here sooner?" he asked, astonishment on his face. "And what makes you finally come in now?"

"The chemotherapy I had didn't work. It just made me sick, just made my hair fall out, and made me think that what was supposed to be the cure would kill me before the disease did. And then the radiation therapy was embarrassing and demeaning, but I told myself I'd be willing to endure almost anything, just to have a shot at my life."

"But if you remember," the doctor said, taking his glasses from his face, "I told you your cancer was terminal. I told you that there was a very slim chance that you would respond to any treatment, but you insisted, so I allowed you to follow that route."

"Well, you were right," Julius said, swallowing some pride. "It didn't seem to work, and I decided I wouldn't make any more efforts to cure myself, nor would I continue to think about it killing me. I just gave up all together. But then, for some reason, when I went to bed at night, I just kept on waking up in the morning. After a while, I didn't have any pain. As a matter of fact, I felt like I was in perfect health. Sure, every now and then I'd get a muscle ache or a runny nose, but it was gone the following day."

"But now?" Dr. Phillips asked, sensing there was more.

"But now I have this cold, this fever, and I've just been feeling like hell for the past two weeks, and I can't seem to shake it. I'm worried it's the cancer again," Julius said, sadly looking down at his folded hands.

"Well, we'll find out what's going on, one way or the other," the doctor said, walking over to him, laying a reassuring hand on his shoulder. "We'll get to the bottom of this."

⚜

Now here was Dr. Phillips standing just inside the door with a manila folder in his hands. There seemed to be no emotions on his face, and if there was one, it was of a man making an effort to hide the true expressions he was actually feeling.

He took soft, cautious steps across the thinly carpeted floor, holding the file in his hands very gently, as if he were carrying Julius's life, and if it slipped out, the man before him would perish that very moment.

Dr. Phillips sat on the edge of his desk in front of Julius, setting the file down gently beside him. "We have the results now. They're right here in this file, Julius."

He had started calling him Julius. He had never done that before, and Julius suspected it was because he feared Julius would tell his patients about the major fuck-up the doctor had made in his diagnosis. Or could it be that he was just a nice guy after all, and he truly wanted to make Julius feel more comfortable, considering all he was going through? He didn't know, and really, it didn't make much difference what the motivation was, because it did make him feel better, as if he weren't in this all by himself.

"I went over them quite a few times to make sure, that's what took me so long. I even called over to the lab, to make sure these were the right results, and not anybody else's."

And now Julius was on the verge of a breakdown. He could feel himself becoming anxious, could feel a cold chill shoot through his spine and a flame ignite at his brow. The results in that file were probably so bad the doctor couldn't believe it. The doctor couldn't believe that a man who was so filled with cancer could actually walk into his office, not aided by a wheelchair or a stretcher, let alone raise enough hell to cause a scene in the waiting room.

"I called and verified everything. Twice. Even went to look at your CAT scan myself," Dr. Phillips said, picking up the folder and letting it fall open, the flaps of either side draping across his open palm.

This was it, Julius thought. He was staring at the doctor as if he were death, as if he had the ability to take his life right there, and even though that was not the case, even though he was just the deliverer of the news, Julius still feared for his existence. So much so that his heart stopped right there, or at least it felt as though it did, because there seemed to be nothing happening within him. His legs, arms, were numb, not his own, and all he could do was close his eyes and listen as the doctor spoke.

"The tests show that your cancer seems to be in remission."

Julius felt as if all of a sudden his heart started beating again, and then he slowly opened his eyes. "What did you say to me?"

A long, thin smile lengthened across the doctor's face.

"We can't seem to detect any trace of cancer throughout your entire body. How does that sound?"

Julius wanted to jump from his chair, leap into that man's arms, and kiss him. How did that sound? All the bad things Julius ever thought or said about this man, he was taking back at that very moment.

Julius took the doctor's hand, and pumped it vigorously, thanking him over and over again. They both smiled and laughed, and then Julius said, "But what about how I'm feeling? That's not the cancer?"

"I'm afraid that's just a case of this persistent flu that's going around. I'll give you some antibiotics for it, and you should be better in a few days."

"But how could this have happened? You said then that the cancer had invaded other parts of my body, my spine, my pelvis, and now you say it's gone?"

"It may have been that you had a delayed response to all the treatment you received. Or, even in rare cases, people with advanced cancer may experience spontaneous remission."

"So what does that mean? I'm cured?"

"No. I don't think we can say that yet."

"But you said you couldn't find any of the cancer."

"I know, but . . ."

Julius grabbed the doctor's hand and shook it, cutting him off from what he was about to say. "I want to thank you for everything," Julius said, smiling. "I'll be seeing you," and then he was turning toward the door.

"Hold it, where are you going?"

"No more cancer. I'm going home to my wife."

"Julius, a remission means the cancer may only be gone right now. There could be a single cell lurking that may cause the cancer to come back. You need to come back for scheduled checkups."

Julius walked back toward the doctor, a sly smile on his face, shaking his head, waving his finger. "No, no, Doc. Last time I came back for one of your checkups, you cut the amount of time I had left in half. Don't take this personally, but I've managed to live an additional five years staying away from you, so I think I'll just continue what I've been doing."

Dr. Phillips was smiling again, obviously happy for the man, regardless of what route he chose to take. "Please, just come in every so often just for a blood test?"

Julius smiled with his doctor. "Sure. I can do that."

Julius didn't go home right away to give his wife, Cathy, the news, even though the thought crossed his mind as he drove away from the medical center, a smile on his face, a feeling of rebirth in his heart. He wanted to be alone with that feeling, wanted to fully thank whoever, or whatever, it was who had given him back his life.

He ended up at the ocean. It was where he went when he needed time to himself, when his thoughts got too jumbled and twisted in his head. This was the place he could let them all out onto the water's surface, and let the waves carry them away from him.

He was sitting, his legs crossed, on one of the large rocks that bordered the water. The gray clouds had cleared, allowing the brightness of the sun to cast down upon him. He lifted his face to feel its warmth, and thought of all the days like this before him. He looked at the water, then closed his eyes, breathed deeply, exhaled, and with that breath came the words, "Thank you."

For so many years, he had not known how much time he actually had to live, did not know if he would drop dead while having dinner, his face landing in his bowl of soup while in mid-conversation with his wife. But now, with this clean bill of health, he felt like a normal person, felt the way he had before he even had cancer, as though he could start living again, start making plans to do something next year, or two years from now. That was something he had never done over the past five years. And when Cathy asked about going on vacation, or commented on a holiday, or his birthday when it was more than a month away, he'd just turn a deaf ear to the idea, because he knew there was every likelihood that he would not be there to celebrate it.

Now things are different, he thought, the huge smile still on his face. But then another thought crept into his mind that made the smile start to disappear. Why had he gotten the cancer in the first place? He knew then, had always known, that it was a punishment for abandoning his

wife and three sons twenty-five years ago. He had known that the moment the doctor had told him, and, although devastated, he hadn't been
all that surprised, because he was expecting something terrible to happen to him, he just didn't know what. That moment, sitting there in that
chair, receiving the news that he would die soon, he realized what a
grave mistake he had made, never contacting his sons after leaving
them so long ago.

So at that moment, he had decided to change that. Yes, he knew that
it was only fear that motivated his actions, that his sons would see that,
recognize the coward that he was, searching them out only because he
didn't want to die alone. But he would make the attempt.

He'd flown to Chicago and located his sons. "Who in the hell cares
that you're dying!" he'd figured his sons would say if he'd told them
about the disease. But the main reason he hadn't told them was because
he hadn't wanted them to take him back just because they felt pity for
him. So he'd kept his illness a secret.

He'd gone to them asking them to take him back, telling them that he
was sorry for ever leaving them, but they'd denied him, both his middle
son, Marcus, and the eldest, Austin. Marcus had grown to hate Julius by
that point, and Julius could understand why. On the other hand, Julius
knew Austin would've taken him back had it not been for Marcus, for
they had always been close, but he chose not to betray his brother's
feelings, rejecting his father as Marcus did.

So there would be no life with his two oldest sons, but he had one
son left, Caleb. The son he had never had time to build much of a bond
with, for he was so young when Julius had left. The son who, by talking with his other sons, Julius had found out, also hated him passionately. But Julius would go to him, he decided. He would go to him
groveling, asking for his forgiveness. It was his last hope, and his decision to do that changed his life.

Now, Julius looked down at his hands, and there lay an envelope, one
deep crease in the middle where it had been folded so he could carry it
in his shirt pocket, where it had been since he'd received it two days
ago. The letter had been sent from Joliet Prison in Illinois.

⚜

Julius remembered being there more than four years prior, in that state prison, seeing his youngest son, now thirty-two years old, behind that thick penitentiary glass. It was his fault, he told himself. His fault his son was there, because Julius had abandoned him, left him without someone to keep him from making the mistakes that landed him behind bars.

He wanted to make that up to his son, needed to be reunited with him before he took his last breath. Because Julius was now desperate, he decided to tell Caleb of his illness, that he would be dying within a year, and of his need to redeem himself for abandoning him.

"Is there anything I can do for you, get for you, son?" Julius asked, looking at his son through the thick prison glass, speaking to him over a phone.

"I don't need anything from you."

"But what about your son?"

Caleb's girlfriend, Sonya, and their son, Jahlil, were left now without a man in their lives, the man that Julius knew Jahlil so desperately needed. He would not allow what happened to Caleb to happen to Caleb's son. In an attempt to make some kind of connection with Caleb, Julius promised he would take care of Sonya and Jahlil while Caleb was in prison. He would move them out to California, where he lived, allow them to live with him, and care for them till Caleb was free.

"But in return for caring for them, I want us to have a relationship. I want to write you, and have you write me back. I want you to know that you have someone out there thinking about you, waiting till you get out. Someone that loves you."

Julius knew it was a lot to ask of his son, considering he had not seen him in twenty-five years, knew the painful feelings that his son was harboring. But Caleb accepted not because he cared to have a relationship with his father, but because he was desperate, because he was thinking of the welfare of his girlfriend and child.

"I think Sonya will wait for you," Julius said, before he left, not knowing if he truly believed the words that were coming from his mouth. But it was what his son needed to hear, and Julius vowed to himself at that moment that he would try his best to keep Caleb's family intact for him for when he returned.

But after two years, Sonya wanted to leave. She said she couldn't take the restrictions, the feeling that she was being held prisoner until Caleb was released, so she packed her things, and Julius's grandson, and left.

As Julius stood in the front of his driveway, watching the cab pull away, carrying Sonya and Jahlil to a place he did not know, he realized just how much this would hurt his son Caleb. This would take whatever desire he had to make it out of prison away from him. This would make him want to roll over and die, and Julius would not allow that to happen.

Even after Sonya moved away, the letters continued coming from Joliet Prison as they had every week. One letter for Julius, one for Sonya. Julius responded to his letters as he had every week since he had visited his son. Julius knew the letters he wrote his son gave him strength, told him to endure, that his father loved him, and that if there was anything his son needed, he would do everything in his power to get it to him.

Although bumpy at first, Julius and Caleb managed to build quite a relationship through those letters, and Julius could feel his son developing a dependence upon him. In the sixth month of letter writing, Caleb started asking questions about his father's health. How was he feeling, when was the last time he had seen the doctor?

Julius wrote him back, telling him he was done with the doctor, that there was nothing the doctor could do for him any longer. And when Julius received Caleb's reply, he could feel Caleb's anger and disappointment through the words on the page.

They screamed of his concern for his child: "Who will take care of Jahlil?" Of his worry for his girlfriend: "And where will Sonya live?" And finally, of his feelings for his father. "You have to keep seeing the doctor to make sure you're okay. I don't want to lose you if I don't have to. Please, Dad, go see him."

Julius had sat in his den, reading that letter, a small lamp burning a dim circle of light in the blackness, as he stared down at it. He held it in both his trembling hands, his eyes concentrating on the word "Dad." This was the first time his son had called him that, and even though it was written and not said, it held just as much meaning. Julius had his son back, at least one of them, and the boy cared, truly cared, about what would happen to him.

Julius had opened his desk drawer, pulled a blank sheet of paper out, and started to write on it.

Dear son,
You no longer need to worry about my health. I will be here for you.
No matter what, I'll be here for you when you get out. That I promise.

It was the only thing he wrote on the page. He stuck it in an envelope and mailed it that evening.

After Sonya had left, her letters from Caleb piled up on the table in the hallway, right near the front door.

"You have to tell him that Sonya is gone," Cathy said, standing over the letters, speaking softly, as if the words in the letters Caleb wrote could somehow allow him to hear what was being said.

"And what good would that do? There's nothing he can do about it, and all it would manage to do is drive him crazy. I can't tell him."

"So you just want to keep him in the dark, let him think that everything is the same?"

Julius nodded his head, ashamed, for there was no other course he could take.

Cathy picked up the letters, stuck the nail of her thumb in the top of one, and started to rip it open.

"What are you doing?" Julius said, rushing to her, trying to take the letter.

"I'm going to write him back."

"But you can't do that."

"You said you want him to think everything is the same. I'll pretend it's Sonya writing the letters. Unless you want to tell him the truth."

"No," Julius said, helpless. "But what if she writes him from wherever she's living now?"

"She won't do that. If she meant what she told me, she never wants to speak or hear mention of Caleb again."

So now, still sitting on the rocks of the ocean, Julius pulled his son's letter from the creased envelope, his eyes dropping down to the bottom, and read the final paragraph.

> *Thanks for the plane ticket you sent me. I'll be released next week, so I'll be there soon. I can't wait to see you, Sonya, and my son.*
>
> > *Love,*
> > *Caleb*

Next week, Julius thought, folding the letter and smoothing his fingers across the crease. The letter had come two days before, and it had probably taken three or four days to get there. He quickly added the days and realized that, give or take a day, his son could very well be getting released that very moment. How would he go about telling his son that he had lost his family? After thinking a long moment, he realized there was no way other than to tell him the truth, and although he could risk fracturing, if not breaking, the fragile relationship they had built, he would tell him.

2

"Get down!" Caleb yelled, and quickly Blue turned to see the barrel of the store owner's shotgun staring him in the eyes. With that, Blue threw himself to the floor. Ray Ray spun around, his eyes ballooned, turning his gun as quickly as he could, trying to shoot the man before he was shot himself. But before he had the gun swung halfway in the direction of the man, the deafening explosion from the shotgun was heard.

Caleb closed his eyes now, trying not to think about what had happened to him and his two friends when they attempted to rob a convenience store five years ago. Caleb was twenty-seven then, and had lost his job, was months behind on his rent, and he and his family were on the verge of getting evicted. He would've done anything in his power to stop that from happening. Not only because he didn't want to see his family homeless but because he had been trying to prove to Sonya that he was capable of taking care of her and their child, after he had failed on a number of previous occasions, by losing countless jobs and by getting into trouble. So if he failed them once again, he would be proving that he was unable to provide for them, and if that happened, Sonya assured him that she would leave and take their son with her.

"We do this one time, Caleb," Blue said, grabbing Caleb by the shoulder, his blue-black face frowning seriously. "We go in, get your money, and be out."

Caleb wanted no part of it. What if something went wrong? What if they got caught? He would lose Sonya for sure. And it was as if Blue was reading his mind, because he said, "If you don't get this rent, Sonya gonna leave you anyway." Caleb looked over at the corner of the room where Ray Ray was sitting, lazily pulling an Afro comb through his long hair. He nodded his head in agreement with what Blue said. Going to his brothers for the money was out of the question, because that would just prove once again that he wasn't able to provide for himself. So this seemed the only way.

But it had all gone wrong, and now, five years later, Caleb closed his eyes, and tried to block the images of that day out of his mind. But he could not rid himself of the painful memory, could not pull himself away from the awful grip the past had on him. He was forced to relive that moment.

After the shots were heard, the bullets sped across the room, finding their way into the soft flesh of Ray Ray's heavy body, into his chest, where there they exploded, tearing through him, sending him crashing into a wall of shelves. His body slowly slid down the shelves, a trail of his bloody insides dripping down over his head.

Blue ran to Ray Ray, stood over his large body a moment, shocked. He quickly, nervously, scanned the area, looking around him, as if there would be something lying about he could use to save his friend's life. Finding nothing, he fell to his knees and took his injured friend's head in his hands.

Ray Ray's chest was torn, blood, lungs, and shattered fragments of his ribs seeping from the wound, as he lay there twisted in the corner of the store's floor. Blue started frantically slapping his cheek, trying to keep him from slipping into death. And Ray Ray was trying not to go there, trying to fight death from taking him. He whipped his head about, his eyes wide, whirling about in his head, as if he was expecting to see the paramedics burst the door open, or Caleb fall to his knees and start CPR, or whatever people do to save the lives of people who have been ripped open by shotgun fire.

But no one would be coming to save Ray Ray, Caleb thought as he stood over him watching him bleed. Ray Ray kept on struggling, his eyes still darting about in his head, as he gagged, choked, and puked up the bloody, meaty insides of his stomach. And Blue was still there, the mess rolling over his hand and arm. "You ain't gonna fucking die. You hear me!"

But Ray Ray was dying, and Caleb knew that. Still, Ray was trying to fight his injury, as if he thought he could control the amount of blood he lost. But he couldn't, because it was flowing out of the huge wound in his chest now, saturating his shirt, the dark jelly syrup–looking stain getting bigger and bigger, like a pancake just poured onto a hot skillet.

"We gonna get you out of here. You hear me? You hear me!" Blue shouted, seeming frightened that Ray didn't hear him, might have died since his eyes had fallen closed. Then Blue grabbed Ray Ray's cheeks, shaking him, inadvertently forcing a huge quantity of blood and vomit out of his mouth. Ray Ray's eyes opened slowly, but they opened. And he smiled, a sick, helpless, sad smile, as if he was hearing what Blue was telling him, and trying to believe him, but couldn't. Then tears welled up in his eyes and started to fall, and at that moment, Caleb knew that Ray Ray realized that he was going to die, that everything was clear to him now, and he was more frightened than he had ever been in his life. Blue must have sensed that Ray Ray had come to that realization, because Blue crawled up under him more, took him securely in his arms, and rocked him a little harder. He spoke just a little louder, but not just so Ray Ray could hear him over the chaos that had to be going on in his head. He was also speaking louder to drown out the sirens that suddenly seemed to be coming from everywhere, and because he knew Caleb would say they needed to run.

"Blue," Caleb said softly, but forcefully.

"We ain't fucking leaving him!" Blue yelled, rocking Ray Ray more, like a mother rocking her slain child.

"We gotta go! The pigs are gonna be here any minute. We can't stay."

"We can't leave him!" Blue said, and tears were running down his shiny black face now. "That ain't right!"

Caleb spun in a nervous, frustrated circle, expecting the cops to burst in through the windows and doors any minute, waving guns, shouting for everyone to get on the floor. There was nothing they could do but get the hell out of there.

"Blue, he's going to die, if he ain't dead already. Now get the fuck up!" Caleb grabbed Blue under the armpits and pulled him from under Ray Ray. Blue was weak, damn near dead weight, as Caleb dragged him toward the door. The sirens were loud and all over the place now, so much that Caleb didn't know from which direction they were coming. They needed to get out of there, Caleb kept telling himself, but something made him stop. Blue was hanging from Caleb, his arm slung over his neck like a beaten prisoner of war, but suddenly Caleb felt the need to stop and take a final look at Ray Ray. When he did, he wished he'd hadn't, because Ray Ray was staring back at him, his face smeared with blood, blood running from his slightly opened mouth, one arm outstretched, his palm open, as if he was reaching to be carried out of there. And his eyes—opened wide and unmoving—were staring at Caleb, and Caleb was frozen. They held him there while they burned the entire image in Caleb's brain, for him never to forget. Caleb didn't know if Ray Ray was alive or dead at that moment, for he didn't move at all. But just when Caleb was about to turn, he saw the corners of Ray Ray's mouth slowly turn up, as if he was smiling, his hand reaching out a little more, the fingers flinching, as if trying to extend all the way over to Caleb and Blue, grab on so he would not be left to die alone. At least, that was what Caleb thought he saw. The screaming sirens wailing louder and louder forced him out, Blue's weakened body still hung over his shoulder, before he had a chance to know if his eyes were telling him the truth or not.

Caleb roused himself from his thoughts, shaking away the awful event that had landed him in the dreadful place he was now finally outside of. He stood there, his hair long, wild, and mussed about his head, patches of facial hair growing dense in some spots and thin in others. His body was lean and muscular, from the little bit of fat he'd lost while eating prison food, and the muscle he'd gained by pumping iron in the yard. He stood as if just coming out of a trance, outside the gate of Joliet, Illinois, State Prison, a massive, menacing, gray structure that sat on a huge compound, a twenty-foot-tall barbed-wired gate sprouting from the ground and stretching around the entire area.

Two huge guards, their chests and biceps bursting out of blue-and-gray security uniforms, stood on the opposite side of the gate. They had just released Caleb, and they were staring at him now, probably wondering why he hadn't moved, wondering why, after spending five years within that gate, he wasn't turning tail and running as fast as he could from the place. But Caleb didn't care what they thought. They couldn't do anything to him now. He was a free man, and his actions were his own, his time was his own, and he could make his own decisions, and what better time than that moment, he thought, for him to start.

Beside him stood another man. A slight, boyish-looking man, of about twenty or twenty-one, with narrow shoulders, who constantly had a look of fear on his face. Even now, it was there, as if he worried that someone would reach out from between the narrow slit in the gate and grab the collar of his T-shirt, and haul him back in.

"So what are you going to do now?" the boy-man said, as if he himself had nowhere to go and nothing to do, which was probably the case. He had no more in his hand than what Caleb had, which was a wrinkled paper bag that held a stack of letters, not much more than he had been thrown in the place with.

"Got a plane ticket. Going home to see my father, my girl, and my son in California."

A look of envy was on the young man's face, but he smiled anyway, obviously trying to deny the emotion.

"That's good, that's good," he said, looking down at the pavement, nudging a crumpled can with the tip of his shoe. "You gonna do that right now?"

"No," Caleb said, staring at the guards standing behind the gate, watching him through their mirrored sunglasses.

"Well, what you gonna do right now?"

Caleb turned to glance at the man, then looked away again. "I'm just going to stand here for a while, so you might as well go on home." Where home was for this man, Caleb didn't know, and he didn't much care, because he had too many problems of his own to concern himself with. He had too many demons to rid himself of before he took another step out into the world.

Caleb drifted back into his thoughts, the same thoughts that had plagued him since the day Ray Ray had gotten killed. He had left Ray Ray there to die by himself. They should have taken him with them. Even though they were caught in the end, they shouldn't have abandoned Ray Ray, thrown him aside like some worthless piece of shit. It horrified Caleb to think of the police finding Ray Ray, walking around his body, glaring down at it, like a dead animal smashed and bloody in the center of the highway, thinking to themselves, or even saying it, "Well, just another nigger dead, eh?"

And then one of his buddies agreeing with him. "That's right. Makes our job all the more easier."

Then another image popped into Caleb's head.

Although he knew it was impossible, he could not shake the image of Ray Ray's parents walking into that store, maybe stopping to get a can of peas on the way home for that night's dinner, and seeing their son slain, coated with dried blood, his eyes eerily open in his head. Caleb could see Ray Ray's mother, blinking furiously, then shaking her head, trying to get that foolish make-believe image out of her mind, but when it would not go, she ran to Ray Ray. She ran to her son and dropped to her knees, burying her face in his chest, grabbing fistfuls of his torn, bloodied shirt, shaking him, beating his dead body, tears spilling onto her son. She was scolding him for putting himself in the position to get shot, because she had told him a thousand times not to go hanging around with "those boys," because they would get him killed one day. And there he was, dead, on that floor. Dead before his mother could even say good-bye to him, before she could tell him how much she loved him, and all she wanted to do was die right there with him. And it was apparent by the way she raised her anguished, now blood-covered face and hands up to the heavens, and yelled out to God, "Please spare my boy! Pleeeaaasssse!" But nothing had happened, and she collapsed onto his dead, stiffening body. And then there was her husband's hand, Ray Ray's father's hand, big on her shoulder, and he was looking down on his son's dead body, no expression on his face, but somehow seeming more torn apart than his wife.

Caleb shook the image out of his head, looked around to find himself alone now. The man beside him was gone, the guards who had walked him out, gone, obviously tired of staring at him, and the sun that was above him had now lowered itself into hiding, taking the daylight with it.

How long had Caleb been out there? It could have been hours, for he had no watch on his wrist to tell him. He pulled an envelope from his pocket and slipped its contents out. It was a plane ticket in his name. A ticket to California to see Sonya and his child. It had been five years that he'd been away from them, five years since he'd held them in his arms, and, on a few occasions, he feared he never would again. He thought many times about the day he would receive the letter telling him that the distance was just too much for her. That he couldn't go on expecting her to wait for him like that, and that it was cruel to put her in that position. But that letter never came, and now he was out. In just a couple of days, they would all be reunited.

He took a step in the direction of the bus station that would carry him on to the rest of his life. Then he halted, thinking once again about Ray Ray, and turned back around, slowly walking down the street in the opposite direction.

Caleb sat on the bus, staring out the window like a child on his first field trip. He sat, pushed up very close to the window, his nose almost touching it, watching as the crumbling storefronts and poorly maintained lower-middle-class homes of Chicago's South Side passed him by. Caleb reached up and pulled the cord to signal his stop. The bus lurched to a halt, and Caleb climbed down and out onto the street. The bus pulled away, slowly leaning this way and that over the uneven, pothole-riddled streets, as it trailed off, leaving Caleb standing on the corner alone. He looked over his shoulder, feeling as though he was being watched, a residual feeling left over from his time behind bars.

No one was coming after him. His getting out was not a mistake. He was free, and he told himself he would have to just get used to it. It was already getting dark, and the lamps hanging over the streets started to flicker above him, so he moved on.

He stopped in front of a small blue-and-brown house, the paint chipping from the gutters and window frames, one of the windows taped over with cardboard to keep the chill Chicago spring winds out. He took slow steps closer to the house, wishing that the lamp that was burning behind the sheer curtains in the front window had not been burning at all. He would have turned away, would have left, telling himself that he had tried, but no one was home. But the light was there, so he was obligated and he continued on, placing a foot upon the first creaking wooden step of the house.

Five steps up, and Caleb's finger was inches from the doorbell. It was shaking, his heart beating so fast that it caused his entire body to tremble. He swallowed hard and pushed the button. He turned his back on the door, looked out on the street, searching his mind for something to say. He should have thought of this while on the bus, he scolded himself. The door opened behind him before he could pull any two words together to speak.

He turned to see a short, slightly overweight, dark-skinned woman standing behind a screen door. Her hair was short and mostly black, but the silver of her roots grew up about an inch out of her head to expose themselves. She was smiling, which Caleb thought meant she recognized him, but she obviously didn't because she asked, "Can I help you?"

Caleb struggled again with what he was going to say, then finally was able to come out with, "I have something very important to talk to you about. I was wondering if I could come in?"

Ray's mother looked at Caleb oddly, as if debating as to whether or not he was telling the truth, or just trying to get inside so he could rob them.

"I grew up in this neighborhood. I lived right down the other street," Caleb said, looking over his shoulder, pointing in that direction. Ray's mother looked as though she was still deciding.

"Well, ma'am?" Caleb asked her again. And before she could answer, a large man with a brown face, shiny and creased like a well-broken-in catcher's mitt, came up behind the shorter woman and said, "You used to live down the street, right? Well, c'mon in, son. It's gettin' a little chilly out there."

The tall man held the door for Caleb as he walked into the small, modestly decorated living room. Caleb was nervous, and he shouldn't have been there, he told himself, as he stared at the man and woman staring back at him.

How do I begin, Caleb thought. What the hell can I possibly say to these people? Then he decided to just come out with it, but the word that was only a moment from dropping from his lips was halted when he caught sight of a picture sitting in a frame on one of the end tables. It was of Ray Ray as a child. Five or six, his head covered by a big, nappy Afro, his narrow body swallowed up by a striped Ernie and Bert turtleneck. Caleb wanted to smile, wanted to laugh, wished that his friend were still alive, because if he were, Caleb would have given him hell for that picture. But he wasn't. He was dead, and that was why Caleb was at his house.

"Do you know who I am, Mr. and Mrs. Collins?" Caleb asked.

Ray's father didn't answer, but his mother said, "You're Esther's boy, from down the street? Right?"

"No, Mrs. Collins," and Caleb lowered his head, not wanting to see the initial response on their faces when they heard the words he was about to speak.

"I'm Caleb Harris. I was a friend of your son, Ray. I was with him when he was killed five years ago." Caleb kept his head down, expecting to feel the big hands of Ray Ray's father grab him around his neck and brutally strangle him, shaking him till his brain rattled in his skull, but there was no such assault, and Caleb almost wished there had been, because the thought of looking back up to see their faces seemed more painful.

When he did look up, the father's face was blank, as if the words he'd heard didn't even register. But Ray's mother seemed to be working at keeping her face together, for the corners of her mouth were trembling, her eyelids fluttered quickly, and her chin seemed on the verge of collapsing. Then a single tear rushed down her plump cheek, and with a thin whimper, she turned and ran for the bedroom, the door slamming shut behind her.

Caleb was left staring the big man in the face, wanting to turn away, but feeling it would be disrespectful.

Mr. Collins gestured toward the sofa. "Sit down," he said, taking a seat himself across from Caleb. "She still hasn't gotten over the loss of our boy."

Caleb wanted to say so much more, something comforting, something that would take away some of this family's hurt, but all that came out was, "I'm sorry."

"No, no, no," the big man said. "It wasn't your fault. I mean, you were there, but he had a mind of his own. And if you had got shot and killed, that wouldn't have been his fault, because you got a mind of your own."

Caleb nodded his head, and continued staring at Ray's father. He watched as he looked up at the ceiling, then down at the floor. He looked as though he was about to cry, and even though Caleb knew at that moment he should have turned away, should have given him his time to grieve, if that was what he was doing, Caleb could not take his eyes from the man.

Mr. Collins quickly got up, turning his back on Caleb, bringing a hand up to cover his face. "I got these damn allergies," he said, his voice shaky. Then he turned around again, after pulling himself together.

"You do all you can for these children . . . you work hard to give them all you got, feed them, clothe them, send them to school, and . . ." He shook his head to finish the statement. "Sad thing was," he spoke softly now, "I always knew it would happen like that. We tried so hard to straighten him out, but he would never listen. Never!" he said bitterly. "He just wouldn't listen. He was always into trouble, juvenile homes, getting picked up by the police. But that doesn't mean we didn't still love him. You know that, don't you?" and he was looking at Caleb now, this look on his face as if he was trying to convince Caleb that what he said was true.

"I know that, sir," Caleb said, then he stood and added, "I just wanted to come here and let you know that I was there with your son, and that . . ." Caleb paused, wondering whether or not to tell the lie. " . . . Ray Ray didn't suffer at all. He went quickly."

Ray's father turned to Caleb, obviously grateful for his words. He placed a large hand on Caleb's shoulder. "Thank you."

He walked Caleb to the door and was undoing the bolts, when the door Ray's mother disappeared behind, opened. She walked out, her face wet with tears, surprise in her eyes.

"Where are you going?!" she asked, anger in her voice, her words directed at Caleb.

"Margaret, now stop it," her husband said, moving back toward her, his palms out, as if anticipating her charging at Caleb.

"I said, where is he going?"

"He is going home. He didn't have to come over here and do this," Ray's father explained. He now held his wife in his arms, trying to keep her from moving any closer to Caleb.

"That man killed my child," Ray's mother yelled, sounding on the verge of hysteria. "If Ray wasn't with him, he would still be alive!"

"He wouldn't still be alive," her husband said, trying to yell loud enough to get through to her. "Because he would've done something else to get himself killed, and you know it. You know that!"

"That's a lie," Margaret said, struggling to get out from within her husband's embrace. "You killed my son," and she was stabbing a finger at Caleb now, reaching out with clawed hands, trying to get ahold of him, trying to escape her husband's grasp, spit flying from her lips. "You killed him and you should have to pay."

And then Caleb spoke, knowing he shouldn't have. But he couldn't help himself.

"I did pay. I paid with five years of my life in prison."

Ray's mother's eyes ballooned so big in her head that they appeared as though they would pop.

"Five years!" she spat. "Five years, but you're standing right here. Where is my son? You did five years for robbing that store, but he did life! He's dead. You may have paid your debt to society, but you still owe me. You still owe me!"

"What do you mean? For five years I thought about your son lying there, dying in front of me, and every day I wished I could've done something. But I couldn't," and there were tears welling up in Caleb's eyes now. "There are times when I wished it was me who had gotten shot instead of him, me who had died, so you wouldn't have to go through this. But I can't change places now, he's gone, and there's nothing I can do about it," Caleb cried. "Nothing!" He lowered his head into his open hands, digging his fingers deeply into his scalp, wishing that he could roll over and die. But then he felt a hand fall gently upon his arm, then another, slowly pulling him in. He let himself be brought forward, and he realized he was in the arms of Ray's mother.

Her cheek was pressed against the top of his head, and she was crying as well. He could feel her warm tears fall to his cheeks. She rocked him there in her arms, as if he were her own.

"You miss him, don't you?" she said, rubbing Caleb's head.
Caleb nodded.
"And you're sorry that he's dead, that you had to see him die?"
Caleb nodded again, wiping tears from his eyes.
"Well, we won't let him die like that. Do you hear me?"
Caleb didn't answer, forcing the woman to take his face in her hand, make him look her in the eye. "Do you hear me?"
"Yes," he said.

"Stay right here. I want to give you something." She moved away from him, leaving her husband standing next to Caleb. His head was down, his hands shoved into his pockets.

She went to a cabinet in the dining room, opened it up, stood on her toes, and pulled something from the top shelf. It was a pamphlet of some sort, and when she handed it to him, he could see that it was a funeral program, Ray Ray's picture in black and white on the cover.

"A mother should never have to lose a child this way. Never. And far too many of us are." The pamphlet remained in her outstretched hand, Caleb seeming afraid to touch it.

"Take it," she said.

Caleb pulled the program from Ray's mother's fingers.

"I don't know how you're going to do it," she said with authority. "But you're going to find a way not to let his memory die. You find a way to actively repent, because you had no choice about spending those years behind bars. You were made to do that. But now you need to do something for Ray because you want to. Do you understand?

"Yes," Caleb said, the tears now dry on his face, the program hanging from his hand, his body still trembling some from his emotional outpouring. "I understand."

Austin Harris pulled his large Mercedes up to the curb in front of his old house, in the upper-middle-class neighborhood of Beverly. He left the engine running for a moment, and thought about reaching behind him, and pulling the jacket of his Armani suit off the hanger that hung from the back window, and throwing it on, but decided not to. There wouldn't be a need yet. And maybe he thought that because he didn't see his ex-wife's gold Maxima parked out front as he should have, and he wanted to try to calm himself down before he jumped to any conclusions.

Austin looked at his watch, even though the dash clock was staring him right in the face—6 P.M., the tiny hands on his watch said. He wrapped his hand around the ignition key, turned off the engine, and let his chin sink into his chest, exhaling sorrowfully.

He was thirty-seven now, and tired of this, damn tired of the games Trace chose to play. He thought about getting out of the car, checking the garage, but if her car wasn't there, if she wasn't home with the kids all dressed, their overnight bags at their feet, happy little smiles on their faces, anticipating all the fun they'd have with their father, Austin feared he would lose it and do something crazy. Something that would land him on the 10 P.M. news highlight reel.

So Austin just decided to sit there, remembering the first time he'd left his wife. They had been married for six years, and from his point of view, things were becoming boring, mundane. His life was becoming typical. Come home from work, have a meaningless conversation with the wife, maybe have sex that was just as meaningless just to say that sex was still being had, then crawl into bed, roll over so that your backs are facing each other's, then fall asleep. He was not being fulfilled, and Trace must've sensed that, for she really seemed to start pouring it on, going to extremes that she hadn't in years, making extravagant dinners, paying him compliments, and sexing him like they were teenagers. But nothing helped.

The night he left was during one of those meals. Trace had gone all out, four courses, linen tablecloth, candles, wine, soft music—she even pulled out his chair for him, and gently placed his cloth napkin in his lap.

If there was conversation that night, Austin couldn't remember it, because all the while Trace was eating and Austin was picking at his food with the tips of his fork, he was thinking of what would be the right way to break the news to Trace that he would be leaving her. But he realized there was no right way, so he just came out and told her. It was somewhere between dinner and dessert and Trace was leaning over to pour him another glass of wine, when Austin said, "I think we need a break."

Trace went crazy for a moment, and later slung a plate across the room that just missed Austin's head; she threatened to club him with the heavy bottle of wine, but in the end she understood he was leaving. "And what about the kids?" Trace asked. Austin's reply was, "I'm leaving you, not them. They still have a father."

So he'd left, because it just wasn't there for him and Trace any longer. He went out and got an apartment, still saw the kids a couple of times a week, but after a few months of that, realized that maybe he had made a mistake. He realized that he had done something similar to what his father had done to him and his brothers, and that was abandon them.

Austin still remembered how much he missed his father when he was a child, how much he'd wanted him there, and although Austin still spent time with Troy and Bethany, he knew that it wasn't the same as if he had still lived with them. But that wasn't what really brought him back. His father had popped into the picture all of a sudden, shown up from nowhere, begging to be forgiven. He seemed to have nothing, seemed to be filled with nothing but regret for all the foolish mistakes he had made. Austin didn't want to be the man his father had become, and he thought about what had made him leave, and what it was he had left behind. He couldn't figure out what made him leave behind a wonderful woman who truly loved him, and was securely in his corner, no matter what. Yes, she had her flaws and faults, but didn't everyone?

Eventually, through a lot of begging and proving, Austin managed his way back into the marriage, and back home. But just two years later, they started to have more problems. This time, though, Austin wouldn't run.

"I have a friend," he said one evening while he and Trace were out at dinner. The kids were with their uncle Marcus, leaving them time to themselves. "She's a counselor," Austin said.

"What kind of counselor?" Trace asked, looking at Austin from above her coffee cup.

"Marriage counselor. I think we should see her," Austin said, then averted his eyes down to his dessert.

"For what, Austin?" Trace whispered loudly, looking across the room, making sure no one heard her.

"Because we need to. We always argue, but we never talk. It's like we're strangers, and we have nothing in common anymore but the kids."

"If that's how you feel, why don't you just take off like you did last time?" Trace said, with attitude.

"I'm not running this time. I made an appointment. We need to do this," Austin said, firmly.

"Fine," Trace said, and that was the end of the conversation. She said no more about it, because she knew, as Austin knew, that she would have gotten loud enough to draw the attention of the entire room, so she let it drop. And that was the reason Austin chose to tell her right then, right there, because he didn't want to deal with her antics, didn't want to experience what he had when he'd walked out on her five years ago. Didn't want to have to deal with her yelling and screaming, didn't want to have to duck and dodge the dinner plates she would whip at his head.

Austin and Trace sat in the counselor's office listening to Austin's friend, a middle-aged black woman, her hair pulled back in a bun, a pair of glasses resting on her nose, and noticeably, no wedding band on her finger. They went through a number of exercises that were designed to find out what their problems were. Trace seemed to have no interest in the practice, making little effort to participate. Austin worked as hard as he could, wanting to give everything possible, realizing just how much he loved his wife, how much he'd missed her when he had left the first time. But seeing that Trace seemed to have no interest in saving their relationship made him lose his desire as well, feeling that the marriage may have been far past the point of saving.

Three months passed, which consisted of a lot of talking at counseling and little to no talking at home. Trace seemed to resent the fact that Austin had even suggested this course of action, and it made her shut down entirely. Nights in the bedroom were perpetually quiet. Not a sound could be heard, not a movement was made. Austin could hear his wife breathing beside him, feel that she was awake, but she always stayed as far away from him as the king-size bed would allow.

For those three months, Austin let Trace have her way at night, telling himself that he would not break down, give in, and beg her to give him what he was sure she was certainly missing herself. The first two months were relatively easy to get past, for he just put his mind on other things, concentrated on work at his law firm, put in such long hours that at night he just fell right to sleep. But after two and a half months, work could no longer keep his mind off his wife, and neither could a private trip to the bathroom, standing over the toilet, a porno magazine lying open on the sink. So he had tried, although only a couple of times, to convince his wife, kissing her about the neck and face, but she simply thwarted each attempt, moving away, telling him, "No!" the way an owner would reprimand a bad dog for trying to eat its own shit. Then she would just roll over, ignoring him entirely.

But this night, he'd had enough. He was throbbing, almost painfully so, and when he turned to face Trace, he felt his tip brush up against the soft flesh of her ass, sending an electric rush up his spine. He slid over closer to his wife, pressing himself against her, but almost immediately, without saying a word, she rolled away from him. Austin would not be put off. He reached up, placing a hand on her soft shoulder, smoothing it, kneading it in his hand, and he could feel himself becoming all the more excited. Then he let his hand roam down in front of her, above the space below her neck, just above her sloping breast, and he could feel how warm she was, feel the rhythmic beating of her heart. He thought he felt it jump, alerting him to the fact that she wanted him as badly as he wanted her, that she was just playing hard to get, and nothing else. So he went for it, full steam, cupping one of her breasts, throwing his face just over her shoulder, kissing her wildly about the neck, and shoving himself blindly in between her legs, hoping to hit the bull's eye.

"No!" Trace cried out, rolling over, clicking on the bed lamp. Then she turned and looked at him as if she knew him no better than a stranger riding on the bus who had miraculously appeared in her bed.

"What is wrong with you? Have you lost your mind?"

Austin was momentarily embarrassed, ashamed about what just happened, till he looked at the situation for what it really was. Then he said, "Have I lost my mind? For what? Trying to make love to my wife? What is wrong with *you*, Trace?"

"What is wrong with me? You're the one that's having us going to see some damn counselor, acting as if there's something wrong with us."

"So that's why you've been holding out on me, playing sex games with me, acting like a damn child, hoping to get me to respond the way you want me to? That is so ridiculous, Trace. I thought you were above this," Austin said, turning to roll over, feeling his erection going down.

"Fine. If that's what's so important to you, Austin, go ahead. If you want to fuck so badly, c'mon. Come get it," she said, throwing the sheets and blanket off her, exposing her fully naked body. She threw herself on her back, her breasts spilling to the sides of her body, then she bent her knees and spread her legs open wide.

"C'mon, Austin. This what you want?"

Austin found himself propped up on one elbow, looking at her now, telling himself that he would not lower himself to that, to jumping on top of his wife, admitting to her that at this very moment sex was what he really wanted. But his manhood said otherwise, for it had grown long and hard, and between the two heads, there was no competition as to which would have the last word.

So Austin sprang up on top of his wife, sank down in between her legs, and slid into her. The feeling was immeasurable, indescribable, and he felt himself becoming weak with pleasure, his arms trembling, his head swimming. But he would hold himself up, because this was the best he ever remembered his wife feeling, and he gently slid in and out of her, wincing against the extreme pleasure, speaking to himself at first, saying, "Ooh, this feels so good." Then he included her, as he sped up his movements. "It feels good, don't it, baby? Tell me it feels good, Trace."

But there was no response from her, and after speaking to her in such a way three or four more times, he opened his eyes to look down at her to see why she hadn't responded. It was because she wasn't even paying attention to him. Her head was turned, her eyes focused on something sitting on the nightstand. Her jaw was tight, as if she was not enjoying this at all, but suffering through it. Austin saw that both her hands were clinched into fists, felt that her muscles were stiff with re-sistance and not with pleasure, and he knew that things would never be the same between them. This was the last straw, all that was left to turn him completely off to her.

Almost immediately Austin felt himself shrinking. He slid out of her, pulled himself off his wife without saying a word. She acted as though he was not there, as she had done during the entire episode. She did not turn her head to acknowledge him, did not lower her legs, just kept them there, as if she were a corpse, a lifeless dummy her husband used, positioned in such a way to receive his maximum pleasure. And he knew that was the way she wanted him to feel. Austin picked up the spread and sheets from off the floor. He pulled his wife's legs down, and covered her up. He went to his bureau, pulled out some sweatpants and a T-shirt, threw them on, turned out her light, and left the room to sleep on the couch.

Eventually, after another month, counseling stopped, and Trace seemed to be happy about it. She was giving him sex again, and Austin did nothing but take it. Not joyfully, exactly, but the way a millionaire would accept a gift of five dollars. He could live without it.

He would pleasure Trace, make her reach orgasm, not caring if he came or not. They no longer spoke about counseling, and Austin never spoke about them needing it anymore.

"Why are you traveling so much more on your job now?" Trace asked one morning, sitting down to breakfast with him.

Austin hadn't thought anything of it till that moment when he looked down and saw the plane ticket on the table beside his breakfast plate, the weekend bag packed at his feet. He had to get up at that moment and start off to the airport or be late and miss his flight, which was the last thing he wanted to do.

"You know how it always gets busy this time of year. Conferences," is what Austin told Trace, standing, grabbing his things, bending over and kissing her good-bye.

On the plane, slumping in the wide leather seats of first class, he sucked at the last little bit of cognac in the bottom of his glass. He felt more comfortable, able to relax, much more so than when he was at home, and he knew that was the real reason he was traveling more. He did it to get away from his wife, to distance himself from a situation that he knew was failing, but he hesitated walking out on again, not sure if he would be making the right decision, unable to know if it was really over.

But that weekend, something happened that made him no longer question whether he should leave Trace or not. Austin bumped into a beautiful, young attorney from Washington who was also attending the conference. He had known her vaguely from two other conferences they'd both attended in the past; both times, Austin felt there was a mutual attraction. Her name was Cynthia Edwards, and after only a day, they found themselves in bed together.

That night they made love longer and more passionately than he and Trace had in over five years. The next morning, Austin awoke to Cynthia sleeping behind him, her body contouring to his shape, a limp arm thrown over his waist. He turned over, gently trying not to wake her. He looked in her face, realizing he knew this woman he just made love to slightly more than he knew the housekeeper who had made the bed they were lying in. But there was a powerful feeling he got, as he caressed her face in his hand. At the moment, it was indescribable, but if he let himself, he could convince himself that it might have been love. It wasn't. But whatever it was, it felt good. It was something that he hadn't felt with Trace in so many years that he thought he'd lost the capacity to feel it at all. And at that moment, Austin knew what it was he had to do.

Riding to the airport, he was fueled with the thought of how he was going to change his life, how he was going to tell Trace, on seeing her, that it was over, that he needed more, wanted to truly love his life, be excited about it. But as he thought about it while up in the air, it was as if he had sprung a leak somewhere, and all those intentions, all that drive, started to spill out of him.

Austin was thinking about his children, about how this would affect them. He thought about how leaving Trace again meant leaving his children. And Austin couldn't help but think about his father's disappearance. He should've been obligated by his father's thoughtless act to stay put where he was for the rest of his life. But there was a difference between the two of them. Austin knew that he would always remain a part of his children's lives no matter what, even though the relationship wouldn't be just the same as if he stayed.

But by the time the plane landed and he made it to the gate, Austin was happy to see his wife and beautiful kids waiting for him. Trace ran up to him, hugging him, kissing him, and he could feel his six-year-old son, Troy, grabbing his right leg, his daughter, Bethany, a year older than her brother, trying to pull his bag from his hand to help him carry it.

As Austin walked out of the airport, his family crowding and smiling around him, telling him how they had missed him, he was all of a sudden overcome with guilt. Had he made a grave mistake by sleeping with that woman? Austin kept telling himself that he was the one trying to save his marriage, but what did he go and do? Sleep with the first woman willing to sleep with him.

He stopped right there, just before they reached the car, Bethany holding one of his hands, Troy holding his bag, and Trace very near to him. He looked her very seriously in the eyes.

"What?" she said, smiling nervously, as if fearing that he was about to drop a bomb of some sort. And that was just what he was about to do. He thought about admitting it right there, or at least putting the kids inside the car, pulling her farther away into the parking garage, and getting it off his chest. Telling her that he'd made a mistake, and the only way that he could continue truly working toward saving the marriage was for him to remain honest with her.

"Is everything all right?" Austin heard her say. He snapped out of his deep thinking. "Yeah, yeah. Everything is fine. Just glad to be back," Austin said, something telling him that disclosing his infidelity would harm his marriage more than help heal it.

Over the next month, Austin compared everything Trace did to how Cynthia did it. He compared how they made love, the size of their asses, their feet, the brightness of their teeth, the kinkiness of their hair. It was terribly wrong to be doing this, and he forced himself to put the woman out of his mind, and focus entirely on his wife. He bought Trace flowers, but she wasn't as impressed as he felt she should've been. He surprised her with a dinner he made one night, and she showed her gratitude by getting sick, locking herself in the bathroom afterward, and puking up every morsel of it. One night, on the spur of the moment, he wanted to go to the movies, maybe even a drive-in, but they couldn't find a sitter. If he and Cynthia had wanted to go to the movies, they wouldn't need a sitter. And then there were times when Austin wanted to make love, but Trace was tired, or when he wanted her to please him in a certain way, and she pretended not to know exactly how. They had been married for so long that Austin knew she should've known these things.

Austin was entertaining those thoughts of leaving again, but before he could let them take their course, manifest themselves into actions, he landed back in the office of the marriage counselor. Trace wasn't by his side, for he had not even mentioned it to her, because he knew how she would respond. But after a month of going by himself, he knew that there was only so much ground he could cover with him there alone. So one night while Trace was slipping on her nightgown, getting ready for bed, Austin mentioned it.

"Trace, I think we need to go back to counseling," Austin said, already in bed.

Trace didn't reply to what he said, didn't even look at him, just slipped under the covers with her back to him, reached over, and turned off the bed lamp.

"Trace," Austin said, staring into the darkness.

"Austin, do you love me?" Austin heard Trace ask him.

"Of course I do."

"And I love you, too. And that's all that matters. We don't need any woman, especially one who isn't married herself, telling us what we need to do to be happy."

"Trace . . ." Austin said, but was cut off. Trace had quickly rolled over, placed herself on top of him, and was holding his cheeks with one of her hands, her lips very close to his.

"There's nothing else to say. And if you just stop it with the damn counseling talk, I'll give you the best sex you had in a long time," she said, softly thrusting her pelvis into his.

Austin didn't think so, an image of Cynthia's naked body popping into his head, but he said, "Yeah, okay." But now he knew for sure, there was no saving this marriage.

Three days later, Troy was having his birthday party. Fifteen smiling and cheering kids were at the house to celebrate his son's seventh birthday. They were all crowded around the table, balloons clinging to the ceiling, party streamers strewn about the walls, the kids wearing party hats and blowing party favors. Trace was leaning against the kitchen doorway, a proud smile on her face as she watched her son about to blow out his candles, and Austin knew what she was thinking, could tell by that smile she wore on her face. She was thinking that all was so good with her life. She was thinking that there was nothing more she wanted, she had it all: two beautiful children, a huge home, no financial worries, and a man who loved her.

She gave her husband a gentle squeeze about the waist when he walked up beside her and something made Austin want to pull away from her. Things weren't as she saw them, and he was angry that she felt they were. Maybe if she realized that the excitement had left, she wouldn't have objected to the counseling, would have made more of an effort to find some way to get it back, rather than settle for things the way they were, and just expect everything to be fine. Going through the motions of life just wasn't enough for Austin anymore, and he would have to put an end to it right now, at the peak of his dissatisfaction, because he knew if he waited, if he gave his mind a chance to rationalize staying, he would.

So as his son closed his eyes to make his wish, Austin slowly leaned his head over to his wife, placing his lips to her ear. He saw the smile that was already on her face start to widen, and Austin knew that she thought he was being playful, leaning into her to tell her something naughty, or nibble on her ear. And then, when Troy leaned forward to blow out the candles, all the kids peering over him, their eyes on the flickering blue flames as they were blown away, leaving them sending tiny gray spirals of smoke in the air, Austin whispered into his wife's ear.

"I've had an affair."

Trace continued to look at her son, the smile still on her face, but faltering a bit.

"What?" she said, not turning to him, but still looking at her son, speaking through the teeth of her smile.

Austin wore a smile, too, and although it was practiced, he figured it did not let on to his daughter, who was now looking right in his face, what was going on.

"I had an affair, and I just thought you should know that."

There would be no dish throwing, no hollering and cursing this time. There would only be Trace standing still, the words slowly seeping into her brain, the realization of it pulling the corners of her smile down and dimming her eyes, till she could no longer hide her pain. She moved her hand to her face to cover the anguish, shield the kids from what she was experiencing, especially on this day.

Trace must've felt Troy look up at her, for she ducked into the kitchen before he could see that his mother was on the verge of tears. Austin quickly walked over to the table, draped his arms around both his children, and cheerfully asked, "So what did you wish for?"

"I can't tell you, Dad. Then it won't come true."

But Austin hadn't even heard what his son said, because his attention was in the kitchen with Trace. It was a game now. But she'd started it, he rationalized, by holding out on the sex because he'd made an attempt to try and work out their problems. It was her fault. All her fault, Austin told himself, feeling a pang of guilt fall over him, wishing, maybe, that he hadn't told her. But it was too late now, and it was probably for the best. There was no going back. She would ask him to leave, and there would be no explanation that he could give her to change her mind. He wouldn't be walking out, she would be putting him out, and yes, he knew it was a coward's way, but it would get the job done. The next time he was weak and groveling for forgiveness, it wouldn't make a shit's bit of difference, because, he knew, in Trace's mind, there was no forgiving this.

That was around three years ago, and now Austin realized, still sitting behind the wheel of his car, that there were advantages and disadvantages to getting the divorce. The advantage was, naturally, that he was no longer in what he considered to be a dying relationship with a woman he was rapidly losing love for with each day that passed. The disadvantage of the divorce was that Trace had the opportunity now to play games with him through the children, keep them from him, make them available only when she saw fit, and Austin knew he could take only so much more of that abuse.

Austin walked up to the front door, knowing he was doing it just to waste time, because he knew she wasn't there. He looked down at his watch again, then rang the doorbell. It was six-fifteen, and he envisioned her on the road somewhere, not heading home, but somewhere else, the kids in the backseat. Trace probably knew exactly what time it was, probably realized that he was there, sitting in front of her house, but didn't give a damn either way.

After ringing the bell two more times and banging on the door with the flat of his fist, he decided to give up and just wait for her. He'd been sitting on the cement stair just below the front door, his chin in his hand, for not even five minutes when he saw Trace's Maxima rolling quickly down the street toward him. She looked as good as she always had, her brown hair curled in a new shoulder-length style, Austin noticed, as he saw her through the windshield.

He stood, took a few steps out where she could see him as he approached. The car pulled up, stopped, and the engine was cut off. At this point, Austin was beyond anger. Not only was Trace late but he didn't see any sign of his kids. Trace jumped out of the car, still in perfect shape, wearing a casual business suit under a lightweight trench. She slammed the door behind her, and hurried toward the house. She wasn't looking at Austin but past him, toward the front door, as if he weren't even there, and that just angered him more. He stood there like a brick wall, his arms crossed angrily over his chest, a murderous look on his face, and she blew right past him, not even acknowledging him.

Trace hunched over at the door, trying, with as much concentration as she could muster, to stick the key in its place and open it, but that proved more difficult than usual because of the odd jumping and dancing about that she was doing.

"Where the hell are the kids?" Austin was behind her now, the same evil expression on his face.

"Not here," Trace answered quickly, finally getting the door open. She dropped her purse and the paper shopping bag she was carrying from some department store on the floor, just inside the house, and was about to sprint away, when Austin grabbed hold of her by the arm.

"I can see that they aren't here. Where are they? I was supposed to take them for the weekend."

"I'll explain in a minute, but right now I have to use the bathroom," she said, her dancing becoming quicker, as if someone sped up the beats per minute on the phonograph that was connected to her bladder.

"No, you tell me right now," Austin said, tightening his grip when he felt Trace trying to pull away. "You tell me right now where they are."

Trace didn't speak, just grimaced, slipping her hands in between her thighs, her knees coming together, as if trying to clamp off the impending flow of urine.

"Are they at Marcus's house again? Did you take them over there?!" If she had, he swore he didn't know what he was going to do. It seemed as though his brother was being more of a father to his kids than he was lately, taking them to the park, museums, keeping them overnight. Even worse, it seemed that was just the way Trace wanted it.

"No, Austin. They aren't at Marcus's!" she spat, her face turning red, her eyes bulging, her cheeks inflating like an overextended balloon about to pop.

"Then where are they?"

"Goddammit, Austin, let me go so I can piss, or you'll never find out!" she said, and from the angry glare in her eyes, she meant it. Austin set her free, and she quickly scurried to the bathroom, her knees still locked together, her hands still forked between her thighs, cursing to herself as she went.

Austin stood by the door, hearing his wife moan in exquisite relief as she emptied her bladder. He heard the toilet flush, the water running in the sink, and then she was standing in front of him, looking evil.

"If I'd pissed on myself . . ."

"Where are the kids?" Austin asked, stepping in front of her.

"Oh, they're spending the night at their friend's house," Trace said, as if she just remembered.

"But they were supposed to spend the weekend with me. We spoke on the phone. Don't you remember?"

"Austin, their little friend was having a sleepover party. They just found out and they wanted to go. Dare I say, more than they wanted to go with you?" Trace said, stepping around Austin and walking into the kitchen. She went to the fridge, pulled out a diet soda, popped it open, and took a sip.

Austin stood there in the doorway, glaring at her, livid.

"Why are you playing games with me?" he said, doing everything he could think of to keep his anger under control.

"I'm not playing games with you," Trace said, her back still turned to him, and he knew she was doing it for no other reason than to spite him.

"Then turn around, goddammit!" he yelled as loud as he could.

Trace jumped, then slowly turned around to face him. She took another sip of the Diet Coke, and looked at him as if he was doing nothing more than interrupting her quality time with her carbonated beverage.

"You don't want me to see my kids. Is that why you do this? Is that why you take them over to my brother's house all the time?"

"No, Austin," Trace said, setting down the can, and raising her voice some. "It's because they happen to love their uncle, and because you always seem to be at work. How many times do you think you can tell them you're going to do something with them and not show up before they don't believe anything you say anymore?"

"What are you talking about? I never miss a date I plan with them."

"Really, Austin?" Trace said, pacing over to him. "Troy's football championship game. You were supposed to be there.

"And how about Bethany's ballet lesson? I had told you that I needed to do something and asked you if you'd be able to take her. You said you would. I asked you were you sure. I asked you that three times. And you said of course. When I went to pick her up after her lesson and the instructor said you never showed, I rushed over to her school. She'd sat out there waiting three hours for you, and when I told her you weren't coming, she didn't believe me. When I tried to pull her away, she started to cry. That child has more faith in you than she should, and you just keep letting her down. One day, you're going to really hurt her," Trace said, shaking her head pitifully, turning away from Austin.

"Those both happened three months ago, and I told you, everything at the office just went crazy, and I got so caught up that I just couldn't make it. I told you that would never happen again."

"Why did it happen the first time?"

"I didn't mark it on my calendar and I overlooked it."

"Overlooked it, Austin. What would happen if *I* just decided to overlook our children? And you act like it comes as a surprise that I would let them do something that they want to do, instead of sit here and wait to see if you come or not. What comes as a surprise to me is that you actually made it."

"I told you that I'd be here. We agreed that I'd take them this weekend," Austin said, feeling more angry with each word he spoke.

"Well, they're gone now, Austin, and I'm not about to go over there and take them away from their friend's house," Trace said, taking a sip of her soda.

"Then I'll take them tomorrow. They can come then," Austin said, his tone low.

"Marcus promised he would . . ."

"No, Trace." Austin cut her off. "I don't want to hear what Marcus promised them. That means nothing to me."

"It means something to Marcus," Trace said.

"Well, who do you think is more important to those kids?" Austin said, and there should have been no question about the answer, but Trace didn't respond right away. She stood there, a wondering expression on her face.

"You are, I suppose. But I'll have to think about canceling the plans with Marcus. They're looking forward to seeing him."

"These aren't just your children, you know. I have a say, too. I am their father," Austin asserted with authority.

Trace simply looked up at him, no expression on her face. "Then act like it."

5

Marcus lay stretched out on his back, across his bed, receiving sloppy, wet kisses over his mouth and cheeks, occasional nibbles on his chin. This was how he liked to be kissed, feeling the warm saliva from a woman's lips smeared across his face. He wasn't into those pecking, dry kisses, those tight-lipped, no-tongue-action kisses. That was for grade school, and he was a grown man. All that other stuff was a tease, and went out with blue balls and eight-track tapes.

But this, he thought, as he rotated his head about, trying to probe his tongue deeper and deeper, using his tongue to wrestle with the tongue that was in his mouth, this was what he was into. And Reecie knew that this was the type of business that got him so bothered he couldn't even speak, couldn't even think, so he would just lie there, his eyes spinning about in his head, enjoying her hot lips on his, her body next to his, her gentle, probing fingers, tracing lines and circles around his most sensitive parts.

Which was what she was doing at just that moment, gliding her pointer finger down the length of his torso, stopping just above his navel, then trailing down just a little farther, circling him, coming dangerously close to touching him there, but purposely not doing it.

She wants me to lose it, Marcus thought to himself. She wants me to bust a load right here in my damn drawers, and what kind of man would I look like then? He grabbed Reecie's hand, rolled her over on her back, kissing her on her neck.

"Oh, you wanna play games like that, eh?" Marcus said, laughing, sliding his hand in between the buttons of her blouse, feeling her hardened nipples through the thin satin of her bra.

"Yeah, I wanna play games like that, because I always win," she said, and then giving out a tiny whine, because Marcus had worked his way into her bra, and squeezed the end of her erect nipple.

"You always win? Is that so?" Marcus was on his side now, gently nibbling on Reecie's earlobe, playing with it using the tip of his tongue. He slid his hand down in between her legs, massaging her there, feeling her body as she closed her legs around his arm and started to rhythmically gyrate with the motion of his hand.

She enjoyed this and he knew it. Knew everything about her body, knew exactly what she liked, what she loved, and what sent her beyond the point of no return. He raised himself to his knees, unbuttoned her blouse, and lifted her bra to fully expose her round, full breasts. He rubbed his face into their fullness, as he undid the clasp on her pants and slid his warm hands into her panties.

"So do you still always win?" he asked, looking up at her, about to take her right breast into his mouth. She didn't respond, for she seemed to be off in that fuzzy, flowery place that women only go when their chords are being plucked just right. So he took her into his mouth, feeling her expand even more against his tongue. She let out a deep moan, her body stiffening, then relaxing.

"Marcus," she said longingly, as if calling him from her sleep.

"Yes, baby," he said, a sly smile on his face.

"Make me feel good," she said, and she was blindly reaching for the buckle of his belt. He pushed her hand away, and said, "Is that what you want?"

"Yeah, I want to feel you," and again her hand was reaching for him, for any part of him that she could lay her hand on. But he playfully dodged her, lowering his head to the level of her waist. Then he slipped his fingers into the waist of her pants and panties, and slid them down together, exposing her smooth brown shapely legs.

He kissed her toes, slowly working his way up her legs to her knees, pausing there for a moment, nibbling the tips of her kneecaps, then continuing up, sliding his hands under both of her thick thighs, as he continued kissing. Now he was kneeling at the edge of the bed, his torso firmly lodged in between Reecie's open legs, his hands filled with her plump ass, and his chin resting on the triangular, neatly trimmed thatch of hair that grew just above that special place.

Marcus looked up at her just before he intended to take his dive, and saw that she was massaging the tips of her own nipples, her eyes closed, still in that tranquil place. He lowered his head, kissed her innermost thigh, and then she said, "No, Marcus. I want to feel you. Inside me."

He disregarded what she said, pushing her legs a little farther apart, wetting his lips with intentions of getting straight to the main course, skipping over the appetizer, when he felt Reecie sitting up.

"No, Marcus. I don't want that. I want us to make love."

And again he tried to take her mind off what she was asking for by burying his face between her legs. But this time, he felt her hand on his head, her fingers digging into the curls of his hair and lifting him out of there.

"Marcus, fuck me!" she demanded this time, and there was no way he could act as though he didn't hear that request. He raised up, leaned over her, and looked down. She had a fistful of the bedsheet, and was still squirming a little, as if seeing in her head an image of Marcus making love to her, but it was quickly fading against her effort to hold on to it.

"I can't do that," Marcus said, disappointment in his voice.

"Why not?" Reecie asked, beyond pissed off. "You're damn near pushing a hole in your pants." Marcus looked down to see that there was no problem there. He was on full bone, and if he had unzipped his pants, his penis probably would have found its own way into Reecie, and pulled him helplessly trailing behind. There was no problem in that department, but he still couldn't.

"I have my reasons," he said, covering the bulge in his pants with his hands, trying to will the erection away.

"What do you mean, you have your reasons, Marcus?" Reecie said, now kneeling in the bed, pointing at her breasts. "My nipples are so hard I could cut diamonds, and I'm so wet I'm about to drown the both of us, and you tell me you have your fucking reasons!" She moved from the bed as quickly as her body would allow her, bending down to pluck her fallen clothes from the floor. She cradled them in her arms as she stomped toward the bathroom door.

"I'm so sick of this from you, Marcus. When was the last time we made love?"

Marcus tried to answer, looking up at the ceiling trying to recall that date to his mind, but it wouldn't come.

"Just like I thought. Fine, if you don't want this, then I'll find someone that does." She spun quickly, her clothes in her arms, not aware that she'd dropped her bra, then disappeared into the bathroom, slamming the door behind her.

Marcus just stared at the door, laughing to himself, thinking that would have been a hell of an exit, worthy of an Academy Award, if she didn't have to come back out to grab her bra. And then, a moment later, the door opened just a crack, then enough to let Reecie out to snatch her bra from the floor.

"I knew I left that out here," Reecie said.

"I know you did," Marcus chuckled to himself.

Five minutes later, Marcus was sitting on the edge of the bed, as Reecie darted about, a cloud of perfume trailing behind her, stuffing crap into her pocketbook, stuff that Marcus knew Reecie had no need for.

"Where are you going?" Marcus said without worry, his arms crossed confidently over his chest.

"I told you. Somewhere I'm appreciated."

"In your condition."

Reecie came to a screeching halt in front of him. "Fuck my condition!"

"Okay," Marcus said. "Don't be out too late," Marcus called to Reecie as he heard her pounding down the stairs. "Curfew's at ten."

"Screw you, Marcus," he heard her call back.

"She's pissed. Really pissed," Marcus said to himself, lacing his fingers behind his head and falling back onto the bed. "But we'll be fine, because we've gotten through a lot worse than this."

His mind wandered off to six months ago. Marcus and Reecie had been dating for five years, living together for four of those. She was thirty-three years old, single, no children, and not engaged, and Marcus could tell that wasn't exactly where she wanted to be. He loved her, too, probably more than he even wanted to admit. But he also had to admit that he was seriously frightened of the idea of marriage. Everyone he had known seemed to have negative stories about their own union, and every man, be he someone Marcus knew, or just some guy at the barbershop, would tell him, as if they were doing Marcus a favor, "Don't do it, man." The warning always sounded the same, as if Marcus was facing some grave danger, and although it was too late for the man speaking, Marcus could still manage to save himself, if he just heeded their warnings. So although Reecie was the first woman he had actually loved, he was fearful of getting married for fear of things not working out, of their getting divorced and hating each other. Marcus knew that with each day Reecie spent with him, a day passed that she could've been using to find the right man, the man who wanted to get married as she wanted, live happily ever after, and all that jazz. That would make her happy, and that was all Marcus wanted for her. So he had no other choice but to end it with her.

He came up with a brilliant plan for how to end his relationship, at least he told himself it was brilliant. He had a friend named Sarah. Well, she really wasn't his friend, but she was a woman who worked down at the print shop on Fifty-third Street. Every time he went in there, she would bat her long lashes at him, run her hand through her frizzy, curly, brown-blond hair, and stick out her large breasts, hoping that Marcus would be taken with her. He didn't know why she had to throw herself at him, because the woman was beautiful—light brown complexion, full sensuous lips, and a shape any man would fantasize about.

"How's it going today, Marcus?" she always asked, smiling wide, looking at him seductively. "What can I do for you today?" And there was always a hint of her willingness to do truly *whatever* it was he wanted her to do for him on any day.

"Hey, Sarah," Marcus would say, smiling back, paying her only enough attention to get her to do the job he needed done. I just need copies of this, or that blown up, or this laminated, he would tell her.

"So when you going to ask me out?"

"I'm in a relationship, Sarah. Sorry."

"Is it serious?"

"Serious enough to keep me from asking you out."

"Well, you let me know if it ever ends, okay? I'll be here waiting for you," she'd say, winking an eye.

"I'm flattered," Marcus would say, then take his materials, and walk out of the store, knowing that her eyes were glued to his backside each and every time he left.

So when Marcus went to the store after he had devised his plan, and was met with Sarah's usual greeting, Marcus replied, "You can have lunch with me." Sarah's eyes lit up, a smile widening across her face. "Okay."

"I'll be back at noon to pick you up."

Twelve-fifteen P.M. and Marcus and Sarah were at Medici, a trendy little restaurant in Hyde Park where college students would gather. Sarah was sitting across from Marcus, excitedly sipping a cup of tea, looking as if he were a famous R&B singer, and she was his biggest fan.

"Tea good?" Marcus asked.

Sarah quickly nodded her head in the middle of sipping from the cup, almost spilling it into her lap. She laughed at herself and dabbed up the little she'd spilled on the table with a napkin.

She's pretty goofy, but she's cute as hell, and she should go along without a problem, Marcus thought to himself.

"So I asked you here because I want you to do something for me . . . I mean with me," Marcus said, catching himself.

"What is it?" Sarah said enthusiastically.

"I don't know if I should say," Marcus said, lowering his head, wringing his hands together as if he were too shy to mention it. "I mean, it's kind of . . . I don't know, forward. You might not want to do it."

"No, no, no. Just ask me. I'll decide if I want to or not," she said, and she was leaning forward in the booth, a look on her face as if she was worried about being left out of the greatest opportunity in life.

"Uhhhhh," Marcus continued to lead her on. "I don't . . . ."

"Just ask me!"

"All right, here goes. I want to pick you up from work tomorrow, bring you to my house so we can make out. I want to do this right around the time my girlfriend comes in the house so she can see us. What do you think?" Marcus asked, looking at Sarah, an unsure smile on his face. She would find what he said ridiculous, he knew. But there was no better way than to just come out with it.

Sarah looked at Marcus, a deeply perplexed look on her face, as if he'd just asked her an ancient riddle that she knew she could never answer in a million years.

"Marcus," Sarah finally said. "I think you got me all wrong. I like you a lot. I think we both know that. But I'd want to have you for myself.

I'm not trying to get off into any kinky stuff. I'm not trying to share."

Marcus was afraid she'd try and get moralistic at the last moment and ruin his plans. He didn't want to lie to her, but this had to happen, and she was the perfect person to make it happen. And it wasn't as if he was telling a total lie. It was only a half lie, and that couldn't be all that bad.

"No, no, no. Now I think you're misunderstanding *me*," Marcus said, smiling confidently, reaching across the table and taking her hand in his, squeezing it, as if to assure her that he could be trusted. "I don't want you to have to share me, either. That's why I want my girlfriend to see us kissing. Not having sex, nothing kinky, just kissing. That way, she'll dump me, move out, and then I'll be open to date you. See what I'm saying?" Marcus stopped, looking intently into her puzzled face, waiting for her to catch up to everything he'd just said.

After a moment, still without showing emotion to let Marcus know whether or not she was game, Sarah said, "Your girl, she's not crazy or anything? She won't pull out a gun and try and shoot me for being with her man, will she?"

"Ohhhhh, no," Marcus said, in his most carefree voice, waving the entire notion off. "She's the most timid little woman. She's a kitten."

After that was said, Sarah was smiling again, a mischievous look in her eyes. "All right then, I'm game."

The next morning while Reecie was getting ready to head to work at Marcus's brother's law firm, Marcus asked, "So you going to be home at the regular time?"

"No," she said, pouring herself a small glass of orange juice. "I have a stop to make, so I won't be home till around six."

Perfect, Marcus thought, and received the peck Reecie gave him on the lips. "Love you, baby," she said, and those were the last words Marcus needed to hear. This woman loved him, and there was no question about that, never was, and his scandalous ass was about to . . .

"Marcus, did you hear me?" Reecie said, interrupting his thoughts. "You were spacing out."

"Oh," he said, snapping out of it. "Love you, too."

"Is everything all right?"

"Yeah," Marcus said, averting her concern-filled stare. "Just something I have to do."

And by ten minutes to six that something was starting. He and Sarah were at his house, sitting on the sofa, watching television. Well, Marcus was watching television, or trying to, because Sarah had her arm around him, her leg casually draped over his right knee, and she kept trying to kiss him on the ear and neck. She was wearing tight jeans to show off her curves, and a thin blouse, with no bra underneath to exhibit her large, perky breasts.

"Sarah, don't you want to watch TV?" Marcus asked, brushing at his neck, as if he were being pestered by a fly.

"No. I want to kiss you," she said, sliding closer to him. "Isn't that why I'm here?"

And she was right about that. Marcus didn't want to do it, but all the plans were made, and all he had to do was play his part, and he would free Reecie to get what she truly deserved, a man who wanted exactly what she wanted. Not one that she only thought did.

Marcus looked at the clock on the VCR. It read 5:58 P.M., and he knew he needed to start this, because Reecie would be pulling up at any minute.

"All right. You want to kiss," Marcus said, swallowing hard, looking at Sarah's full lips the way a sick child glares at a spoon of cod liver oil floating before his face. "Then let's kiss."

Marcus slowly moved toward Sarah, but was quickly grabbed by the back of his head by both Sarah's hands, and pulled forward till their lips locked. He was trying to give her Hollywood kisses, do the rotation bit, but keep his lips closed. Sarah, however, wasn't having it, and pried his lips open with her tongue, sinking it into his mouth.

It was hot and sweet, and tasted of peppermint, and Marcus had to tell himself not to enjoy it, keep his hormones in check, because he knew he could rise if he let himself. He continued kissing her, rotating his head so he could peer at the clock—5:59 P.M. it said, and he told himself, only a couple of minutes more, and it'll all be over.

But this wasn't right. It's just not right, he was thinking, and started to feel guilt, and wondered why it was attacking him now. Marcus tried to tell himself he wasn't cheating, but then again, he was doing this so it would appear that he was, and what sense did that make?

Everything seemed to blur in his head, and now he was questioning whether or not he should even go through with it, when all of a sudden, he heard a car pull up in his driveway, no doubt Reecie's. It was too late. There was no turning back, because if he backed out now and tried to tell Reecie what was really going on, she would say that was just a weak ass excuse for getting caught, and she would walk. Damned if he did, and damned if he didn't.

Marcus continued to let Sarah kiss him passionately, as she breathed hard, pressed her breasts into him, rubbing the back of his head, as if she were auditioning for a love scene in a major motion picture. Marcus was still more excited than he should've been, but it was waning now because his mind was on where Reecie was on her journey from the car to the house.

He heard the car door slam shut and he jumped.

"Just let it happen," he heard her say, their lips still pressed together. But in his mind's eye, Marcus saw Reecie's progress now, could damn near hear her high heels clip-clopping across the pavement. Twenty feet from the driveway to the walkway of the house was the distance, and Marcus envisioned that she was halfway across.

Sarah ran her hand down Marcus's back, was raking her nails up and down the length of it, and although he didn't want any part of it, this movement was trying to pull his attention from where Reecie was. But it wasn't strong enough, for now he saw her just outside the door, taking the last step up onto the porch. She was right there, sliding her key into the lock, or at least that's what he saw in his mind, and for that reason, his heart started to beat like crazy, his body tensed up in a mess of tightened muscles, and Sarah must have mistaken this for his being turned on. And somehow, before Marcus even knew what happened, Sarah was up on his lap, straddling him, her legs spread out over his thighs, kissing him and thrusting her pelvis into him, as if they were screwing through the clothes they were both wearing. Then Sarah drew her face away from Marcus's, reached down, grabbed her shirt, lifted her blouse to expose those two huge breasts, and pushed them forward into Marcus's face. At that very moment, the door opened, and Reecie walked in.

Marcus was in mid-motion, trying to lift Sarah off him before it was too late, his hands hiked up under her armpits, but then again, it could have looked like he was trying to pull her farther down on him. Either way, he wasn't fast enough. Reecie's purse dropped from her hand, the keys hit the floor with a sharp metallic crunch, and she just stood there, frozen, wide-eyed, in shock.

Marcus pushed Sarah aside and slowly rose from the sofa, realizing the immense damage he had foolishly created.

"Who the hell is that?" he heard Sarah say from somewhere far behind him, playing the role to the very end.

"Shut up!" he said with a wave of his open hand, and then concentrated on Reecie. He kept his eyes intently on her, moving very slowly, his palms open, arms out to his side, as if confronting a small, frightened animal he was trying to capture.

"Reecie, it's not what it seems. I can explain," he said, and he took another step, which caused Reecie to stumble backward and fall toward the open door.

Marcus raced over to her, catching her in his arms, but she fought her way out of them.

"Reecie, let me explain," he pleaded.

"Don't explain. It's over," she said, anger and pain wavering in her voice. "It's over," and she turned to run back toward her car, but stopped just outside the house and turned back around to face Marcus, tears now running down her face.

"Let me just tell you one thing before I go," she said, her voice quivering with emotion. "I just came from the doctor's office. We're two months pregnant, but I'll fix that, since you have other things to do." And then she turned and raced to the car.

"Reecie, no!" Marcus said, running after her. But she jumped into the car and locked the doors before he could stop her. He ran into the house as she was pulling out of the driveway, but by the time he found his keys and ran back out to his car, she was gone, leaving no clue as to which direction she'd escaped in.

6

It had been a full week since Marcus had seen, or spoken, to Reecie. These were days filled with anguish for him, just staring at the
walls, wondering if she was all right. He sat at his drafting table many
times, a colored pencil in his hand, an illustration taped in front of him,
but he was unable to concentrate on anything but Reecie. What a fool
he was to think that he could end it with her like that. What a fool he
was to think that he could end it, period. He knew he loved her, but
now, now that he'd lost her, it was so painfully clear that he could never
live the rest of his life without her.

For the first two days she had been gone, Marcus did nothing but
stand over the phone, hoping it would ring, hoping it would be her. He
wasn't able to leave his house, for fear that she would call and he'd not
be there. But after so much of that, he realized she would not come to
him, he would have to go out and get her.

Marcus wondered just where she could've gone, where she could've
been staying since she'd left his place, and the first place he ended up
was at Reecie's best friend's, Keera's, apartment.

Marcus knocked, the door opened, and Keera stood there, her short
hair all pinned up on her head with a million bobby pins.

"You fucked up," was what she said, shaking her head, giving Marcus
a pathetic look.

"Is she here?"

"Come in," she said, stepping aside for him to enter, not answering his question.

Once inside the small apartment, Keera started on him. "She loved you so much, was willing to give you everything, and look what you do to her."

"Keera, is she here?" Marcus said again, looking around the place, hoping to find some sign, a piece of her clothing, her address book, to let him know that she was staying there.

"It's just like men, to have everything, a beautiful, educated woman who cares the world about them, and then throw it all away for some skank, some hoochie, some piece of stank ass that they can screw a couple of times and toss away because they're too afraid to make a commitment to a real woman."

But Marcus had heard all that he was going to hear from her. He rushed at her, gripped her shoulders, and shook her till a couple of the pins in her head fell to the floor.

"I asked you a question, Keera. A fucking question! Is Reecie here?"

Keera looked up at Marcus, shock on her face. "She ain't, but she was."

"And where did she go?"

"I don't know," Keera said.

"Where did she go?!" Marcus demanded, shaking her again, but not as hard as before.

"I said, I don't know." Keera raised her voice, angered at being man-handled. She yanked away from Marcus. "I don't know because she knew if she told me, I'd probably tell you. And she was probably right." She looked at Marcus, wrapping her arms around herself.

"I hate what you did to her, Marcus. But I've always liked you. I think you're a decent man, but you're just kind of fucked up in the head. Like most men are. When it's time to make the big decision, time to stand up and behave like a man, you guys wet your pants, start to cry, and turn into babies. If you only knew how much of that we have to go through before we find someone we feel is worth investing in, giving our lives to. She found that in you, Marcus," Keera said, walking over to him, standing face to face with him.

"She's a good one, Marcus. And I'm not just saying that because she's my girl. You don't want to lose her."

"I know," Marcus said. He moved toward the door and was on his way out.

"And, Marcus, if she comes back, I'll call you and hold her as long as I can. Okay?"

"Thanks, Keera." Marcus walked back over to her and kissed her on the cheek. "Sorry about shaking you."

Keera waved him off. "Oh, I know you're upset. That's the only reason I didn't knock your ass on that floor. Now get out of here and find my girl." She smiled.

"Are you sure she's not staying here, Keera? Positive?" Marcus said, making one final attempt at getting her to tell him the truth.

"Marcus, I wouldn't lie to you. She's not here. But have you checked her mother's place?"

Not a half hour later, Marcus ended up at Reecie's mother's house. Dorothy stood in the small opening of the door, the security chain roped across the narrow gap, looking like an older version of Reecie, with the same caramel complexion and brown highlighted hair. She stared at Marcus as if he were a stranger, or some delivery guy asking for her signature on a package.

"Reecie's not here," Dorothy said, through the opening.

Marcus didn't get it. The entire time he and Reecie had been dating, Dorothy just loved him. Every time he would see her, she would pull him into a hug, kiss him as if he were her favorite nephew, and say, "So when do I get to start planning for Reecie's wedding?" But now she seemed hesitant to even look Marcus directly in the eyes.

"Can you open the door, so I can see for myself if she's here or not," Marcus said, trying to look past her through the narrow opening for any sign of Reecie. Dorothy just moved her head, blocking his view of the inside of the house.

"I told you, she's not here. And even if she was, which she's not, I wouldn't open the door so you could see for yourself. I can't believe you even had the nerve to come looking for her, after what you did."

"But I . . ." Marcus said. And before he could say another word, the door was slammed in his face. He stood out there, knocking on the door occasionally over the next fifteen minutes, but decided to leave when he heard Dorothy call through the door, "I've phoned the police, and they should be here any minute."

When he got home, Marcus called Dorothy's house, but all he got was her voice mail. He could see Reecie's mother in his mind, standing over the phone as it rang, looking down at the caller ID displaying his number, and at that, refusing to pick it up. Reecie was there and he knew it. Where else would she go? Where else but to their mothers' house, do all women go after their men crap all over them the way Marcus did, he told himself.

That night Marcus drove back over to the house, pulled up, and parked close enough to monitor it, but far enough not to be noticed by anyone. He sat in that car until six in the morning, his body aching, his mind frazzled, hoping not to, but expecting at any moment, to see a car drive up, some guy behind the wheel, Reecie in the passenger seat. They'd park just in front of the house and start kissing and necking like high school kids. The windows would fog all up, and then Marcus would have to go over there, and the way he was feeling at that moment, kick the damn glass in, drag whoever the man was out, and beat him into a bloody mess. But that never happened. Nothing did.

He drove home, weary-eyed, his lids wanting to shut on him, his body desperately needing sleep, for he hadn't slept much at all since this started. But when he got home, he didn't stumble up the stairs to his room and fall into bed, fully clothed, and allow himself to be snatched away by sleep. He sat at his desk, placed a couple of sheets of blank paper before him, thought for a moment, then started to put down all of his feelings, all of his fears, and exactly what had happened the other day. He explained it all, his fucked-up line of reasoning, how he'd felt he was doing her a favor by allowing her to leave him so she could find someone who wanted the same things she did, and how much he loved her, truly loved her. He wrote it all.

Afterward, he drove back over to Reecie's mother's house, feeling more exhausted, barely able to keep the car moving down the center of his lane without veering over to the other side. Once there, he knocked on the door. It opened, the chain on again, and there was Dorothy's face staring at him from the narrow slit.

"I told you . . ." she started, but Marcus finished.

"I know. She's not here, and hasn't been here, and if I don't leave, you're going to call the police," he said in a groggy voice. "But would you just please give her this." He extended the letter toward her, but didn't let go, held it there, hovering just in front of her face. "Give this to her. Don't just toss it in the trash. All right, can you, please?" Marcus said, his eyes begging the woman for the slightest bit of mercy. "If your daughter's happiness means anything to you at all, you'll give this to her. Because regardless of how you now feel about me, your daughter loves me. And if she doesn't want to be with me, let that be her decision, not yours. Okay?"

The mother didn't answer, just stared at him, as if waiting for him to say more.

"Okay?!" Marcus said again, shaking the letter a little before her eyes, as if to shake loose whatever was stopping her from responding.

"Yes. All right," Reecie's mother said, and something about the way she answered led Marcus to believe that she would actually do it.

So it had been a week without word, Marcus thought as he walked down the street. He had taken this evening walk to try to get his mind off Reecie, to get out of the house so he wouldn't go crazy, start hating himself for what he had done, and begin yanking down curtains, flipping tables, and toppling TV sets. He had to calm himself and reflect on the foolish thing he had done, and more important, start to accept the fact that Reecie was gone. She hadn't called to get her things yet, and each time he walked into the house, he would check her drawers for her clothes, to make sure she hadn't gotten in and out without his being there to try to stop her, but he knew it was just a matter of time.

Marcus turned the corner, his hands shoved deeply into his pockets, his head dragging, putting him on the block his house was on. He continued slowly moving, only lifting his head occasionally, not wanting to trip over anything, when he saw a car parked in front of his house. He didn't pay it that much attention, dropping his head again, continuing to wallow in self-pity. But for some reason, he felt compelled to look up again. The streets were dark, making it somewhat difficult to see what kind of car it was from how far away he was, but he picked up his pace a bit, in an attempt to more quickly identify it.

As he moved closer and closer, his strides became faster and longer, till he was fifty or so feet away, and then he stopped. Just froze in the middle of the sidewalk, as if he was afraid to continue, because the car that sat there was Reecie's silver '88 BMW, and there seemed to be a shadow of a person behind the wheel.

Marcus swallowed hard and took one step forward. A cautious step, like a baby trying its legs for the first time. After that, two more steps, and before he knew it, he was striding toward the car as if it were on fire. He slowed just before it, not knowing which was the best way to approach, the passenger's or driver's side. He stepped to the passenger's side, feeling that, for some reason, if he was too aggressive moving to her side of the car, she might feel threatened and speed off.

He lowered himself, peering into the darkened car. Reecie was looking up at him, and even though he had no idea what was to come, how relieved he was to be staring into her face again.

She reached over and opened the door for him. "Can I get in?" Marcus asked, only ducking his head into the car.

"Yes," Reecie said, and there was absolutely nothing Marcus could read in her voice that would let him know where he stood with her. He sank into the low seat of the car and turned to Reecie, wanting to spill his guts, wanting to tell her everything, but he was stopped by the fact that she was just looking quietly out of the front windshield, as if he weren't there at all.

Marcus sat there watching her, feeling very anxious, knowing that she was probably reliving the day that she had driven up to the house, tracing the steps from the driveway to the door, thinking about the moment she'd stuck the key in the lock, turned the handle, and then . . .

"Reecie," he said now, trying to stop her mind from seeing that excruciating image once again, if that was actually what she was thinking.

"Reecie, I'm sorry."

Reecie didn't respond right away, but after a moment, in a very small voice, she said, "So I got your letter."

"Reecie, I'm so sorry," Marcus said again, hoping she would believe him.

"Was it that bad, Marcus?" she said, turning to him, then quickly looking away, as if the image of his face was too painful for her.

"No. It wasn't bad at all. It was wonderful," he said, scooting closer to her, as close as the bucket seats would allow, as close as he felt he could without sending her running, screaming, from the car.

"Then why did you go through all that? Why couldn't we have just been together?"

"Because I was a fool. Reecie, I love you so much," and then Marcus ventured to take her hand. She jumped a moment, then tried to tug it softly away from him, but he held fast to her, wrapping both hands around hers.

"I told you all this in the letter, but I was just afraid of loving you so much, of getting married, loving you even more, and then losing you."

"And why would you have lost me?" she said, turning to him.

"Because it happened that way with my father, seems to happen that way with everyone."

"But we aren't your parents, and we aren't everyone else, Marcus. Why can't you see that?" She shook her head, as if her attempts at trying to prove that to him had failed, and always would.

"I see that now. I see it, I'm past it, and I want us to be together."

"And the frizzy-headed girl?"

"Just like I told you in the letter, she meant nothing. It's you I want. It's you I want to spend the rest of my life with."

Reecie looked away, staring out the windshield again, and then without looking at him, she said, "I don't think so, Marcus. Because you say how much you love me, but your actions say something entirely different."

"You want actions?" Marcus said, and he was going into the inside pocket of his jacket. "It was that day that I went out to get this," he said, fishing something out. It was a small blue box. Reecie still was looking away from him, but he took her hand and placed it on the soft fuzzy surface of the tiny box.

"Look at it, Reecie. Go ahead."

After a moment of resistance, she took the box in her hand, and brought it up before her face.

"I knew that very moment that I wanted you forever. Hell, I knew when I heard your car pull into the drive that I had made the biggest mistake of my life. So after you left, I told that girl that I was sorry about dragging her into a situation I wasn't man enough to handle, and then I kicked frizzy-head out."

Reecie cracked a thin smile, but it quickly disappeared after she realized that Marcus had probably seen it.

"I drove straight to the jeweler's after that. Well, aren't you gonna open it?"

Reecie stared down at the box, then up at Marcus, then back to the box. With her other hand slightly trembling, she cracked the top of the ring box. It snapped open, and Marcus could hear a short gasp escape her. Her lips parted slightly, her entire face seeming to soften at the sight of the brilliant, one-carat solitaire.

"It's beautiful," she breathed. "But I can't." She closed the box and passed it back to him, turning her head to look out the window, as if staring at it too long would make her want to take it back.

"And why not?" Marcus asked, alarmed.

"Because . . ."

"Because you don't love me?" Marcus interrupted. "Is that it, because that's the only reason I'm accepting. Tell me now, the truth, and I'll forget all about this."

Reecie didn't look at him, nor did she reply at all. Marcus took that as her admission that she did still love him.

"So that's all that matters. Marry me, Reecie. Marry me, and make me the happiest man in the world. It would be wonderful," and his mind was filling with all the pictures of them jumping the broom, and soon after that, her giving birth to his son. He would be the proud father, the great father that he had never had, but knew now he wanted to be.

"Marry me, and we'll have a wonderful life. Just you, me, and our child," Marcus said, looking lovingly down at Reecie's midsection. "Imagine how it'll be to raise our . . ."

"Marcus," Reecie called, interrupting him.

" . . . to raise our boy. It will be a boy you know, don't you?" Marcus said, smiling.

"Marcus," Reecie interrupted again, her voice filled with sadness.

"What?" Marcus asked, his smile disappearing, seeing the sadness that was on Reecie's face. That look put something on Marcus's mind, something that Reecie had said that she would do when she found Marcus and Sarah together. But no, Marcus thought, feeling a pain in his heart. She wouldn't have done that.

"What, Reecie?" Marcus asked again, fear in his voice. "Tell me you didn't do it. Tell me you didn't kill our baby."

Reecie said nothing, just stared at him, the sadness still in her eyes. He reached across the car and grabbed her by the shoulders.

"You didn't. You didn't do that. Tell me you didn't do it," Marcus said, filling with anguish, looking at Reecie, down at her belly, wondering how she could allow someone to cut their child out of her.

"You say that you love me, were always talking of getting married, and when you get pregnant, the first thing you do is run down to the damn clinic to get it cut out of you! What kind of woman are you?!"

"Don't you dare talk to me that way," Reecie said. "As though you have no guilt in this. When I was told by that doctor that I was pregnant,

I was so happy, I couldn't wait to get home to tell you. The entire way home I thought about how you would look when I gave you that news, how happy you'd be, and how you would take me in your arms, and we'd jump around with joy, because we were having a child. But when I opened the door," Reecie said, shutting her eyes, putting her hands over her face, as if the image was ever present, and there was nothing she could do to rid herself of it, "I saw you and some bitch straddled across you, pawing at you, kissing you. And the first thing I thought was, all the years we've had together meant nothing. At that moment, all I wanted to do was get that baby out of me. Rid myself of anything that had to do with you, because you didn't love me, never did, or you wouldn't have done such a thing. You brought us here, Marcus. No one but you."

And there was nothing Marcus could say about that. His vocal chords were frozen with guilt, with the fact that she was right. And that guilt sank down into his chest, into his belly, making him double over with the pain that it was he who'd actually killed their child, or at least, put her on the path to wanting to kill it, and that was the same thing.

A red-filtered image of Reecie in that doctor's office, her legs held open, heels elevated high, strapped into stirrups, came into Marcus's head. He could not see the doctor's face, just the top of the paper surgical cap he wore. He saw his head duck down in between Reecie's legs, then heard the burr of some sort of tool, a saw, or knife, or vacuum, and at that moment, hot tears came to Marcus's eyes. He reached over, fumbled for the door, quickly hung his head out of the car, and felt as though he wanted to vomit, but just coughed hard, his back painfully arching up with each false eruption. Then he jumped out of the car, staggered away from it on wobbly legs, while wiping the tears from his face.

"You killed our child," he kept saying over and over again, his hands to his face, moving in no specific direction but where his legs chose to push him.

Reecie raced up behind him, following him, taunting him.

"How does it feel to love something so much that it feels like a part of you, then all of a sudden you lose it?"

"You killed our child," Marcus said again, not knowing where Reecie was, but trying to move away from her voice.

"Now looking back on it, did it make sense to do what you did?" she spat at him.

"Get away from me," Marcus shouted.

"Was it worth losing all that you did, just because you were afraid of the future, afraid of commitment?!"

"I said, leave me alone."

"I will. I'll leave you alone," she said, slowing, then stopping behind him. "But tell me this. If you had a chance to do it all over again, to take everything back, would you?"

Marcus stopped, pulled his hands from his face and turned to walk to her. His eyes were puffy with the tears he'd spent, and he sniffled as he approached, trying to pull himself together.

"Would you do that to save us?" Reecie asked, looking up into his eyes.

Marcus swallowed hard, cleared his throat, and spoke without any hesitation or indecision. "I would give my life for us and that child, if I could take it back." Then he leaned slightly toward her, like he was going to take her in his arms, or kiss her, but stopped himself, shaking his head, as if something within him told him it was too late for that, and then he turned and started to walk away.

"Marcus," he heard Reecie calling behind him, but he ignored her, continued moving toward his house.

"Marcus," she called again, this time adding, "Our baby is not dead. I never said that. You just assumed it. I could never do such a thing. Your child is here, still growing inside me." She placed a hand on her belly.

Marcus turned, not knowing what to say, what to think. But he ran to Reecie, grabbing her up in his arms, squeezing her tight, then quickly pulling himself off her, for fear of crushing their child.

"Don't worry. You won't hurt her," Reecie said.

Marcus showered Reecie with kisses all over her face, her neck, even bending down to kiss her on her stomach.

"You aren't lying to me, are you? You didn't do it?"

Reecie shook her head. "No." She smiled.

"I'm so sorry, sweetheart," Marcus said, taking her face in his hands, and kissing her lips. "I'm so sorry."

"I know that. I could tell. But I don't ever want to go through this again."

"Then does this mean you'll marry me?" Marcus said, excitement in his voice.

"Yes," she said. "I'll marry you."

That was six months ago, but his wife hadn't changed a bit. Marcus moved one of his arms from under his head and held it before his eyes. He stared up at his watch and figured Reecie had been fuming long enough. He walked down the stairs, threw on a jacket, and opened the front door of his house. He looked outside a moment, stepped out, and pulled the door closed behind him. He took the stairs, not slow, not fast, but as if he was about to take a leisurely walk about the block.

He walked out to the curb, bent down, and tapped on the passenger window of Reecie's car. She manipulated a switch on her side, and his window mechanically slid down a crack.

"Can I get in?" he spoke into the small space, a knowing smile on his lips.

"What makes you think I want you to come in?" Reecie said, not looking at him, but through the front windshield.

"Because you said you were going somewhere where someone wanted you, and after driving all over the world, you realized that place was right here. And besides, you always come out here when you have something on your mind."

Reecie unlocked the door, then readjusted herself in her seat, which she did with some difficulty, considering she was eight months pregnant and her stomach sat big and round in between her legs, like a large laundry bag filled tight with wet clothes.

Marcus sank into the low seat of the car and smiled over at her.

"Don't you be smiling at me. I'm mad at you," she said, crossing her arms over her huge belly. "Are you seeing someone else?"

"Of course I'm not seeing someone else."

"Then why won't you make love to me? Why haven't you made love to me in I don't know how long?" Reecie said, pulling the halves of her jacket over to try and cover the roundness of her belly. "Is it my condition?"

Marcus leaned over and tried to lay a kiss on Reecie's cheek, but she quickly pulled away.

"No, don't try that lovey-dovey stuff on me. Tell me the truth. You don't want to make love to me because I'm pregnant, do you?"

"Kinda like that."

Reecie looked shocked by his response, and began fumbling for the handle of the door to let herself out of the car.

"Hold it. Hold it, Reecie," Marcus said, grabbing her arm. "It's not like that. It's just that I'm afraid . . ." He lowered his head in embarrassment.

"Just tell me, Marcus," Reecie said, perturbed.

"It's just, look at your stomach." He laid a palm on its tight roundness. "All this is baby up here, and I don't know how far down it goes, but I'm imagining pretty far. Now, I'm pretty big," Marcus said, nodding his head, as if to reassure himself of that fact. He was sliding his hands all around the surface of her belly now, as if measuring a piece of furniture to make sure he could fit it through a narrow doorway. "And what would happen if I go . . ."

"Oh no," Reecie said, shaking her head and laughing. "You're not about to say what I think you're about to say."

"No, this is serious. What happens if I go slipping and sliding all up into you, with our baby sitting in there?"

And now Reecie was bursting with laughter.

"This is serious. I could poke him in the ear, or put one of his eyes out," Marcus tried to explain, but Reecie was laughing so hard, she could barely pay him any attention.

"It's like that magic trick," Marcus said, holding his hands in front of him as if he were holding a balloon. "You know, when the magician slides these huge knitting needles into a balloon, and the entire audience is holding their breath, knowing it's going to pop. What if that happens to our baby?" Marcus asked, with more than a little concern in his eyes.

Reecie calmed herself down as much as possible, smoothing away a tear from the corner of her eye with the tips of two of her fingers. "Babies don't pop, Marcus," she said, letting out the last of her laughter, and she leaned forward, took his face in her hands to give him a kiss on the lips. "But you are so sweet for making sure they didn't before you slipped and slid your big ol' self up in me," she said, starting to laugh again.

"All right, now you're making fun," Marcus said, waving a scolding finger at Reecie. "But now that you say it's okay, I think I'm about to get me a piece of that long overdue lovin' right now." He lunged over his seat toward Reecie, grabbing her in his arms and kissing her all over.

"Ever done it in a car, Mama?" he asked, while undoing the top button of her shirt, but he flew backward, almost jumping out of his skin, when a knocking came at the passenger-side window.

Marcus whipped his head around to see who it was, thinking it would have been a policeman standing there, preparing to flash a bright light in their faces, but it wasn't. It was a man, thin and neglected, his clothes hanging off him as if they were two sizes too big. The man bent down to look in the car, making Reecie move quickly to pull her jacket over herself, even though the only part of her that was exposed was the tiny bit of skin just behind the undone top button of her shirt.

The man's face looked dirty, for all the strands of hair that grew there, long and curly about his chin and cheeks. And his hair was long, and it was mussed, as if a comb had not been dragged through it in years.

Reecie was pushed as far away up against the opposite window as she could have been, Marcus daring to move a little closer to the man outside the car so he could say, "Who are you? And what do you want?"

"Marcus," the man said.

And at that moment, Marcus realized who it was. The man looked almost just like him. They were of the same light brown complexion, had the same brown curly hair, although Marcus's was neatly cut, and they were almost the same height, but Caleb was much thinner, as he had always been.

"It's me, Caleb," the man said, moving his face just a little closer to the window to give his brother a better look.

"That's Caleb," Reecie said, waving at him, but Marcus quickly grabbed her hand and forced it down.

"You didn't tell me he was getting out of prison," she said.

"That's because I didn't know," Marcus said, pushing her out of her side of the car, and for some reason, going through the effort of contorting his body this way and that to get out on that side as well.

He walked Reecie around the car, keeping both hands on her hips, as if wanting to control her actions.

"Man, you guys are having a baby," Caleb said, excited, and reached out to touch Reecie's belly as she came near him.

Marcus felt her start to move toward his brother, but he redirected her away from him, and gave her a little shove toward the house.

"Go on in. I'll be in there in just a few minutes." Reecie looked at Marcus as if he were crazy, then took steps toward the house, stopping on the porch.

"So how's it going, big brother? If I didn't know any better, I'd say that you weren't glad to see me," Caleb said, his arms out, open, as if expecting a hug.

"You walk up to my car, sticking your head in like you were trying to steal it."

"Well, I didn't know you all would be out here boning." Caleb chuckled.

Marcus's face was stone. "That's not funny, and you look like shit. Have you seen yourself?"

"Appearance isn't my highest priority after being in prison for five years."

"It doesn't appear to be," Marcus said, with no regard for Caleb's feelings. "So why are you here?" Marcus asked, looking over his shoulder to see Reecie standing on the porch.

"What do you mean, why am I here? I haven't seen you in something like four and a half years."

"That's not my fault," Marcus snapped.

"Whatever. I just came to spend time with my brother. I'm headed somewhere tomorrow, so I was thinking, if I can crash here until . . ."

"No. You can't."

Caleb paused, a disoriented look on his face, as if his ears weren't working.

"What do you mean, I can't?"

"Just what I said, Caleb. You can't crash here, you can't do anything here. And to tell the truth, I'm done wasting my time, so I'll catch you whenever," Marcus said, turning his back and walking toward the house.

Caleb ran up to him, grabbed him by the arm, but Marcus spun, swatting Caleb's hand away, taking an adversarial position.

"What the hell is wrong with you?" Caleb said. "You don't want to see me?"

"Did you want to see me, Caleb?" Marcus said, anger and hurt in his tone. "We haven't seen each other in four and a half years, because you wouldn't take my visits. Do you remember that? Do you remember me going up to that prison, calling on you, and you telling them that you didn't want to see me?"

"I was going through something when you came that time."

"And how about the next five times after that, Caleb? And the five times after that? Were you going through something then?" Marcus said, walking up very close to his brother. "And when I sent you letters asking you just what the hell was going on, was there anything in the world that I could do to help, was there so much going on that you couldn't even lift a pen to respond?"

"Yes," Caleb said, his voice hard and low. He was staring directly into his brother's eyes, not six inches between the two of them.

"Bullshit, Caleb. There couldn't have been that much going on that you couldn't even write me back a goddamn letter."

"And how the fuck would you know, Marcus?!" Caleb exploded, and in the distance, Reecie took one step forward, as if worried for her husband.

"How would you know how bad something is behind bars?! When was the last time you spent five years, hell, five minutes, locked up in prison? Tell me, Marcus. Tell me. How the fuck would you know?!"

Marcus didn't back down, did not move an inch from where he was standing, just stood there, still staring in his brother's eyes. He took a moment before answering, searching those eyes, seeing that there was some hurt in them, but they could not equal the hurt that he himself was feeling for being abandoned by his brother. Caleb couldn't know how worried Marcus had been about him then. Wondering if he had gotten sick, was injured, was dead. Marcus had gone up there on ten separate occasions asking to see him, and when he was turned down, tried everything to persuade the guards to get Caleb anyway, drag him out there kicking and screaming, but they would never do it. He tried to tell them that they didn't understand, and they didn't. Because Caleb was his little brother, had always been, and had always been his responsibility, but Marcus had let him get away from him. Marcus had let Caleb end up in prison, and that was bad enough, but now he had lost contact with him altogether. It tore at him for months and months, till he decided that he could not let that bother him if it didn't bother his brother. And on that day, he abandoned Caleb, as he felt Caleb had abandoned him.

"All that I did for you coming up," Marcus spoke slowly, softly. "All that I tried to do for you. Do you remember?"

"I remember, Marcus," Caleb said.

"There was no one more in your corner than me. I would've given anything to you, my little brother. Would've sacrificed anything, but look how you repaid me."

Caleb looked away, as though he was trying to avoid the accusations thrown at him.

"No. Don't look away, because you know it's true. Yeah, you say that you were going through some things, and if you say they were bad, then I'll believe you. But you could've let me know something. Let me know that you were okay, that you even recognized the fact that I was trying to help you."

"Well, I'm sorry," Caleb said, but to Marcus, the apology seemed hollow, as if Caleb felt he really had nothing to be sorry for, but was just saying it for his brother's benefit.

"I'm afraid it's too late for that, Caleb. After Mother died, I was all about keeping you, me, and Austin together as a family. One of the reasons was because I promised her I would. But the other was because I just wanted to, I felt we were worth it. But now, I have to accept the fact that I've failed Mom, and that I no longer care about us being a family anymore. I'm tired of worrying about what happens to the two of you, and bending over backward to try and help. I'm concentrating on my family now. So if you'll excuse me, my wife needs me." Marcus turned to walk away from his brother, not looking at, but past Reecie, who was now behind the screen door, as he approached the house.

"So it's like that now, huh, Marcus?"

"Yeah, Caleb. It's like that. It's just like that," Marcus said over his shoulder, not turning back. He climbed the stairs, walking through the screen door, stopping in front of Reecie, for she wouldn't let him by.

"You can't just let him leave like that."

"Yes, I can, and I will," Marcus said.

Reecie turned. "Caleb," she called, and attempted to push her way out the door.

Caleb turned, too, stood there in the middle of the lawn, as if wanting a reason, any reason, to be let in the house.

Reecie pleaded with Marcus. "Why are you doing this?"

"Because it has to be done. I can't take care of them anymore. I have my own family to care for, and you should appreciate that more than anyone," Marcus said.

"But he's your brother. Do something."

"And you're my wife, so let it be," Marcus said. "Just let it be."

"Fine. Have it your way," Reecie said, leaving Marcus standing there at the door. He watched her walk through the house and up the stairs. When she was out of sight, he slowly turned to see his brother walking off into the darkness of the street. He placed a hand to the screen, wanting to call him, wanting to push through the door, run and get him, and bring him back to his home, set him down, and be his brother once again. But as Marcus had told Caleb, it was too late for that now.

7

Austin paced about his high-rise condo, a snifter of cognac in his palm, taking an occasional drink, trying to calm himself down, still thinking about how he was being treated by his ex-wife. He was an attorney, a divorce lawyer, no less. Why had he never taken his wife to court, sued for custody of the children? Because it would never work, he told himself, taking another sip of the alcohol, wincing a little as it heated his palate. It would never work because the custody laws were made for women, because even though there would be no children without the contribution of the man, men were seen as expendable when it came to raising them.

So he could say that she beat them, that she left them in the house all night by themselves, or that she was an alcoholic. But he didn't have the nerve to lie like that, he thought, now standing over his bar, pouring himself another shot. Yes, he hated how he was being treated, how he was being denied his children, but Trace was a good mother, and he would never do anything to take those children from her, even though it seemed she was trying to do that to him.

He turned to walk back toward the huge floor-to-ceiling windows, when the house phone rang.

"Hello," he said, picking the phone up.

"Hello. Is this Austin Harris?" a male voice asked.

"Yeah. Who is this?"

"Guess."

"Look, I'm not in the mood for games. Tell me who this is, or you're getting the dial tone," Austin said.

There was a long pause, then he heard the voice again.

"You ain't changed a bit. All right, it's Caleb. Your brother, man. Remember me?"

"Caleb," Austin said, excited. "The apartment is 2809, okay?" He pressed the button on his phone that activated the security door downstairs. Austin went to the front door, opened it and stood by it. He knew it would take a moment for Caleb to walk to the elevator, and another few moments for it to carry him up, but Austin was excited to see him, so he waited there, playing different images across his mind, wondering what his brother would look like after more than four years of not seeing him.

Austin heard the sounds of the elevator being lifted up to his floor, saw the doors open, and watched as his brother walked out and into the hallway. Caleb looked down the wrong end of the hall upon exiting the elevator. "Down here," Austin called. Caleb turned, then walked in his direction.

He looks like hell, Austin thought. As if he had been not in prison but on the street, and had fights there, and lost most of them. Caleb extended a hand to Austin, but Austin just looked down at it, grabbed it, then pulled his brother into an embrace. Austin felt him struggle just a bit within his arms, fighting, no doubt against the awkwardness, the surprise of being hugged by the brother who never seemed to care anything about him, but Austin held him close and tight.

"It's good to see you, Caleb. No shit. It's good to see you."

"Yeah, okay," Caleb said, his voice muffled, his face pressed very close into Austin's shoulder.

Austin took his brother inside.

"Want a brew?" Austin asked, standing with his hand on the refrigerator door.

"Yeah," Caleb said.

Austin walked over to Caleb, handing him the imported beer.

"So when did you get out? Why didn't you let me know?" Austin said, taking a swallow of his drink.

"I got out today, and I'm letting you know right now," Caleb said, checking out the label on the beer. "Yup, you ain't changed. Plain old Budweiser is never good enough. You have to buy stuff you can't even read the label on because it's in German."

"Well, only the best will do," Austin said, smiling, taking another swallow. "So tell me. How was it?"

"How was what?"

"Prison," Austin said, with the enthusiasm of a child.

Caleb walked over to the large windows of Austin's condo, stared down at the speckled lights of the illuminated city below him.

"You got the place here, man," Caleb said, ignoring Austin's question. "You doing all right for yourself. I guess Trace ain't got all your loot."

"She tried," Austin said. "But you still didn't answer my question. How was it?"

Caleb turned to look at Austin, a serious look on his face, as if he might still have been reliving the hell that he'd endured while he was in prison.

"I don't want to talk about it, if that's all right with you."

"Oh, okay. I mean, my fault."

"Naw. It's cool. It's just after physically being there all that time, I'm in no hurry to go back mentally, know what I'm saying?"

"I understand," Austin said, smiling uncomfortably. "So how did you find me?"

"The letters you sent me. The return address."

"Well, since I didn't get any answers, I figured you never got them," Austin said, sitting down, draping an arm over the shoulder of the sofa.

Caleb walked over to the chair opposite Austin and sat there, rolling the fat bottle of his beer in the palms of his hands.

"Well, I was going through some things at the time, and . . ."

"Hey, hey, hey, Caleb," Austin said, leaning forward, sticking a hand out, as if to stop him from saying another word. "You were going through something and you couldn't write me back, I understand. You were in prison, while I was out here chillin'. Trust me, I understand, man."

"Too bad Marcus don't feel the same way. I just came from there, and he act like he don't want nothing to do with me."

Austin chuckled a bit at that, thinking of Marcus and his new approach to family matters. "Marcus is on a different page of his life now. He doesn't have many words for me either, since I divorced Trace. But he sure has all the time in the world for my kids." Austin receded into his thoughts, thinking of his children walking happily down Michigan Avenue on either side of Marcus, him holding their hands, pulling them along as if he were their father. "But I'll handle that with him later," Austin said, a hint of jealousy in his voice.

"Things sure did change around here since I was away, hunh?" Caleb said.

"Yeah. To think he was the one that was always fighting so hard to pull you and me together, to keep the three of us a family, and the minute he decides to stop, boom. Here we are, you and me, sitting around having a drink. How ironic is that shit?" Austin said, laughing just a little, but when he glanced over at Caleb, he was not laughing, he wasn't even looking in Austin's direction.

"What's up?" Austin asked.

Caleb turned to face him. "Why couldn't we be like this earlier? I'm thirty-two years old," Caleb said.

Austin had nothing to say, a look of regret on his face. He remembered all the evil words that were spoken between them, all the hateful things they did to each other, and at that moment, Austin wondered the same thing.

"Naw, I'm not asking that question of you, like it was your fault. I acted like an asshole toward you, just like you did me. I'm just putting the question out there, because I guess I wish we coulda been like this a long time ago."

Austin looked thoughtfully into his little brother's eyes, and raised his glass toward Caleb. "Well, me too, lil bro'."

Caleb raised his bottle and gently tapped his brother's glass in a toast. There was a complete and awkward silence after, which prompted Austin to stand up from the sofa and say, "All right, that's enough of that. We don't need to be shedding no tears here during our brotherly moment."

Caleb laughed at the remark, getting up as well.

"I have a guest bedroom over this way," Austin said, walking toward a narrow hallway in the opposite direction of the kitchen. "And you know you're welcome to stay as long as you want."

Caleb was following behind him, but stopped. "I appreciate that, Austin, but I'm outta here tomorrow."

"Tomorrow?" Austin asked, disappointed. "Where you going so soon?"

Caleb started to say something, then held it back. He turned around, facing away from Austin, taking a step toward the living room. He halted there for a moment, looking around, then made a straight line for one of the end tables beside Austin's sofa. Under a lamp sat an old photograph of their mother, Mary, and their father, Julius. In the picture they were young, smiling, standing arm and arm. Caleb picked up the framed photograph and examined it lovingly.

"I remember this," he said. He held it up to Austin as if he got a prize for making the proper identification of the couple. "I didn't know you still had it."

Austin walked over to his brother, looking over his shoulder, gazing down at the picture as well. "Yeah, I never let go of it. It's really the only thing I have of either of them."

"You still miss Mom?" Caleb asked, setting the photo down very carefully.

"Yeah, I still miss her," Austin said, pacing around his apartment. "It's no longer painful to think about her, because it's been so long. But I still miss her. You?"

"Yeah, I do. I think about her every now and then, but I have to stop myself, because I'll wonder how it would've been if she hadn't died when we were kids, and that makes me pretty sad."

"I know what you mean."

"And what about the old man? What do you think about him?" Caleb said, his question formed very carefully.

"Hmmm," Austin replied, rubbing his chin, devoting much thought to the answer. He remembered the last time he saw him five years ago, when his father was all but begging for his forgiveness. He apologized for leaving them, for never being there, and he wanted to be back in his sons' lives. Austin would've taken him back, had actually decided to do it, but Marcus was so much against it that Austin couldn't betray his brother.

"I've been here for you when he was gone," Marcus said. For all the bad times, Marcus had been there to support him, when his father was nowhere to be found, and now Julius wanted to walk back into their lives as though he had not missed a single day. In so many words, Marcus told Austin it was either him or their father, and although it wasn't, that decision should've been a no-brainer. Austin had to deny his father, even though he wanted nothing more at the time than to take him back.

"I miss him, too," Austin said. "Back when the whole thing went down with you and the robbery, he was trying to come back into our lives, but it didn't work out. I guess I never told you about that, hunh?"

Caleb shook his head at the question. "So you haven't spoken to him since?"

"Naw. I thought about trying to find him, but so much has been going on with me, Trace, and the kids, that I told myself I didn't have time. And I feel that if he really wanted to be a family again, he wouldn't have been discouraged so easily, so I just said the hell with it."

"Is that how you really feel about him? You don't care?"

Austin looked at Caleb peculiarly. "Why are you asking me all these questions about Dad all of a sudden?"

"No reason," Caleb said, backing away from Austin, as if something was showing on his face and distance would stop Austin from identifying it.

"We're just catching up. Remember, the toast and all that?"

"Yeah, just catching up," Austin said, still a bit suspicious. "I think you're keeping something from me. I think you have something to say," Austin continued, walking up to his brother, pinning him in the small space of a corner. He looked deep into Caleb's eyes, and yes, there it was. What it was, he couldn't tell, but there was something. Although he hadn't always been close to his youngest brother, he knew him well enough to know when he was hiding something.

"Spit it out," Austin said, grabbing a fistful of Caleb's mangy, oversized jersey.

Caleb didn't speak, just stood there fidgeting, seeming to wrestle with what was in his head.

"Tell me, Caleb, and stop fucking around," Austin said, shaking him a little.

"I shouldn't be telling you this," Caleb said, shaking his head, as though he were about to make a grave mistake.

"Tell me anyway."

"Well, you probably didn't know this, but for the past five years," and then, all of a sudden, he stopped.

"What? What!" Austin said, pissed off, shaking him again. "Tell me."

Caleb closed his eyes, then opened them. "I just wanted you to know that for the past five years I was thankful that you got that other attorney and helped represent me, and tried to save me from going to prison. I really appreciated that, Austin."

Austin regarded him strangely, slowly undoing his fist from around Caleb's shirt. "That's all you had to tell me?" he said, looking at Caleb through slanted eyes.

"Isn't that enough? I'm spilling my guts here."

"Yeah, it's enough," Austin said, less skeptical, hugging his little brother.

"Defending you wasn't a question. I just wish I could've saved you from going away," Austin said, drawing away from Caleb to look into his face.

"It's no big deal. It's over now," Caleb said, trying his best to smile. Austin smiled as well. He slapped Caleb on the shoulder, and said, "Well, I guess you're right." Austin turned and headed toward his bedroom.

"You can do what you want to. Watch TV, raid the fridge, whatever, but I'm about to hit the sack."

"Oh," Caleb said, catching Austin before he walked out of the room. "You think you can take me to the airport tomorrow afternoon?"

"Airport? You leaving the city?" Austin asked, surprised. "Where you going?"

And again, Caleb took a moment to gather himself. "When I was in prison, I met this guy, and after a while, we got to become pretty good friends. He has a place out in California, and he said he really wants me to come stay with him."

Though sad to see his brother go, Austin smiled at the thought of Caleb starting a new life. "That's cool. But are you sure that's what you want? You aren't leaving here because you don't have a place to stay, because I told you, you're welcome here for as long as you want."

"Naw, I'm cool, Austin. For real."

"All right. We'll get breakfast in the morning, finish catching up, and I'll take you out there. But only on one condition."

"What's that, Austin?" Caleb said, sounding as though he knew it would be something terrible.

"We stop off at my barber, so we can get you a cut and a shave and have you looking like a human being again."

"All right," Caleb said, grabbing a handful of the nappy, mess atop his head. "You got a deal."

8

"So where are we going?" Julius asked Cathy from the passenger seat. She was happily wheeling her white Volvo station wagon about the streets of L.A., making turns that Julius had never seen her make, down streets that seemed unfamiliar to him, even thought they weren't twenty minutes from their home.

"I'm not telling, sweetheart. But you'll be glad I took you when we get there. Trust me," she said, squeezing his hand, and there was nothing else that he could do, or wanted to do, he thought as he sat there staring lovingly at her. She was the most beautiful woman in the world to him, all five feet and two inches of her. And even though she'd developed a few more wrinkles over the years, a couple more gray hairs here and there, he was still in love with her orange-brown eyes, and her sweet smile. She had always come through for him, had always been there for him, regardless of the circumstances. She'd never thought twice about her love, or her devotion to him.

He remembered when he'd tried to leave her because he was supposed to die.

"We should just break up now, and go our separate ways," Julius had told her one night, while they were sitting alone in their dark living room. His heart was breaking at that very moment, but he'd had to do it.

"Break up?!" Cathy said, getting up from the couch. "We've been together more than twenty years, and you want to break up now? What the hell's going on?"

"Come back here," he said softly, grabbing her hand, trying to pull her down, but she would not come.

"No. You tell me why you don't want us to be together anymore."

"Cathy, because I'm dying," he said bluntly.

"Julius, I know that. And I still love you."

"But it's not like one day I'm here and healthy, and the next, I'll just keel over and die. This is a disease growing in me, and it's going to . . ." He paused for a moment, an image of his sickened, deteriorating body creeping into his mind. He shook it away and continued. "This disease is going to slowly eat away at me. There'll come a time when I won't be able to walk, or feed myself, or even . . . even wipe my own ass, and I don't want you to go through that."

"You have no choice, because I'm going to be there, holding you up, spooning you food, and wiping your ass, whether you like it or not," Cathy said, lowering herself back down on the sofa next to Julius.

But he stood up, shaking his head. "Don't you see? I don't want that. You're still young, not even fifty-five yet, and I don't want you spending your life caring for a dying old man, when you can be out there finding someone else that you can be with."

"What did you say?" And Cathy was up again, all five feet two inches of her, but she was standing there in front of Julius as if she were a full two feet taller and was about to pound on him.

"Find someone else and do what, Julius? What am I going to do with someone else?"

"Get married," Julius said sadly. "That's what you always wanted, isn't it?"

"Yes. But to you."

Julius lowered his head, knowing he should have taken this woman so long ago and made her his wife. But he let fear of the future, fear of the possibility of his doing to her what he'd done to his first wife, stop him.

"Well, it's too late for that," he said.

"Who says? We're both still here."

"What are you talking about?"

"Julius," Cathy said, taking his face in her small, warm hands. "You're the only man I've truly loved, the only man I'll ever love. This just makes sense."

Cathy took hold of Julius's left hand, and lowered herself to one knee.

"Julius Harris, will you marry me?" she said, grinning up at him.

He'd looked down at her, asking to give herself to him, after all the years he had never asked, and something broke inside of him, allowing all his fear to come to the surface. He felt unsure on his feet, wobbled backward, and lowered himself onto the couch.

Cathy leapt to his side, shaking him. "Julius, what's wrong? What's wrong?"

"I'm going to die. I'm scared," he said, barely able to get the words to come out. He was shaking, and he knew Cathy could feel his fear, for her eyes were filled with worry and concern.

"I've been trying to be brave, to be strong, but I'm not ready. I'm just not ready," he gasped, wrapping himself around her tightly, burying his face in her shoulder. She had no words to comfort him, he figured, for what was there to say? Nothing.

"Julius," he heard her call, and she was reaching around her back to unclasp his hands.

"Look at me, Julius." And when he did, she smeared the tears from his cheeks.

Cathy drew a deep breath, exhaled, then spoke. "I love you, and I want nothing more than you to be here for the rest of my life, but that's not going to happen, so you have to be strong."

Julius turned to look away, but she held his chin and pulled him back.

"Do you hear me? You have to be strong, because everything happens for a reason. And if now is not the time that you're supposed to go, then we'll be together a little longer. But if it is," Cathy said, struggling with her emotions, "then you'll just have to be strong and go. Can you do that for me?"

Julius nodded his head.

"Now say it with me, so I know you mean it."

"I'll be strong," they both repeated.

"But until then, Mr. Harris, I still believe you owe me an answer to my proposal." Julius said yes.

The day Julius heard the good news from Dr. Phillips, he stayed out by the oceanside the entire day. For those hours, he was oblivious to all that was around him, and when he finally pulled himself out of whatever state he was in, he noticed that the sky had darkened around him, the air becoming cool. When he finally got home, there was just a single lamp burning soft and gold behind one of the living room windows.

He walked in to see his wife standing at the window, the curtain parted slightly, as if she were still looking out at him, and hadn't noticed that he was standing there beside her.

"Cathy," Julius said, and she practically jumped out of her skin. She turned toward him as if he were a ghost. She pulled her nightcoat around her, wrapping her arms over her chest.

"Baby, what's wrong?" Julius said, worried.

"I've been here all day, thinking what if it was the cancer that was making you sick. I was thinking how much I love you, how much you've become my life, and that I'm not ready to lose you. I'm not strong enough, Julius. I won't be able to take it." A tear spilled out of her eye and raced down her cheek. "I kept trying to tell myself not to think like that, but you were gone all day, and I . . ."

"Cathy," Julius said, extending his arms, stepping toward her, but she turned away from him, quickly moved to the other end of the room, still keeping her back to him, as if she thought that if she didn't face the bad report, it wouldn't be real, its power would die, not able to affect them.

"You were right. I'm sorry for making you go see the doctor. If you . . ."

"Cathy."

" . . . just would've stayed home, we would've never known and things would've been . . ."

"Cathy, I'm fine," Julius said. She turned to him, a look of bewilderment on her face. "It's gone, baby," he said.

"What do you mean?" she asked, her voice still wavering some.

"I mean, the doctor ran a full battery of tests, and there is no trace of the cancer left in my body. Those were his words exactly."

Cathy turned to face him fully now. And by the look on her face, she seemed to be trying to decipher some riddle she must have felt was there.

"Julius?"

"What?"

"You're not lying to me?" Cathy asked cautiously.

"No, baby," Julius said, slowly shaking his head from side to side, a huge grin widening across his face. But it couldn't compare to the one Cathy wore. She ran toward him, jumped into his open arms, and squeezed him with all she had.

"This is a miracle!" she cried, tears streaming down her face again, these tears of joy. "It's a miracle, baby," she said, leaning away from him to look in his eyes. "You know that?"

"Yes," he said, nodding his head, then kissing her. Yes, he knew.

So why was he so surprised when Cathy's Volvo pulled up and parked across the street from a huge church?

"Why we stopping?" Julius said, looking up and down both sides of the street, knowing that they couldn't have been stopping to go to church.

"Don't play blind, Mr. Harris. You see that church standing over there as big as anything. Now get out, before I have to drag you by your ear as if you were eight."

Julius stood just outside of the door, looking up at the church. It was big, beautiful, and majestic, with its towering steeple, and the vibrantly colorful stained-glass windows reflecting the sun's rays. But what difference did it make how beautiful the place was? It was a church, and it had to have been fifty full years since he'd been in one, other than to get married, or maybe play some cards.

"C'mon," Cathy said, yanking Julius by the arm.

"But why?" Julius said, pulling back, stopping them.

"Oh, how soon we forget. Just the other day, we agreed that you being cured was a miracle, right?"

"Yeah," Julius agreed.

"Well, it's time that you give thanks." And without giving him a chance to answer her, she was yanking again, dragging him up the walkway.

They stopped in front of the church door.

"What makes you think it's open?" Julius said, hoping it was closed.

"Oh, it's open. Every day, baby," Cathy said, and then she walked behind him, placed both her hands on his shoulders, and marched him to the door.

"But we're going to be late for picking up Caleb from the airport," Julius said, speaking over his shoulder.

"We have three hours before his flight lands, and you know it. Now I want you to walk through these doors, walk right up to that altar, kneel down, and thank God for the miracle he gave us."

"Me?!" Julius squealed, turning around quickly to Cathy, as if he feared she might have disappeared in a puff of smoke just that fast, leaving him alone.

"Aren't you coming? Where are you going to be?"

"I've been coming, Jay. All those walks I've been taking every morning? Well, I've been coming here to pray. For you, and for us. Now it's your turn."

"But . . ." Julius tried to fight.

"It's your turn," Cathy said again, sternly now. And then she opened one of the huge wooden doors, and out of it blew the eerie darkness and unsettling calmness of the church's insides. Julius felt like a vampire at that moment, and thought if he walked into the church, he would go up in flames, or at least, one of the church people would come out of one of their dark offices, wearing a black suit with the white collar, waving a cane about, yelling for him to get the hell out of his church.

"Cathy," Julius pleaded one more time. But she shook her head, pointing into the dark, holy place, then giving him a shove forward in the small of his back. Julius stumbled into the church.

"I'll be right out here in the car whenever you're done," Cathy said, then let the door fall closed. Julius watched it slowly swing shut on its hinges, blotting out the sunlight behind it. He shivered when it shut completely, as if it was the cover to his casket, and not just the door on this church.

Julius turned slowly around, took the huge room in. He tilted his head, marveling at the beauty of the huge stained-glass ceiling that hung, what looked like a hundred feet high, above the floor of the cathedral. The light outside burned through its blues, greens, reds, and yellows, making them electric, as if powerful bulbs sat just behind it. He looked at the long rows of wooden pews before him, then up at the altar, and all of a sudden, he felt his fear go away. He took one step forward, looking about for a moment, then walked all the way up to the altar. He stood there, staring at the figure high before him, arms spread, feet, one above the other, nailed to the cross. His body hung there, his head fallen a little to the side, his eyes looking down upon whoever stood under him. And in those eyes, Julius saw peace—he saw forgiveness, infinite understanding, and divine righteousness.

Without knowing it, Julius had lowered himself to his knees and bowed his head. His mind was racing, as was his heart, thoughts scrambling about. Then he slowed himself, breathed deeply. "I don't know where to start. I've never done this before," he said aloud, his voice echoing throughout the room, even though he was speaking very softly.

"But I know I have reason to do it now. You have saved my life, and have given me back one of my sons, after I had thrown them all away. You have given one back to me, and allowed me to live so I can be with him. And I guess I have to ask you. Why did you do it? I don't deserve it. I don't deserve to be here after what I did. I don't deserve to have a good woman like Cathy, after abandoning the good woman that I had. I don't deserve to be so happy, don't deserve to have my life spared, when there are so many good people who are sad and are dying for no reason at all. Why? Why did you do it?" Julius said, then he fell silent. Then after a moment, he lifted his head, peered up into the eyes that looked down on him, and asked again, "Can you tell me why, because I need to know?"

Half an hour later, when Julius made his way out through one of the huge wooden doors, Cathy saw him, and pushed the button to raise her seat up, for she had been leaning back while waiting for Julius.

He walked toward the car, no differently than how he normally walked, and there was nothing on his face that betrayed anything he was thinking, or anything that may have happened while he was in the church. Cathy unlocked the door for him. He got in and sat beside her, looking at her plainly, but not saying a word.

"Well, what happened?" Cathy said, a bit eager to know.

"I just got some things off my chest, that's all."

"Do you feel as though you got something from it?"

Julius's eyes rolled up, as if he was visually searching his mind. "I can't say for sure right now, but I have a feeling I will."

9

 Caleb had to look down at his boarding pass twice to make sure he was in the right place, after walking only a few paces into the plane and finding the number that corresponded with his pass was above a wide leather seat with full armrests, a tiny video screen folded down into one of them, an air phone in the other.

When the voice had come over the PA calling for first class, Caleb had just continued looking down at his magazine, knowing they didn't mean him. But there he was now, standing there looking at the seat, then the ticket stub, and then the seat again.

"Can I help you, sir?" a smiling flight attendant, dressed in the airline's blue and red, asked him.

"Am I in the right place?" he asked timidly, handing her the ticket stub.

She looked down at it, then up at the number, then said, "Yes, sir—4B."

"You sure?"

The attendant smiled, nodded, then hurried off down the aisle to attend to someone else.

"The ol' man sprung for first class. Ain't that some shit?" Caleb said to himself, as he lowered himself into the comfortable confines of the seat. The few belongings he did walk out of prison with, all of Julius's letters, all of Sonya's letters, both bound in separate, thick stacks, held by their own wide brown rubber bands, he now had in a mesh Adventure Green Eddie Bauer backpack Austin had bought him on the way to the airport. He slid the backpack under the seat in front of him, and then settled back into his own.

He leaned back a head that was now neatly cropped, tapered lightly around the temples and neck, his face clean-shaven. He wore baggy jeans, an extra-large FUBU T-shirt, the same clothes that he had when released from prison.

Austin wanted to stop and buy him some new things, but they would have been late to the airport, so instead, he dropped Caleb a fistful of twenties and tens that equaled almost two hundred dollars.

"Man, I can't take this," Caleb said, his backpack on, standing at the gate.

"Why not?" Austin said, "Because you got too much money already?"

"Because I just can't."

"Take it anyway," Austin said, shoving the money in Caleb's jeans pocket. "You got all my numbers. Need anything, just call. Now I got to get to work." Austin grabbed his brother and squeezed him, Caleb hugging him back.

"I love you, man," Austin said.

"Damn, you gettin' mushy all of a sudden. You don't got to say all that," Caleb said, laughing it off.

"Yes, I do," Austin said seriously. "I lost you to prison without telling you that. But nothing will ever happen to you again without your knowing it. You got me?"

"Yeah," Caleb said, nodding his head, touched. "I feel you. And I love you, too."

"I know. Now get your big-head butt on that plane," Austin said, popping the back of his brother's head, then wrapping his arm around his neck and drawing him in for a last quick hug.

"Would you like something to drink before we take off?" another flight attendant said now, pulling Caleb out of his thoughts. This one was thin and brown, with long hair pulled back in a ponytail, and looked too much like his girlfriend Sonya for his mind not to start working and his body not to start reacting just a little. He squirmed in his chair some when he said, "Like what?"

"We have juice, soda, coffee, tea, beer, wine, and mixed drinks."

Caleb wanted a shot of something, but didn't want to spend any of the money Austin gave him, especially on something like alcohol, considering he didn't know what the situation would look like in California.

"I'll have a Coke," he said, looking up at the beautiful brown twin, as if uncertain of his answer.

"There's no charge for any of it," she said, her voice dropping some to be heard only by him, as if she had taken in the look of his clothes, realized he might not have been accustomed to flying first class, therefore didn't know this tidbit of information.

"Oh well," Caleb said, rubbing his chin in his hand. "All of a sudden I changed my mind. I think I'll have a shot of cognac. And I did know that it was all free."

"I know you did," the attendant said, smiling at him.

It didn't take long after the plane was in the air for the two generous glasses of cognac to put Caleb straight to sleep. His chair was reclined as far back as it could go, and the airline's thin blue blanket was stretched out over him and tucked up under his chin. At first he was sleeping soundly, his body still, his breathing steady, as he dreamed of Sonya, the thoughts, no doubt, brought on by the attractive and attentive flight attendant, whom Caleb watched every time she passed by him. He thought of seeing his son, of the three of them spending time just holding each other, tangled up in a big ol' ball of love and comfort.

But then Caleb started to shift around in the wide seat. Only a little at first, the movements almost unnoticeable. But then the tranquil look on his face turned to that of fear, then anger, then pain, and he started jerking, the muscles throughout his body spasming now. In his mind, he saw the image of Ray Ray stretched out across that convenience-store floor, an ever-widening circle of his blood seeping out beneath him.

"Don't leave me. Don't leave me," echoed through Caleb's head. Caleb saw himself standing in the courtroom, saw the large, white-bearded judge sitting high before him.

"Guilty, Your Honor," he heard himself say. Then he heard the closing of the jail cell door the first night in prison. He saw the blackness before him, as he sat embracing himself in a corner of the cell. He heard men's voices in the dark, some laughing, some talking, some moaning in self-pleasure, others in mutual pleasure, others crying in pain.

Still sleeping, Caleb quickly spun in the chair, his left hand snapping, a corner of the blanket jumping off him, folding over on itself.

In his dream, he saw countless faces, mostly black, flashing before him. Then he saw blackness again, with intermittent flashes of light. And he heard voices once again, echoing, angry voices. He saw quick, indistinguishable movements and snatches of what he thought were body parts. He saw hands moving quickly, feet, elbows. He saw torsos writhing, muscles tightened in effort, or against effort. And then he saw the hands again, moving even faster now. Faster and faster, and coming closer until he felt them, and they were grabbing him, here and there, holding him. A hand on his shoulder, shaking him. He heard voices. "Hey. Hey." And then the grip tightened, and he tried to pull away, tried to . . .

"Hey. Wake up."

Caleb snapped out of his sleep, drawing away from the hand that was on his shoulder, the hand of the flight attendant.

"Are you okay?" she asked, a worried expression on her face.

Caleb nodded meekly. But he wasn't, for his face was glossy with thick sweat, his body pushed against the window next to him, as if he feared being attacked.

"Are you sure?" she said.

"Yeah," Caleb said, looking around, making sure nothing from his dream had followed him and was sliding out from under one of the chairs, or creeping down from one of the overhead bins.

"Here," the attendant said, handing him a cloth napkin. "Wipe your face with this. And I'll be back with a bottle of water for you."

"Thank you," Caleb said, but she had already left.

By the time the plane had landed and Caleb was walking out of it in a flow of other passengers eager to see friends and family, he had put the dreams behind him, as he had done every time he had them. He was out now and all that was past him. He was about to start a new life, and everything that happened in the past would remain in the past, he thought, as he looked over the heads in front of him, seeing his father and a woman by his side.

10

Julius caught sight of his son, and he was filled with both excitement and dread. Excitement at the fact that he hadn't seen him in five years, and dread because he had to tell him that his son and girlfriend were not at home, as he had expected. He took hold of Cathy's hand, afraid to venture any farther without her support, and she looked at him, as if knowing exactly what he was feeling.

Julius pulled his wife along, stepping through the crowd of people, as he saw his son doing the same. The closer they got, the wider the smiles on all of their faces became, until they stood right in front of each other. Julius had to just pause and admire Caleb, mentally engrave this moment in his memory before he could do anything else.

He could reach out and touch him, take him in his arms if he wanted to, unlike the last time he saw him, when he wanted so much to do so, but was hindered by the thick penitentiary glass standing between them. His heart thumped heavily in his chest, his hands trembled, his palms secreting sweat. He took another step forward, closing the distance between the two of them and quickly pulled his son into an embrace, feeling Caleb's arms wrap tightly around him.

"It's so good to see you again, son," he said, erupting with emotion.

"It's good to see you too, Dad," Caleb said, smiling, looking over his father's shoulder. He pulled away from his father, looked him up and down, his eyes resting on his father's face.

"You look good, are you all right?" Caleb said softly, only loud enough for the two of them to hear, as if Cathy had never known about the illness.

"I'm fine. But I'll tell you about that later," Julius said, his volume as low.

"Are you sure?" Caleb asked again, and Julius could see that the question wasn't posed the way most people ask it, using it as a greeting of sorts, never really actually concerned with the answer. His son truly cared about him, and seemed as though he would give thought to nothing else until he made sure all was right with him.

"Yes, son. Everything is okay," Julius said, looking his son deeply, proudly, in the eyes, holding the back of his head in the palm of his hand, as he'd done the first time he'd held him as an infant.

"Then why does it look like you're about to cry?"

"Because I'm just so happy that you're back in my life again," Julius said, blinking back any tears that may have been ready to fall. "And I never want us to be apart again."

"Then we won't be," Caleb said, squeezing his father's arms, as if trying to reassure him of that fact.

"Do you mean that?" Julius said, hopeful, feeling now that there was nothing else he could want in life.

Caleb nodded. "Yeah."

Julius stared in his son's eyes a moment longer, as if he was too good to be true, as if he were a dream, and Julius had to make sure that he was awake and this was all real. And then he grabbed Caleb again, and the two men embraced for a long time.

Cathy stood there, smiling, looking as though she was about to cry at this show of emotion. She walked up to them, placing her hand softly on Julius's shoulder, rubbing him there.

"I'm Cathy," she said to Caleb. "You've never met me, but I feel as though we're old friends."

Julius released his son. Caleb extended a hand to Cathy.

"Oh, forget that, and give me a hug," she said. Caleb and Cathy embraced, then Julius wrapped his arms around both of them, thinking how the moment he had been waiting for for five years had finally become reality.

Julius pressed the accelerator of the Volvo a little harder than he usually would, thankful that there wasn't much traffic on the normally-clogged California freeway. He wanted to get out of the car as soon as possible, feeling as though he was trapped in the cramped space. Sitting like that would give them nothing to do but talk, and that would lead to Caleb asking about Sonya and Jahlil again. He had asked about them twice on the walk to the car through the airport, but Julius was able to switch the conversation once by asking him if he was hungry, which he was, and then pretending that he had forgotten where he had parked the car.

"I thought I put the car right here," he said quickly, after Caleb had said something about hoping that Sonya and Jahlil would be there when they got back.

Their conversation over most of the trip had consisted of nothing but small talk, until Caleb reached over and placed a hand on his father's shoulder, and said, "Well, how has it been to be a grandfather over the last five years?"

Caleb looked at Julius, smiling proudly, as though he had known the gift of Jahlil, and was now waiting to hear how in love his own father was with his boy.

Julius glanced up into the rearview mirror, seeing Cathy's eyes there. He gave her a look, for he had no clue to what to say. The same expression was in her eyes, but one that also suggested caution.

"It's been great," Julius said, which wasn't fully a lie, for he had taken care of him for two years.

"And how is my boy doing? I bet you he's big, isn't he?" Caleb said, musing to himself, his focus directed on an image in his mind.

"I'll let you see for yourself," was all Julius could come up with.

Julius drove down the neatly manicured street he lived on in the city of Torrance. A row of trees on each side of the street shaded the block from the hot sun above, as he pulled up in front of his large, beautiful home. Caleb excitedly looked out the window.

"Is this it?" he asked, wide-eyed.

"Yeah. This is the place," Julius said, with as much enthusiasm as he could muster.

Caleb leapt out the car first, grabbing his backpack. He walked quickly toward the house, like a child expecting a birthday party inside, and waited by the door. Julius walked around and held the car door as Cathy climbed out of the backseat.

"What am I going to do?" he whispered to his wife out of the side of his mouth.

"There's nothing more we can do," she whispered back. "We have to tell him the truth."

"Come on." Caleb waved them up. "I haven't seen my family in five years."

Julius slowly marched himself up the walkway toward the house, trying to find something in him, some words he could string together to inform Caleb of all that had happened, and make it make sense, make it not hurt his son, but nothing came to him.

He nervously extended his hand to open the door, the key in his fingers, when he stopped.

"Caleb, I have something to tell you."

"Yeah?" Caleb said innocently.

Julius looked at his son, then at Cathy, but try as he might, the words just would not come. "Nothing," he said, defeated. He slid the key in the lock, turned the knob, and pushed. Caleb was through the door before it had fully opened, and was standing in the living room, his backpack on his shoulder.

"Sonya. Jahlil." He spun around, looking up at the ceiling, as if expecting to hear the patter of their feet just overhead, then hear them moving toward the stairs and appearing at the top of them, but there were no sounds.

"Sonya. Jahlil," he called again, but this time louder, as if they might have heard him the first time, but refused to respond. And he was turning slowly in that circle again, glancing at the closet door, as if it could have been a room they were waiting in. His eyes moved over the sofa, toward the kitchen.

"They aren't home?" Caleb said, not looking at Julius and Cathy, but taking steps toward the hallway. He disappeared down the hall, coming back only after a second, a look of worry on his face. It was a look that said he knew that something was wrong, and when Julius stood there and didn't answer him, he sensed that his son was putting things together in his head.

"Where are Sonya and Jahlil?" Caleb said, now appearing both dreadful and angry.

"Well," Julius said.

"Well, what?" And Caleb walked over to him, stood just in front of him.

Caleb gripped his shoulders. "Tell me what's going on, please," he said desperately.

"They left, Caleb," Cathy said, sparing none of his feelings.

"What do you mean, they left?" he said, releasing his father, looking to Cathy. "What time are they coming back?"

Cathy walked over to Caleb, gripping his forearm just above the wrist. She said the words gently. "They aren't coming back. Sonya left and took Jahlil three years ago."

Caleb stood frozen, his eyes closed, as if the confession were spoken in a foreign language and he was busy trying to decipher its meaning. His teeth clamped down tight, and the muscles over his jaws were visibly tensing. His hands slowly rolled into his fists and started trembling, and he looked as if he were bracing against some impending explosion. Then he said, in a voice that was both painfully restrained and fearful, "What did you just say?"

"That they left three years ago," said Julius. He had pulled Cathy from in front of Caleb, fearful that Caleb would release his anger and hurt her.

Caleb shook his head, as if none of what he heard was true. "No. No, they didn't leave," he said, reaching for the backpack and snatching it off his back. "They didn't leave. I know they didn't." And now he was tugging at the zipper, peeling it back, and shoving his arm into the bag, pulling out a stack of letters. "Because I have proof." He threw the bag into a corner, quickly sifted through the thick stack of letters, and pulled out the second one from the top. He plucked the letter from the envelope, popped it open with a determined snap of his wrist, and proceeded to read from it.

"It's been too long. I can't wait to have you home. See you when you get here. Love, Sonya.'"

He held up the letter so they could see what he read was real.

"It's got this address on it, and it's dated just a week ago."

"It's not real, Caleb," Julius said with a voice gentle enough to coax a man off the ledge of a building.

"You're lying. She wrote this," he countered, raising his voice.

"Look at the handwriting closely. You know that's not hers, don't you, son?"

Caleb looked down at it quickly, up at his father, then grabbed it between two tortured fists, and took a longer look at it. The top edge of the page vibrated with the trembling of his hands.

"I wrote the letters, Caleb," Cathy volunteered.

Caleb looked up slowly, his eyes like those of a bull's ready to charge.

"You did what?"

"I wrote the letters," Cathy said, shame in her voice.

"For how long?" Caleb asked, in a way that sounded as though he could believe none of this was true.

"For as long as they've been gone."

"You did that?" Caleb said incredulously, even more angered, taking a step toward her.

"We knew you needed those letters to make it through, Caleb," Julius said, trying to calm his son.

"And how did you know what to put in them?" Caleb asked, and when Cathy didn't answer right away, he answered himself, as if just coming to the realization.

"You read my letters to her, didn't you?" And this angered him all the more, causing him to explode.

"Who gave you the right?! Who do you think you are, reading my personal letters, pretending to be my girlfriend, and making me think that she's waiting here for me, when she's not?"

"Caleb, I'm sorry, but I thought . . ."

"You thought!" he yelled, waving his hands crazily about his face. "Who are you to fucking think anything about me?"

"Now, Caleb, that's enough," Julius said, moving toward his son.

"You don't know me. You're just some bitch who married my father, and now you think that you can play mother to me, but you're wrong."

And with that, Julius grabbed Caleb by his shirt, shook him hard, and pushed him backward. Caleb tripped over his feet, and fell to the floor.

"This is my wife," Julius said, standing over his son. "And don't you ever speak to her like that again, or you will not be welcome in this house. Do you hear me?"

Caleb looked up at his father, shocked and angry.

"Yeah, I hear you," he said, pulling himself up from the floor, snatching his backpack, throwing it over his shoulder, and heading for the door. "I hear you loud and clear." He opened the door and took off down the street.

Julius ran to the door after him, stopping there, wanting to follow him, but didn't. Cathy walked up behind him, placing a hand on his shoulder, watching as Caleb turned a corner and disappeared.

"I'm so sorry, baby," Cathy said. "I should've never suggested writing those letters.

"It's not your fault," Julius said, his eyes still focused on the corner. "He's just angry about his girl and his child. But he'll calm down, and when he does, he'll come back." Something inside Julius didn't believe what he said, as much as he wanted Cathy to believe that he did, and that saddened him. After all those years of waiting, anticipating having his son back, it looked as if he were losing him all over again.

11

Caleb sat on a green paint-chipped park bench, folded over at the waist, as if he would be violently ill. He wrapped his arms around himself and rocked gently, mourning the loss of his family. Not as if they had left him, possibly never to be found again, but as if they had been in a terrible, head-on auto collision, consumed in a torrent of flames, and then obliterated in a powerful explosion.

It wasn't that bad, Caleb thought, but what difference did it really make, because they were still gone forever. Pictures of Sonya's face, of his son's face, kept flashing through his mind. The first day he'd met Sonya in line outside of the Regal Theater, how she'd smiled brightly at him, the first time he'd made love to her, the feeling he'd felt then, knowing that this would be the woman he would spend the rest of his life with. He remembered the roundness of her belly when she was pregnant with Jahlil, the point when the doctor told Caleb that he saw the head, and Caleb yelled the news to Sonya, who was lying on the delivery table, covered in sweat, breathing madly. Caleb saw in his memory the first time he held his son, the first time his son took a wobbly step toward him and smiled his toothless grin when he fell forward into Caleb's arms. And the images kept coming, flashing at him faster and faster, as if he were about to die, giving him one last look before he took his final breath.

No, he wasn't dying, but something inside him wished he had, questioned how he would be able to continue to live without his family. It was them that he'd thought of every single day he was behind those bars. It was them he saw when he closed his eyes at night, and only that image, the feeling he got in his heart when he thought of them, would calm him enough to allow him to fall into sleep.

Caleb remembered rushing to get his mail every Wednesday, tucking it under his arm, and quickly heading back to his cell, looking over his shoulder, as if someone would try and take the letters from him. Once there, he would sit and eagerly open them, always one from his father and one from Sonya. Caleb would read Sonya's second, devouring it quickly the first time he read it, wanting to find out what was going on with her, his son. Then he would go over it again, savoring every word, as if she were speaking the letter to him, right next to him, in his ear, and he could hear each word as she clearly spoke it, could hear her breathing as she paused, inhaled and exhaled, could feel the warmth as the air pushed out from between her lips and tickled the fuzz on the rim of his ear. Caleb would read over that letter at least four or five more times before the day was done, and one more time just before lights out. It was the next best thing to having her there with him, him being there with her, because they were her words, her thoughts, or at least that's what he'd thought.

Caleb bent further forward, embraced himself tighter, pressing his upper body closer against his thighs, thinking how for the last three years that he was in prison, believing that Sonya was still loving him, still waiting for his release, none of this was happening. An additional pain came when he thought about all the things he'd written to her, his feelings, his desires, his fantasies about after he was released. He preferred the letters to the phone, knowing that hearing her voice would only make him feel ashamed for what he had done, and only make his time away harder for him to endure. He could remember once scrawling words sloppily across a sheet of paper with one hand while masturbating with the other, telling her exactly what was happening, and that he always thought of her when he did that. Somehow, the moment came off very intimate for him, and he'd figured she'd feel the same way about it. But she would have never seen it, Caleb thought angrily, because it was Cathy who opened it, and Cathy who read it. Caleb could see Cathy looking over the words, her reading glasses balanced on the tip of her nose, then halting all of a sudden, reading over the last sentence, and then calling Julius.

"Come here and take a look at what your son's doing for fun behind bars." He could see them arm in arm, both holding a side of the page as they read it over, then throwing their heads back with laughter.

Caleb pulled himself up, reached across the bench, and grabbed his backpack. He dug into it, pulled out the letters that were written by Cathy, and held them in his fist. He looked up and saw a wire garbage basket twenty feet from him. He saw himself standing, walking over there to throw the letters away, then lighting a match, and setting the whole thing ablaze, but something stopped him. Even though the letters were phony—what Cathy probably thought Sonya would say—something in Caleb wanted her to be right. He wanted the words on those letters that had Sonya's name signed to them to be the truth, and he worried that throwing them away, or destroying them, might somehow lessen the chances of this being the case.

Caleb slid the letters back in the bag, and looked around, not knowing what to do now. Caleb had run out of the house as quickly as he could with intentions of finding Sonya and Jahlil, and bringing them back, as if they had only a twenty-minute head start on him, and not three years. He ran for two or three blocks, fueled by his urgency, but this urgency in no way aided him in which direction to go, because he had never been here before, had no idea of which way to turn.

He stopped, breathing hard on the corner of a busy intersection, looking around, as if, by chance, he might see them, walking hand in hand, crossing the street. Then Caleb saw a cab, flagged it down, and got in.

"Where you go?" the dark-faced African cabdriver asked, looking into the rearview at Caleb.

And that was the million-dollar question. He had no idea where he was trying to go, where he should go. He thought briefly, thought about where they could be, where she could afford to take them with the little money she had, and even though things could have changed since he'd been away, he assumed they hadn't. He thought about the poor neighborhoods in Los Angeles that he saw in movies and heard about in rap songs, the neighborhoods where black folks lived.

"South Central," Caleb directed.

"Where in South Central?" the cabby said, now turning halfway to look in Caleb's direction, but not directly at him.

"Doesn't matter."

When they arrived within the city limits, the cabby slowed the car and neared a curb. "This good?"

Caleb looked out his window, saw the littered street, the run-down storefront buildings, the shabby people who ambled aimlessly about, their heads hung low. How much it resembled his old neighborhood in Chicago. This was where they could be, or a place like this, and Caleb was about to get out, when he thought, where would he go next? What clue could he follow now? Would he go door to door, trying to read the faded, rain-blurred names on mailboxes? No, he couldn't do that.

"What time is it?" Caleb asked.

"Three o'clock," the cabby said.

"Take me to a school."

"What kind of school?"

"An elementary school, where kids, nine or ten years old would go. Do you know where one is?" Caleb said, leaning over the backseat, digging anxiously into the upholstery.

"I think I do. Sit back."

When the cab slowed and pulled to the curb for the second time, they were sitting in front of a school. It was as run-down as the street they had stopped at, the lawn in front of it, or what was supposed to be a lawn, just a slate of firmly packed gray dirt. The bricks of the building looked old and ready to crumble away if they were brushed up against too hard. The playground off to the side was littered with the fossils of what used to be a swing set, monkey bars, and other things that now lay unrecognizable after being vandalized, or just plain neglected.

Caleb paid the cabby, gave him a decent tip, then jumped out of the cab. He walked up to the school's door, wrapped his hand around the handle, and pulled, but was surprised when it wouldn't open. He tried the second door just beside it, and that too was locked. There was another set of doors at another entrance, which Caleb assumed was probably the main entrance. He tried both those doors, and they, too, were locked.

Caleb turned away from the door with frustration, thinking the school couldn't be closed and everyone gone yet. So he turned back to the door and started to knock. Politely at first, his knuckles tapping lightly against the metal of the door. Five, ten knocks, then the force increased, till he was rapping hard enough to feel the pressure vibrate through his fingers and into his hand. And the longer he stood there and knocked, the longer the door stood unanswered, the longer it made Caleb feel as though this was truly the door that he should be knocking on. That his son stood just behind that door, and all Caleb had to do was get behind it and his search would be over. Caleb abandoned the polite knocking, and began swinging his arm over his head, as if he were throwing a hammer, beating on the door with the butt of his fist and yelling, "Somebody open the door. Will somebody open this door!"

When the door was finally opened, a middle-aged woman, her hair braided and pulled back, stuck her face out, asking, "What's the problem? What's going on?"

Caleb felt only a little embarrassment, rubbing the flat of his fist with the other hand, then said, "Is this an elementary school?"

"Yes, Booker T. Washington Elementary. Can I help you?"

"I'm looking for Jahlil, my son, Jahlil Harris. Is he here?" Caleb asked excitedly, barely able to control himself at the possibility that he could be.

"I'm sorry, Mr. Harris, but school let out almost an hour ago."

"I know, I mean, that's fine, but does he go here? Is he a student here, at this school?"

"Well, sir, if he is your son, shouldn't you know that?" the woman said, moving a little farther behind the door, closing it slightly.

"Yes, I know, but I've been away. I just want you to check to see if he goes here, so I'll know." And then Caleb saw that, for some reason, she seemed scared of him, as if he wasn't who he said he was, and he imagined her closing the door in his face before she even moved to do it.

So when she quickly said, "I'm sorry, sir. I can't help you," and started to pull the door shut, Caleb grabbed the edge of the door with one hand and tried to keep it open. But she was using both hands, and he was using only one, and when she gave it that last tug, it slammed shut, catching the tip of Caleb's middle finger. He cried out in extraordinary agony, shoving the hand into his armpit, trying to stifle the pain. Then he hurled himself against the door again, banging it harder than before with his shoulder, telling himself that his son was surely there, just behind that door, and he had to do everything within his power to get inside. It took him only five more minutes of banging to realize that Jahlil wasn't behind that door, that he probably wasn't even a student of this school, that is, if he even still lived in California. So Caleb abandoned his efforts, and walked slowly over to the playground, folded himself up on the very end of a green bench.

"What will I do now?" he asked himself aloud.

He had left Julius's home, the home that was supposed to be his home from now on. But he was glad he'd done that, because he now hated the man for breaking his promise and letting his family get away. Caleb took a deep breath, then exhaled, and thought for a moment, and realized that deep down, he didn't hate his father. Truth was, he loved the man. Yes, he had left him and his brothers when they were children, but Caleb had accepted that everyone made mistakes in their lives, but not everyone came back and tried to repair those mistakes. His father did. He could have come back sooner, Caleb thought, and maybe he wouldn't have ended up in prison if he had, but regardless of that fact, Julius had tried to do whatever he could to help his son, giving Sonya and Jahlil a place to stay. Was it his dad's fault that Sonya didn't want to stay there any longer? Caleb asked himself. He could see Sonya yelling at Cathy and Julius, cursing them, her things in a suitcase, dragging Jahlil by the hand. "I'm tired of this, tired of your damn rules, and feeling like I'm under some microscope because you're saving me for your son. I can't live like this no more!"

That was Sonya, Caleb knew. He remembered the one time she came to see him in prison, before she went to live with Julius in California.

"I can't do this anymore," she'd said, looking down to avoid Caleb's eyes. "How am I supposed to go on in this relationship with you behind bars? How are you supposed to be a father to Jahlil like this?"

He'd told her that he would never make it without her, but she'd left him anyway. Thankfully, Julius at least convinced her to come stay with him. "I think she might even wait for you," he'd told Caleb. He didn't say he was sure, or that he guaranteed it, and even if he had, Caleb couldn't actually expect him to be able to. So why the hell was he mad at Julius? And although he didn't know Cathy very well, he knew what kind of person she was, knew that she'd been there for his father through his entire illness, knew that she'd waited on him hand and foot when he couldn't do things for himself, and knew that she probably would have shared half his illness, even if that meant her dying early with him, rather than living on years without him.

In his heart, Caleb knew that Cathy wrote those letters because she'd thought, along with Julius, they were the only things that would probably get him through life in prison. She knew he'd be mad as hell at them when he got out of prison, but at least he'd be out, and would eventually come around when he'd had the chance to think about it. She was right.

12

"⚓ This is it," Caleb said, tapping the front seat of the cab. He paid the cabdriver, got out of the car and shut the door, and when he turned around, he was surprised to see his father stepping out onto the porch, as if he was expecting Caleb home soon and decided to wait outside for him.

Caleb froze for a moment, not knowing what to do. Should he walk on up to the house, or jump back in the cab? But then his latter option started rolling down the street away from him, leaving him with only one choice. As he took cautious steps toward the house, Julius walked toward the front of the porch, waiting there at the top of the stairs.

"I need to apologize to Cathy," Caleb said, stepping onto the first stair, resting a hand on the rail, "for what I said."

Julius looked down at his son, seeming as though he was holding back a deluge of emotion, like a child who never expected to see his runaway dog again, only to find it one day, sitting there at the foot of the stairs.

"Cathy's not here. She went to the store, but she'll accept your apology. She understands what's going through your mind." He extended a hand for Caleb to climb the stairs, and then placed a hand on his son's back, directing him into the house. He closed the door behind them, then turned to see Caleb glancing around anxiously.

"I'll just wait around till she comes back so I can say I'm sorry, then I'll leave, if that's all right," he said softly.

"Leave? What are you talking about?" Julius said, concern filling his voice as he took steps closer to his son.

"I can understand if you don't want me to stay here, after what I said to your wife. It was wrong and . . ."

"Caleb," Julius said, embracing his son. "You were furious because of what happened to your family, and I understand that. You were expecting to see them after five years, believing, knowing that you would, and when you get here, you find out that all of it was a lie. A pathetic lie, thought up because I was too much of a coward to tell you the truth," Julius said, letting go of his son, turning away from him in shame for a moment, then turning back to face him.

"You should be angry, and if anyone should be apologizing, it should be me to you. I should've never told you that I would take them. I should've never tried to guarantee something that I knew I couldn't. But you have to know," Julius said now, seeming to plead with his son, "that I was only doing it because I was desperate. Because I needed for you to take me back, because I wanted so badly to make up for all the years that I had lost for leaving you in the first place, for failing as a father. I apologize to you, son, but I was just trying to help you. Seems as though you would've been better off if I had never reentered your life." Julius turned and paced away from his son.

Caleb stood there, looking at his father's back, wondering how the man could feel as though he failed him, could feel as though Caleb hadn't benefited in any way by having him in his life again.

"You saved my life," Caleb said softly, and he was transported back into prison, back to the time soon after the incident happened, back to the time when he hated himself for being there, blamed himself for being so foolish, and wanted nothing more than to stop the nightmares that crowded his dreams at night, to silence the voices, the laughing, the yelling that continued to echo in his head, following him from the place it all occurred.

He had closed himself off from everyone as much as he could, didn't take any visitors, didn't return any letters, and didn't speak to anyone he didn't have to speak to.

His life wasn't worth living, and so after little thought, he realized that there was only one thing that was left for him to do. That night, after lights out, Caleb pulled out a spoon that he had managed to steal from the mess hall. Over the past few days, while outside in the yard, he would stand near a wall of the prison, and hiding his actions behind his back, he would slowly slide the curved side of the spoon back and forth against the cement of the building. At the end of the day, just after lights out, he would pull the spoon out of his sock, and carefully slide a thumb across the increasingly sharp edges, telling himself that in a couple more days they would be sharp enough.

At the end of that third day, an hour after lights out, he pulled the spoon out once more, ran his thumb across the sharpened edge, and it felt more like a knife, more like a razor, than a spoon. It had managed to cut his thumb, drawing a little blood. He stuck his thumb into his mouth, tasting his own blood, and told himself that it was now time to do what needed to be done.

Caleb pulled himself out of his bunk, and sat on the edge of it. The faint, thin strip of light that always splashed into his cell from a nearby spotlight glowed on the ground near his feet. He held the spoon in one hand and placed the wrist of the other into that faint light, allowing him to better see what needed to be done.

He would take the spoon and slice through the artery of his left wrist, and if he had enough strength, he would grab the spoon with that injured hand, and slice the other wrist as well, so it'd be twice as hard to save his life, if someone happened on him before he was dead. This had to be done, Caleb told himself, placing the shaking, sharpened edge of the spoon against his trembling wrist. It had to be done to stop the thoughts he was having, the dreams from constantly tormenting him. He would do this and it would allow him to pass into death where he wouldn't have to hate himself any longer, where no one would have to be burdened by his worthless existence.

Caleb steadied the hand that held the spoon, and lowered the edge onto his wrist. It would be over soon, he told himself, kept telling himself, in an attempt to stop himself from crying, stop himself from chickening out, because this would be for everyone's good, including his. So he pressed the blade farther down onto his skin, until he felt its sharpness, until he felt that his skin was on the verge of splitting. He didn't stop there, but pressed down even farther, sliding it slowly, a short way across his wrist, until he felt something warm escape the cut, and spill up onto his skin. He looked down and saw his blood, dark and thick on the edge of the spoon. He felt his insides flip, and thought he was about to lose whatever was in his stomach. He turned away from the sickening sight, the corner of an unopened letter, peeking out from under some other papers on his table, catching his eye.

That day was mail day, and he'd received the usual two letters he always did, one from Sonya, one from Julius. He had opened hers for some reason, and it said the usual things, how she had missed him, how it was hard for her and their son being without him, and how she hated waiting for him to be released. It did nothing for him but assure him that he would be doing the right thing by taking his life. But he had not opened his father's letter, because he didn't want his father's words stopping him from doing what he knew he had to do. But now, for some strange reason, he had to read that letter, had to know what was written on that page, and if nothing else, it would bring some sort of closure to his life.

So Caleb pulled the sharpened spoon from his wrist, looked at the wound, and seeing that he hadn't cut himself too deeply, wrapped a towel around the cut, and snatched the letter from the desk. He opened it and sat back down on his bunk. He read through three-fourths of the letter, unmoved by the words, till he read . . .

I haven't heard from you in two weeks now, so I imagined something must be on your mind, or something must've happened that is causing you not to write me back. Whatever it is, son, you have to know that you are not facing it alone. I am here for you. I know it sounds crazy, but sometimes I just think about the day you get out, the day I get to see you again, and we stand face to face, father and son. I wonder what I'll say, wonder if I'll try to be cool, and extend a hand for you to shake, or be true to myself, and race toward you and try and pick you up and hug you like you were four again. I think about that a lot, about us just being in each other's company, not saying a word, just appreciating the fact that we are family, and that we love each other, regardless of all that has happened. You are the reason I can have those thoughts, it is because of you I smile so many times in the course of the day. Whatever it is, son, don't let it get to you, because soon it will be all over, and you will be where none of it can touch you any longer.

Love, your father, Julius

P.S. Thank you for letting me be your father again. It gives me reason to keep on living.

Caleb set the letter down, wiped the tear from his eye, and immediately began writing his father back. It was a ten-page letter, telling him everything, every emotion he felt, every thought he had. When Caleb finished, the lights were coming up in the prison. It was morning, but he was not tired, nor depressed.

"What did you say, son?" Julius said, now facing Caleb.

Caleb pulled himself out of his thoughts. "I said, you saved my life."

"What do you mean?" Julius said, looking bewildered.

"The letters, Dad. The letters you wrote me, they got me through," Caleb said, laying a hand on his father's shoulder. "You gave *me* a reason to keep on living."

Saturday night, the sky outside was dark, but the dome light in the roof of Marcus's Accord slowly brightened as he pulled the key out of the ignition. Austin's kids, Troy and Bethany, sat in the car with him, Bethany, in the front seat, Troy leaning forward from the back. They both wore hats from Marriott's Great America, and each clung to huge stuffed animals that Marcus probably paid double for in the children's attempts to win them.

He turned to the kids, smiling. "You guys have a good time?"

"Yeah, Uncle Marcus, it was great," Troy said, both his arms thrown over Bethany's seat. "When can we go again?"

"You'll have to ask your mother that."

Bethany swatted at Troy's arms, trying to push them back over her seat.

"Would you stop!" she said, looking upset.

"Bethany, what's wrong?" Marcus asked her, canting his head to look up into her downturned face.

"He keeps on messing with me."

"I do not," Troy objected.

"No. I think it's something more than that. You seem like there's been something on your mind all day. Tell me what it is, okay?" Marcus said, lifting her chin so he could better see her face.

She didn't speak right away, but looked about the car, as if trying to find anything else to talk about, but when she couldn't, she said, "We were supposed to see Daddy today. Why didn't he take us?"

Marcus shouldn't have even asked her, because he knew that she missed her father, had missed him since he left for the last time. Troy, on the other hand, seemed unaffected by the divorce. He just took things as they came, saw his father when he was able to, and never commented either way when he didn't. But Bethany seemed deeply wounded, as if a life-sustaining organ had been removed from her body. He could not blame her, for he had some experience with how she was feeling. That was why he was spending as much time with them as he could. Marcus remembered what it was like to grow up without a father, and he wasn't going to let his niece and nephew experience that just because Austin decided he no longer wanted to be there for them.

No, Marcus wasn't trying to replace Austin, be the kids' new father, but he wanted them to have someone to turn to if they needed someone, and he wanted them to always feel loved regardless of what happened.

"Well, what am I, chopped liver?" Marcus said, trying to make light of the situation.

Bethany looked up at him. "What is chopped liver?" she said apathetically.

"You don't know what chopped liver is?" Marcus said, with all the enthusiasm of a clown entertaining a room full of cheering children. Then he turned to his nephew and asked the same question. Troy shook his head.

"Oh, I don't believe this. I'm not only going to tell you what chopped liver is, but I'm also going to tell you where it comes from and how to make it," he said, gesturing with his hands, like a two-bit magician preparing to pull flowers from his sleeve. "You ready?"

Bethany lamely nodded her head.

"Chopped liver is a delicious little treat, and you get it from inside your belly," Marcus said, reaching over to Bethany, "and you chop it up by tickling it real fast with your fingers." And he started tickling Bethany, making her curl up in defense, trying to push his hands away and wipe the laughing tears from her eyes at the same time."

"Stop, Uncle Marcus!" she laughed helplessly. "Stop!"

"Am I chopped liver? Am I?" He continued tickling her.

"No!" Bethany laughed and screamed some more, and continued even after Marcus stopped. She slowly sat up, her chest and belly heaving, her face pink and wet with tears. She smeared them away, then looked toward her uncle.

"Listen, guys," Marcus said. "I know what you're going through, and I know you miss your dad sometimes, but he's not going anywhere. He loves you just as much as you love him."

"I know that," Troy said, smacking on a wad of bubble gum, as if he never doubted the fact to begin with.

"He loves you as much as you love him," Marcus said again, giving more attention to Bethany this time. "And he would never think of leaving you, or hurting you, because he loves you too much. Just like your uncle Marcus," he said, smiling proudly. "Okay, Beth?" Marcus said, looking into her eyes to make sure she understood.

"Okay," she said.

"Now give me a big hug. Both of you."

Bethany leapt into Marcus's arms, and Troy pushed himself through the narrow space in between the two front seats and squirmed his way into the embrace as well.

Marcus held the kids there in his arms, them squeezing him tightly around the neck for a long moment, until he started to make exaggerated strangling sounds.

"Uhhhhggggg, I can't breathe. I can't breathe," he played.

"Then what if we squeezed harder?" Bethany said.

"Then I might have to make some more chopped liver."

"Okay, okay, we're letting go," Bethany said, quickly releasing her uncle. Troy pulled away as well, but they remained in Marcus's arms.

"Now, is everybody okay?"

"Yeah," the kids said together, smiling.

"And who loves you more than anything in the world?"

"You, Uncle Marcus," the kids chimed again.

"And don't you forget it." He kissed them both quickly on the cheeks, and moved to get out of the car.

When the front door opened, Trace smiled at the sight of her children.

"You guys have a good time?"

"Yeah, Uncle Marcus won us these toys," Troy said, sliding around his mother and into the house.

"Sorry for getting them back so late. You know how the kids are, once they start having fun."

"You sure they weren't the only kids having fun?" Trace asked, smiling slyly.

"Well, I can go no-handed on the roller coaster, you know," Marcus bragged. "Anyway, I'd love to stick around but I need to get back and make sure my pregnant wife didn't decide to have the baby without me."

"Can you hold on just a minute, Marcus?" Trace said, grasping his hand to stop him from moving toward the door. "I just want to start the kids getting ready for bed, then I'll be right back down."

"Okay."

Marcus watched as Trace ushered the kids upstairs, and even though he knew it was wrong, he couldn't help but notice her body, her slim waist, her curvaceous hips, and the fleshiness of her round behind as she took the stairs. She was a beautiful woman, and he just didn't get what the hell was on his brother's mind deciding to leave someone like that. He had thought about it a thousand times, each time he came to pick up the kids, or each time Trace dropped them by, always looking better than the last time, always as sweet as ever. Marcus wondered at what point Austin just up and decided that she was no longer what he wanted. Did he realize now what a mistake he'd made?

Marcus would never let anything come between him and his wife, let this happen to his family-to-be, because they were the most important thing to him in the world now, and he could no longer imagine living life without them.

"Thanks for waiting," Trace said, coming down the stairs. "I just wanted to talk to you for a moment." Marcus noticed that she looked worried, that something seemed on her mind.

"What's wrong? Is everything okay? Are you making out okay with money?" Marcus said, his hand already wrapped around his billfold, moving to crack it open with the other hand and give whatever was needed to make her problem go away.

"No, no, no, Marcus," Trace said, shaking her head, placing her hand again upon his, pushing the wallet back toward his pocket. "We have all the money we need." She turned, took steps away from him, bringing her flattened hands up to her lips, as if she were praying.

"I don't know what to do with their father. If I'm doing the right thing, handling this the right way."

"Trace, you're a good mother," Marcus said, quickly moving over to her to make his point. "And you can't question your decisions. You make them for a reason, and you have to know that they're right."

She turned back to face Marcus. "But I know it's wrong to sometimes keep them from Austin. If both of them behaved like Troy, if Beth was able to shrug off her father not showing up when he was supposed to and go play video games, I wouldn't be so adamant about protecting her. But she's not," Trace said, shaking her head, as if her child's unlimited love for her father was some sort of illness. "She loves him so much, and not that I do it intentionally, but when I say something against him, she's right there, defending him, telling me to take it back, that it's not true. If I didn't think that it would sound cold and inhuman, I would almost say she loves him too much. And something just tells me that one day, she's really going to be hurt by him."

Trace threw her arms around herself, as if bracing against the confused feelings she was experiencing. She moved toward Marcus, into his space, the space right in front of him, right below his nose. He reached out, placing his arms around her.

"Trace, whatever you do, it will be the right thing, because you're doing it for those children. Austin walked out on you and put you in this position, so don't you go feeling guilty because you have to make decisions concerning them. Do you hear me?"

Marcus felt her head bob slightly up and down, her soft curls rubbing against the coarse stubble of his two-day unshaven face. These were harsh words he spoke against his brother, but Marcus felt he deserved them because Austin was behaving like an irresponsible child, stepping in and out of the lives of his wife and children, as though it had no effect whatsoever.

Marcus grabbed Trace by the arms, leaned her away from him so he could look into her eyes. "And I want to tell you that I'm here. If you're having any problems, if you need me to take the kids for an hour, a day, or a week, you let me know, and I'm there. If you need me to baby-sit, I'm on my way over with pajamas and board games. And if one day you need me to tell Troy about the birds and the bees, well, I'll have to get a book and read up on that, because obviously I'm a little slow, if I'm just having my first baby at thirty-five."

That little joke managed to get a smile out of Trace, which, aside from comforting her, was all Marcus wanted to do. "I love your kids. Being with them is making me look so forward to being a father myself. So whatever you need. I just want you to know that I'm here."

"You don't have to tell me that, Marcus, because for me and the kids you're always here, and I love you for that," Trace said, kissing him on the cheek and giving him a warm hug. Marcus wrapped his arms around her, hugging her as warmly, but quickly jumped away from her when he looked up and saw Bethany standing on the stairs in her night-gown, staring down at them, her fists wrapped around two of the ban-isters, looking through the wooden poles, resembling a prison inmate.

"Bethany," Marcus said, spinning Trace around to see her daughter. He felt hot with embarrassment, nervous with guilt, but knew he had no reason to.

Perhaps it was because his niece had been standing there, for just how long, he did not know, spying on him, as if he was doing some-thing wrong, something to be ashamed of.

"Bethany," Trace said, turning around to see her daughter. "Get your butt in the bed, before I come up there and do it for you."

"Well, I guess I should be going," Marcus said, feeling even more guilty.

"Okay," Trace said, and leaned over to kiss him good-bye on the cheek, but he clumsily jerked away, looking up to see that his niece hadn't listened to her mother and was still staring strangely down at him.

14

When Marcus stepped into his house, all the lights were off, save for a faint glow, pouring around the upstairs corner, and spilling weakly down the stairs. Marcus took the stairs quietly, trying not to make too much noise, in case Reecie was sleeping. When he got upstairs, Reecie was not in bed, but in the bathroom, standing in front of the full-length mirror, her nightgown hiked up just below her breasts to expose her round belly.

"Now that's what I'm talking about. Striptease," Marcus said, sticking his head in the door.

"Oh, shut up, Marcus," Reecie said, not turning around, not dropping her gown, and not taking her eyes from her stomach.

"Well, how about a table dance?" Marcus stood behind his wife, kissed her on the neck, then wrapped his arms around her and rubbed her smooth belly. "How are my babies tonight?"

"I'm fat, Marcus," Reecie said, staring at herself, a look of disgust on her face.

"Maybe if you just stop swallowing babies."

"I'm serious. I look disgusting. I can't wait for this to be over," Reecie pouted, letting her gown fall back over her belly. "I'm tired of not being able to do things because I'm pregnant. I wanted to go to Great America."

"Did you see Dr. Thompson?"

"Yeah," Reecie said, walking toward the toilet.

"Nothing was wrong, was there?" Marcus asked with concern.

"No. She said my pressure was low, that's why I was feeling a little lightheaded," Reecie recited, as if it was no big deal. "She gave me some pills to take."

"Did you take them? Where are they?"

"In the cabinet."

Marcus opened the cabinet, looked over the shelves of bottles, tubes, and short, fat jars, and saw the orange-brown prescription bottle of Reecie's medication. He picked it up, moved his head out of the cabinet, and closed the mirror to find Reecie sitting on the toilet, her elbows on her knees, her face in her hands, a tiny, muffled tinkling sound echoing in the bowl beneath her.

"God, Reecie!" Marcus squawked, covering his eyes. "Must you do that in here?"

"It's the bathroom. Where else am I going to do it?" she said plainly to him.

"Well, you could've warned me, made a sound, rang a bell, somethin'," Marcus said, setting the prescription bottle down and walking out of the bathroom, his hand still covering his eyes.

"Marcus, you have to get over that. We've been together for years and you're still acting like a child," Reecie called out to Marcus, who was standing just outside the door, his back to the door frame. "Where are you going to be when I'm giving birth?"

"As long as you aren't giving birth while sitting on the toilet, I'll be right there," Marcus called back.

"Very funny, smarty pants," Reecie said, flushing the toilet. Marcus heard the faucet water running, then watched as his wife walked past him.

"Don't worry, I won't touch you. I don't want to give you cooties. And, oh yeah, Austin called."

That was just what Marcus needed, bad news to top off a perfectly good day. He exhaled deeply, pulled himself off the door frame, and walked into the bedroom.

"Why did that man call here? He knows I have nothing to say to him."

"He has something to say to you," Reecie said, lifting the blanket and sheet and sliding under them, sitting up in bed. "He wanted to know where you were, and if his kids were with you."

"You didn't tell him, Reecie, did you?" Marcus said, rushing over and sitting on the edge of the bed.

"Of course I did."

"Why did you do that?"

"Because they're his kids, and he has a right to know," Reecie said, sounding somewhat angry at him. "And you know what else? I have a few words to say to you about the way you treated Caleb the other night."

"We had that discussion, remember? It was you bringing it up, and me telling you that it was none of your business."

"What?" Reecie said, disbelief on her face as if she knew her ears were lying to her. She threw the blanket off her, and was slowly, carefully, climbing out of the bed.

"Reecie, what are you doing?" Marcus said, standing, wishing he'd never spoken the remark he just had. "Just get back in bed, and let's talk about this later."

"No, Marcus," Reecie said, waving a finger before him. "We'll talk about this now." She sat down on the edge of the bed, then pulled on his hand, directing him to sit next to her. She looked at him, straight into his eyes, without saying a word, and Marcus could read deep, serious concern. He smiled, wanting, hoping, that she would smile, too, that they would laugh, change the subject, and forget about this, but she didn't. The stare became a bit more intense before she said, "I'm really starting to worry about you." She still had his hand, and now she was rubbing it, gently, soothingly, like someone would stroke the fur of a sick dog that was fully aware somehow that it would soon be put down.

"Your brother has been locked away for five years. This was probably the first place he thought to come to. He asks you can he stay the night, and you turn him away like he was some stranger, some homeless street man you never laid eyes on. Are you aware of the way you looked at him? Are you aware of what you did when he tried to touch my stomach?" Reecie said, standing, resting a hand there. "I thought you were going to grab him and throw him in some sort of choke hold, like he was a criminal."

"It wasn't that bad," Marcus denied, under his breath.

"It was that bad, Marcus. It was. Did you think he was going to hurt the baby? Hurt me?"

Marcus just looked down, not acknowledging the questions.

"I am his sister now. I am his sister, and this child will be his niece or nephew. And then what are you going to do? Are you going to bar him from seeing our child, or will you never let our baby know who he is?"

Marcus didn't respond.

"Well, Marcus?"

"I haven't decided which yet," he replied smugly.

"Don't get smart with me," Reecie snapped. "I mean it."

"And I mean it, too. I haven't decided yet." He looked seriously into her eyes, then away.

"And I don't even want to talk about how you're treating Austin. You avoid his phone calls, you don't accept his invitations to see him, you don't speak two words to the man, but you can spend days and weekends with his children, as if they're your own."

"Troy and Bethany are my niece and nephew, I have the right to spend time with them."

"But they are his children. Give him the time to see them himself."

"That's not my business," Marcus said, shaking his head. "That's between him and Trace."

"Then tell me why are you shutting out your brothers? Because you were hurt before?"

"I have my reasons," he said plainly.

"We've all been hurt," Reecie said, raising her voice, turning to him. "But this is your family."

"I have my reasons," Marcus recited coolly again.

"So what do you plan on doing, disowning them like you did your father after he hurt you? Never seeing them again? Telling yourself that you no longer have any brothers? Hunh?"

And there she was with his father again. He wished Reecie had never been around when all that went down, when Julius tried coming back into his life. Reecie saw a very vulnerable side of him then, saw just how much his father's leaving him had affected him, how wary it made him of being left by everyone else. It was something that he never wanted to admit, but she'd figured it out, and even though it had been five years since that man walked out of Marcus's life for the second time, whenever he got angry, whenever he was irritable, she always had to ask if it was because of his father.

How Marcus hated that man the last time he saw him. How he wanted to hurt his father, wanted him to feel the pain that Marcus had felt all his life, the uncertainty of wondering whether he was abandoned because of something he'd done wrong, or because his father was just a worthless bastard.

"That's right. I'm never going to see them again," Marcus said in the same cool tone, and from the look in his eyes, there could be no mistake that he was dead serious.

Reecie shook her head at the sound of his reply. "I see now. Marcus disowns his entire family because he simply no longer likes them, because they let him down one too many times, and he doesn't want to have to deal with anyone ever again. Do I have that right?"

Marcus nodded his head. "Yes."

"But they're your brothers, Marcus. Why can't you just act like it?" Reecie said.

"I was worried about Caleb in prison, but he wouldn't even see me. And when I went to Austin to talk, to try and find a way both of us could see him, he was too busy to sit down with me for five minutes. All that I've done for them, always around when they needed me, but they couldn't act like brothers the one time I needed them, so I'm done."

"Well, I don't like it, and I don't think it's right."

Marcus got up, stood right in her face, and spoke softly. "To be honest with you, Reecie, on this one, it really doesn't matter what you think." Marcus noticed her taking offense to what he was saying already, but it didn't make any difference. This was none of her business. She was only an outsider looking in. She did not know all that he knew, didn't know his brothers like he did. "This is my family, and I'll handle this the way I think is best," he continued, looking her directly in the eyes. "And all you can do is accept that."

"Is that right?" Reecie said, as if there were a million more things she could do.

"That's right," Marcus replied, turning away from her, walking into the bathroom, and closing the door behind him, telling himself this was the last he would say about it.

15

First thing Saturday morning, Austin called over to Trace's house, hoping that Trace would decide to let him have the kids for the day and overnight, but when he spoke to her, she said, "I'm sorry, they've already left with Marcus to go to the amusement park."

Austin couldn't speak—he just held the phone tightly, angrily, next to his ear, a dumbfounded, betrayed look on his face.

"And you couldn't even tell me? You said you'd think about letting me have them!" he yelled into the phone.

"Austin, calm down," he heard Trace instruct.

"Why are you doing this to me?"

"Austin, we already talked about this," she began, and she was right. All she would do was give the same excuses, make the same tiresome points. So he slammed the phone down. It was all he could do not to curse her, say something that he would surely regret, and probably lessen his chances of seeing his children even more, if that was possible.

After a moment of thought, Austin quickly picked up the phone again, punched in the numbers to Marcus's house, hoping they had stopped there first before going on to the park. He stabbed the numbers quickly, purposefully, as if he was racing against the clock, as if he knew at just that moment, Marcus was rounding up his kids, "Everybody out!" holding the front door open, waiting for them to run out to the car. Austin had to catch them before they had gone.

"Reecie!" Austin breathed into the phone, upon hearing her familiar voice. "Where's Marcus, is he there?"

"No, I'm sorry Austin. He took the kids to Great America. I wanted to go, but I was feeling . . ."

"How long have they been gone?" Austin said, cutting her off.

"At least an hour," she said, then paused. "I'm surprised you didn't know . . ."

"Thanks, Reecie. I'll talk to you later."

Austin didn't call back to Trace's or Marcus's house till well after six o'clock. When he phoned, Reecie picked up the phone, the same sincere, regretful voice, informing him that her husband had not returned yet, but when he did, she would be sure to pass on the messages. He called Trace again, but there was no answer.

Austin waited, not being able to leave the house for fear of missing his opportunity to catch either one of them at home, and not being able to sit still, furious at his ex-wife and his brother. And after a second of thought, he could almost understand why Trace was behaving as she was, even if he didn't agree with it. He knew she was partly motivated by revenge, angry at his leaving her in the first place.

But his brother—for his own little brother to act the way that he had been, to not return his phone calls, to avoid him at all cost, as if they didn't share the better part of their lives together, bathe together in the same tub. Austin wanted to smile at that image, but couldn't bring himself to, because of the stranger Marcus had now become. He had sided with Trace, and Austin knew if Marcus wasn't there to give her emotional support, cheer her on, tell her that she was right to do the unthinkable things she was doing, she probably would have come to her senses long ago and stopped this mess. But she had not, and Austin felt he could blame his little brother for that fact.

Austin waited a few more hours to call, and it took all his willpower to do that. He stood over the phone, watching the second hand of his TAG Heuer watch slowly tick round and round, till the watch read nine-thirty, then he picked up the phone, dialed his wife again.

"Hello," Trace said.

"I don't even want to speak to you, Trace. Just let me talk to my kids."

"*Your* kids. I believe . . ."

"Goddammit, Trace!" Austin yelled into the phone. "I'm tired of your bullshit. I am their father. Now let me talk to one of the fucking children."

There was no response at first, then Austin heard her voice meekly respond, "Beth is brushing her teeth. Here's Troy."

Austin spoke to his son, the angry scowl on his face replaced by a huge smile the moment he heard his little son's voice. But after five minutes of talking to him, the smile had sunk back into a frown, for every other word out of his son's mouth was about Marcus. Uncle Marcus did this, won us that, said such and such.

Then Bethany came on the phone. "I love you, Daddy."

And those were the words he was longing to here.

"I love you too, sweetheart. Did you have fun at Great America?"

"It was okay, but I wanted you to be there," she said sadly.

"I know, baby. And I wanted to be there, too, but maybe next time, okay?"

"I hope so, Daddy, because Uncle Marcus is all right, but you're more fun than he is."

Austin was smiling from ear to ear after that comment from his daughter. "I know, sweetheart. But you should still be thankful that he does all the things with you he does. He can't help that he's no fun," Austin said, still smiling.

"So did anything else happen?" Austin asked.

"No, Mommy just made me go to bed when I saw her and Uncle Marcus kissing," Bethany said.

"What did you just say?" Austin said, not believing his ears.

"Mommy made me go to bed."

"Not that part, baby. The other part," Austin forced, feeling himself becoming anxious.

"Uh, when Mommy and Uncle Marcus were kissing?"

"Yeah."

"They were kissing, and hugging, and Mommy said she loved him."

Those were the words that rang over and over in Austin's head, as he pushed the big Mercedes in the direction of Marcus's house early the next morning. He stopped himself from speeding over there the moment after he heard the news, for fear of killing the man, grabbing him by the throat, strangling him till his face turned bright red and then exploded like a stressed blood vessel.

He would sleep on it, he told himself, which resulted in a lot of rolling around, tossing and turning, trying to blank out images of Trace kissing his brother, or Marcus holding his wife, of them together—he couldn't think about it, or he would just go crazy. So when seven o'clock rolled around, Austin was out the door, not showering, not caring to comb his hair or brush his teeth. He threw on a pair of old jeans and a hooded sweat top, and raced to his car.

The Mercedes screeched to a stop in front of Marcus's house, the back end hiking up with the quick halt of momentum. Austin jumped out of the car, walking quickly at first, then almost running. He punched the little illuminated button beside the door, once, then twice, then three more quick times.

Reecie opened the door, her middle big and round, but appearing as radiant as a pregnant woman in her eighth month can look.

She looked at Austin, and obviously could tell what he was thinking by the look on his face. She said, "You want to see Marcus, don't you?"

"Very good, Reecie. Would you get him, please," he said, straining a smile.

She turned back toward the house, then turned back around to Austin. "You can come in if you want."

"No. I'll just stand out here."

Moments later, wearing sweatpants and a T-shirt, Marcus reluctantly walked up to the door to face his brother.

"We need to talk," Austin said, suppressed anger narrowing his eyes.

"You know I don't have anything to say to you," Marcus said, focusing over Austin's shoulder to avoid looking in his eyes.

"Well, I have shitloads to say to you," and Austin grabbed Marcus's arm as if he were not a thirty-five-year-old man, but his little ten-year-old brother again. Marcus squirmed some, resisted a little, but probably realized that it was useless, considering his older brother had at least twenty pounds and four inches on him.

Austin dragged Marcus down the walkway, then stopped where the walk fed into the driveway, looked around a moment, then headed down the drive, still pulling Marcus along.

"Austin, what are you doing! I have nothing to say to you."

They stopped in front of the garage door, just beside Marcus's car, which was sitting there.

"Open it," Austin directed with the authority of a dictator.

"What?"

"I said, open the garage door! Reecie doesn't need to hear this. And if you were smart, you wouldn't make her have to," Austin said, releasing Marcus, pushing him against his car.

Marcus looked at Austin as if he didn't know what he was talking about, but deciding not to take any chances, he reached into the car, punched the button on the remote garage door opener that hung from the driver's side visor.

The garage door slowly, mechanically, rolled up to reveal an empty room, save for tools of every sort that hung on the walls, and a couple of oil stains on the center of the floor. Austin shoved Marcus under the rising door, and once in, reached over and smacked the button on the side wall. The door paused for a moment, then started to roll in the opposite direction.

"Now, what the hell is this about? What can't Reecie hear?" Marcus said from across the room.

Austin stood there, his attention not on Marcus, but on the decreasingly smaller space under the garage door. When it closed completely with the finality of a stone wall closing on an ancient tomb, Austin rushed over at Marcus, grabbed him by the front of his T-shirt and slung him across the room, where he slammed into a pile of boxes and plastic bags filled with garbage.

"You son of a bitch!" Austin hissed, lurching toward him, his fists heavy and tight at his sides.

Marcus wrestled with the debris falling about his head, clouding his vision, then pulled himself up, only to find himself being grabbed by his brother and tossed across the room again, this time, landing on the floor, falling on his hands and knees, sliding a foot or two across the smooth, dusty cement top.

Fear in his eyes, Marcus turned to see his brother still coming. "What the fuck are you doing?!" he gasped.

Austin was on him again, yanking him up by the now stretched-out collar of his T-shirt. Both his fists were filled with the cotton shirt, as Austin forced his brother backward, tripping, stumbling over his own feet, till his back hit hard against the garage wall. Still holding Marcus by the collar, Austin tightened his grip, pressing his knuckles into Marcus's neck, as if he wanted to push his fists through his brother's throat.

"You're fucking her, aren't you!" Austin spat, fury on his face, in his eyes.

Marcus struggled to speak, opening his mouth, but nothing came out.

"I said you're fucking her, aren't you! Answer me! Say it!"

Marcus drew on whatever strength he had left and batted Austin's arms away, then said, "If you get your damn hands out of my throat, maybe I could." He then bent over, dropped his hands to his knees, breathing hard, trying to catch his breath.

"When did it start?" Austin asked. His voice had lowered, filled less with anger now, more with sorrow.

Marcus didn't stand, but looked up at his brother. "When did what start?" he asked, shaking his head. "And what the hell is all this about, you throwing me around like you lost your fucking mind?"

"You know damn well what I'm talking about. How long have you and Trace been having an affair?"

Marcus looked back up at his brother in amazement. He looked down again, and when he looked back up, a silly smile was on his face. He slowly lifted himself upright, leaning against the wall, giggling a bit, then laughing.

"What! Trace and me having an affair? Where in the hell . . . ooohhh," Marcus then said, throwing a hand to his face, shaking his head. "You spoke to Bethany, didn't you?"

"That's right, and she told me. What the hell is so funny!?"

"Austin, it was harmless, man. You have to believe me. She was feeling bad about what was going on with you and the kids, and she was just thanking me."

"For what?!" Austin said, his voice pure anger now.

"She wanted to know if she was handling things the right way with you and the kids, and I told her . . ."

"You told her, damn right she was, didn't you, Marcus?" Austin said, throwing his hands up in frustration.

"I told her I supported her in whatever decision she makes."

"Who the fuck are you to support my wife," Austin yelled, jabbing him in the chest, "in a decision she makes about my kids!"

"She's your ex-wife," Marcus said, under his breath.

Austin threw his arms over his head, latching on to the back of his skull with his fingers, and paced away from his brother, growling with rage.

"I'm sorry, Austin, but you put yourself in her shoes." Marcus spoke in a small but righteous voice. "If you'd just stayed with your family like I told you, worked on your relationship. But you weren't hearing any of that, because it's always about departure with you. If you aren't feeling a situation, then there's no hope for it, regardless of everyone else involved. If Austin says it's over, it's done."

"Who the hell are you to talk about ending relationships?" Austin bit back. "Caleb has been gone for five years," Austin said, holding up as many fingers in front of Marcus's face, as though he wouldn't understand without the visual aid. "He gets out of prison, and guess who he comes to see first? That's right, you," Austin answered for Marcus. "And then he has to come to my house telling me that you treated him like shit, like you didn't even know him, but then again, I shouldn't have been surprised, considering how you've been treating me. What the hell is that all about, Marcus?"

Marcus lowered his head. "I have my reasons."

"No, no. Fuck your reasons," Austin said, standing in his face now, pointing a trembling finger directly between his eyes. "How dare you disassociate yourself from me and Caleb, as if we were no more than acquaintances you can dismiss on a whim. We are your brothers, and I'm sorry to inform you, but you cannot pick and choose us as you please. And whether you like it or not, we are your brothers for the rest of your life, and you will treat and respect us as such." Austin felt his very soul rattling with fury, but he suppressed it, not wanting to lay another hand on his brother. "Now talk."

"I told you," Marcus said, with a hint of anger now in his tone. "I have my reasons, and if that's not good enough, then tough," he breathed defiantly.

Austin looked sternly in his brother's eyes. Marcus shot the same look back at Austin.

"I'm tired of you. Just fucking tired," Austin spat, then walked away seething. "All that we've been through," he yelled, his head facing up, as if he were not talking to his brother, but to the world, asking them to listen to his argument, see just how trifling his brother truly was. "All the hell that we've been through, Dad leaving, Mom dying, taking care of ourselves, and now, when I'm having problems, need to rely on my brother, he's on the side of my ex-wife, trying to keep my kids from me, trying to hurt me in a way that nothing else can. Do you know what this is doing to me?" Austin said, turning to his brother so he could see the pain in his face. "And then having the one person I always thought would be there just abandon me as though I make no difference to him at all. Thanks a lot, Marcus," Austin said, walking toward the button on the wall, preparing to push it.

"What am I supposed to do?" Marcus yelled, Austin's hand in mid-air, just an inch from the button. Austin lowered his hand, and turned toward his brother.

"How many times have I been the giving one, the caring one, laying myself on the line, always there for everyone, but when I'm in need, there's no one there for me!" he barked at Austin. "Why's that?"

But Austin didn't give him an answer, because he knew Marcus didn't want one.

"I'm the one that's tired. And you talk as though you never abandoned me, as though Caleb never did. What happened after Mom died? Do you remember that, Austin? You went away to grad school. I was just turning eighteen, and you left me there to take care of Caleb. Left me there to deal with the feelings of losing her, walking around in the house she used to live in, raised us in, being reminded of her every day, walking past her door, expecting to see her walk out of it, expecting to see her standing in the kitchen. And did you know I used to hear her voice echoing through those halls sometimes," Marcus said, looking up as though he could almost hear her voice now. "No. You wouldn't know that, because you weren't there. You didn't have to deal with that, and neither did Caleb, because he left to move in with some older woman he barely knew. Didn't take him no time to realize that he didn't want to be there either, and guess what that left me? Alone. How do you think it felt to wake up to that every morning, hunh," Marcus said, stabbing a finger at Austin.

"But I got over it, still accepted you two as my brothers, realized the importance of keeping us together as a family, even though the two of you couldn't stand each other. I was there for the both of you, helping you when you split with Trace the first time, helping Caleb with bills, his rent. I even gave him the down payment for a car. But somehow he still managed to go to jail. And what happens when I go to see him, when I go to tell him that I'm still there for him, that whatever he needs, I will get him? He won't see me. I continue to come, he won't take my visits. I try to call, he won't take those either, won't return my letters."

"He said he was going through some things," Austin said.

"I don't give a damn what he was going through!" Marcus yelled. "I was his brother!" Marcus lowered his head, calmed himself some, and continued.

"So, I didn't want to, but I came to accept the fact that, for some reason, he wanted nothing to do with me anymore. That was hard to deal with, Austin. Very hard, because he was my little brother. But you wouldn't know any of that, because when I tried to come to you with it, you were too busy, too."

"I was in the middle of getting a divorce, Marcus. I had my problems, too," Austin said, but Marcus seemed deaf to his reasoning.

"So I was abandoned twice by the two of you, as if it wasn't enough to be abandoned by our father, then left by our mother. I couldn't take it anymore. I won't take it anymore. It hurts too much, Austin. Those are my reasons."

"So what are you saying? That you're never going to have anything to do with me or Caleb again?"

It took Marcus a moment to answer, but when he did, it was with conviction.

"That's what I'm saying."

"That's a bit harsh, don't you think?"

"I don't care if it's harsh. I'm through with you."

"So that's the kind of ball we're playing, hunh?"

"That's right," Marcus said, no remorse in his voice.

"I gotcha," Austin said, taking steps away from his brother, then turning back to say, "Well, if you're through with me, you're through with my kids, too. There will be no more picking them up from Trace's house," he said, taking a step toward Marcus. "There will be no more outings." He took another step. "No more spending the nights." Still another step he took. "And no more going for ice cream or movies, or anything of that nature," Austin said, taking the final step that put him face to face with Marcus again. "I don't want you calling over there, don't want you sending anything over there, I don't want you speaking to them, don't want you fucking thinking about them. And if you do, if I hear mention from them that they have even heard mention of you, I swear, you'll be sorry. You can't deal with me, you can't deal with them," Austin said with finality, then turned, and pounded his way to the door. He slapped the button; the garage door slowly started to rise.

"Austin, you can't do this. You can't deny me them," Marcus called behind him. "What about when Trace is at work, you know I work at home. I have the time to take them. You know how much time you spend at your firm. Austin, they'll suffer for this. You can't do this."

The garage door rolled up entirely in front of Austin. "Watch me," he said, turning to Marcus. "I'm their father, and I'll do whatever I want."

16

Sunday morning, Julius stood in the middle of his driveway, the sun beaming down warm and bright on his back, as he stared up at the window over his garage. He wanted to move, wanted to walk toward the garage, walk around back to the stairs that led up to the guest house, knock on the door, but he didn't know how he would be received. He didn't know if Caleb would come to the door, exhausted from not sleeping, and dismiss him, tell Julius that he didn't feel like talking to him, not even look at him after the news Julius had given him.

The night before, when Caleb came back, after Julius and he had talked, Julius walked him through the house, taking him out the back door, and into the backyard.

"I want to show you where you'll be staying," he said, escorting him around back to the stairs that led up to the guest house. Julius didn't know why, at the time he was climbing those stairs, his son behind him, the backpack still on his back, he didn't think that seeing the place could have an affect on Caleb. It was because Julius was so excited, because he had cleaned the place up, made it comfortable for his son, and all the while he was doing that, he thought of the very moment that he was in now, climbing those stairs with anticipation of opening that door, and seeing the look on Caleb's face when he saw how nice it was, how big it was. And Julius would say, "You can stay here as long as you like, son. And if there's anything you need, I'll be right next door. How about that?" he would then say, elbowing Caleb in the ribs. "We're neighbors."

But it didn't quite work that way. Julius opened the door, stepped back, and let his son step through the doorway. Caleb looked around the two-bedroom guest house. It was huge, with a large living room, open dining room flowing into a half-kitchen. Windows were every-where, making the space feel very open. The furniture was somewhat plain, but clean and well kept. A large television sat in front of the couch, a small portable stereo sat on the shelf just below the TV.

"So how do you like it, son?" Julius said, stepping in behind Caleb, closing the door. But Caleb didn't answer, just walked slowly farther into the living room, pulling off his backpack, sitting down on the couch without thought as he continued observing the place. Julius no-ticed that he was looking at the apartment strangely, as though there was something wrong with it, or as though he might have been there before.

"Son," Julius said, "what's wrong?"

It took Caleb another moment to answer, but he turned around, a lost look on his face, and said, "Is this where Sonya and my son lived?"

It had been, and although Julius had been the one to clean it up af-ter she took off in such a rush, he'd never thought to prepare himself for that question, this moment.

"Yes, Caleb, it was," Julius said, feeling like a heel, wishing now that he had somewhere else that Caleb could live, an extra guest house or a basement, so he wouldn't have to deal with the memories he was no doubt beginning to be bombarded by already.

Caleb moved into the kitchen, stopped there for a moment, turned around, looked down at the floor, up at the ceiling, then all of a sudden, reached up and opened one of the cabinets. He peered in to find it empty, then he closed it, and opened the one beside it, closing that, and doing the same to the remaining cabinets above and below the sink. He stood in front of the fridge, opened it. It was stocked with food.

"Cathy went grocery shopping for you the other day," Julius said, with the caution and softness of a nurse assisting a doctor during a complicated surgery. But Caleb closed the fridge almost immediately, not interested in the food. Still not speaking, he took quick steps through the dining room again, and disappeared into one of the bed-rooms. He was in there only a moment. Julius heard the closet door opening and closing, heard the pull of a dresser drawer, then heard it being pushed back, the wood of the drawer sliding into its wooden housing.

Caleb walked out, but then ducked into the other room. Julius heard him performing the same ritual, then Caleb was standing in the doorway of the bedroom, long-faced, forced into inaction, for there were no more cabinets or closets to open, and no more drawers to pull.

"This was her room, wasn't it?" Caleb said sadly.

Julius wanted to answer him yes, but the lump in his throat was too big to speak past, so he just nodded his head.

Caleb exhaled deeply, loudly, and with the breath that was pushed out of his body seemed to come all his hope and strength as well. He walked over to the couch, sat himself down, leaning forward, resting his elbows on his knees, his hands dangling in the space between his open legs, his head hanging low.

Julius looked at his son, wanting to do something, touch him, say something, but he had never been in this position with his son before. He was not there when Caleb's heart was broken by his first girlfriend, was not there when he told a woman he loved her but she felt different; he wasn't there for anything, so he had no idea how to respond to Caleb, how Caleb would respond to him. So all he could do was push himself forward, over to the couch, and sit beside his son.

Caleb didn't acknowledge him, and his position did not change the slightest bit. Then after a few moments, he said, not even looking up into his father's face, "Why did she leave?"

And this was the question Julius never wanted to answer, but always knew he would have to. He knew it on the day Sonya left, and as she disappeared from his sight that day, he saw this exact moment, sitting in front of his son, having to have to deal with it. Julius told himself he would put off thinking about it till tomorrow, always tomorrow, never coming up with what he would tell his son, and now, he believed the reason he'd done that was because he didn't want to lie to his son. He wanted to be forced to tell him the truth, not have some elaborate story to fall back on. But now, sitting there, watching as his son turned his face toward him, seeing the sadness in his eyes, knowing just how much what he had to tell him would hurt him, he thought about telling that lie now. Nothing complicated, something as simple as, he didn't know. He just didn't know why she left. There was every reason to say only that, for Caleb wouldn't know if it was the truth or not, and it would save both of them a lot of pain—Caleb the pain of knowing the reason, and Julius the pain of witnessing his son as he found out what the reason was.

Caleb looked deeper into his father's eyes, wanting to know the answer.

"It was because she wanted to see other men and I wouldn't let her."

Caleb closed his eyes and turned away, crushed, putting a hand to his forehead and squeezing.

"Goddamn," Caleb said, under his breath.

Julius reached out toward Caleb's turned back, his hand hovering just over his shoulder, hesitating to comfort his son, then finally letting it rest there.

"I'm sorry that it had to come from me. I didn't want it to be like this."

"No, no," Caleb said into the hand that was now cupped over his face; he sniffed, wiping his face and nose with his hand, then turned to his father.

"No, I appreciate you telling me. You could've told me a lie, told me what you thought I wanted to hear, but you didn't, and that means a lot to me."

"Son, I didn't want her to leave," Julius said, full of sorrow.

"I know you didn't."

"But maybe if I just would've let her see other people, she would've stayed," Julius said more to himself than to Caleb. "But I couldn't let her do that to you right in front of my face. I just . . . I don't know," Julius said, shaking his head, confused in his own indecision.

"She might have stayed here, but not for me. You did the right thing, Dad," he heard his son say, sadness in his voice.

Julius looked up, and there was something resembling a smile on his son's face. He knew it was purely for his benefit, but his son seemed to be making the effort to put the awful past behind him, so Julius decided he would do the same. He lifted himself from the couch with as much spring as he could muster and said, "What do you say about your old man cooking us up a couple of my famous fat burgers?"

"No, Dad. I don't think so. Not tonight."

"I'm telling you, son. You don't know what you're missing. I put beer in them," he said, trying to muster a smile as well.

"No, really, Dad. I just think I want to be alone tonight. Is that all right?"

"Yeah, son. That's fine."

That night, Julius stood in his pajamas at his bedroom window, looking through the curtain.

"What is he doing up there?" He posed the question to Cathy, even though he spoke it at the window. "It's after one A.M. I wonder if he's all right?"

"Julius, he's doing whatever he needs to do." Cathy's voice came from behind him, then he felt her holding him by the shoulder and about the waist, trying to pull him from the window.

"Come on. It's time for you to get to bed," she said, pulling down his side of the blanket as if he were six years old. "I'm sure there are just some things that he has to get right with," Cathy said, slipping into bed herself, reaching over and turning off the lamp. The room went dark, and she leaned over, feeling for Julius's face, and gave him a kiss. "He'll be fine in the morning."

Julius took the final stair that placed him right in front of the guest house door. He folded his fingers into a fist, raised his hand slowly, then knocked lightly on the door. Three times, then paused, then another three times more, a hair harder than the first. He waited another moment, then after no answer, he took the opportunity to turn and walk away, telling himself that his son probably didn't want to hear from him or speak to him anyway. But before he descended the first stair he heard the lock turning from behind the door, and then the door opened. Julius turned back, not to see his son, but the door softly swinging open. Julius pushed the door open, and walked in.

Caleb was sitting at one of the stools, pushed up near the breakfast bar, looking exhausted from thought and lack of sleep. He was tired, and it didn't take much imagination after seeing the sheet that hung from the sofa cushions and spilled onto the floor to know that he had slept on the couch.

Julius closed the door softly behind him and stood at it, looking for what to say or do next.

"Again, let me tell you, I'm sorry about yesterday."

"It's no big deal," Caleb said, the words barely audible from under his breath.

There was silence for quite a while, and Julius couldn't stand it, couldn't stand to see his son suffering like that. At that point, Julius knew that Caleb could do nothing about the situation, no matter how much he tried to search his mind for a clue that would lead him to Sonya and his child. He also knew that the more Caleb sat around and tried to find a way to find her, the more he would come up with nothing, and the more depressed he would become. Julius couldn't stand by and let that happen.

Julius pushed himself from the door, walked across the room, picked the sheet from the floor, and started rolling it around his arms into a ball. He fluffed the pillows, and placed them back neatly on the sofa. Caleb looked up briefly at Julius with little interest, then back down to the blank space of counter he was paying so much attention to before him.

Julius stuck the sheet in the linen closet, closed the door, and said, "Okay, so we have to decide what we're doing today." His voice was as high and chipper as he could possibly make it, considering the situation.

Caleb looked up at Julius again, the heel of his hand smashed into his cheek, no interest on his face whatsoever.

"C'mon, son," Julius said, walking over and standing in front of him. "There are some things I want to do with you today."

"Not today, all right. There's a lot on my mind."

"Sonya."

"Yeah," Caleb said, softly.

"So what are you going to do, son? What have you thought of?"

"I have some ideas," Caleb said, leaning forward on the stool. "But there's nothing I can really do with them till tomorrow."

"Then what good would it do you sitting around moping on this beautiful Sunday? Get washed up and hang out with your old man. What do you say?" Julius prodded him playfully with a shove of his elbow.

Caleb shook his head, doubt on his face, then said, "Naw, I don't think so."

But Julius wasn't taking no for an answer. He marched into the bathroom, yanked back the shower curtain, turned on the water, adjusted it to warm, then marched back out to his son.

"I'm your father right, son?" Julius said.

Caleb didn't answer.

"I'm your father," Julius said again, this time it being said as more of a statement than a question.

"And this is the first time that I'm exerting that authority in thirty years, but you are going to go in the bathroom and shower. There are some of my old shirts that I washed and put in your dresser drawers. You come out, get dressed, and we're going to go out, do some things, have some fun. Do you hear me?"

Caleb looked into his father's eyes, not blinking, not agreeing nor disagreeing with what he said.

Julius softened just a little when he realized that the drill sergeant approach wasn't going over very well. "Son," he said, placing a hand on his shoulder. "I'm as sorry about Sonya and Jahlil as you are, but don't worry, something tells me you're going to get them back. But in the meanwhile, sitting up here in this house mourning their loss won't do anything for you. We have this beautiful day, I'm here, you're here, and we've been waiting to be together for five years now. What do you say we do that? Not harp on what we don't have, but celebrate what we do. What do you say, son?"

Again Caleb looked into his father's eyes without speaking a word, then he just got up and walked into the bathroom. Julius stood there a moment, looking toward the bathroom door, then after another moment, he heard the shower curtain rings slide across the metal pole, and heard the tone of the water change as it no longer hit the bottom of the tub, but crashed against Caleb's bare back.

After Caleb was clean, wearing a light blue, button-down-collared oxford shirt he didn't appear too comfortable in, or proud to be wearing, Julius and Caleb walked down the stairs and out into the backyard.

"You've never seen my pride and joy, have you?" he said to Caleb, as he went about unlocking the side door of the garage.

"Un, uh," was all Caleb said.

They walked into the dark garage. Julius flipped a switch on the wall, the dome on the ceiling lighting up to expose a small tarp-covered automobile.

"You ready for this?" Julius said, excited, leaning over and wrapping his fists around two bunches of the tarp.

Caleb nodded his head coolly, but Julius could see some curiosity and excitement creeping into him as well.

Julius yanked the tarp off, and what lay under it was a shiny Mercedes-Benz roadster. Its shiny red metal sparkled brilliantly, even under the dim light of the garage, as though it had just been meticulously waxed and buffed lovingly with an infant's warm cloth diaper.

"Wow," Caleb said in astonishment, and the word slowly seeped from Caleb's lip like air from a slow leak in one of the tires.

"You like, hunh?" Julius said proudly, rolling the tarp up, sticking it on a shelf, then walking over to Caleb. "It's a beauty, hunh?" Julius said. "It's as old as you are, but she's in mint condition. All her records are up to date, never been hit, everything is original." Julius smiled. "You like her?"

"I love her," Caleb said, looking down in awe, a distorted, reversed image of his face smiling back at him from the passenger-side fender.

"Then I think you should drive her."

"What!"

Julius tossed Caleb the keys. They jumped in, Caleb relaxing slowly into the leather seat, letting his fingers gently curve around the steering wheel.

"You sure about this?" Caleb asked, smiling slyly. "You know I haven't driven in five years. Is the speed limit still ninety-five?"

"Very funny. But I'm not worried about you. I know you'll treat her just like she was your own," Julius said confidently. "And one more thing." He went into his back pocket, and pulled out three fifty-dollar bills and handed them to his son.

"I can't. Besides, I already have a little money."

"Well, take a little more. Consider it the start of the weekly allowance you never got."

It was a beautiful day, the sun was out, warm and bright, so they let the convertible top down. Julius rode beside his son, allowing the wind to blow in their faces, as they laughed about things that required no thought, and held no consequence.

Julius was happy, happier than he had been in a long time. But what was more important was the joy he knew his son was feeling. He looked across the seat to see Caleb carefree as a child, a huge grin on his face, as he wheeled the car quickly down the long stretch of almost-vacant highway before them. Not even a week ago, his son was imprisoned behind bars, in a place Julius could never truly imagine, never fully understand, and never appreciate. There were things that could have and might have gone on in that prison that no man should have to suffer through. But now his son was free of that, and to see him as he was at that moment made Julius feel blessed, and he realized that if it were all over at that very moment for him, he would die a very happy man.

That afternoon, they stopped at a huge park, the grass thick and green, stretching far around them as they tossed a football back and forth lazily through the air. It had been what Julius dreamed of for so many years, the picture-perfect image of a father and son sharing a sunny Sunday afternoon.

After that, Julius gave Caleb directions as they drove to a house. It was a huge house in the valley, the driveway clogged with nice shiny cars, convertibles and coupes, sedans and SUVs.

When they jumped out of the car, Julius paused a moment, looking at the house.

"What do you think about this place?" he asked his son.

"It's beautiful. Why, is it mine?"

"No, son. But it's one of the places my company built before I retired," Julius said proudly.

"It's nice, Dad. Really nice," Caleb said, smiling at his father, and that made Julius even more proud.

They walked up and rang the bell and a gentleman with salt-and-pepper hair and a brown-gold face opened the door. From around him rushed the sound of men's voices loudly cheering, and an announcer calling football plays.

The man smiled when he saw Julius, reached out and gave him a huge hug.

"Old man!" he laughed, clapping him on the back. "Where you been, you missed almost all of the first quarter."

When the embrace ended, Julius said, "With my son, just hanging out."

"Of course," the man said, looking at Caleb with the same huge smile. "Come here, boy." And when Caleb extended his hand, the man grabbed it, and yanked him forward into a hug. "Your old man has told me so much about you," he said, slapping Caleb on the back the same way he did Julius. "It's so good to finally meet you. Come in. Come in."

There had to be twenty-five men there, sitting on sofas and chairs and stools, leaning against walls, and copping squats on the floor. Some were older, Julius's age, some Caleb's. Many of the fathers had their sons with them, and every one one of these men Julius knew. Julius walked through the crowd of men, stepping over them, trying not to bump any arms so as not to shake the suds lose from the heads of any of the beers they were holding. Julius was greeted by, or greeted, everyone they passed, and afterward, he'd say proudly, "And this is my son," as he pressed a hand into Caleb's upper back and kind of pushed him forward. They would shake Caleb's hand, the younger men, coolly, casually, seeing him as brother, the older men, firmly, with authority, seeing him as a son, all of them smiling warmly, saying, "Good to meet you. We've heard so much about you." And that was the truth. Julius had always boasted about the fact that his son would be home soon. And he did not lie, didn't say he was coming from college, or the military, or from a trip around the world. He was coming from prison, but he was his son, and he loved him no less for that, maybe even more.

And as these men greeted Caleb, as they all sat around and cheered at the game, laughed at each other, and ate food and drank beer, Julius could see that Caleb realized that his father was proud of him just for being his son. And during one brief moment, when a touchdown was made, and everyone threw their hands into the air, cheering, slapping high fives, Julius turned to find his son in the crowd. At the same time Caleb had to have been looking for him, and their eyes met, and with no words, they exchanged their feelings—Julius letting his son know how honored he was to have Caleb back with him, and Caleb telling him thank you for having him back.

That evening, when the sun started to set, the men began to file out of the house, into their cars, and drive off. Julius walked toward the driver's side of the car. Caleb fished the keys out of his pocket, and tossed them to his father.

By the time Julius drove into the parking lot at the oceanfront, the sun had pretty much set entirely. The weather was still warm, the stars were out, and a gentle breeze stirred occasionally, then died off.

Both men stepped out of the car, Julius walking slowly toward the large rocks that bordered the water, his son following two steps behind. They climbed up on one of the huge square rocks, stood looking out, as the gentle breeze ushered the water in, pressing the waves into the rocks beneath them.

Caleb looked down, then up at his father. "You come here a lot, don't you?"

"All the time," Julius said, not looking at his son, peace in his voice, as if he were farther away than his eyes could see at that moment.

It was late when Julius finally walked into his bedroom, Cathy sitting up, under the covers, reading a novel, the television on. Julius was beaming like a child with his A-grade test paper pinned to his chest.

"Well, aren't you the night owl," Cathy said, setting her book down in her lap.

Julius didn't say a word, just walked to the bed, leaned over her, and gave her a passionate kiss on the lips.

"Whoa," Cathy said, looking up after Julius drew away. "You must've had a good time today."

Julius was in the bathroom now, taking off his clothes, noticing as he caught a glimpse of himself in the mirror that he was still smiling. He didn't think he could wipe the smile from his face if he wanted to, he was feeling so good. He slipped into his pajamas and walked back into the bedroom.

"It was one of the best days of my life," he said, standing in front of the bed.

"Father and son day," Cathy said, smiling sweetly, seeming as though she knew all that was in his head, in his heart, without his having to say anything more than, "Yup."

"Well, come to bed, cowboy, so we can have a husband and wife night," Cathy said seductively, batting her eyelids, turning down his side of the bed.

But when Julius bent down to get into bed, a quick, sharp bolt of pain stabbed him in the lower back, causing him to gasp, and move a hand back there.

"Are you all right?" Cathy asked, alarmed, sitting up.

The pain passed almost immediately. Julius exhaled, cautiously stood upright, then bent down the same way, testing himself, and when nothing happened, he crawled into bed.

"Yeah, I'm fine," he said, snuggling closer to his wife. "It must've been from tossing the football around today with Caleb and sitting on the floor. It's nothing," he said, dismissing it. "Now, what were we supposed to be doing?" he said, kissing his wife, as he reached over to click off the lamp.

17

Caleb wanted to sleep in either of the bedrooms, but couldn't bring himself to do it. He stood just above Jahlil's bed, looking down, almost afraid to sit on it. He lowered himself, feeling as though he was doing something wrong, something harmful, like sitting on his son, instead of just his bed, smashing the boy there under him.

Caleb pulled himself off the bed, turning to look back at it again. He wouldn't sleep there, something telling him if he did, it would just further limit the chances of his son coming back to sleep in it himself.

He walked out of the room, over to what had been Sonya's bedroom. He stopped just outside the doorway, both his hands gripping its frame, not able to bring himself to even walk in there. It would bring him closer to her, he thought, sleeping in that bed. Maybe he would feel her somehow as he slept, maybe he would smell her scent in the mattress, be able to visualize her better in his dreams if he slept in her bed. But there was a reverse to that, too. Maybe he would smell more than just *her* scent, Caleb thought, as he saw a faint image of her naked body above the bed. She was rolling over onto her stomach, rising to all fours. She hiked her behind up in the air, looking over her shoulder, licking her lips with lustful anticipation. And then from behind Sonya, a naked male slowly contoured his body to hers, slinking one arm around and under her, cupping one of her dangling breasts, the other hand losing its fingers in Sonya's thick hair, pulling her head back.

"No!" Caleb gasped, feeling all his breath escape him, as if he had been hit in the gut with a hard punch. He slumped some in the doorway, his face turned away from the bed, afraid to look back at it for fear the pornographic movie would continue to play out in his mind.

His decision was made for him, and he dragged himself to the closet again, pulled out the linen his father had put away, and began spreading it across the sofa cushions.

She wanted to be with other men was the way his father put it, Caleb thought, pausing just over the sofa now, two corners of the sheet in his hands. And when he really thought about it, that didn't surprise him. He had been gone for five years. Did he really expect Sonya to be celibate that long? Did he think she'd have no sexual urge, no needs? Yes, he would have wanted it that way, but he didn't expect it. So knowing now that she was with someone else angered him, made him jealous beyond comprehension, but it wasn't something he didn't expect, and something he couldn't ultimately get over.

He would have to get them back, he told himself, now tucking the sheet under the cushions of the sofa. He would have to physically go out and search for them, because he had tried the phone book, and her name wasn't in it. He had tried dialing information and was told there was no listing for that name. So he would have to devise some sort of plan, come up with some strategy to find her and their son, so he could at least let her know that he was out of prison again.

But then a quick wave of fear flashed through him, as three questions posed themselves. Would she even care that he was out again? Was she living a life now that she enjoyed more than the life she lived with him? And was she with a man whom she loved now more than she had loved him? Caleb didn't know what the situation would be when he found his girl and his son, but he forced himself not to think about it, because one way or the other, he was going to get his family back.

The next morning, Caleb was out on a dual mission: find his family, and find work. Yes, his father had given him money, and was prepared to continue giving it to him for as long as Caleb needed it. But Caleb couldn't be a leech like that. He had his pride. So he was wearing the light blue button-down of his father's that he had now grown to like. A pair of his father's slacks hung loosely off his behind, but not too loose, precisely the size he would have bought for himself at the store. He looked pretty professional, he thought, as he stepped out of the cab, except for his shoes, which were still the tennis shoes he had walked into prison with. His father's foot was bigger than his, and there was no way he was going to walk about town, his feet flip-flopping, slapping the pavement, as if he were wearing clown shoes.

"Then go buy yourself some shoes," Julius had said, reaching into his wallet again, forking out one hundred dollars and handing it to his son.

"You already gave me money, Dad," Caleb said, raising a hand in protest.

"That was for you. This is for shoes. Now take it before I have to drag you to the store and buy the shoes for you, like you were a child."

Caleb took the money, because he knew he would need it later, but didn't buy the shoes. He wanted to look professional, but still wanted to remain comfortable, and the idea of squeezing himself into a pair of those hard-heeled, pointy-toed deals was far beyond him.

Caleb closed the cab door and stood on the curb, looking at the public elementary school that sat before him. It was Booker T. Washington again, and even though he was pretty sure that Jahlil wasn't a student here, Caleb could think of no better place to start, and he had to make some form of effort.

He took a seat on one of the benches within the play area. He looked down at the old Timex his father let him wear, since he didn't have a watch of his own. Its huge white face spun on Caleb's wrist, since the band was far too big for his narrow bones. Soon it would be time for recess, and he would have the opportunity to see if Jahlil was actually a student there or not.

Fifteen minutes later, scores of children ran past Caleb in a blur. Smears and smudges of what seemed identical smiling brown children's faces raced passed him, just after the bell rang to announce recess.

Caleb stood in the middle of the school's grounds, turning in dizzying circles, trying to pick this one child, his child, the child he had not seen in five years, out of what seemed a river of children. Caleb felt saddened at that moment, to think that he could not immediately identify his own child. A picture of Jahlil emerged in his mind. It was how he last remembered him. Four years old, short, round, pudgy, his facial features softened by baby fat. But now he would be older. Nine years old, and Caleb tried to alter the image in his mind, age it. He would be taller, thinner. But as Caleb tried to change that image in his head, it began to fade and distort and become the child who was standing only a few feet from Caleb. Then it changed again, and became the boy the other boy was talking to.

Caleb shook his head quickly, shaking away that moment of confusion, telling himself, convincing himself, that when he finally laid eyes on his child, he would know him. But the real question would be, Caleb thought, as he slowed to a stop and continued looking about at the screaming, laughing children, would Jahlil know him?

Caleb dug back into his past with his son. Two years after Jahlil was born, Caleb went to prison for two years for possession of marijuana. When he was released, Jahlil was four years old, and Caleb was with the boy every single day, till six months later, when he was sent back to prison for the five years he'd just completed. Caleb quickly did the math in his head, and realized that out of his son's entire life, he had only known Caleb for two and a half years of it. So what made Caleb think the boy would recognize him after not seeing him for the last five years, and even if there was some hint of recognition, why would Jahlil care that he had returned? He had lived this long without his father, had only really had him there when he was an infant, which was a time that he was sure his son had forgotten by now. So why should he feel his life could be improved by the addition of Caleb?

It was a question Caleb wanted to work out in his favor, but he couldn't, for someone caught his eye. It was a boy running, a thin, brown-skinned boy, his baseball cap turned backward on his head, and although Caleb could only see the side of his face, he looked just like his son as he remembered him.

Caleb immediately took off after him, dodging through a maze of talking children. Caleb hoped he wouldn't draw attention to himself and scare his son off before he could even reach him, but it was too late. When the boy looked over his shoulder again, he caught sight of Caleb racing toward him. Caleb saw the boy's eyes bulge in his head, as he picked up speed and changed direction. He was running away from the school now, looking back over his shoulder every few seconds at Caleb.

He's scared of me, Caleb thought, as he pressed himself harder, pumped his legs, his arms, faster, slowly gaining on his son. He's scared of me, thinks I'm some stranger trying to grab him and do who knows what. And Caleb thought of stopping, just giving up and finding him another day, rather than scaring him like this, but he couldn't.

"It's me, son," Caleb yelled, still running as fast as he could. "It's me, your father, and I'm not going to hurt you." But Jahlil wouldn't listen, so Caleb continued to close the distance between them, until he was so close that he could hear his son panting, breathing heavily, just in front of him. Ten more steps, Caleb thought, as he reached out his arm, the ground passing quickly below his feet. Then five more steps and he could grab him.

The boy looked over his shoulder again, but by this time, Caleb's fingertips were already dancing, grazing the surface of the boy's shirt. Another moment later, Caleb had him, grabbed him by his shirt, and dragged him to the ground, where they both fell, Caleb wrapping his arms, his body around him, trying to spare him from the unyielding surface of the ground. When they finally rolled to a stop, Caleb on the ground beneath the boy, his arms still wrapped tightly around him, the boy struggled, kicked, and punched to escape.

"I ain't got nothing! Let me go. I ain't got nothing!" he yelled.

"Jahlil," Caleb said, holding tight to him, for fear he would run if he let him go. "Jahlil, just hold it. It's me," Caleb said, maneuvering to his feet without letting go of the boy, then turning him around so they could face each other. "It's me, Jahlil, your father."

The boy looked oddly at Caleb, then said, "You ain't my father, and why you keep calling me Jahlil? My name is Stevie."

Caleb's grip weakened with the disappointment and realization that this actually wasn't his son. Stevie pushed away from him, looking at Caleb for a moment, a bitter scowl on his face. Then he turned and started to slowly walk away. Not run, not even walk quickly, appearing to have lost all fear of Caleb, because he was not some strange stalker anymore trying to abduct little brown boys from school, but a crazy man who thought every boy was his son, and ran them down till he found out that they weren't.

Caleb got up, dusted himself off, and looked around, hoping that no one had witnessed this. No one had, and for the final time, he told himself that this definitely wasn't the way to find his son.

Caleb walked off the school grounds, his head lowered, fists sunk into his pockets, feeling as though he had failed. He didn't find another cab, but walked the streets, trying to think of what he could do next to find his family, but nothing came to him. There seemed to be absolutely nothing he could do, but wait, and hope that somehow something would come up that would lead him back to them.

Meanwhile, he had to focus on gaining some sort of employment. He had been in this position before, walking the streets, looking for a job, any job, he recalled, as he passed by the run-down storefronts, watching as his reflection stared back at him.

He still had no skills though, knew no trade, except the little he knew about filing computer disks that he'd learned from his last job before he went to prison. But judging by the look of the small businesses he passed on that street, they probably didn't even use computers.

He passed by small clothing stores, barbershops, a butcher's shop, two or three currency exchanges, and a gas station, and nothing appealed to him. Yes, he was desperate for work, but something about these places didn't seem very desirable to him. He knew he shouldn't be thinking like that, because if he were to walk into any of these stores asking for a job, they probably wouldn't hire him. And it could be for a number of reasons. Maybe they wouldn't like his look. Maybe because he had no experience, or maybe just because they weren't hiring at the time. But then there was that one reason he knew would always come up, and always give an employer a reason to tell him no. He was an ex-convict. And considering all the brothas out there out of work who had no records, what was the chance of his getting work with one? His situation seemed hopeless.

After an hour, all of the walking and thinking made Caleb hungry and thirsty. He stopped at the door of a small convenience store, opened it, and walked in. And there, just inside the door, something seemed to loop itself around his throat and squeeze, halting his breath. Immediately, he felt coated with a thin layer of cold sweat, his hand trembling on the handle of the door, his mind telling him to turn and run back out, but his legs refusing to respond.

It was exactly like the store, the one that he, Blue, and Ray Ray tried to rob, the same one that Ray Ray died in. Everything eerily the same, from the placement of the shelves, the counter, and the register, to the amount of lighting overhead, and the scarred gray floor tile underfoot. Caleb turned back to the door, the window shade striking him in the face, and he was transported back five years ago when he looked out behind the shade of that other store, taking watch.

He nervously, clumsily, fumbled to open the door, pushing it when he was supposed to pull, running into it. He took a step back, prepared to open it again and get out of there, when he heard someone behind him.

"Whatcha need, young man?"

Caleb didn't move, just held tight to the door handle.

"I said, whatcha need?"

Caleb slowly turned around to see the old, thin man standing behind the counter. He was a raisin-faced man, his skin black and shriveled, his body narrow, delicate, fragile, with at least what looked like sixty-five years.

"I was just a little hungry and thirsty," Caleb said, softly.

"Well, you gonna buy you something to eat, or not? I got everything, and drinks is in the back."

"Oh, okay," Caleb said, taking slow, unsteady steps down the snack aisle, grabbing the first package that caught his eye. He walked toward the back of the store, and then he was struck again. He was standing just over the spot where his friend had fallen, where he spit his insides out, where Caleb dreamt his parents found him.

Caleb had to ask himself what in the hell was going on? Why was all this happening? Why was he being tortured like this? And it hit him, as an image of Ray Ray's terrified eyes, his blood-covered lips and teeth, came into his mind. Then he saw Ray's mother, felt her arms around him, heard her remind him what he'd promised her, and it all made sense to him now. A place just like the one he'd robbed, a place just like the one in which his friend died, was where he should start to pay back his debt to her and to her son. How could he have not seen that from the moment he walked in the door?

Caleb took a large step over the area he imagined his friend lying in. He opened the glass door of the cooler, pulled out a bottle of grape soda, then headed back to the counter and the old man. Caleb didn't place his items on the counter, but held them in his hands.

"This your store?" Caleb asked.

"Yeah, it's my store," the old man said, seeming offended by the question. "Who else's store would it be? It's mine, and been mine for forty years now." He dabbed a crumpled handkerchief across his wet brow and neck.

"Who else works here with you?"

"Nobody. It's my store, and I'm all who works here," the old man replied. "You want that food or not?"

"Yeah. But I was wondering," Caleb said, setting the grape drink and Hostess cupcakes on the counter. "You need some help around here? I'm looking for a job and . . ."

"Don't need no help."

"I knew you might say that. But there seems to be a lot of work to do around here," Caleb said, turning to look about the store. "And I'm good with my hands."

"Don't need no help, I said," the man repeated, grabbing the cupcakes and flipping them over, looking for the price. When he found it, he punched the number into the ancient cash register.

Caleb just looked at the man, who he knew was avoiding looking at him. He had to work here, and taking no from this man wasn't even an option.

"Look, sir," Caleb said. "I'd do anything to work here. It's very important, and it would mean so much . . ."

"Can't you people hear!" the old man shouted, slamming the cupcakes against the counter, flattening them under his hand. "Everybody want me to stop working or take on help," he said, directing his anger at Caleb, though Caleb knew he was probably aiming it at a slew of other people as well. "It's my store, and I can work it. I'm old, but I ain't dead yet," he said softly, to himself almost. "Now go back there and get you another cupcake, 'cause I ruined this one. And when you come back up here, don't be askin' no more about no job."

Caleb walked back down the aisle, his mind on what else he could do or say to convince the man that he should work there. His mind was not on where he was stepping, so he jumped when he accidentally brushed up against a display of canned beans, toppling them over, sending them crashing and rolling about the floor.

"I'm sorry," Caleb said, spinning to apologize to the man.

"You did that on purpose, wanting to make yourself look useful," the old man barked. "But it don't make no difference. You pick up every one of those cans, stack 'em back, and I ain't giving you a cent for it."

Caleb was already bent over, his head buried below the shelves, chasing down the fat cans of beans. He had lowered himself to all fours, was reaching beneath one of the shelves to retrieve one of the errant cans, when Caleb heard the door of the store open and shut, then heard someone say, "Give me all of your money, you old motherfucker!"

Caleb couldn't believe it. He froze there, his arm outstretched, his fingers grasping for a can. What was this, he wondered, some kind of weird joke? Was he in the damn Twilight Zone?

Caleb quickly, silently, got to his feet, crouching, still below the surface of the shelves.

"I said now, motherfucker. Move!" and Caleb saw, as he raised himself just high enough to see over the shelves, that it was just a boy of maybe fifteen or sixteen, shoving a gun in the old man's face. The boy was trembling, as he should have been. He kept looking back and forth between the door and the man, which told Caleb he was most likely in this alone, having no one to act as look out for him.

What to do? What to do? Caleb asked himself, his mind racing. He could let this go down, not get involved, let the boy get the money and run. Then Caleb could buy his soda and his cupcakes and be out, and that would be the end of it. But what if it didn't go down smoothly? What if the old man got heroic and said something like, "I ain't givin' you shit, you little fucker!" which was exactly what Caleb heard the old man say.

"What! What!" the boy yelled, jabbing the gun farther into the man's face, as if he were going to shoot him, and that's when Caleb knew he had to do something. Not because he truly felt the boy would shoot the old man, because something in his voice told Caleb that wouldn't happen. But he had been there before. He knew it could go nowhere. Knew whatever little money the man had in the register wasn't worth the price the boy could pay.

"You don't want to do that," Caleb said, now standing tall within the aisles, so that he could be seen.

The boy whipped the gun around, looking wide-eyed at Caleb, the fear in his face now growing more intense.

"Don't move, or I'll blow you away."

"Just put the gun down," Caleb said calmly, even though he was shaking inside as badly as the boy was. He eased forward on feet he could not even feel now, seeing his open hands rise up before him, as though they had a mind of their own. "I don't got nothing. I just want to talk to you."

"Stay back, man. Or I swear, I'll do you."

"Naw, you ain't gonna do that," Caleb said, working a phony smile on his face, as if there was nothing to worry about. "You don't want to shoot nobody, and you don't want to rob nobody."

"Yeah, I will, if you keep comin' at me. Now stop right there and get on the floor," he ordered.

"I'm not getting on the floor," Caleb said, shaking his head, his hands still before him.

"Why not?"

"Because I just got off the floor, and I don't feel like getting back down there. And besides, I know you ain't going to shoot nobody, because you don't want to. And you really don't want to be in here trying to rob this store, but there's something going on that's making you feel like you have to, right?" Caleb said, reading the exact thing in the boy's eyes. "Am I right?"

The boy had weakened some, and Caleb knew he was getting through to him, saw the gun drop just a little, but after a second, the boy said, "You don't know shit," then raised the gun back up.

"I do, son," Caleb said, still slowly closing the distance between them. "I do because I was where you are right now. I was there five years ago, and I tried robbing a store, but it didn't work. My friend got shot and he died, and I don't want that to be you. I don't want you to die like he did. Do you want that?"

The boy didn't say anything, but Caleb thought he saw him shake his head.

"I spent five years in prison for trying to rob that store, and I don't want that to be you, either. Bad things happen in prison, let me tell you. I know what you're going through, and it don't have to go down for you like it did for me. Now why don't you just give me that gun?" Caleb said, extending one of his hands in front of the boy.

The boy looked deeply into Caleb's eyes, as if questioning whether or not he could believe him. Caleb knew that was exactly what he was doing, and he tried to appear as sincere and nonthreatening as possible, as he carefully extended his open hand a little farther toward the boy.

"C'mon, you're doing the right thing here," Caleb said, in as cooling a voice as he could speak. "Everything's going to be all right."

He lowered his gun a little farther, something in his eyes telling Caleb that he was about to surrender the weapon to him, when Caleb saw the boy's eyes quickly dart in the other direction, stopping on the old man.

Caleb followed the boy's eyes, and caught the man just as he was raising up from beneath the counter, a shotgun in his hands, pointed at the boy.

The boy quickly turned the gun on the old man, yelling, "I'll fucking shoot you! I'll fucking kill you!"

"And I'll fucking kill you!" the old man yelled back, both of them wide-eyed, shaking with fear, while Caleb stood in the middle of it, fearing that he would be the only one shot.

He had to stay in control, he couldn't lose it here, not now, because there was no telling how badly things could turn out. He would remain focused on the boy, because he seemed to have already covered some ground with him, and he knew the old man felt justified in protecting his own business and would never put down his weapon.

"Listen," Caleb said, turning back toward the boy, both his palms open and held up before the boy. "Just forget he's standing there, okay. Let's just do what we were doing, and just go ahead and give me the gun."

"So he can turn around and shoot *me,*" the boy said, his voice cracking with fear.

"He's not going to shoot you," Caleb yelled, becoming frustrated. "Are you?" he yelled over his shoulder to the man.

"I'm gonna blow his fucking little head off," the old man threatened.

"He didn't mean that," Caleb quickly said to the boy, cursing himself for even asking the man the question. "Now, c'mon, what do you say. I'm pissing my pants here, why don't you just give me the gun, and we can both walk out of here, it'll be all over."

Beads of sweat started to roll from the boy's brow down on to his face. He was scared to death, and becoming even more frightened with every moment that passed. The gun was shaking madly in his hand, and Caleb focused on his trigger finger, saw that trembling as well, and knew if something didn't happen this very moment, this would all quickly spiral downward, and somebody would end up dead.

"Fine," Caleb said. "Both of you motherfuckers want to shoot each other. Then do it. I'm the fuck out of here," and he started walking toward the door, on legs he felt would collapse under him with each step he took.

"Hold it. Where you goin'?" the boy said, his eyes on Caleb, but his outstretched arms still holding the gun on the old man. Caleb looked at the boy, then looked at the man, the shotgun still directed at the boy, and said, "I'm going to let you all do what you want to do. You want to shoot that man, right?"

The boy didn't answer.

"I asked you a question," Caleb said, raising his voice some. "You want to shoot that man, and take all that money he has in that cash register, because you know he got a lot, right? Selling candy bars and sodas all day can make you a lot of money. Can surely make enough that it would be worth killing someone over, right?" The boy still didn't answer. "So go ahead and shoot him."

After the boy still didn't say or do anything, Caleb yelled at the top of his lungs. "Go ahead and pull the fucking trigger!"

The boy jumped, the gun landing on Caleb. Caleb's heart skipped a beat, but he did not show his fear, and kept as cool as he possibly could.

"Oh, so it's me you want to shoot, now," Caleb said, trying to convince the boy he had no fear. "Then go ahead. I'm tired of this shit."

He walked in front of the boy, placing his chest right up to the barrel of the weapon. "Go ahead, big man. You got the gun. You ain't afraid to pull the trigger, then pull it. Pull the damn trigger. Kill me, have that old ass man with the shotgun, who ain't got much time to live himself, kill you, and we'll all be done. Or you can just be smart, and do what I've been asking you to do, and give me the gun." Caleb said the last part softly. "Give it to me, and I promise the old man will let us walk out of here. He won't call the cops or nothing, will he?" Caleb said, directing the question to the old man, with a cautionary tone, demanding he answer the question correctly this time.

"Naw, I won't," the old man said.

"So what do you say?" And again, Caleb was holding his hand out for the gun.

The boy looked up into Caleb's eyes one more time, then slowly handed him the gun.

"Good deal," Caleb said, taking the gun, emptying the bullets, then placing them on the counter before the old man.

The old man grabbed Caleb's arm. "You still want that job, you can have it. All right?" the man said, straining a smile.

"Thanks," Caleb said. "I'll think about it." Then he walked over to the boy, wrapped his arm around his shoulder, saying, "You did the right thing. Trust me," as they walked out the door.

18

After drawing the line on Marcus last Sunday morning, telling him he was not to set foot near his kids, Austin directed a blazing course over to his ex-wife's house to inform her of the same news. Upon reaching her house, he jumped up the stairs two at a time, fueled by the anger built up from dealing with his younger brother.

It was still early, nine in the morning or so, Austin guessed, without even caring to look down at his wristwatch. What difference did it make anyway? he thought. He bypassed the doorbell, choosing instead to rap harshly on the window beside it, for the forceful sound of the glass rattling in its frame under his knuckles better conveyed the mood he was in, rather than the polite "ding-dong" of the doorbell.

Austin was preparing to knock again, harder this time, when he heard from behind the door Trace's muffled voice saying, "Okay, okay." The sound of locks being undone, the doorknob turning, and Trace was standing in front of him, her hair piled atop her head, pulling a robe closed around her waist.

She blew a sigh, obviously not pleased to see him, but Austin didn't give a damn.

"What are you doing here? You aren't supposed to see the kids today, and even if you were, they aren't awake."

"I'm not coming to see them. It's you I want to talk to," Austin said.

"Well," Trace said, standing behind a screen door.

"Can't you at least let me in?"

"I'll come out," she said, opening the door, and stepped out onto the porch, brushing a hand over her hair, looking out at the street.

Austin wanted to ask her had it gone that far, did she hate him that much now that she did not even want him in the house, but he stopped himself, because at that moment, he was so angry that it didn't even matter to him. He was there for one reason, and that was to let her know that, "Marcus is not to see our children anymore."

"Hold it," Trace said. "Where did all this come from?"

"Marcus doesn't want to deal with me, then he doesn't want to deal with my kids."

"No. You can't do that," Trace said, stepping into Austin's face. "He loves those kids and they love him, too. If he doesn't want to have anything to do with you, that's between the two of you. You can't go bringing the kids into that, playing games with them to teach him a lesson."

"I can't?"

"No, you can't."

"And what in the hell do you think you're doing?!" Austin yelled, his loud voice disturbing the serenity of the quiet early morning. Trace scolded him with her eyes, as if cars were stopping on the street before her house, and windows were being lifted on all the neighboring houses, heads sticking out to see what all the commotion was about.

"You're the one playing games," Austin said, lowering his voice some. "We aren't together, and you want to punish me for that by keeping the kids from me."

"I'm not doing that," Trace said, folding her arms over her chest. "I told you what this is all about. I'm protecting them, doing what's best for them."

"By allowing Marcus to see them more than me. Are they confused yet, Trace?" Austin said, looking her dead in the eyes. "Have they mistakenly called him Daddy yet?"

"Don't be stupid," she said, looking at him as though he were behaving like a child.

"He's not to see them. I'm serious, Trace. That man is not to see my children," he said, turning to descend the stairs.

"It's not your right to make that choice."

Austin stopped midway down the stairs, turned, and looked angrily back up at Trace. "It is as much my right as it is yours. And if you make me, I'll do what I have to to enforce that right. Don't make this uglier than it already is, Trace."

Trace seemed to heed his warning and didn't say a word after that.

"And just so you'll know not to make any plans, I'm taking the kids next weekend for Troy's birthday. So have them out here in front by one o'clock next Saturday, since you don't seem to want me in the house."

"It's too late," Trace said, "I've already made plans. He's having a birthday party."

"Cancel it," was all Austin said, then confidently walked down the stairs and jumped in his car, not bothering to look back at her before he drove off. He meant business this time, and he felt she knew that.

But if she knew, why, when he pulled up that Saturday morning, did he see no sign of the kids outside of the house? And he noticed that, even if the kids were out there, he wouldn't have seen them right away, because of all the cars that crowded the curb, and packed the driveway of Trace's house, one of those cars being Marcus's Honda Accord.

Austin couldn't believe this, knew this wasn't happening. After he spoke with his wife, and gave direct orders to his brother, they both just said the hell with him, and did what they wanted to do anyway. Austin stopped his car beside Marcus's, punched the hazards and jumped out. He grabbed the gift-wrapped box he had for his son from the backseat, and slammed the car door. He stopped in front of Marcus's car, looked down on it, and saw the seething, furious reflection of himself in the passenger-side window. He wanted to do damage to the car, wanted to vandalize it, and thought it would probably be a good idea, possibly save that fate from happening to his brother. But instead, he turned and marched toward the house.

As he neared the door, he heard the rise and fall of cheering, gleeful voices. Those of children and adults, and judging by the level of loudness and the number of cars parked around him, he figured there to have been at least twenty-five to thirty people in the house. But it didn't make a difference to Austin. They would just all be witnesses, he thought, as he whipped open the screen door, and made his way inside.

From the moment he stepped into the hallway leading from the front door, he was surrounded by adults leaning against the walls, holding tiny, colorful paper plates in one hand, party food stacked on top of them, Styrofoam cups in the other, red Kool-Aid swooshing around, which they were trying not to spill as they attempted to eat and drink and stand, all at the same time.

Austin continued marching down the hall, the huge birthday gift still tucked under his arm, and as laughing, playing children, darted in front of him, jumped up and down around him, and brushed up against him, he made only mild attempts at avoiding them. He was wearing blinders now, saw only the tunnel he'd follow to lead him to where everything was happening, which would be the kitchen. This was where the high-est concentration of noise was coming from, where most of the people would be.

A couple of people recognized Austin as he took the final few steps toward the kitchen. He heard them greeting him, addressing him, but he paid them no mind, did not nod his head, nor turn to acknowledge them in any way as he pushed past them. Now the blinders were closer together, his field of view tighter, focused on his daughter, laughing and squirming as that man—that's how Austin felt about him now, that man—tickled and hugged Bethany, pulled her tight into him, kissed her on the cheek, whispered something in her ear. And the fury, the ex-treme rage, which was only simmering in Austin's belly a moment ago, was now boiling over, threatening to erupt as he gently set Troy's gift down on a counter, and reached down to pull Bethany away from Mar-cus. Austin was suppressing what rage he was feeling now, hoping his daughter couldn't see it, hoping that he wasn't holding her too tight, even though he wanted nothing more than to rip her away from his brother.

She looked over her shoulder, and seeing Austin, she smiled wider and said, "Daddy!" But Austin simply set her aside, because there was something else he had to do.

His brother was obviously caught off-guard, for when he saw Austin, his eyes widened, he pushed back in his chair, as if that were a route he could take to escape. But when the back of the chair hit the wall, Mar-cus stood up, looking as though he wanted to say something, looking as though he was trying to stop Austin from what he was preparing to do. But there was no stopping Austin, because the punch had already been released, and it was now cutting through the air, all his force be-hind it, directed toward Marcus's eye, or his cheek, or his jaw, any of these places just fine for Austin. And when it connected, hitting Marcus flush against the space just below his left eye, Marcus flew off his feet, up onto the card table he was seated next to. A huge swell of astonished voices filled the room, as the card table flattened under Marcus's weight, sending cups of Kool-Aid and plates of birthday cake flying into the air.

"I told you to stay away from them!" Austin yelled, pointing down at Marcus, who lay atop the collapsed table, his clothes pasted with white cake frosting and dyed red with Kool-Aid. "I told you," and he was moving toward Marcus, with intentions of picking him up, and further drilling the point home, when he was grabbed from behind.

"Come with me," he heard Trace demand. His eyes were not on her, but still set vengefully upon his brother. He was yanked away from him, trying to get at Marcus again, Marcus scrambling to his hands and feet, pushing himself backward through the mess around him.

"I said, come with me, goddammit," Trace said, lowering the volume on the curse word, so only Austin could hear it, and none of the surrounding, gawking kids.

Austin allowed her to draw him toward the front of the house. He was falling out of the anger-induced rage he was in, finally allowing himself to look at all the people standing still with shock, staring at him accusingly, as if he were a murderer being carted off to jail. He was able to hear the complete silence, save for his little girl crying somewhere in the space behind him.

Austin was pushed through the screen door, and again he and Trace ended up on the front porch.

"What is your fucking problem?" Trace spat, a stiff arm up, pointing into the house. "Coming in my house, during that child's birthday, and tearing it up like it was some bar."

"I told him to stay away," Austin said slowly, looking around as if he was just coming out of a sleep, as if he had been the one who had been punched and was just coming to.

"So you come in attacking him?"

"He was with Bethany."

"He is her uncle." Trace raised her voice.

"And I am her father!" Austin said, raising his voice louder, stabbing a thumb in the center of his chest. "All I want to do is spend time with my children without being put through all sorts of hell by you. Why can't that happen? Why!"

Trace stood there, staring at Austin hatefully, looking as though she weren't going to answer, not seeming as though she felt she had to, until they both heard a voice say, "Answer him, Mommy."

It was Bethany, standing behind the screen door, her tiny hands on it, as if she were being held captive, her face puffy and wet with tears.

Trace whipped her head around. "Get in the house, Beth. This is between your father and me."

"No, sweetheart, come out here," Austin said, opening the door to let her out. He stood her in front of her mother, Austin resting a reassuring hand on her shoulder.

"Answer her question, Trace."

Trace looked down at her weeping daughter, then shook her head. "I'm not answering anything in front of her. You can't use her like this, Austin."

"Fine, Trace. I've been trying to avoid doing this, but I will sue for custody of my children. Do you want that to happen? Do you want them to be put through that, just because we can't seem to work this out? We don't want to do that, Trace," Austin warned, pushing Bethany in front of him so his ex-wife could get a good look at her. "Because if you think this is bad, you ain't seen nothing yet."

She didn't say another word, and Austin figured he must have hit the right note with the threat of dragging her into court. But it was just a threat, and nothing more, and if she knew more about the law, she would've realized that, because there would've been no way that he could've beaten her. Trace was a very good mother, and even Austin himself would have to testify to that. She had the house, a good job, and had done nothing hurtful or neglectful to their children.

But those weren't the only reasons why he knew he couldn't win. When her games first started, he'd actually consulted with a child-custody attorney, a good friend of Austin's, Kevin Ackerman. And Kevin had told him that his chances were close to impossible. "The only thing you'd accomplish would be to put those kids through more hell than they've already been through," he'd said, pushing his glasses back up on his narrow nose. "Now if that's the goal, I'll take your money and we can start today." That definitely wasn't the goal, but leading Trace to believe it was, was to his advantage.

Trace stooped, putting herself level with her daughter. She looked sorrowfully into her eyes, and wiped the tears from her cheeks. "All right," Trace said, softly, surrendering. "Next Friday, after school. You can take them overnight."

Austin smiled, not at his wife, but down at his daughter, who was smiling meekly up at him. "You hear that sweetheart, next week we'll hang out, okay?"

"Okay, Daddy," Bethany said, throwing her arms around her father's waist and squeezing him tight.

"Now go on back to your brother's birthday party."

"Are you going to come in?"

"No, sweetheart. I don't think I'm wanted in there, but I'll call you, and I'll see you on Friday."

"You promise?"

"I promise," Austin said, kissing her, then sending her back in the house. When he raised himself back up to look in Trace's face, she turned away from him, suggesting that she was forced to submit to something that she knew was wrong.

"I want to thank you," Austin said, knowing that no other words would be said if he didn't say them first.

A second later, Trace's eyes focused on Austin. "I'm not doing this for you, and I'm not doing this for them, because I don't think they'll benefit from it. I'm doing this so they won't have to go through what you threatened me with."

"Well, whatever," Austin blew with a carefree tone.

"Do you actually think it makes a difference to them if they see you or not?" Trace said, her face balled up in a bitter scowl. "You've been so in and out of their lives that they've all but forgotten about you. And just because Beth cries and says that she wants to see you, don't let that fool you. Understand, they're children, and you're like an old toy to them. A toy that they've lost interest in, so they haven't seen it, or played with for a while. But when someone comes, threatens to clean house, take it away, that's when they kick and scream. Like all children, they want something most when they're told they can't have it. But believe me, if you were to leave, and never come back, they'd be fine. They'd treat you like just another lost toy under the bed and never care if they saw you again."

"Whatever you say, Trace," Austin said, turning and walking down the stairs, as though he thought nothing of what she had said. But he did, and the words echoed in his head all the way home.

19

"That bastard," Marcus growled as he sat behind the wheel of his car at a red light. He looked up at himself in the rearview mirror, pulling the dripping bag of ice cubes Trace gave him from his face. The space below his eye, and a little to the side of it, had already grown puffy and tender, and it was changing colors, from purple to an almost black. He touched it with his finger, and winced from the pain, asking himself, after the fact, why he chose to do that. Because he was a glutton for punishment and he enjoyed pain, he told himself. And maybe that was the reason why he continued to see Austin's kids, even though he had been warned against it.

Marcus was honked at by the car behind him. He gave the teenage girl a wicked stare through the rearview, applied the slowly melting bag of ice cubes back to his face, then accelerated the car on its way.

Yes, Austin had told him not to see the kids again, but Marcus didn't think he was actually serious, at least not black-eye serious. Didn't Austin know he was doing him a favor? He was trying to fill in where he left off, but Austin couldn't appreciate that, probably thinking that he was trying to fill his shoes or something, and that was the most ridiculous thing Marcus had ever heard.

He could have said something, Marcus thought, making the turn to put him on the street his house was on. He didn't have to just come in there swinging, as if Marcus were some kind of pedophile, trying to get his rocks off fondling Austin's child. He threw punches first, and never even bothered to ask questions. But if he thought that would scare Marcus away, he was wrong. Troy and Bethany were Trace's kids, too, and if she still had no problem with Marcus seeing them, then he would continue doing it.

Screw what Austin thinks, Marcus thought, as he pulled his car up in front of his house. And screw Austin, too, for that matter. Now he knew he never wanted to see his brother again. He never wanted to hear his name, never wanted to hear mention that they were even related. This was it. The thought of Austin would never enter his mind, or the mind of anyone who was near to him from now on.

Once inside the house, Marcus called out to his wife.

"Reecie. Wait till you see what Austin did," he said, walking into the kitchen, dropping the bag of ice in the sink, and drying off all the water that ran from the bag down his arm. He called out again, "Reecie," but there was no answer.

He went to the freezer, yanked it open, and pulled out a frozen steak and placed it against his eye.

"Where are you at, Reecie?" Marcus said, to himself. "Your butt is too big to go anywhere." He looked through the living room, dining room, poked his head into the bathroom. But no Reecie.

"Reecie," he said, taking the stairs, one hand grabbing at the banister, the other still holding the frozen meat to his eye. He checked all the rooms up there, still not finding her. He ended up on the edge of the bed, trying to remember if she'd told him she was going somewhere, but she'd told him nothing. Oh well, he thought. It was probably for the best anyway. Marcus would have told her everything that happened, and her Benedict Arnold ass would have probably sided with Austin.

He leaned back, letting himself fall across the bed, but reached under his back when he heard something crumple beneath him. He pulled out a piece of paper, held it before him, and realized it was a letter from Reecie.

Marcus,

I don't like the way you've been treating your brothers lately. It's not kind, and it makes no sense whatsoever to me. You're supposed to love them. They're your family. So until you can find it within your

heart to do whatever it is you need to do to get things right with them,
I won't be coming home. But that shouldn't matter to you, since it
doesn't matter what I think, and since I have no choice but to accept
whatever you say to me.

Reecie

P.S. When you do regain your damn sanity, you can reach me at
Austin's. You know, your brother.

"What!" Marcus screamed, shooting up to examine the letter better, making sure this wasn't a joke of any kind.

He couldn't believe this. Austin was wrong about all of this. He was the one who couldn't be reached when Marcus needed help dealing with the fact that Caleb wouldn't see him. He was the one who left his wife and children, practically ignoring the poor kids, as if they weren't even his. Austin was the one who socked the hell out of Marcus, forcing him to walk around with a piece of cold, hard beef pressed to his face, which he pulled down and angrily slung across the bedroom.

Marcus reached for the phone and pushed in his brother's number.

Two rings, and Marcus heard his brother's voice. "Hello."

"Put Reecie on the phone, Austin," Marcus said, trying to control his anger.

"I told you to stay away from them, Marcus. If you had just done what I told you, I would've never had reason to hit you."

"You didn't have reason to hit me, and I said put my wife on the phone."

"That is, if she wants to talk to you."

Marcus listened, strangling the phone in his hand, pressing it up to his head hard enough to cause himself a bit of pain. He heard Austin drop the phone hard against the table and he knew his brother had done that on purpose, as if punching him in the face wasn't enough. After a moment, Reecie finally made her way to the phone.

"Hello," she said, and the tone she delivered made it sound as though she was being taken away from something that she would have rather still been doing.

"Reecie, what is your damn problem? What is this note about?"

"You read it, right?"

"Yeah, I read it."

"Then you know what it's about. You're not acting like yourself, Marcus. You're acting evil, and when I tell you I don't like it, that I'm worried, you tell me it doesn't matter to you what I think, and it's not my business. I thought I was your wife."

"You are. But you don't understand," Marcus tried to explain.

"I understand that the man I met and fell in love with loved his brothers, would've done anything for them, but now has up and changed. You want nothing to do with them, and by the looks of it, sounds like you might up and change on me, too."

"Reecie, he's the one that told me I couldn't see his kids anymore."

"He told me about that, and considering what he was going through, I agree with him on that."

"You agree with him!" Marcus screamed, moving the phone away from his face to stare at it, as though she could see his crazed look through the receiver. "Do you know that he hit me today, just for being with my niece?"

"Yeah, he told me that already. We had a long talk, and he explained himself."

"Oh, really?" Marcus said, feeling a flash of jealousy pass through him. "And what else were you all doing, fucking?"

"What did you say to me?"

"I said, what else were you all doing, fucking!"

There was no reply.

"Hello," Marcus said. But still nothing, then he heard a couple of clicks, and then the dial tone.

"Oh, so you want to hang up on me now, hunh?" Marcus hissed to himself, as he dialed Austin's number again. Hearing Reecie answer, he said, "What are you doing hanging up on me?"

"What are you doing talking to me like you don't have any damn sense? I only packed a weekend bag, but I can come back for the rest," Reecie said with attitude.

"Look, I'm sorry. But imagine how I feel. All the wrong that Austin's done, and you're taking his side."

"You're taking Trace's."

"But you're my wife," Marcus squealed.

"And you're his brother."

Marcus paused for a long moment, thinking about what she'd said, and even though she was right in theory, he wasn't feeling very brotherly of late.

"Look. I know things haven't been just right between me and him, but I shouldn't have to live without my wife just because of it, and you know it. If you want to curse me out, or tell me that I'm wrong, please, just do it from the same house, will you?"

There was silence on Reecie's end, and Marcus knew she was thinking over his request.

"Under one condition. You apologize to Austin."

"What?!" Marcus squawked, his voice high. "If you could see my face."

"But I can't, and I want you to apologize."

"For what?"

"For being mean to him. For not seeing him. Now, if you want me to come home, you'll do it."

"But . . ." and before Marcus could say another word, he heard Reecie giving the phone to Austin.

"You got something to say to me?" Austin said.

Marcus gritted his teeth, curled his fingers into fists, did everything in his power to stop himself from saying what he really wanted to say to his brother.

"I'm sorry for being mean to you. I apologize." It didn't sound like an apology, but a confession forced out by means of torture.

"I'll think about accepting it," Austin said. "But I still want you to stay away from my kids." He was off the phone, and before Marcus could blow up at him as he was prepared to do, Reecie was on the other end.

"Good. I'll be home soon," Reecie said. "And, Marcus, you may not know it now, but this is the start of putting you and your brothers back on the right track."

"Whatever you say, Reecie," Marcus said.

20

Julius looked at his reflection in the bathroom mirror, toothpaste foam clinging to the outside of his mouth. He just stood there, his face long, his eyes tired, letting the water, paste, and saliva mixture ooze down his chin. He was tired, exhausted, and he looked it. Just brushing his teeth managed to wear him out so much that contemplating bending down to cup water in his hands and rinse his mouth made him want to turn and crawl into bed.

He did it anyway, feeling a bit shaky on his legs, feeling the pain that had been bothering him for a week now attack his lower back when he bent over the sink. It was the same pain that had struck him last week, the night after the wonderful day he and Caleb spent together. It was because of the energy he exerted that day, the football tossing, the squatting on the floor, he told himself. And when he woke up the following morning, barely able to turn over without grinding his teeth together, wincing through the pain, he told himself it was because of the love he made to Cathy the night before. He was doing things he hadn't done in a while, putting forth a bit more effort. He was happy, about life, about his love for his son, for his wife, and he'd wanted to show her. But the next morning, he'd just lain there in bed, feeling chained down by the sheets and blankets that covered his arms and legs, as she pulled herself up, and looked down at him, seeing his eyes open, but his body remaining still.

"You gonna get up, or do you want a little more from last night?" she'd said, slyly.

And to think of even contorting his body the way he had last night caused Julius to feel a bit more pain, even though he hadn't moved an inch.

"No, baby. You go ahead. I'm just going to take a few more minutes, and I'll meet you downstairs for breakfast." He was getting worse. It was getting worse. But the question was, what was it? Could it be . . .

No! He wouldn't think like that, he'd told himself, as he quickly halted, a sharp pain stabbing him in the back; he'd thrown his legs over the side of the bed. He'd bit down, squinting his eyes tightly shut, trying to suppress the cry that was beating at his clamped teeth to come out, for Cathy probably hadn't even descended the first stair yet. If she'd heard him, she would have rushed back into the room, found him doubled over in pain, and questioned him as to what was going on. And when Julius said he didn't know, it would have all started again, the prodding to find out what was wrong, and God forbid, the push for him to go back to see the doctor.

He had decided to hide whatever discomfort he was feeling until it passed. It was a muscle strain, or a flu of some sort. He would wait it out, and as long as Cathy wasn't suspicious of anything, he would be fine. But Julius had never thought it would get to the point where he would be considering forcing himself to go to the doctor to find out what was really going on. It had crossed his mind once, but he'd dismissed the thought, telling himself the pain would pass.

Now, Julius leaned over toward the hand towel hanging on the rack in the bathroom, and wiped off whatever toothpaste was left in the corners of his mouth. He looked back in the mirror, very closely now, and with his thumb under one eye, the pointer finger of the same hand under the other, he pulled down on the skin beneath each eye, revealing the moist pink insides of his lower lids. He didn't know what good it would do to examine that space, but he'd seen it done in the movies and he thought giving it a shot would reveal something that would clear his mind. It didn't. He then opened his mouth, stuck his tongue out, and said, "Ahhhhh." If that was supposed to tell him something, he didn't know what it was either, so he closed his mouth, and pulled his face away from the mirror.

He turned to move toward the toilet, then stopped, and looked in the mirror again. For a long moment he just stared, then said, his lips

moving slowly, the words barely audible, "You're fine, Julius. Everything will be all right." And then he thought about the last time he'd
visited the doctor, when the man had smiled and told him that all
traces of the cancer were gone, and when Julius focused back on himself in the mirror, he found that he was smiling now. He was fine, he
told himself again.

"What are you doing in there, Julius, preparing for a portrait?" he
heard Cathy calling from the bedroom.

"I'll be out in a minute," Julius said, now stepping away from the mirror, stopping in front of the toilet, lifting the seat, then pulling himself
out over the elastic band of his pajama bottoms. "I just have to take a—"
he called out, releasing the muscles in his bladder, allowing the urine to
leave his body. But nothing happened. Nothing was coming out. He
looked down at himself as if to verify this, looked into the clear water of
the toilet to make sure that nothing at all had spilled from his penis. But
he knew he had to go, could feel his bladder tight with what had to
come out. This was not happening. Immediately Julius's mind rushed
back to more than five years ago, when he was standing in his bathroom, trying to go, and he couldn't. This was not that day, he told himself, shutting his eyes, shaking his head, trying to put the thought out of
his mind.

Pain, and/or trouble urinating. It was a symptom, Julius knew. It was
in all the little pamphlets, marked—THINGS YOU SHOULD KNOW ABOUT
PROSTATE CANCER, so he knew this couldn't be happening to him, because
he was cured. He knew he was, the damn doctor had told him so. So he
would urinate and prove to himself that the doctor was right.

He took hold of himself, directed himself toward the center of the
bowl, and concentrated on the fluid flowing. And when after a few seconds it still hadn't, he concentrated more, telling himself that this had to
happen, that he would not go to bed tonight before it did, that this and
only this would clear him of all the terrible things that were shooting
around in his head. So he concentrated harder, shutting his eyes, gritting
his teeth, and bearing down as if he were pushing against a persistent
bout of constipation.

And then it happened, a quick spurt of fluid exited the tip of his penis, hitting the rim of the bowl. Julius smiled some, feeling the rest
about to follow, but when it did come, it felt as though boiling acid
were racing through his urethra, burning the tip of his penis, the pain

shooting back through the shaft, burrowing deep into his center, and erupting in an explosion of agony high in between his legs.

He doubled forward, shoving a hand into his gut, wishing he were able to push through the skin, through his organs, and squelch the pain. Urine was still flowing forcefully, painfully, out of him, for he could not make it stop. And when it finally did, he stood hunched over the toilet, his head hot, dripping with sweat, his stomach in a burning tight little knot, his eyes clamped shut. He didn't want to open them, for fear of what he might see, of the color that would fill his eyes, the sign that would let him know, without question, that it was back again.

Julius trembled there for a moment, summoning whatever bravery there was inside of him to force him to raise his lids, and when he did, it was what he had thought, what he had feared. Blood. Blood was sprayed all about the toilet, on the rim, in the bowl, on the floor, some still clinging to the head of his penis. And this time, unlike more than five years ago, what came out of him wasn't pink, the blood diluted with urine. This time the blood was a thick rich red. Some of the drops on the toilet's rim were fat and heavy-looking like dried drops of wax, letting him know that most of what he expelled was blood.

Julius crumpled to the floor on his knees, amid his own blood, wanting to die right there. Why try and live any longer, he asked himself, because he was going to die now. This was the confirmation. Of this he was sure.

After cleaning up the blood and urine, Julius slowly made his way back through the door and into the bedroom. Cathy was sitting on the edge of the bed, wearing a low-cut satin nightgown. The better portion of her upper breasts were showing, and the way she was sitting, her arms spread out behind her, her chest shooting up and out, made it apparent that she was in the mood. Her legs were crossed, the gown, falling back to reveal the soft thigh of the raised leg, the foot of that leg, dangling carelessly, sexually, almost waving him toward her.

"Want to mess around?" Cathy said seductively, her voice low, raspy.

Normally Julius would have leapt and dived into her. He would have gone after her with the vigor of the other night, and seeing her now made him think of that, made him hear her passionate voice call his name, smell her sweat scent, feel her dig her fingers into his lower back. But that was when he was well, at least when he thought he was well, and this was now, and although it was only a week ago, it felt like an eternity to him.

"No. I'm really kind of tired," he said, walking around her, trying not to look at her. He climbed into bed on her side, leaving her sitting on his. He climbed in, not caring about the pain that radiated through his bones, telling himself there was no need to treat himself gingerly now. The truth was out, and there was no way he could rationalize against it.

"Is everything all right, Jay?" Cathy said, leaning softly across his shoulder, her hand draped over him, rubbing lightly the blanket that covered his belly. "You sick?" And the question came with the innocence of her wondering about a cold, or a little upset stomach. He wanted to tell her, knowing that if he did, she would hold him, tell him not to worry, that it could be something else, and no matter what, she would always love him. But he couldn't give her that news yet, drag her senselessly down that path again, if he wasn't absolutely sure.

"No. It's nothing," he lied. "Just sleepy. But I'm sure I'll be fine in the morning." He leaned up, a bolt of pain raging through his spine, to kiss his wife.

"I love you, baby. And I always will," Julius said, sounding graver than he wanted to.

Cathy looked at him oddly for a moment, then smiled. "Aw, baby. I love you, too."

The next morning, Julius pulled open one of the double doors that led him into Dr. Phillips's office. The same aging, white-haired people were lurching over in their waiting room chairs, staring up, squinting at the television in the high corner of the room. He turned to see Susie casually sitting behind her desk, and recognizing him, she fixed herself into a more defensive posture, her body becoming tighter, lowering herself a bit in her seat, like a turtle retreating into its shell. The carefree look on her face was replaced with something approaching dread, and she swallowed hard as Julius approached her desk.

"Dr. Phillips in?" Julius questioned.

"He's in with a patient at this moment, but I'm sure he'll see you as soon as he comes out. As soon as he comes out," she stressed, as if worrying he'd flip the desk, trash the office, and take her as hostage, if he wasn't pleased.

"Is that okay, Mr. Harris?"

She remembers my name, Julius thought. "Yes, that'll be fine."

Five minutes later, Dr. Phillips exited the office, shaking the hand of a graying, rather healthy-looking man. They were smiling as they walked, the man pumping the doctor's hand thankfully.

"Okay, Mr. Reegan, see you next time."

The doctor turned toward Susie's desk, obviously not seeing Julius, but had to have been quickly informed that Julius was standing just on the other side, for Dr. Phillips turned around, scanning the room. When he caught sight of Julius, he smiled, saying, "Hey, hey, how's the miracle man?"

Julius took the hand the doctor extended, and they shook.

"Can I have a minute with you, please?" Julius said.

The doctor led him into the office, and closed the door.

Dr. Phillips walked behind his desk, plopped down in the seat, leaned back, and said, "So, how are we doing?"

"Not great," Julius said, his voice low.

The doctor leaned forward, the amused expression falling from his face. "What's up?"

Julius lowered his head. "It's back. The cancer is back."

Dr. Phillips came from around his desk, sat in the chair beside Julius. "How do you know. What makes you say that?"

"It's all the symptoms," Julius said, looking up at the doctor. "I've been weak, experiencing incredible pain in my back and hips, where you said the cancer had spread to last time, and . . ." Julius trailed off.

"And what?" Dr. Phillips said.

"And I urinated a lot of blood last night."

The doctor looked deeply into Julius's eyes for a moment, as if searching for something there, then turned away, sorrow on his face, as if he knew exactly what was going on in his body. But he said, "We'll run the tests again," anyway. "We'll find out what's going on, Julius."

The following morning, Julius sat alone in Dr. Phillips's office. He was waiting again, like the last time, for him to make his way in with the re-

sults of the tests. Julius had kept trying to convince himself that the doctor would have good news. That everything, every pain he was feeling,
every symptom he experienced, had a logical explanation that pointed
away from cancer. But his mind would not steer him clear of his worry,
for he knew what it was, and knew that this time, there would be no
happy ending.

He looked toward that seat beside him and envisioned his wife. He
had thought all night about bringing her, had considered it when she
asked him where he was going that morning, but realized that the news
would be better coming from him, in their home, than from some doctor in the cold, sterile surroundings of a medical office.

The door opened, making Julius jump. Again upon entering the office, the doctor in no way hinted at what the news would be. His face
was blank, his demeanor as normal as ever, as he took his place beside
a view box hanging on the wall.

"Will you come up here, Julius?" the doctor asked politely. In his
hand he had Julius's medical records in the manila folder, and a larger
brown file, marked X rays. He dug his hand in the X-ray jacket, and
pulled out an eight-by-ten-inch radiograph. He hung it on the view box.
On it were two hazy, miniature X rays of skeletons.

"This is your bone scan, Julius." He pointed to dark areas, little
patches of black in his lower spine, around his hips, in his pelvis, with
the sharp tip of a number-two pencil. He ran a line down the length of
both the skeleton's legs, tapped lightly at a place on either of the upper
arms. Then the doctor turned to Julius, his face long, saddened, seeming burdened, now betraying all he was about to say.

"Why don't you have a seat?" he said, extending an arm toward the
chairs.

Julius looked over to them, then turned back to the doctor.

"No. I want to stand. Just tell me," Julius said, calling forth what little
bravery his fear had not already taken.

"These areas I pointed out," the doctor began, "are metastatic bone
disease. The cancer is not only back, Julius, but it has spread all throughout your body."

Julius stared at the doctor, certain what he'd said, but not believing it,
or not wanting to. All of sudden he felt lightheaded. The room took one
huge, quick spin, and Julius felt himself heading toward the floor. He
felt the doctor's arms around him, before he hit, helping him over to the
chair.

"Are you all right? Let me get you some water," the doctor said, turning to go. But Julius caught hold of him.

"No. No. I'm fine," he panted. "But tell me how. How can there be nothing, and two weeks later it's back, all over? How can this be?"

"I don't know, Julius," the doctor said, shaking his head, his expression full of sorrow. "If I knew I would tell you, but honestly, I haven't the slightest idea."

21

Caleb stocked all the shelves with the new groceries, swept the floor, cleaned all the glass windows in the front of the store, in the front door, and on the refrigerated cases in the back of the store. He wiped down the counter, grabbed his backpack and the keys to Cathy's car from under the counter, and yelled into the back room, "Okay, Mr. Olin. I'm gone."

Caleb heard the volume of the portable black-and-white TV lower, then Mr. Olin's voice.

"All right, Caleb. See you tomorrow, and don't go gettin' into any trouble," the old man called back. Caleb didn't know if he meant that as a joke, or if he was serious, considering all the trouble Caleb had gotten into in the past, considering the trouble he was almost in, in old Mr. Olin's store.

Caleb had told Mr. Olin everything about his past, about Blue, Ray Ray, and how everything went down just before they'd decided to try and rob that store. He talked to Mr. Olin a lot while stacking cans or unpacking bags of dog food. The gig didn't pay much, and didn't do much to hold Caleb's attention. Neither did it give him much of a feeling of satisfaction, but it was something to do to put some money in his pocket, and keep his mind off the fact that he had lost his family and still couldn't think of a single way of finding them.

Caleb would busy himself with whatever he could find to do around the store, because there really wasn't much, and Caleb now saw that old man Olin was telling the truth when he said he didn't need any help. But Caleb figured he gave him the job anyway because he was able to talk the boy out of robbing the store.

It had been a week already, Caleb thought, as he jumped into the white Volvo wagon and started it up. Cathy insisted on his taking it now that he was working, and she smiled as she handed him the keys, saying, "Now this'll give me a reason to drive Julius's Mercedes."

Caleb thought about the boy. After he had convinced him not to rob the store, he remembered walking him outside, his arm around his shoulder, and stopping in the middle of the sidewalk.

"You did the right thing in there," Caleb said, looking him in the eyes. "You know that, don't you?"

The boy didn't say a word, just looked at Caleb as though he'd heard what he'd just said, but didn't really agree with it.

Caleb gripped his shoulder and shook him just a little. "Did you hear what I said? You just made a decision that will affect the rest of your life."

"Great. But what am I supposed to do about right now?" the boy said, pulling away from Caleb and walking away.

"Hey," Caleb called, catching up to him, walking beside him. "What is your name anyway?"

"Why you want to know? So you can call the cops, turn me in?"

"I told you," Caleb said, stopping the boy from walking. "I just got out of doing five years of hell in prison. You think I want to see another young brotha go through that? Why you think I went through what I did to talk you out of robbing that old man? So you wouldn't get caught up with the police. Now what is your name?"

"Thomas," the boy said without ceremony, starting to walk again.

"Well, mine's Caleb."

"Didn't ask," Thomas said, his eyes straight ahead, as if no one was there walking beside him.

"Hold it," Caleb said, grabbing Thomas by the arm, stopping him once more. "What were you robbing the store for anyway?"

"What difference does it make to you? You played Batman, saved the day, so why would you care?"

"I care," Caleb said. "That stuff I told you back there. That was no bullshit. I was right where you were, where you are, needing money and not being able to get it. I had people who were willing to help me, which is the worst part about it, because I was just too damn foolish and full of pride to take their help. So I know what you're going through. Now tell me why you were hitting the store. Maybe I can help."

Thomas looked at him long and hard, as if testing the validity of his words, then said, "I don't think so." He turned and walked off again, but Caleb jumped in front of him, blocking his path.

"Just try me."

Thomas exhaled a long sigh, then said, "It's my moms. She's real sick, and the drugs she needs cost a lot of money."

"Can't you go to the county hospital or something for that?" Caleb asked.

"They'll pay when she has to come into the hospital, and they pay for some of the drugs, but it's that generic garbage, and that shit don't work. I was robbing the store so I could get some money to pay for her medication."

The boy was telling the truth, Caleb knew, could just tell by what was in his voice, and for a brief moment, Caleb wished he had never been in that store, wished that the boy had gotten away with the money so he'd be able to buy that medication.

"Don't you have a job?"

"Uh, yeah. Part-time moving packages at this warehouse, but that don't make nothing," Thomas said, dropping his head.

Caleb looked quietly at the boy for a moment then said, "How much is it?"

"How much is what?"

"The medication. The drugs."

"Like two hundred dollars," Thomas said, gravely.

Caleb thought about the one-fifty his father gave him for his so-called allowance, the hundred he had given him for shoes that morning.

"C'mon," Caleb said, starting to walk in the direction of the Rite-Aid down the street.

"Where we going?"

"You know the name of the stuff you supposed to get?"

"I got the prescription in my pocket," Thomas said, scurrying up behind him.

"Well, I got enough money. We're going to buy it for your mother."

After Thomas bought the medication with the money Caleb gave him, they left the store. They were walking quietly, side by side, down the street, Caleb noticing that Thomas hadn't said anything since taking the money from him.

"You all right over there?" he asked.

Thomas didn't answer, just kept walking, his hand shoved deep into the pocket of his baggy jeans, where he had stuffed the medicine. He wasn't ignoring Caleb this time, but Caleb could see by the intent look on his face that his mind was elsewhere.

"Thomas, you still here on earth?" Caleb said, loud enough this time to catch his attention.

Thomas turned to him, a disturbed look on his face.

"What?"

"What's going on? You ain't say shit to me since I gave you that money. You ain't say nothing, not even thank you. What's up?"

Thomas stopped in the middle of the sidewalk, looked Caleb square in the face for just a moment, then pulled the medication out of his pocket and extended it to Caleb.

"I can't take this. Here."

Caleb looked down at the boy's hand, then up in his face.

"What are you talking about you can't take it? Your mother needs it, that's why I bought it for you, so she can have it. Now stop talking crazy and put that back in your pocket."

"Why did you give me that money? What's up with you? What do you want? I ain't got shit. And I ain't lettin' you fuck me, or nothing like that."

Caleb spun his back to Thomas, shaking his head in disappointment.

"Haven't you heard a word I've been saying to you all day?" Caleb said, turning back to him. "Don't you get it?"

"Naw, I don't fucking get it!" Thomas said, emotion filling his voice. "Ain't nobody done shit for me my entire life, and here you come along, stop me from knocking off that store, and just hand me two hundred dollars because I need it. And you shaking your head, look-ing at me funny, because I want to know why."

"All right, that's cool," Caleb said, raising both his palms to the boy, as though he meant no harm by what he said. "You want to know why? It's because you're lost. You're at a crossroads, little brotha, and if somebody don't take your hand, if somebody don't show you the way, you're gonna end up dead. And when I look at your life, and that funky two hundred dollars I gave you, there ain't no comparison. I'll see that much money again, at least I think I will," Caleb said chuckling. "But there's only one Thomas." Caleb placed his hand on the boy's shoulder. "So now you get why I gave you the money?"

"I guess," Thomas said, looking sadly toward the ground.

"Well, damn. You could be a little happier about it. Your mama's getting the medicine she needs, your ass ain't going to jail for robbing a store, and you even made a friend out of the deal. I mean, we are friends?" Caleb said, checking himself.

"Yeah, I guess we can be friends," Thomas said, his head still turned downward, but a smile starting to appear on his face.

"Well, all right then. That's what I want to hear," Caleb said, extending his hand to the boy. "Now give me some dap, so you can get home and get this medicine to your mother. Thomas smiled wider, grabbed Caleb's hand, and they shook.

"C'mon in," Thomas said, waving Caleb through a weathered front door. They walked into the living room of Thomas's house, and Caleb couldn't help but notice the dilapidated condition of the place. Thomas had insisted that he come, considering what Caleb had done for him, and Caleb thought Thomas would've seen it as an insult if he were to reject the opportunity to meet his mother. So as Caleb continued through the house, he tried to keep his eyes on the boy before him, but the tattered furniture in the room kept stealing his attention. He noticed the bedsheets that hung nailed over the windows of the room, and the four columns of milk crates that supported a large, flat piece of plywood, which was obviously used as a table. There were dishes coated with old, drying food, glasses on the table left filled with molding juices, and Caleb quickly turned away as he caught sight of a single roach scurrying about.

The boy walked through the room, stepping around trash as if it weren't there, and at his request, Caleb followed behind him. The house was as quiet as a tomb. The only light was what filtered through the soiled, beige bedsheets hanging over the windows, dragging on the floor below.

They stopped just outside a closed door, and now Thomas was whispering.

"I'm gonna give my mother the medicine you bought her. I want you to come in and meet her, okay?"

"No, no, I changed my mind," Caleb said, shaking his head. "If she's sick, she needs her rest. Just give it to her."

"She's not sick all the time. Sometimes she feels a little better, it just depends. But I want her to know who got the stuff for her."

"I really shouldn't," Caleb said, wishing there was some way he could just disappear.

"C'mon, it's cool," Thomas said, taking his arm. And before Caleb could even try to refuse, Thomas had already pushed open the door, and was pulling him into the dark room. The air was tight and thick with sickness. Caleb wanted to gag, wanted to cough, but held it down.

Thomas walked over to his mother, who was lying in bed, a thin, small woman, who looked to be in her late thirties. She was covered by a mountain of thick blankets, and although there was very little light in the room, Caleb could see that her forehead was wet with a fair amount of sweat.

Thomas must have seen it too, for after hugging her and kissing her on the cheek, he pulled the washcloth from a basin of water that sat at her bedside. He squeezed most of the water out of it, then dabbed her brow and cheeks.

"Momma, I got your medication," he whispered to her, a smile on his face. "And not that cheap generic shit—I mean, stuff, either. But the good stuff."

Thomas's mother turned her head slowly to him, and opened her mouth as if she hadn't in days. "How'd you get it?"

Thomas turned to Caleb, waving him over. Caleb didn't move.

"C'mere."

Caleb walked over to the bedside, and smiled as best he could down at Thomas's ailing mother. And even though she appeared to be pretty sick, she was smiling back up at Caleb, which made him smile a little more.

"This is Caleb, Momma. He bought the medication for you. He's my friend." Caleb saw movement under the layers of blankets, and saw Thomas's mother's hand peek out from under them. She extended it to Caleb.

"I can never thank you enough," she whispered. "And maybe when I'm better, we can sit down and talk?"

"Your appreciation is all the thanks I need," Caleb said, holding the woman's soft, small hand in his. "And that would be fine. But you just take your time."

Two days later, Thomas visited Caleb at work and announced excitedly, "She's outta bed again!"

Caleb was taking out the trash in the back of the store, and Thomas popped out from behind one of the Dumpsters, almost scaring Caleb to death.

"What are you doing back here, Thomas?" Caleb said.

"I just wanted to tell you that my mother's feeling a lot better, thanks to you. I couldn't come in the store or that old man would kill me, so I came back here."

"He won't kill you," Caleb said, dumping the trash. "I told him everything, and yeah, he's still a little mad, but he'll get over it. What are you doing out of school anyway?"

"Uhhhh, it's lunchtime," Thomas answered quickly.

"What time is it over?"

"One o'clock."

"Where do you go?"

"Uhhhh, Fisher High."

"Isn't that like two miles away?" Caleb said, looking down at his watch. "How you going to make it back there in ten minutes?"

"I can be a little late for my next class," Thomas said.

"No, you can't," Caleb said, setting the can down, taking off the thick work gloves he was wearing, and reaching around his back to untie the work apron he had on.

"What are you doing?" Thomas said.

"I got my lunch break coming up, and I'm taking you back to school."

"You don't have to do that," Thomas said, jumping in front of Caleb, trying to stop him from walking back into the store.

"Yes, I do. We're friends. You said so yourself, and friends are supposed to help each other out. So that's what I'm about to do."

"But I don't need your help."

Caleb stopped and turned to Thomas, who was standing just outside the doorway now. "Never be too proud to allow someone to help you. I told you, I learned that the hard way. Now let's go."

Caleb pulled the car up to the curb of the high school. "Is this fine?"

"Yeah. That's the door I go in. Right here is cool," Thomas said, looking out the window at the school. "You didn't have to do this, you know," he said, turning back to look at Caleb.

"Yeah, I know, but c'mon," Caleb said, reaching over to muss Thomas's hair. "Everybody needs someone to look out for them, and now you got me."

"Great," Thomas said. "Now I gotta be all on good behavior and stuff."

"Damn right. What time do you get out?"

"Ummmm, like three-forty, and no, you can't come pick me up. My moms don't even do that."

"I wasn't trying to pick you up, Thomas. I just wanted to know if you wanted to do something later on. I don't know, play some video games or catch a movie. What do you think?"

"Okay," Thomas said, perking up. "What time do you get off? I'll meet you back at your job."

Caleb and Thomas hung out every day for the rest of the week, and at first Caleb wasn't sure if this was just because neither of them had nothing else to do, or if it was because they actually enjoyed each other's company. But Caleb realized now, as he wheeled the Volvo down the street, that he truly liked the boy. At first, Caleb thought that he was just hanging out with him because, in some way, he felt responsible for him, because the kid reminded him of himself when he was his age, and because of the debt he still felt obligated to pay to Ray's mother. And yes, all of that was true, but there was something more to it than that. The boy was funny, had Caleb rolling every minute they were together. He was a good kid, had dreams of becoming an architect. Sometimes when they were walking down the street, he would just stop. He'd grab Caleb's arm to get his attention, then point toward the sky at the top of a building and comment on the design, or the curve of one of the windows.

Caleb was trying to deny the other reason why he enjoyed being around Thomas, and that was because it reminded him of what being a father was like. He missed that so much, not having his son around, and although there was a part of him that felt as though he was betraying Jahlil somehow, he allowed Thomas to fill that void, if only for a while, if only till he found his son again.

Caleb reluctantly told Thomas all this one day, while they were sitting at an outdoor table on Venice beach, eating hot dogs.

"Well, I guess that's cool," Thomas said, not seeming to make much of a big deal about it. "You kinda remind me of what it feels like to have a father again. I mean you're old enough," Thomas said, smiling, taking another bite of his hot dog.

"Hey, I'm only thirty-two," Caleb said, throwing a french fry at him.

So there was this bond developing between the two of them, and it felt good to Caleb to have a friend again. Caleb was getting used to seeing Thomas, which was why he was now heading his car in the direction of Fisher High, even though they hadn't made plans to hang out that day. Caleb wanted to surprise him, and knew they'd have no problem finding something to do.

Caleb looked at the car's dash clock, and it read 3:25 P.M. He was early. Thomas got out at 3:40, so Caleb parked the car near the door Thomas said he usually came out of, and waited for the bell to ring.

There were kids walking around the small campus carrying book bags, talking to one another, a boy walking with his arm around a girl, seeming as if he were trying to convince her to let him do a lot more than that. Caleb slumped in his seat some, music playing softly from the car's speakers, entertaining himself by watching these kids do their thing.

Caleb caught sight of another boy a good distance down the street, wearing a hooded sweatshirt, just standing on a corner. He was so far away that Caleb couldn't see his face, but something held Caleb's interest. Maybe it was the way the boy's head was turning left to right, as if he were on the lookout for something. There seemed to be an uneasiness in his stance, as if he didn't belong there.

Caleb saw another figure approach him, the second body equally as unidentifiable as the first, but a short conversation took place, that of four or five words at best, and then an exchange was made. Something was given by and something received from both individuals, and Caleb didn't have to guess what it was. He was from the streets. He knew when he saw drugs being sold.

There was a time when drugs didn't bother Caleb. Back when he

didn't have a son, or back when it seemed the most common thing being peddled was a little pot, which he himself smoked on occasion,
though never sold. But now things were different, and not just because
he'd quit smoking after he got sent away, but because he did have a son
to worry about. And today it wasn't just weed being sold on the street,
but crack, and cocaine, and whatever else someone could fool people
into spending money on. Caleb might have let it go this time, but he
was outraged that this was taking place right in front of a high school.

No, it wasn't cool in the heart of the projects either, but it was even
more evil to sell here.

Immediately Caleb thought of Thomas. He had managed to escape
one major pitfall, but what if he got involved with drugs? What if that
bastard up there selling managed to convince Thomas to start using?

Caleb simply couldn't have that, he told himself as he turned on his
car's ignition. Thomas was his friend now, and he would not allow
some fool whose life was already ruined to ruin the life of his friend.

Caleb raced the car forward, coming closer to the boy. He was
making another exchange, his back to Caleb, and Caleb would take
advantage of that. He rolled right up to him, not drawing the boy's attention, and put the car in park. He jumped out of the car, left the
door open, sneaking up behind him, grabbed the boy, ready to shake
the shit out of him, but when he spun the boy around, he was looking
in Thomas's face.

"You're fucking selling drugs?!" Caleb yelled, throwing his hands up, as
he paced angrily across the alley in front of Thomas. It was the first
place Caleb saw to pull the car over after he had thrown Thomas into
the front seat and sped off.

Thomas didn't say a word. He was cowering against the wall of one
of the buildings that enclosed the two of them in the small, narrow,
trash-lined place.

"Answer me," Caleb yelled even louder, walking up to Thomas.

"Yeah," Thomas whimpered. Then said, "I gotta take care of my
moms."

"And what about that money I just gave you? Didn't that take care of
her?"

"For right now," Thomas said, still cowering against the wall. "But she
needs that every month."

"Then if you're out here selling drugs, why did you even ask me for the money, why were you trying to rob that store?"

"Because I needed it. And even though it makes more than any other job I can get, it still don't make enough. Not the kind of money I need. My mother doesn't work. I take care of her. I take care of everything."

Caleb paced away from him, not knowing what to do about the situation, not knowing what to do with his anger.

"Are you even in school, or are you just there to sell drugs?" Caleb said, turning back to him.

"What do you think?" Thomas said smugly.

Caleb ran back up to Thomas, stabbing a finger in his face.

"Don't you get smug with me. You're the one in the wrong here. And let me tell you, it's going to stop. Right now, Thomas. This shit is going to stop."

"I can't stop. I told you, I have to take care of my mother."

"You sure as hell aren't going to do it selling drugs," Caleb said.

"Then what am I going to do, flip burgers, wash cars, work at a damn convenience store?"

And Caleb knew that remark was meant to hurt him, but he ignored it.

"At least you wouldn't have to worry about getting killed or being sent to prison. And besides, you said selling doesn't pay anything anyway. What difference does it make?"

"Well, I'm making a little more than I'm supposed to be making, and that makes a difference," Thomas said, his voice lowered.

"What did you say?" Caleb said, grabbing his shirt. "Are you skimming?"

"I have to," Thomas said, allowing himself to be handled.

"Are you crazy? You're going to get yourself killed if you're found out."

"I won't. I know what I'm doing. Me and this guy, we talk a lot, and he don't have a clue."

"I don't care. You're stopping right now," Caleb said, releasing him.

"Then what am I going to do?"

"I don't know," Caleb said, turning away, his arms crossed, trying to search his mind for an answer. "We'll do something. Don't want you to end up like me. If you knew how much I regret every day what I did," Caleb said, his mind drifting, thinking of his family. "I would do anything to get Sonya and Jahlil back," Caleb said, more to himself than to Thomas.

"What did you say?" Thomas said, a look of interest on his face.

"I said, I regret every day . . ."

"No, no. Those names. Who are they?"

"Sonya and Jahlil," Caleb said, nearing Thomas, curious about the look on his face. "They're my girlfriend and my son."

"Your girlfriend. What does she look like?"

"I haven't seen her in about five years, but then she was kind of thin, brown skin, nice eyes and she wore her hair in a ponytail all the time."

Thomas had a perplexed look on his face. "But is there anything else more specific?" he said.

Caleb closed his eyes tight, concentrated, then said, pointing to the space just above his top lip, "And she has a . . ."

"Mole right here," Thomas said, finishing for him. "That's her."

Caleb's heart stopped at even the possibility that this boy knew where Sonya was. This had to be some evil joke, some way Thomas had thought of to get back at him.

"That's who?" Caleb said, his entire body trembling with anticipation as he moved very close to Thomas now.

"That's Curtis's girlfriend."

"Who is Curtis?" Caleb said, still excited, but hurt to find out that Sonya did find somebody else.

"The guy I work for, sell drugs for."

"And my son, Jahlil. You've seen him? He's there with them?" Caleb asked, slowly clutching Thomas's shirt with both his fists.

"Yeah. I seen him."

Caleb's heart was pounding in his chest, sensing that he was so very close to being reunited with his family.

"Now this is very important, Thomas. Do you know where they live?"

"Yeah. I've been to their house."

Their house. The phrase stung Caleb, thinking of them living together, a happy little family.

"Can you take me there?"

Thomas swallowed hard, then nodded his head. "Yeah," he said, in a small voice. "I can."

22

Sonya turned the corner onto the Compton block on which she lived. She rolled the sporty Lexus SC 400 slowly down the street, hating what she saw, hating that they had to live here. But she told herself not to harp on it. "Take the good with the bad, baby, and keep on living," she told herself, as she drove the shiny black car up in front of the deteriorating single-floor home.

The damn house needs a paint job, needs new windows and landscaping, Sonya thought, looking up at it through her car window. No, what that house really needs is a new house. But Sonya knew neither of these would happen, the new house or the repairs, because their house was just the way it was supposed to be. That's what she was told.

Sonya slid her key out of the ignition, and was about to open the door, when she looked about the street, and saw the four or five "strays," as she liked to call the homeless addicts, look in her direction. There were always strays out on the street where she lived, and that was another reason Sonya hated living there. Whether it be eleven at night, or eleven in the morning, the sun shining down on them hot and bright, these people, old and young, male and female, stood out on the street, absent looks on their faces, as if waiting for the number-four bus to roll through. Some of them, Sonya imagined, were trying to score; others were just standing out there because they had nothing else to do with themselves. Either way, she didn't like them, didn't like dealing with them, didn't like looking at them through her car windshield, or her house window. They looked like the creepy people in Michael Jackson's "Thriller" video to Sonya, with their tattered clothes hanging from their bodies, their faces dirty, and their hair all about their heads. She would have left a long time ago, if she didn't have 100 percent assurance that she didn't have anything to worry about when it came to them.

Sonya jumped out of the car, walked around it, and started taking the bags out of the trunk. One of the strays dragged herself up to Sonya, a woman forty-two or forty-three, a good ten years older than Sonya was. She grinned, black holes appearing in her smile, running a dirty hand with chipped fingernails, and chipped fingernail polish on top of that, through her hair, as if trying to make herself presentable.

"You need some help with yo' bags?" she asked, looking up at Sonya.

I want you to disappear, Sonya thought. I want you to turn around, start walking, or hobbling—or even crawling if you have to—down the street, and keep on until you disappear, until I never have to see your pitiful face again. That's what Sonya thought at that moment, and what she wanted to say to the woman.

But instead, Sonya leaned over to her and extended one of the bags for her to take. The older woman looked up, a bit surprised, as if not expecting to be taken seriously, took the bag happily from Sonya's arm, and stood there, awaiting instruction.

Sonya slammed the trunk. "Follow me," she said, and heard the "sssppp, sssppp, sssppp," of the woman's dragging feet. She was wearing house slippers over sweat socks. That could be me, Sonya thought, as she approached the stoop of her house. I came so close to being who she is, so close to that being my life, Sonya said to herself, as she turned to the woman, who was still smiling, her back hunched a bit now.

"Set it down right there."

The woman slowly, very gently, set the bag down on the stoop, as if it were a bag of bombs, not bread, bananas, and bacon. Sonya set her bag down as well, and went into her purse. She pulled her wallet from the bottom of her purse, but not entirely out of it. She undid the little clasp, and a wad of money popped up. Sonya fingered the one-dollar bill out of the clump, and was about to give it to the woman, when she looked up in her face.

How did you get here? Sonya wanted to ask her. What did you do to ruin your life like this? Sonya let the dollar bill drop, looked back into the purse, and freed a fifty. Sonya took the woman's dirty hand, and placed the large bill in it. Then she looked into her eyes, and spoke slowly, loudly, to her, as if she were deaf as well as badly off.

"I hope this can help you," Sonya said compassionately.

The woman didn't even look down at the denomination of the bill, just closed her fingers over it, happy to have something there. She turned and slowly walked away, leaving Sonya there torn, not knowing whether she wanted to go out there, grab her shoulder, and lead her back into her home for coffee and a heartfelt girl-to-girl, or shut and bar her doors forever, and never set foot back outside.

Sonya picked up the bags and let herself into her home. She closed the big door, which seemed to separate more than just outside from inside, to separate universes. The exterior of the house was deteriorated and falling apart, while the inside was beautifully decorated. It looked like something out of *Better Homes & Gardens*. Sonya had half a dozen of the magazines at her side when she was directing the designers and decorators about the one-time gutted home. It was just the way she wanted it, her home, the home she had always dreamed of, except for the outside. But that couldn't be changed, she was told over and over again. Curtis had made a deal with her. She could do whatever she wanted to the inside, as long as the outside stayed the same. Considering that Sonya could have been a lot worse off, had been, for that matter, she didn't complain. No, it wasn't a perfect life, Sonya thought as she walked into a huge chef's kitchen, designed in black and silver, an island sitting in the middle of the room. But the house was nice, and she and her son were being taken care of.

She set the bags down, pulled out soda and Twinkies, things for her son that she would never eat. Sonya made a point of staying thin, her waist small, hips shapely, but not flabby. Her man would probably notice if she put on a pound, but she kept it off more for herself than him.

Sonya closed the cabinet on the last of the groceries as she heard the front door open and close.

"Mom, I'm home," nine-year-old Jahlil said, running into the kitchen, a book bag on his shoulder, his baseball cap turned backward on his head. He blew right past his mother and attacked the fridge door, standing in front of it, as if he expected a meal to jump out, prepare itself, and place itself in his hands.

"You better close that door, little man, and give your mother a hug," Sonya said, her hand on her hip.

Jahlil closed the door and gave his mother a hug. "Sorry, Mom," Jahlil said.

"That's what you always say, but you do the same thing every day. What's up with that?"

"I just be forgetting," Jahlil said, looking sheepishly up into his mother's face.

"You mean, you just forget," Sonya corrected him, pulling the cap off his head, and hanging it on the back of one of the kitchen chairs. "I told you, if you don't speak correctly, I'll pull you out of that public school and stick your butt in a military school. I bet you won't just be forgetting then, will you? Now sit down, so I can make you a sandwich."

Not even five minutes later, Jahlil was done scarfing down the bologna sandwich. Nothing was left on the plate but crumbs, which he was trying to pick up with his thumb and forefinger and put in his mouth.

"C'mon, dinner'll be in a few hours," Sonya said, removing the plate from in front of him. "Now go to your room and study for that test you have tomorrow."

Sonya was standing in front of the sink, placing the dish there, expecting to hear the sound of Jahlil's chair sliding out from under the table so he could go to his room and study as she'd told him, but she heard nothing. And when Sonya turned around, Jahlil was still sitting at the table, looking as if he had no intention of moving.

"Boy, what are you doing?" Sonya said, walking over to him, placing herself just in front of him.

Jahlil looked down at his folded hands, then up at his mother. "The Basketball Jam party is today."

"Yeah . . . and? I know that," Sonya said. "But you have a major science test tomorrow, so you'll have to go to the next Basketball Jam party, okay? Now you know we talked about this already. Didn't we?"

Jahlil nodded his head.

"I said, didn't we?"

"Yes, Mommy."

"So you shouldn't be disappointed, because you knew far in advance that you weren't going. Now give your mother a hug, and maybe after you're done studying, we'll get some ice cream and rent a movie."

Jahlil gave his mother another hug, then slowly walked toward his room, stopping and pausing longer than he normally would in between each step.

Sonya stood and watched him, her hands now submerged in soapy dish water.

"What are you doing?" Sonya said, looking at her son as if he had lost his mind.

"Nothing. Walking to my room," Jahlil said, trying to appear as innocent as possible.

"Then go on!"

But just when he was about to take his next step, the doorbell rang. Sonya dried her hands on a cloth and walked toward the front door. She pressed her face to the door to look out the peephole, and saw the distorted shapes of three little boys. Immediately, Sonya's blood started to boil. She knew exactly what they were here for.

She pulled the door open and blocked as much of it with her narrow body as she could, so they could not see in. They were all dressed in the same baggy jeans, large enough to fit another little boy in, baseball caps, all turned backward, and extra-large jerseys that hung down past their waists like little skirts.

"Hello, Miss Brooks," one of the boys said. "Is Jahlil ready?"

"Ready for what?"

The boys looked at each other, exchanging bewildered glances, as if Miss Brooks needed to get with the program.

"The Basketball Jam. Is he ready?"

"I think he forgot about it, boys."

"No, he didn't," one boy, who had a particularly large head, said. His cap fit so snugly, that Sonya thought his eyes were about to pop out of his face.

"And how do you know that?"

"Because he told us today at school that he was able to go."

"I see." And without turning around, without needing to raise her voice, because she knew her son was right behind her in the shadows, listening to everything that was being said, expecting that his friends coming and calling on him would make a difference in her decision, she called her son.

"Jahlil," Sonya said softly. And she saw him there in her mind, cowering a bit, not wanting to come forward for fear of being shamed in front of his friends, or of facing his mother's anger. So she called him again.

"Jahlil. Come here." And two seconds later, he was beside her. "Now tell them what I told you, what I told you a week ago."

"I ain't goin'," he said pathetically, hanging his head.

"Sorry, guys," Sonya said, closing the door on the boys and their chatter, and all the fun Sonya knew her son was thinking they would have without him. When she turned around, Jahlil was already dragging himself toward his room.

"We talked about this, and you told them that you could go anyway?"

Jahlil kept on walking, as if he had not heard a word his mother said.

"Boy, you stop when I'm talking to you!" she said, her raised voice filling the narrow hallway.

He stopped, and after a moment, he slowly turned around.

"Now why did you tell them that lie, after I said you couldn't go?"

Her son looked as though he wanted to speak, actually parted his lips to do so, but then said nothing. Sonya waited another moment for him to give her some excuse, but when he didn't, she questioned him again.

"I said, tell me," and her voice was even louder now.

"I don't feel like talking about it," Jahlil said, blowing her off, as if they were the same age, husband and wife, rather than mother and son. Then, he turned again, and was pushing open the door to his room, when Sonya yanked him around by the arm and threw his little body up against the wall.

"What did you say to me?!" Sonya said, and she was fuming now, bending down her face inches from her son's.

"I said, I don't want to talk about it," he said again, staring her right back in her eyes, until Sonya reared back and slapped him across his face. She knew it had to hurt him, for her palm stung with pain, but he just looked back at her with defiance.

"Oh, I see. You're a big man now," Sonya said, undoing her belt buckle, sliding it through the loops of her jeans. "Let's see how big you are now."

Sonya pulled the belt fully out, doubled it, holding the end in one of her fists.

"Now, are you going to tell me why you just disregarded what I said and lied to those boys, or am I going to have to whoop your little tail, and then you'll tell me?"

Jahlil still stood there, not saying a word, but he was trembling, and a tear had fallen from his eye.

"Fine," Sonya said, gripping him by the shoulder, spinning his behind toward her, raising the belt, preparing to swat him, when Jahlil finally said, "Because Curtis said I could go!"

Sonya slowly lowered the belt and turned her son back to face her. "Because Curtis said you could go?" she repeated, as if she didn't hear him the first time.

"Yeah," Jahlil said, with attitude, as if this would save him from his mother's rage. He smeared the tear from his face.

"But I said you couldn't. I'm the one that makes the decisions when it comes to you," Sonya said, shaking him. "Curtis is not your father."

"He might as well be," Jahlil said, under his breath, but loud enough for Sonya to hear.

"But he's not. You have a father."

"I can't remember him, because he's always in jail. What kind of father is that?" Jahlil said bitterly.

And he was right, Sonya said to herself, still holding a handful of the boy's shirt in her fist. Caleb was this child's father, but how could that mean anything to Jahlil from behind the bars of a penitentiary in another state? Maybe if she had stayed in Julius's house, written Caleb religiously, as she had when he was first sent to jail . . . ? Maybe if she had sent Jahlil to Chicago over the summer so he could stay with Austin and sometimes visit his father. In her heart Sonya knew she couldn't have done these things, couldn't attach herself, her son, to a man who she knew would forever be popping in and out of their lives. But now, for some reason, she wished she *had* taken those steps, because if Caleb were ever to hear the words his son just spoke about him, Sonya knew it would kill him.

"Do you really mean that, son? Do you know how that would hurt your father?"

Ashamed, Jahlil dropped his eyes to the floor.

"You still love your father. Doesn't matter what kind of father he is. He's the only one you got. Do you understand?" Sonya said, holding his cheeks in her hand. Jahlil looked in her eyes, and she knew he did understand, but was just hurt, angry at the fact that Caleb wasn't there for him, and lashing out probably made him feel as though he was hurting his father, as his father was hurting him.

"So next time you listen to what I say, because Curtis is not your father."

"I'm not?" Curtis said, surprising Sonya, coming in from work early.
He was standing, muscular and bald, behind her, wearing jeans and a
long-sleeved shirt, stretched taught across his muscular torso. He smiled,
as if what she just said was some kind of joke, and he was just dying to
hear the punch line.

Sonya had met Curtis about three years ago. It was right after she'd
moved out of Julius's place. She had managed to find a small one-bed-
room apartment in Watts. It was roach-infested, and a rat would scurry
across the kitchen floor on occasion, but it was hers. She no longer had
Julius peering over her shoulder, nosing into every single thing she
wanted to do, wanting to know if it would do anything to disrespect his
son's name.

The neighborhood was rough, much rougher than the one she lived
in now. Drugs were sold out in the open, prostitutes stood on practically every corner from some time after noon to well into the morning
hours. When Sonya would come home from work in the evenings from
J. C. Penney, where she sold women's clothing, she would hear gunfire,
hear police choppers overhead, see the spotlight flashing down, searching for their suspect.

She would get anxious on the four-block walk from the bus stop,
thinking about Jahlil, worrying if he was all right, even though she knew
he was safe at the baby-sitter's apartment, a little old Hispanic lady who
lived next door to Sonya.

Once when Sonya knocked on Mrs. Delrosa's apartment door, she
was particularly worried, having-heard about one of her coworker's
daughters who had been killed the night before by drive-by gunfire.
From work, Sonya called Mrs. Delrosa four times that day.

"Has Jahlil been dropped off from school yet?"

"No, Sonya, and for the third time, when he is, I'll call you at the
store, okay, sweetheart?" she said, in her heavy Hispanic accent, Sonya
hearing her confidence through the phone. "Don't worry, your boy is
fine."

But Sonya did worry, for the rest of the day, while sitting at the bus
stop, wondering why the damn thing was taking so long. All the way
home, she continued to worry, and now while waiting outside of her
baby-sitter's apartment she worried as well.

"Come in," Mrs. Delrosa said, motioning her into a dimly lit apartment, overcrowded with old furniture, with countless pictures of Jesus hanging from the walls.

"Jahlil," Sonya called, the moment she stepped in, needing to see her boy, know that he was all right.

"Jahlil!" she called more frantically after he didn't answer, a vision of him lying bloody against a street curb popping in and out of her mind.

"He's just outside on the playground," Mrs. Delrosa said. "I told him to be in by seven-thirty when you got here."

"But it's seven-thirty now, and he's not here," Sonya said, truly worried now that something terrible had happened. "Is it safe out there? Couldn't something happen?"

"It was safe enough for my children, and now for my grandchildren," Mrs. Delrosa said, smiling, as if there was no reason to worry at all. "Jahlil is fine."

Sonya stared down at her watch for another grueling six minutes, not wanting to seem as though she didn't trust what the baby-sitter had told her. But after that, she couldn't take it any longer. She hurried to the door with the intention of storming out of it, rushing down the stairs, out onto the playground, and rescuing her son from whatever distress she was sure he was in. But when she pulled the door open, there was Jahlil, a little dirt smeared across his face and the knees of his jeans, but otherwise just fine.

That night, after Sonya put Jahlil to bed, and made sure the six dead bolts on her front door were secure, she made certain no roaches were in the tub, scrubbed it, then took a bath. She sank down in the bubbles, a glass of wine in her hand, focusing on the candle that flickered on the basin in the dark bathroom. She concentrated on it, trying to ignore the sounds from the two apartments on either side of her. The sound of two young babies crying hysterically on the right side of her, and the sound of a couple to the left of her, obviously experiencing the best sex they ever had in their lives.

His cries, her screams, made Sonya think about the last time she had sex, and that had been more than two years ago with Caleb. Her intentions were to save herself for him when he got out of jail, and even though she would allow herself to be taken out every now and then by some guy, she would only allow a friendship to develop and nothing more.

But now, as she lowered her free hand into the water and in between her legs, she realized she couldn't do it. She was so lonely, so disappointed in herself for landing where she was, that she needed someone, practically anyone, to tell her that things weren't as bad as she thought they were, as she saw they were.

The noise continued from the left of her, the headboard banging rhythmically against her wall, the grunts, and moans of extreme pleasure, and then the two voices howling out together, and then silence.

If Jahlil hadn't been put to bed two hours ago, he would've heard that, she thought, and this angered her. He was already receiving a far too accelerated education by living in this building, seeing the events that took place on these streets, and interacting with the hardened kids out there. He didn't have to know what sex sounded like firsthand, and she didn't need him asking her, "Is that man hurting that woman over there?" whenever they decided to start fucking like animals.

Sonya pulled her hand from out between her legs. What she had been thinking turned her off, made her not want to satisfy herself as she had intended, as she had been looking forward to doing all day. She thought about not giving herself that pleasure, but what else did she have? She didn't have another single thing that she was able to look forward to, and that disappointed her even more.

But this would change. Somehow, some way, it would. Sonya lowered herself deeper into the water, letting her head fall back, her hand find its place back in between her legs, and told herself this would be the last time she would have to do this for herself.

The next morning, as on every morning, she waited till Jahlil got picked up by the school bus, then Sonya walked the four blocks to the bus stop to wait for her bus to work. She sat there, and as on every morning, a black Range Rover pulled up to the curb, the tinted passenger-side window rolled down, and the good-looking, bald guy behind the wheel smiled and said, "C'mon, Sonya, can I take you to work *this* morning?"

This had happened every morning since the first morning two weeks ago when he rolled past her, damn near broke his neck checking her out, then made a wild U-turn to try and get her number.

Although he was cute and well built, she turned him down, because she knew from the first time looking at him with his expensive jewelry draped around his neck and wrists, what kind of business he was in.

But this particular morning, Sonya didn't care about any of that, because it wasn't as if she would take anything more from him than a ride to work.

"Yeah, you can," Sonya said, getting up from the bench.

Curtis looked shocked at first, then quickly reached over and pushed the passenger door open. And that's how it started. For a week he continued to pick her up at the bus stop. The week after that, he began meeting her outside her apartment, and then Sonya found herself cooking breakfast for him and her son.

Jahlil immediately took to Curtis, almost as fast as Curtis took to Jahlil. It was because there was no man in the boy's life, Sonya thought. And oftentimes she would feel a moment of guilt while she stirred the eggs, and saw how Curtis and Jahlil were growing on each other, when Jahlil's father was in jail somewhere, probably wondering why she'd stopped writing him.

After a month of seeing Curtis, they ended up in his bed. During sex, she knew she sounded like that woman in the apartment next door to her, but she couldn't help it. It was so damn good that she wanted to let the world know that she was finally getting some dick again.

"I want you and Jahlil to come live with me," Curtis said afterward, pulling her naked body close to his.

"We can't," Sonya said, without even giving it a moment of thought. The first thing that popped into her head was Caleb. He would be getting out in three years, and even though that was a hell of a long time, she wanted to at least be unattached for him. She wanted to at least be able to give them another try without having to worry about some other relationship getting in their way.

"Why not. You don't love me?" Curtis said, somewhat hurt.

If Sonya could've said no to that, she would've, on the spot. But she had to admit that over the time they'd spent together, she was falling in love with this man.

"It's not that."

"Then what is it?"

"I just have my reasons," Sonya said, squirming away from him some.

"And what about how you're living? This ain't the best place in the world, but it's better than where you're living now. It's safer for Jahlil, safer for you."

And he was right about that, right about so many things, but it wasn't enough to force her away from there, not yet.

Over the next two months, Curtis tried to do everything in his power to convince Sonya that she and Jahlil should be with him. He spent so much time with the boy that Jahlil couldn't stop talking about him when Curtis wasn't around. He had become the father figure that Jahlil was missing, but not only that, he had become what Sonya herself was missing. His companionship had made her life now worth living again. If she had a problem, if he didn't resolve it on the spot, he would talk it through with her, make her feel better about what was bothering her to begin with. He supported her in decisions she made, and comforted her when those decisions didn't work out. Whatever she or Jahlil needed he bought for them, and he even tried to buy her a car, but Sonya wouldn't have that.

"Then I'll just have to not only take you to work but pick you up, too."

And Sonya would've been fine to turn that down too, if on one day when she and Curtis knocked on Mrs. Delrosa's door, the old woman didn't say, "Sonya, don't be alarmed, but Jahlil is not here."

Immediately Sonya panicked. "What do you mean he's not here?"

"There was a shooting outside. Jahlil's was taken to the hospital."

Sonya felt weak, felt she would fall, and grabbed Curtis's arm for support.

"My baby got shot!" Sonya said, hysterically.

"No. He didn't get hit," Mrs. Delrosa said, quickly.

"Why is he at the hospital then?" Curtis demanded.

"Because he was hurt when all the other kids were trying to get away. I'm so sorry," Mrs. Delrosa said.

And that was it, Sonya thought as Curtis raced them to the hospital. If she was wavering before, she was certain now. She would take Curtis up on his offer. It wasn't her fault Caleb was in prison, and she wouldn't let it be her fault if Jahlil got hurt, just because she was trying to save herself till Caleb got out.

And now, three years later, Curtis stood in the doorway, looking down at Jahlil proudly, as if he were his own son.

"Did you tell this boy that he could go to that party today, Curtis?" Sonya asked.

"Yeah, I told him," Curtis said, smiling, as if her questioning was of little to no importance. He reached over and ran a playful hand over Jahlil's short hair.

"How's it going, little man?"

Jahlil said nothing, just looked up at him pleadingly, as if begging to be saved.

"This is no joke. I told him he couldn't go."

"Well, I told him he could," Curtis said, the smile still hanging on his face, but his voice undoubtedly more forceful.

Sonya halted for a moment, measuring that tone, angered that he was trying to check her in front of her son. She would take care of that shit later, she said to herself, but now she said, "You know he has a big science test tomorrow that he has to study for."

"But, Mom . . ." Jahlil tried to speak.

"Shut up, child," she said, her attention on Curtis.

"Jahlil is a straight-A student," Curtis said, in Jahlil's defense. "And he'll score an A on the test tomorrow, even if he goes to the party."

"That's because he's in this house studying like I tell him to every day. Not out at some party, like you'd let him be," Sonya said.

"I don't want him slipping and messing up his grades. I don't want him ruining his chances to get into a decent school and end up doing what you do."

What little smile remained on Curtis's face had now disappeared. The friendly, easygoing disposition he had walked in with was now replaced with something angry and adversarial. He crossed his big arms over his chest and gave her a disapproving look.

"What I do? You don't want him working as a shipper in a warehouse?"

Sure, that's what he'd told her, and he was always gone most of the day as if he actually worked at some warehouse, but she wasn't fool enough to believe it. The money he made, how they lived, the words she heard on the street. No, she knew the deal.

"Jahlil, go to your room," Sonya said, still looking at Curtis, but blindly pushing her son toward his door.

"But can I still go to the Basket—"

"Do what your mother tells you, son," Curtis's heavy voice demanded, and with that Jahlil obediently disappeared into his room and closed the door.

"I didn't mean to say that," Sonya apologized.

"So you don't want him growing up doing what I do," Curtis said, draping his big arm around Sonya's neck. "Like there's something wrong with what I do," and now he was leading her down the hallway, toward the living room window.

"Reach over there and open these blinds," he instructed. Sonya ducked beneath his arm, which he held there, floating in air, as if she was still there under it. She turned the wand that opened the vertical blinds and revealed the outside street. Then she placed herself back under his arm.

"See that out there?" Curtis said, pointing a finger out the window.

"Yeah," Sonya said, seeing him pointing at her car.

"What I do paid cash for that car for you. You didn't see anything wrong with that." Curtis spoke casually. He turned them around smoothly, in one motion, his arm still around her, as if they were performing a choreographed dance move, facing them toward the living room and the rest of the house.

"These African pieces of art on the walls, the Italian leather sofas, the Persian rugs," he said, slowly walking them through the room, giving her a tour of her own house. "What I do made all this possible. And if I recall correctly, I don't remember you seeing something wrong with what I do when we bought these either."

The tour ended in the den in the back of the house, the room he spent most of his time in, a huge entertainment center pressed up against the far wall, housing a thirty-six-inch flat screen TV, huge speakers, and all sorts of components. He removed his arm from around Sonya's shoulder, and to her, it felt as though a corpse were just lifted from her neck.

"And I ain't even gonna talk about where I got you from, ain't gonna think about where you would be right now, if it wasn't for what I do," Curtis said, standing before her as if he had full control of the situation. "But let me tell you this much. If you have a problem with it now, or if you have a problem with me telling your boy something, even though I'm laying down loot to take care of him as though he was my own, then you can pack up the little shit you came in here with, and you can bounce," he said smugly, as if he cared nothing about what her response would be.

Sonya looked up at Curtis for a few moments, trying to read what was behind that smug, apathetic look in his eyes as he sucked on his teeth. She couldn't tell, but it didn't make a difference, because the only thing going through Sonya's head at that moment was a voice saying,

This motherfucker must think I'm crazy. He must think I'm desperate and can't live without his ass. But how surprised he will be when I . . . And before the thought could fully be expressed in her own head, she was walking dutifully past him, in the direction of their bedroom.

Sonya pulled one of the huge floor-to-ceiling mirrored doors back to open the closet, then walked in, not bothering to tug on the light switch string that swung around her head.

"What do you think you're doing?" Sonya heard Curtis saying. He was behind her, standing in the doorway, looking furious.

Sonya emerged from the dark walk-in closet with a worn, denim cloth multicolored overnight bag. It was covered with many different colored patches, and looked as though it was originally made from a number of pairs of old blue jeans. It was the "little shit" Curtis said he had found her with. She had never thrown it away, never unpacked it even, expecting that one day, this occasion would come. She shouldered the bag, marched toward the door of the bedroom. She stopped in front of Curtis's six-foot-three, two-hundred-and-forty-pound body. He was blocking as much of the door as he could, and when Sonya tried to squeeze through on his left, he moved left. When she tried the other side, he blocked that, too.

"What are you doing, Sonya?" he said, and now there was concern in his voice.

"You a bad motherfucker now, Curtis?" Sonya said, rage in her eyes, a burning in her chest and throat. "You throwin' your weight around here like you own me, like you own my son?"

"Sonya, no," Curtis said, backing down some.

"You think I'm some ho you buying? That will do whatever the fuck you say, just because you spending a little money? No. No. Hell, no!" Sonya said, waving an angry finger in his face.

"Now get out of my face. I'm taking my son and walking out of this, bitch!"

Sonya was trying to push the big man aside, trying to squeeze through the small openings, but she could not escape.

Curtis grabbed her shoulders, pulled her kicking and fighting back into the room, and closed the door behind them.

"Sonya, stop," he said, holding her, her back to him, trying to calm her, but she still fought. "I said, fucking stop!"

But Sonya didn't stop. She saw his arm just under her chin, lowered her face, and sank her teeth deep into the flesh of his arm.

Curtis howled out in agony, releasing her, almost throwing her away from him. Then he whipped her around, swatting her across the face with the back of his hand.

"You bitch," he said, at the exact time he struck her.

She spun on her feet, spiraled on her way to the bed, falling there, face down on her belly.

When Sonya rolled quickly onto her back, she saw the big man moving toward her, pressing a firm hand over the place she bit him, as if it were bleeding. It wasn't. She knew she hadn't bitten him that hard, and if she had, she would have tasted his blood in her mouth.

He kept coming closer to her, sending Sonya scurrying across the bed, pushing herself up in the corner of the wall. "Don't come near me," she warned.

"I'm not going to hurt you. I just want to know, what the fuck's got into you?"

"You don't own me!" Sonya yelled.

"I didn't say that I did," Curtis said, moving his hand away and examining his arm to see the circle of Sonya's teeth depressions.

"I just don't get you. All I've done for you, all the fucking money I spent."

"Money only buys things. It doesn't buy me or my son."

"That's not the way you acted when I was spending it," Curtis shot back.

"That's it," Sonya said, reaching for her bag, prepared to go.

"No, no, Sonya, don't," Curtis said, stepping in front of her, holding his hands to stop her. "The money's not even the important thing. I love you, and you know that. I bought you that expensive-ass engagement ring six months ago and you got it at the bottom of some drawer somewhere. You don't even wear it. And Jahlil, you know how much I love him, how much that boy has become a part of my life. I want you to be my wife, and make Jahlil my son, because you know I love him like one."

"He's not," Sonya said. "He has a father," and she didn't even know why she was saying that, why she was defending Caleb's right to his son, but somehow it just seemed the fair thing to do.

"He has a father," Sonya said again.

"Sittin' behind bars."

"I told you, we don't talk about that," Sonya said, the image of Caleb drifting in to her brain.

"Whatever," Curtis said. "I love you and Jahlil. You've changed my life, made me feel like I got a reason to live now. It just makes me mad when you act like I don't even mean nothin' to you."

"You mean something. You mean a lot. I love you, Curtis," Sonya said truthfully. "But you don't own me, and when it comes to my son, I know what's best. Do you understand that?"

"I understand. If that'll keep you two here."

Curtis moved toward her, extending a hand to her, gesturing her to get up from the bed. Sonya did, but took her time doing it. "I love you, baby. And I don't think I can stand losing you or Jahlil," he said, holding her close. "Tell me you'll never leave, that you'll never take Jahlil from me."

Sonya's arms were around Curtis's neck, a blank expression on her face. She didn't answer him, because she really didn't hear him from where her mind was.

"Tell me that you won't leave," Curtis said again, tightening his arms around her waist some, prompting her to answer.

"I won't," Sonya said, but there was little if any meaning behind it.

23

On Friday, Austin was supposed to pick up his kids after he left work. He had been excited about it all week, cleaning a little bit of his condo each day, not wanting to get the entire place clean in one night, leaving him with nothing to do around there but wait anxiously for Friday to come.

He'd bought new spreads for the twin beds that sat in his guest bedroom. Austin could remember when he'd left Trace and gone looking for a place he could call home. He made sure he'd have a large enough second bedroom to accommodate his two children. The first time he was with them after he had moved in, he took them shopping to buy the types of beds, nightstands, lamps, and curtains they wanted. He fixed the room up perfectly, just for them. As he stood in the doorway of the children's room Thursday night, after laying the new spreads across the beds, he thought about what a damn shame it was how little time they actually spent in those beds, in his house, in his life.

But that would be different now, or at least, for the moment. He sat behind his desk, looking down at his watch—3 P.M. In a couple of hours, he'd be with his children, his smiling, laughing children, and he'd be able to put aside the pain he had felt, having to endure not seeing them because of the games his ex-wife was playing.

After he thought about it more, the smile that he'd been wearing on his face was gone, replaced with something that resembled pain. He had to beg her, then threaten her, his child had to shed tears, and then and only then did Trace say it would be okay. But hold it, Austin told himself. All that was true, but he was still seeing his children, which hadn't happened in far too long. He should leave it alone, not stir already troubled waters. He was getting what he ultimately wanted, regardless of how it came about, so why would he try to sabotage that?

No reason, Austin said, standing up from his desk, only trying to allow part of his brain to answer. He had no reason, so he wouldn't mess it up. He told himself to go to his closet and pull his jacket out, and that's exactly what he did. Now go and lift your keys from your desk drawer, and leave your office, so you can pick up your children. He spoke to himself as though he were a child, as though he were simple, and the slightest distraction would divert him from what he should do, what he must do. And he knew that distraction was the other part of his mind, the part that held the real reason he wasn't skipping effortlessly through his office, a toothy grin on his face.

That other side of his mind sat there heavy in his head, like the devil sitting on his other shoulder, countering the angelic reasoning that was trying to get him out of that office and to his kids.

"You're no more than a toy to them, Austin," that other side of his brain said, speaking in Trace's voice. He saw her face, the evil scowl it wore, hate motivating her words. "Believe me, if you were to leave and never come back, they'd be fine, and they'd never care if they saw you again."

The memory of those words halted Austin in his tracks, as he was stepping away from his desk, his keys in his hands. He knew why Trace said that. It was to hurt him. It was the type of relationship they had now, seeing who could cause the other the most pain. But that wasn't the only reason she said it, and it wasn't the worst reason. It was also because she believed it. She truly felt that their children could live without him, that it wouldn't make a difference if he was in their lives or wasn't, and that angered him to no end. Seeing how coming from a family where there was no father had affected him, how in the hell could she think that it would make no difference?

He was beyond anger now, reaching over his desk, accidentally knocking his pen set and paper clip holder to the floor below as he lunged for the phone. He stuck it to his ear, leaned over to punch in the numbers to Trace's workplace, but stopped himself when he saw his finger trembling over the first digit. He was so angry that he was shaking, so angry that he didn't even know what he would have said to her when she did pick up the phone. He probably would have come out with a long stream of nonsensical raging and ranting that would have just been gibberish to her, and if he did manage to convey what he was feeling, would she have even listened? Would she have even cared? Hell, no, Austin thought, lowering the phone back into its cradle.

She would have said something like, "I don't care about all that. Are you coming to get the kids or not?"

And all he could have said was, he'd be there, like a good little doggie. He'd be there to snap up the scrap she threw down for him. He'd be there, and it would have been just what she expected, probably exactly what she's expecting. She probably thought she'd allow him to see the kids only when he was good and pissed, ready to cause a serious ruckus, only after being denied five or six times, and that would be the trend from now on. But it would have to stop, he thought, looking down at his watch, the time pushing closer to the time he was supposed to be picking up his kids. It would have to stop right now, and what it took to stop it might not be pretty, but it would have to be done.

And with that, he moved behind his desk and dropped down into the executive chair, realizing what he must do. He would not pick his children up. He would not call to inform them or his ex-wife that he would not be coming, since Trace was so sure they could live without him, and they would simply forget about him, if he weren't there to remind them. He'd make her see how wrong she'd been.

24

Some time later, Trace walked over to the window, the one she could see the street and the porch from. That girl is too much in love with her father, she thought. Bethany was sitting patiently on the porch, looking down at the little watch on her wrist. She seemed sad, as if she were sitting out there and didn't even know why. After an hour of waiting for her father inside, she'd asked her mother if she could wait outside.

"What difference does it make, baby? When he comes, we'll know about it."

"I just want to wait outside. Can I?" she pouted.

Trace turned to her son. "Do you want to wait outside, too?"

Troy shook his head, not seeming to care either way. "No, but can I go upstairs and play video games till he comes?"

"Go ahead," Trace said, dismissing him, then watching him tear tracks up the stairs. It was where Bethany should have been heading, too, doing something to take her mind off when her father was going to come. That is, if he was going to come at all.

"Okay, go ahead and wait out on the porch. But take a jacket." That was over an hour ago, and now Austin was two hours late. Trace tried calling his firm, and his home, but there was no answer at either. She left two messages, trying to sound polite at first, hoping he'd pick up if he was there, and if not, hoping that he'd realize that there was no longer venom in her voice, and it would remain that way if he'd just come and pick up the children as he had said he would. The second time she called both places was only fifteen minutes ago. She was angry, standing by the window, watching her daughter look down the street for her father.

"Austin," she said as calmly into the phone as she could, "these children are waiting for you. You'd said you'd take them tonight, so what is your damn problem?" She paused, looking for something else to say, but was so angered by the sight of her daughter sitting on the porch, her hands folded between her knees, a look of hope struggling to stay on her face, that she just hung up.

Why does my girl have to go through this? Trace thought. Austin said when they split, he wouldn't do this to the children. The two of them getting a divorce was supposed to be better for the children than their staying together, because the children wouldn't see their parents fighting, wouldn't see them unhappy. And he swore things would be just as they always had been between him and the kids. He'd just live somewhere else.

At 7 P.M. Bethany looked down at her watch and thought, Snoopy had to be wrong.

Bethany looked up and that flickering in the streetlights began to happen. It was the same flickering that would dictate it was time for her to go in for the night, like so many days in the past. Her mother came out for the umpteenth time, this time bringing with her some chocolate chip cookies wrapped in foil. She handed them to Beth, then sat down beside her. She ran a hand over her hair and stopped on top of her head. "Why are you doing this to yourself, honey?" She looked concerned, and Beth wished she wouldn't look that way.

"I'm not doing nothing to myself. I'm just waiting on Dad," she said, crunching one of the cookies.

"Beth, baby, you've been saying that for the past few hours. Now I hate to tell you this, but I don't think he's going to make it."

"He's coming, Mommy. He's coming." Beth started to feel anxious, because she knew what was going to be said next.

"Bethany, he's not. Now it's getting dark out here, and I think it'd be a good idea if you came inside."

"Mommy, I can't. Don't make me, please."

"Why can't you?"

"Because it'd be like I gave up on him if I went in. And if I do that, he really won't come." Her mother could see the seriousness in her daughter's eyes, and hated that she was giving so much of herself to a father who wasn't even there to receive it.

"Beth, it is seven P.M. now. If that man does not show up in one hour, you're going in the house. Period. Do we understand each other?"

"Yes, ma'am."

Her mother stepped inside after kissing Bethany on the cheek. She ate another cookie, counted four left, and wrapped them up for later, sticking them in her coat pocket. One hour, she thought, and hoped whatever her father was doing and wherever he was, he could finish and be there within an hour's time. "I'm not givin' up on you, Dad. I'm not givin' up on you," she said, looking down the street.

It was fifteen minutes to eight, and Bethany had resorted to standing very near the curb, looking for headlights coming in either direction, hoping it was her father. Every time she saw a pair, her heart would fill with all the hope in the world. She would scoot to the side of the street and pray it was her father. But when the cars just kept on passing her by, her heart would break, till the next pair of headlights appeared.

Her mother watched it all from between a slightly parted curtain. It was killing her, and all she wanted to do was run out there and grab her girl in her arms and carry her inside; rescue her from all that false hope that her father has somehow instilled in her. If she could just tell her how much of an inconsiderate, self-loving liar her father was. If she could tell her not to love that man, because all he would do was take those feelings and trample all over them. But she couldn't do that, because that would be bad-mouthing him when he wasn't around, and Beth didn't go for that. So Trace would stay quiet, and wait the fifteen minutes till she would have to drag that poor child in and lie to her, tell her that her father really was thinking of her, even though he didn't come when he knew his daughter thought the world of him.

Trace decided she'd wait those last fifteen minutes with her. She pulled a sweater out of the closet and stepped outside. Bethany heard the door opening and immediately checked her watch—7:45 P.M. She quickly looked both ways up and down the street, where she saw the glimmer of a pair of headlights again. A smile slowly materialized on Beth's face. Trace walked down the walkway, toward the street, looking to see if it was actually Austin.

As the headlights brightened, Bethany became more anxious. Trace could see her jumping with anticipation, as if she were poising her body to jump right into her father's arms.

"Come back a little bit, baby. You're too close to the street," Trace called, worried, picking up her pace to close the distance between her and her child. But it was as if Bethany couldn't even hear. The lights got brighter and brighter, Bethany becoming more and more anxious, more excited, till she stepped off the curb and into the street.

Trace quickened her pace even more now, and when she looked down the street, she could have sworn she saw that pair of headlights swerving. "Beth, get out of the street!" she yelled, but the child still wasn't listening. She was too caught up with what was happening in her head to hear or notice that the headlights were approaching much faster than they should have been, swerving wildly. Beth was caught in some kind of trance, her eyes wide, staring down the street at what she was sure was her father, a huge smile glued to her face. "Beth! Beth, get out of the street!" Trace yelled, running to the child with everything she had. But Beth was standing nearly in the middle of the street now, the bright lights bathing her in whiteness. And as Trace ran toward her child, she could not hear a thing. She couldn't hear the revving of the car's engine, couldn't hear the loud squealing of the car's brakes, she couldn't even hear herself scream out when she realized that she would never make it in time to save her baby from getting run over by that car. All she could do was think that she would never forgive Austin if she lost her child because of him.

Something caught hold of Trace's foot, sending her to the ground, landing just short of where the car impacted with her daughter. She heard a loud thud, then she heard the high-pitched squeal of her child. She looked up and saw her baby's body land beside her, crumpling like a rag doll. The car did not stop. It sped on at the same frenzied pace, if not faster, leaving Bethany's body twisted and bleeding on the side of the street, where Trace cried hysterically over her.

"Help! Somebody, please help my baby!"

25

Marcus sat beside his wife, watching television. He didn't know what was on, and it really didn't matter to him, because his mind was more on the thundering silence that played on between him and his wife than what crap was on the tube. He wanted to talk, really talk, instead of trade one-word answers as they'd done before she turned the TV on.

But then again, there hadn't been a whole lot of conversation since she'd come back from Austin's. Marcus just accepted her back when she walked through the door, never bringing up the issue again. And Reecie paused only a moment, after stepping in the house, at the sight of Marcus's eye. She didn't comment on it, saying that he should have stayed out of his brother's business, but she sure as hell didn't throw her arms around him, offering to get him something to put on it to take the swelling down, or simply offering to kiss it to make it better.

They were civil to each other because, he was sure, they both felt they had to be, considering they were husband and wife, and that they were about to bring a child into the world.

Marcus inched his fingers over toward the television remote that lay by his thigh, and secretly pulled it over toward him, without alerting Reecie. They had to discuss what was going on, because he didn't like how they were living, how they'd been, or hadn't been, relating to each other, and Marcus felt things that happened outside of their household, like what was going on with his brothers, shouldn't be allowed to disrupt the harmony inside.

Marcus hit the remote, and the picture that was before them shrunk into a little bright speck in the center of the tube.

"Hey," Reecie said, turning to Marcus, an aggravated expression on her face. "I was watching that."

"Don't look at me," Marcus said, releasing the remote, and holding up his empty hands. "I don't know what happened. I'm just as pissed as you. I just bought that TV."

Reecie exhaled loudly, turned to her husband, and said, "What do you want to talk about, Marcus?"

"Nothing. I just wanted to tell you that I'm glad you're back, that's all."

"I see. Do you know why I left?"

It took Marcus a second to answer. "I don't know. Because you like Austin better than me?"

"Yeah, that's it," Reecie said sarcastically. "Marcus, this situation is important, and I needed you to recognize that."

"So you leave?" Marcus said. "This was between just me and my brothers. It had nothing to do with you."

"But it does, Marcus. And not just me, but our child, too. I don't know if you ever heard this expression before, but it goes, 'A man will only treat his wife as well as his mother.' Heard that?" Reecie asked.

"I don't know. Maybe."

"Know what it means?"

"Yes, Reecie. But Austin's not my mother, nor is Caleb."

"It doesn't make a difference. They're your family, and if you can all of a sudden switch on them because you feel they've slighted you, what will you do to me if I make a mistake? What will happen if you and our child get in an argument, or she doesn't behave the way you say she should? You gonna disown her, too?"

"I'd never do that, and you know it."

"Judging by your actions, I can't be sure, baby."

"So because of that, you just sided with him, went over there, and left me here alone."

"No. I went over there because, although Austin tries to play the big independent role, he's not. He always needs someone there. That person used to be you. But because you canceled on him, I felt the least I could've done was be there for him. I owed him that much."

"Owed him that much," Marcus said incredulously, getting up from the sofa, walking an angry circle in front of the coffee table. After he was done with his dance, he turned back to her, hands on his hips, and repeated himself. "Owed him that much. Why because you work at his firm? You don't owe that man a damn thing," Marcus said, anger in his voice.

Reecie just looked at Marcus, shaking her head, as if her husband had not a clue. "That wasn't what I was talking about, Marcus."

"Then what were you talking about?"

"I owe him for you. I owe him for us. You may have forgot, but your brother Austin is the reason that we're together, that we're married. He's the one who suggested you call me, remember? If it wasn't for him, none of this would be here. You, me, or our child," Reecie said, lovingly smoothing her hand over her belly.

And oh, what a fool Marcus felt like at that moment. For some reason, he had forgotten about that, and couldn't even remember if he ever thanked his brother for his wife, for his life.

"When I think about what a big part he has played in our lives, I just think it's ridiculous for you to be treating him the way you are. But that's not even the biggest reason you need to repair what's wrong between the two of you, Marcus," Reecie said, extending her hand for him to take. When Marcus took it, she pulled him down back beside her. "He is your brother," she said, pausing between each word. "You, and Austin, and Caleb. You all need each other. And if he's too thickheaded or too childish to realize and accept that, you have to be the bigger one. You've done it all of your lives, so just keep on doing it, okay?" Reecie said, cuddling closer to him.

"Okay," Marcus said, leaning in to give his wife a kiss.

Just then, the phone rang.

"I don't want to get that," Marcus said. "Let's just let it ring."

"No, sweetheart. Maybe you ought to get it. It might be important."

Marcus pulled himself from the sofa, walked over to the cordless phone, and picked it up. It was Trace, crying hysterically on the other end.

26

When Austin stumbled through the door of his condo, it had to have been past midnight. He didn't know for sure, for trying to stop the little numbers on his watch from floating about would take too much concentration, much more than the three double shots of cognac would allow him. He wasn't totally drunk. He'd managed to make it home without swerving too wildly about the road, and had even passed a cop car without drawing its attention.

Austin walked through the living room, leaving one of his shoes in the middle of his floor, and his jacket a few paces after that. He stopped at the doorway of his room, threw both his arms out, catching himself in its frame. He eyed the red illuminated numbers floating in the darkness somewhere deep in his room. They read 12:42 A.M. He stepped on the back of his shoe with his stocking foot, and left his other shoe in the doorway, as he pointed and pushed himself in the direction of where he knew the bed was. He didn't bother with the lights, because he didn't want to see anything. He didn't bother with the rest of his clothes, because he knew he was tired enough to sleep without having to take them off. It would take too long, and all he wanted to do was lose himself in slumber, so he could forget about what he had done to his children. It was wrong, he knew that now, knew it when he'd finished the last drop of his second shot. At the bar he had gone into, Austin closed himself in a stall, and called Trace on his cell phone to tell her that he was still coming, that something had come up, but to have the kids ready, because he was on his way. But she didn't answer. He didn't bother to leave a message, because he hadn't thought of an excuse, and whatever he did say he knew would sound exactly like that, an excuse. So he just hung up the phone, and wobbled back to the bar to have another drink.

Lying across his bed on his stomach, his arms hanging over either side, feeling his body being slowly pulled into an alcohol-induced sleep, he contemplated what he would tell Trace tomorrow. It didn't take him long to decide he would lie to her. He would say that something very important came up, and the kids just slipped his mind. He thought a moment. Yeah, it was bad. He would need more than that. And if something important did come up, by the time he got home, his kids would have occurred to him again, wouldn't they? Of course, he told himself, and at that moment, he would be calling Trace to explain. So that was what he would do.

Austin inched himself slowly across his bed, like a dying worm on hot pavement. He reached out, his hand blindly fumbling across his nightstand, till he hit the phone. He clutched the receiver, brought it to his ear. He punched the talk button and heard the broken dial tone, informing him he had messages. Trace, he thought, not wanting to hear her voice screaming at him, but he dialed his service anyway.

"You have four new messages," the recorded voice informed him. Austin pressed one to listen to them.

"Austin!" It was Trace, and he winced against the sharp, abrasive tone of her voice. "These children are waiting for you. You said you'd take them tonight, so what is your damn problem?" There was a long pause, then a click.

"Great," Austin slurred at the message. The date and time the message was recorded was announced, and then the next message began. It would be Trace again, Austin knew, and when he heard the sound of her voice, he shook his head and wanted to hang up, because this time she had seemed to have lost it. "Austin, where the hell are you?" Then the next message.

"Austin! Austin!" she screamed into the phone. Hearing the intensity of her voice drew Austin up from his lying position, so he was sitting on the edge of the bed. He expected her to be angry with him, but something sounded desperately wrong in her voice.

"Austin, Beth has been hit by a car. Somebody hit her and kept on going," Trace screamed into the phone. She was hysterical. Austin could hear the crying in her voice, the shock. "We're in an ambulance going to Northwestern Memorial right now, but she's not saying anything. She's not conscious! God, Austin, I don't want our baby to die," she cried, then said, "Wherever you are, come as soon as you can!" And she stopped speaking, but she was still on the line. Austin heard the paramedics saying things, medical things, their voices seeming almost as frantic as Trace's. Austin pressed the phone tighter to his ear, hoping he could hear something, hoping he could make out if his daughter was okay or not. And then he called out.

"Trace. Trace! Are you still there?" And then the phone went dead. Austin threw the phone down, sprang from his bed, fumbled desperately for his shoes, threw on his coat, and ran out as fast as he could.

27

Julius sat in a chair, pushed up in the corner of a run-down, Sunset Boulevard motel room, a look devoid of emotion in his eyes. But inside him, there was turmoil. His thoughts were colliding, searching for an answer, a remedy, but there was nothing he could do. There was nothing he could do, and he'd been telling himself that since he woke up that morning, grateful to see another day, but immediately deflated when he thought about how it was among a decreasing number of mornings he had left to see. This thought caused panic, anguish, anxiety in him, but he had to accept it, had to calm his body, and let that realization flow through him, because fighting it was useless now, even his doctor had told him that.

"Well, do something," Julius had demanded of the doctor yesterday morning, five minutes after the doctor told him that the cancer was now raging through his body. It took Julius that long to fully understand the fact that he was dying, again, and that by the doctor's blind estimation, it could happen within weeks.

"I beat it before. I can beat it again," Julius said, trying to convince himself, even if he wasn't able to persuade the doctor. And he knew he couldn't, just by the look on Dr. Phillips's face. It was something between sympathy and sorrow. He shook his head some, looking down at his hands, then back up at Julius, not responding to Julius's demand.

"Well," Julius said, wanting action, knowing that every second that ticked by without it he'd be one second closer to his death. "Put me on some sort of treatment, radiation, chemotherapy, something," Julius said, now flipping through his medical records, as if he could help the doctor devise some plan in treating him.

"Julius, don't," Dr. Phillips said, standing in front of his desk, Julius off to the side, still going through the file. Dr. Phillips didn't even turn to look at Julius when he spoke, just stood there, his head turned downward, as if he knew there was no chance for his patient.

"Don't?" Julius said, moving over in front of the doctor, the thick file extended in his hand. "Then you do it. Call someone. We need to do this now."

"There is nothing we can do, Julius. Don't you understand what I said? The cancer has metastasized all over your body. It's in your bones, Julius. In some of your organs. If we were to try to treat you with radiation, we'd be burning practically your entire body. Chemotherapy? We'd have to use so much on you that the treatment would probably kill you before the disease did," Dr. Phillips said sadly.

"I don't care. I want to try something. I need to try something," Julius said adamantly, raising his voice. "I'm not just going to let this disease take me. I'm not just going to die."

"Yes, you are," the doctor said over Julius's voice, and afterward, he looked a bit surprised at himself, as though this was what he'd been thinking but had had no intention of saying out loud. "I'm sorry, Julius. You have no choice. Now, I can't stop you from going out and trying every treatment under the sun to try and save yourself, but you'll just have to go to another doctor to do it. Because I know what will happen. I've seen it when a family can't accept the fact that their mother or father is dying. I tell them, let the man go home, relax, spend his last weeks or days with his family, in bed, not being carted to some hospital, among strangers every day, pumped full of drugs, and shot full of X rays. But they insist, Julius," the doctor said, speaking softly, slowly, looking directly in Julius's eyes.

"They insist, not because they think the treatments will help, but because they're too afraid to let go. It's too painful for them to sit by and do nothing, while their loved one is dying right before their eyes. So they'd rather put that person through the hassle, through the pain, of receiving treatments, not for the good of that patient, but for their own good. They rack up needless costs, and prolong pain that nothing can be done about. And worst of all, they strip whatever dignity that patient has left, till he's just a lifeless, mindless body, no longer truly living, but just existing, and barely at that. Don't put yourself through that, Julius. Don't put your family through it. It seems as though I was wrong last time, but this time, I'm positive about your prognosis. It's going to come," the doctor said, resting a hand on the side of Julius's arm. "Just let it, and face it bravely when it does."

Face it bravely when it does, Julius thought, still sitting in the corner of the hotel room. Easy as fuck for him to say, he wasn't the one who was dying. He wasn't the one who was scared as hell of going off to who knows where, of dealing with thoughts about what comes next, if anything. There had to be something that he could have done, something more, something that would have given him even the slightest chance, a 1 percent chance.

Julius would've gone to another doctor for a second opinion, but Dr. Phillips was the leading specialist in his field, and as much as Julius didn't want to face it, something deep within him told him that Dr. Phillips was right.

After leaving the doctor's office, Julius sat in his car for almost an hour, just staring into space, his mind occupied with nothing but the rising and falling of his chest, the breathing that he had taken for granted all of his years, the breathing that would, one day soon, cease.

He thought of going home, telling Cathy, but he couldn't bring himself to do that, not yet. Then he thought of going home, but not telling her, saying that he had been out to the park, or to the store. But he knew she would see right through him, question his solemn behavior, his long face, and press him till he could no longer keep it from her. She would push him till it all came out in a fit of sobbing and tears. He thought about calling her, but after a moment, he dismissed that as well. He would do nothing. He wouldn't go home, he wouldn't even speak to her until he'd worked out what to say, or at least until he himself was able to accept his fate without wanting to break down and cry.

Upon entering the room of the motel, he'd closed the door behind him, walked to the middle of the room, and looked around, as if there was something that he was supposed to be doing but he had forgotten what it was. It was the standard cheap motel room, and not even a brand-name one at that. Looking around the room, the queen-size bed in the middle of it, the TV in front of that, a chair off to a side, a chill ran up Julius's spine as he realized that this was what people did when they planned suicide. They would check into a motel room for some reason, and there they would take the bottle of pills, or swallow the barrel of their gun, or hang themselves from their belt or their necktie. He shook the thought and shivered some against the chill, telling himself he didn't have to go through the worry of finding which was the best way to take his own life. That decision was made for him, and he sure as hell didn't think it was the best way.

Not knowing what to do, realizing that he wasn't actually there to do anything, but to avoid doing something, he walked over to the chair and sat. He wasn't hungry, wanted to eat, but knew that, even if he did try, his stomach would reject it. That is, if the food made its way past the series of knots his stomach was now tied in. He wasn't interested in watching television, had no interest in anything but valuing the time he had left.

He glanced over at the clock. It was nearing 10 P.M. He then looked at the phone, thought of calling his wife again, at least letting her know he was okay, for he knew she was probably worrying herself to death already. But then, he thought, maybe it was best if she didn't know. Maybe his strange absence would prepare her for what was to come. It was a cowardly excuse for avoiding her, but it worked for him at that moment. He walked over to the window and pulled the thick, rubber-backed curtain fully across it. He blotted out most of the electric lights that glowed outside, leaving that space black, save for a sliver of light that peeked through at the far end of the window.

Julius sat himself down in the chair, reached over to the nightstand, and clicked off the light. He sat there in the dark till he could no longer hold his head up or keep his eyes open. Then he dragged himself to the bed, where he slept atop the blankets in his clothes.

28

Caleb sat, slumped down some behind the dash of the Volvo. He had parked the car only two doors away from the house that Jahlil, Curtis, and Sonya lived in. Caleb looked at the piece of paper he had written the address on and they matched. This was the place.

He had been sitting out there for at least an hour, watching the house for movement, and trying to find the courage to walk up to the door and see if anyone was home. He had been telling himself not to go, wondering if she even cared to see him anymore, and he knew if he never put himself in front of her, he'd never have to hear that she didn't.

But the waiting was killing him, so he climbed out of the car, walked over to the house, and just stood in front of it. He stared at it for a long moment, wondering what would make her decide to come to such a place, to drag his child with her.

Caleb climbed the stairs, wanted to turn back around and drive off, the second he arrived at the door, but he fought himself.

He rang the doorbell, forcing himself to wait for someone to answer, but no one came. He looked down at his watch and saw it was approaching 4:30 P.M. He rang the doorbell again, two more times, then turned around and looked out toward the street. He had no idea where Sonya was, because he had no idea what her schedule was. And for that matter, he didn't even know if this was really her house. All Thomas had said was that the man he sold the drugs for had a girlfriend named Sonya who looked just like Caleb's description of Sonya, and she had a son named Jahlil. And yes, that was a hell of a coincidence, Caleb thought, giving up, and walking back toward his car, but coincidences did happen.

He opened the car door, preparing to climb back in, when a black Lexus rolled past him, slowed, then drew up and parked right in front of the house he'd just come from.

Caleb didn't get a look at who was driving the car, but it was a woman, and he knew it had to be Sonya. He threw himself into the front seat of Cathy's car, pulling the door closed gently behind him, as if any loud noise would have him discovered.

He peered over the dashboard, his breath coming quick and hard now, as he waited to see just who emerged from that car.

Caleb saw the brake lights flash on the car, then the white reverse lights, as the person shifted the car into park. A second later and the door was swinging open, and Caleb prayed to himself that it was Sonya who would get out of that car, and that somewhere in there, she would have his son as well.

A foot hit the ground outside the car, and Caleb intently watched, waiting to see more of this woman. What would he do if it wasn't Sonya? Even more important, what would he do if it was? He focused his eyes on the car in front of him again, saw the woman backing out of the car. She looked to be taking a bag from inside it. She was almost all the way out of the car, Caleb's eyes locked on her, waiting to see her face, to confirm whether or not he had found the woman he loved, when the other door all of a sudden swung open, and a child bounded out of it.

Caleb's attention was snatched from the woman backing out of the car to the child, who Caleb now saw with his own eyes was his son, Jahlil. Although he had grown taller, and thinner, this was the same boy from before Caleb was sent to prison. Caleb felt a wave of pride roll over him, seeing how well his son had grown up, then he saw Jahlil say something and look over the roof of the car. Caleb's eyes followed Jahlil's stare, and then he saw the woman, for she was standing entirely outside of the car, and yes, it was Sonya.

Caleb leaned farther forward in his car to get a better look at his family. How beautiful Sonya still was. He looked as closely as he could into her face, trying to see something in it to tell him if she was happy or not, if she missed him or not. But how ridiculous was that? he thought.

He looked at his son again. He was a small man now, and all of a sudden, Caleb felt a quick flash of regret, knowing that he missed those all-important childhood years, those years that would never return.

They were walking to the door now, Sonya swinging her purse on her arm, saying something to Jahlil, her hand resting on his shoulder, as he carried a shopping bag.

Caleb didn't know what to do. He wanted to take a minute, think it over, and try to come up with something to say to them, but feeling the way he did at that moment, that would take forever. He needed to move now, he told himself. So he climbed out of the car, stood outside it, feeling as if he were someone else, feeling as if the world he was in at that moment wasn't even real. He slammed the door of the car with enough force to draw their attention, but they didn't turn. They were just in front of the door now, Sonya digging through her purse, fishing for her door key, when Caleb said, "Sonya."

He said it softly, as if he was testing his voice, and when she didn't turn around, he called her again, this time loud enough for her to hear.

"Sonya."

Sonya turned around, looking in the wrong direction at first, then turning again, catching sight of the car, then the man who stood beside it. Caleb could tell that at first, if only for a fraction of a second, she didn't recognize him. Then he saw her mouth drop open, her eyes expand, and a hand fall to her heart.

"Oh, my God," Sonya breathed. Jahlil reached for her hand, asking, "Mommy, what's wrong?"

The boy followed his mother's line of sight.

Sonya gently pulled her hand away from her son, still looking at Caleb.

Caleb found the courage to walk from the car, up onto the sidewalk, and over to the house. Something held him from walking down the walkway of the house though, walking up toward the porch, and he didn't know if it was fear of being rejected by Sonya and his son, or if it was just because he felt he didn't belong there, didn't have the right to trespass on this property.

Sonya, atop the stairs, was still eyeing Caleb as if she were seeing a ghost. The look on Jahlil's face told Caleb the boy didn't know who the hell he was, but he would find out soon enough, Caleb told himself.

"Can you come here?" Caleb asked timidly, afraid that Sonya's answer would be no. She looked down at the boy, as if wondering whether or not he approved, then nodded her head without speaking, and started slowly down the stairs.

Moments later, Sonya was standing just before Caleb. He was looking in her face, in her eyes, and he couldn't believe that after five long years this was actually happening. He wanted to throw his arms around her, hold her tight, but he didn't dare. Things had changed, she was living with another man now, allowing this other man to raise their child, he assumed.

Caleb had nothing planned to say. He was at a total loss for words, so he just said what was in his heart.

"I missed you." His voice was soft, but sure. He was looking into Sonya's eyes to see if any of this registered, if any of it mattered to her, but he didn't care. He just had to let her know these things, so he lowered his eyes and spoke.

"I missed you, and so many times, the only thing that got me through was knowing that I would see you again." He paused, swallowing hard, then said, "I love you, Sonya. Always have, and I'll never stop."

Caleb was afraid to look up after saying those words. She would tell him he could leave now, that she had no longer felt that way about him, but when Caleb finally, slowly, lifted his head to look into her eyes, tears were running down her face.

"What's . . ." Caleb said, about to ask her why she was crying, when she threw her arms around him, squeezing him in a tight embrace. Caleb was caught off-guard, but he wrapped his arms around her, holding her tight as well. He looked over Sonya's shoulder to see his son up on that porch, a worried look on his face, his body fidgeting, as if he didn't know whether or not to come down and try and save his mother from this man hugging her.

"I missed you, too, Caleb. But things . . ." Sonya tried to say through her tears. "But . . ."

"But what?" Caleb said, drawing away from her, so he could look into her face.

"It was just so hard, and . . ."

"Don't worry about it," Caleb said, giving her arms a comforting squeeze. "My father told me everything. But I understand. It's okay. I just want you and Jahlil to come home now." And that must have been the wrong thing to say, for he felt her hold on him weaken.

"What?" Caleb asked.

"Caleb, it's a long story. I don't know if I can just up and leave like that."

"What do you mean, you don't know if you can? Do you want to?"

"Caleb, it's not that simple."

"Why isn't it that simple? Can't you just grab your things and my son," Caleb said, pointing to Jahlil, "and come back with me?"

"Caleb," Sonya said sadly. "I don't even think he remembers who you are."

And even though Caleb thought the same thing when he saw the look on his son's face, he never imagined that hearing the actual words would hurt him so much. He turned again to face his son, who was looking somewhat frightened there on the porch.

"Jahlil," Caleb called. "Can you come here a minute?"

Jahlil looked scared, then looked to his mother for help, for some form of advisement. She didn't say a thing, just looked pained by what she imagined him going through at that moment.

"Jahlil, look at me. It's okay. Will you come down here? I won't hurt you, I promise," Caleb said, his arms open, as if expecting the boy to just run into them.

Jahlil looked to his mother again, and she nodded, sensing the question he was asking her. He descended the stairs, and walked forward toward Caleb, an uncertain look on his face. He stopped there in front of Caleb, his head down, looking as though he was waiting to be punished.

"Jahlil, look up at me."

The boy raised his face.

"Do you know who I am?" Caleb asked, simply.

And once again, Jahlil was looking to his mother for answers.

"No. Don't look at her. Answer me. Do you know who I am?"

Jahlil looked up at Caleb, a sad expression on his face, shaking his head. "No."

"Are you sure?"

"I told you, Caleb. He doesn't know," Sonya said.

Caleb shook his head, disappointed, feeling somehow he was to blame for this.

"It's not your fault," Sonya said, reading his expression. "It's because you've been gone."

Just then a black Range Rover raced up and screeched to a halt in front of the house. The door swung open, a big bald man rushing out and across the lawn toward Sonya.

"What the hell is going on?" he said. "Who the hell are you?" he barked at Caleb.

That had to be Curtis, Caleb thought, the man Thomas had mentioned. The drug dealer. The big man walked closer to Caleb, looking as if he was prepared to fight.

"Who the fuck are you, I said?" Curtis spoke, right in Caleb's face now.

Caleb didn't speak right away, but he didn't take a single step back either. He sized the man up, measured how big he was, the anger on his face, the willingness he seemed to have to fight. He was trying to punk Caleb, trying to intimidate him, but Caleb had been in prison long enough to know that you don't back down from situations like this, you stand your ground, and get your respect.

"I'm Caleb. Sonya's man, and the father of her son," Caleb said, looking the bigger man directly in the eyes. "And I just came to get them, so if you just move your big ass aside, we'll be out of here in no time."

At that remark, Curtis threw his head back and laughed. He walked a small circle in front of Caleb, holding his middle, as if the remark was that hilarious, then ended up back in Caleb's face, the laughter now gone.

"I don't think so, motherfucker," Curtis said, his voice low, cautionary. "If you was Sonya's man, you ain't no more, because I am. And that goes the same for Jahlil. That's my son now, so you might as well carry your narrow ass on."

"Don't work like that," Caleb said, walking over to Sonya and grabbing her hand. "Sonya, go in the house and get your stuff, so we can go." But Sonya didn't budge. That started Curtis laughing again.

"She ain't going nowhere with you, motherfucker."

"Sonya, c'mon," Caleb said again.

"I told you. She ain't going nowhere," Curtis said, storming over and tearing Caleb's hand from Sonya's.

Caleb couldn't believe that she'd stay with this man, that she'd allow a man who sold drugs to raise their child.

"Sonya, you can't stay with him," Caleb said. "He's a drug dealer. You know that, don't you?"

Caleb watched for Sonya's reaction, but there wasn't one. She just stood there, as if he had said nothing at all.

"Did you hear me, Sonya? You can't stay here, anymore. He sells drugs. How do you think that's going to affect Jahlil?"

"I don't sell no motherfucking drugs, and she knows that," Curtis cut in.

"You know a boy named Thomas, don't you?" Caleb said to Curtis.

"He works in my warehouse moving packages."

"He sells drugs for you," Caleb said, pointing at Curtis. "He told me, and I saw him doing it." Caleb turned to Sonya. "You can't stay with this man, can't let him raise our son!"

Still Sonya didn't reply, but just stood there, looking at Caleb sadly.

Curtis wrapped his arm around Sonya. "Tell this fool what he wants to hear, baby."

Sonya didn't respond.

"I said tell him," Curtis said, squeezing her into him.

"Curtis doesn't sell any drugs, Caleb," and the words came out with absolutely no sincerity, but as if they had been taught to her, and re-hearsed over and over again.

"Now, you heard all you needed to hear. So if you'd get off my prop-erty and leave my family alone," Curtis said, ushering Sonya toward the house. He grabbed Jahlil's hand as he passed him, bringing him along as well.

Caleb couldn't believe what he was seeing. This man was stealing his family from him, right in front of his eyes. He couldn't allow it.

Caleb ran over to them, grabbing Sonya, pulling her away from Cur-tis.

"You can't go with him, Sonya. You can't," Caleb begged.

"Are you stupid?" Curtis said, turning on Caleb, pushing him away from Sonya. Caleb tumbled backward, landing on his back in the grass. But he was up immediately, reaching for Sonya, for his son, trying to pull them away, pull them toward his car.

And this time, when Curtis attacked him, it wasn't a push, but a punch in Caleb's stomach. Caleb folded and collapsed to the ground, throwing both his arms around his burning middle.

He tried to pull himself up, but before he reached his feet, Curtis struck him again across the jaw, sending him spinning into the grass, landing on his face.

"Curtis, stop!" Sonya cried.

But Curtis walked right up to Caleb, stood just over his body, his leg drawn back, as if he was about to kick him, when Jahlil pulled away from Sonya, threw himself into Curtis, grabbing his leg with one arm, beating him in the back with the other.

"Stop it!" Jahlil cried. "Don't do that!"

Curtis turned and plucked Jahlil from his body, tossing him aside.

"Take this boy, before he get his little ass hurt," Curtis yelled over his shoulder at Sonya. Sonya ran over, grabbed Jahlil in a protective hug.

"I told you, motherfucker," he said, turning back to Caleb. "They ain't your family no more, they mine. What you think, that you could just leave for five years, hang the fuck out in prison, not provide for them, not take care of them, and then come back and find them waiting for you? No, motherfucker. They got somebody now that cares, that takes care of them, and yo' ass should be happy. So don't let me see your ass around here again, because next time, you won't get off so easy."

Caleb tried to get up again, but he needed oxygen to do that, and still none had reentered his body.

"Sonya," Caleb coughed.

He lifted his head, saw her standing there, seeming as though she wanted to come to him, comfort him, but Curtis grabbed her, pulled her away.

"Sonya, you can't stay with him. You can't let him raise our son," Caleb yelled. But she probably didn't hear him, because Curtis had forced her and his son into the house.

29

"Ms. Anthony," a voice called from the other end of the emergency waiting room. Trace looked up to see an overworked doctor with the face of a boy standing at the other end of the room.

When the ambulance had arrived at the hospital, the EMTs had raced Beth into the emergency room, Trace following frantically behind her, pulling Troy along, the boy tripping and stumbling, trying to keep up with her pace.

She was met by a male nurse, his hands raised, stopping her after the stretcher was pushed past him into one of the triage rooms.

"I'm sorry, but you'll have to wait out here. A doctor will be with you in just a minute."

"You don't understand," Trace pleaded. "That's my daughter in there. I have to make sure she's all right."

"I do understand, ma'am. And that's exactly what the doctors are try- ing to do. Make sure she's all right. Now, if you'd help them by waiting right out there," he said, directing her toward the waiting room chairs.

It was two hours of Trace, Marcus, and Troy sitting, saying not a word to one another, all of them worrying about Bethany, not daring to spec- ulate just how bad her injuries were. And now Trace looked across the room to the doctor who was calling her name. Marcus had arrived at the hospital not even half an hour after she had called him. She'd phoned him right after she'd called Austin. Her first intention, in fact, was to call her brother-in-law instead of her ex-husband. But she fought that urge, telling herself that it was only right to call Austin first. She was not surprised that it was Marcus, not Austin, who showed up.

"I'll watch Troy for you," Marcus said, taking him, as if the boy was his own. "Go see what the doctor has to say."

"I'm Ms. Anthony," Trace said, walking over to the doctor, her legs moving stiffly below her, fear in her heart, just knowing that the doctor had bad news for her. It was what she was thinking all the while she was waiting, fighting to keep the thoughts out of her mind.

The doctor extended a hand, which Trace shook.

"I'm Dr. Bryant," he said, then pulled off the glasses he was wearing, rubbed the inside corners of his eyes with his thumb and forefinger, then placed a hand on Trace's shoulder. Trace knew that always meant the worst. He's preparing me for bad news, she told herself.

"Your daughter's going to be all right, Ms. Anthony. She's banged up pretty bad, broke her arm and left leg in two places. We ran tests, an MRI to see if she had any type of concussion, but turns out she doesn't, just some pretty deep cuts that we had to stitch up. But overall, she's going to be fine. We're just going to keep her overnight for observation. Okay?" he said, giving her a reassuring squeeze on her shoulder. "So don't you worry. I'll be back out a little later and let you know what room she's in."

Little metal numbers were tacked to the door—515. Trace stood outside, almost afraid to go in, looking to Marcus for strength. He still held Troy in his arms, the boy's sleeping head on his shoulder. With his other hand, he took Trace's hand and said, "You want me to go in with you?"

She gave it a moment of thought, then said, "No. I'll be okay, but thanks."

She braced herself for the worst, then slowly entered the room. She wanted to cry when she saw Bethany lying there, her head bandaged up, only leaving a small square opening for her face. Her right arm was in a cast, supported by pillows. Her left leg was also elevated, covered in a cast as well.

The room was dark, save for a fluorescent lamp that hung over her head, casting down a light onto her little girl's face that seemed far too bright. Trace stepped closer to her and bent down and kissed her on the cheek, then sat down by her bedside.

"My baby, my sweet baby. I'm sorry all this has happened," Trace said, reaching to touch her head, then pulling her arm back, cautious of the bandages.

"But you're going to be all right. That's what the doctor said. And soon, someday soon, you'll be back on your feet again, running around like nothing ever happened."

Trace took a long look at her daughter again, the casts, the bandages, and it saddened her, filling her with a pain she'd never thought possible.

"Why did you have to go out there?" Trace cried, her face slipping down into her hands. "I told you not to go. I tried calling you, but you wouldn't listen. If you just would've listened," Trace said again, crying more now. And even though the doctor said she would be all right, she wasn't at this moment, and Trace felt it was all her fault.

30

"Can you tell me what room Bethany Harris is in?" Austin asked a sleepy-eyed, middle-aged black man sitting behind the information desk. He tapped the keyboard of his computer sitting before him and looked at the screen, as he blindly reached for a visitor's pass and slid it across the counter to Austin.

"Room 515," he said. Austin took the pass and headed quickly down the hall to the elevator corridor. He stabbed the UP button twice. The elevator took far too long to come, and once he was on it, moved far too slowly and stopped far too many times, letting on a little old lady on the second floor, an overweight, dark brown woman wearing a food-stained white uniform on the third floor, and then on the fourth floor the doors opening just for the hell of it, letting no one off or on.

By the time the doors opened on the fifth floor, Austin was wound up with frustration, ready to literally sprint down the hall. He moved as fast as he could under the bright fluorescent lights overhead, paying attention to the room numbers—501, 503, 505—as they blurred by him. He moved quickly now, speeding to an almost-run, then stopped at a wall, the hallway breaking off in two directions. A sign tacked to the wall before him led him either to the left, toward room numbers 535 to 560, or the right, to rooms 510 to 534. Austin quickly took the right turn, but froze after only the first step, staring at his brother ten feet away from him, holding Austin's son in his arms.

Marcus was rocking Troy gently, had kissed him on the head, and only saw Austin standing down the hall after he raised his eyes.

The look that Austin saw cover his brother's face was that of concern and caution, and he took a step back, turning slightly, as if to shelter Troy with part of his body, as if Austin would attack Marcus, and possibly attack his own son.

Austin walked down to Marcus, slowly, nonthreatening, unlike the way he'd last approached him.

Austin was trying to open his mouth to say something to his brother. What, he didn't know. He stopped himself when he saw Marcus's face up close, the damage he had done to it, the blue-black smear that colored the large mass of inflated skin that hung under his brother's eye.

He made another attempt to speak, nothing coming out except the vague start of a word, but, again, he faltered.

"Whatever, Austin," Marcus said, seeming as if he wouldn't have listened to the words Austin had to say even if he was capable of producing any.

"Just go in there and see your daughter."

31

Trace gently stroked the blanket that lay over her daughter's unin-jured leg. It was the only place she felt safe touching the child. She didn't want to cause Beth pain. Trace wondered if she was actually in any pain, and hoped she wasn't. She knew that the doctors had given her something for it, but Trace just wanted to know that it was working, that her daughter, although asleep, wasn't suffering. She adjusted the blanket a little when she felt a presence enter the room, someone walk-ing up behind her. Then she felt a hand on her shoulder, felt it trem-bling there. Trace turned around, and it was Austin.

He was standing there, looking as though he had been through all hell, dark patches under his eyes, short hairs starting to sprout from his face. His shirt was wrinkled, his tie undone. He looked exhausted, and when Trace looked in his face, it read sorrow.

She wanted to attack him. She wanted to rip his eyes out, right there, for what had happened to her daughter. But she couldn't. It wasn't just her child, but his, and she knew she wasn't the only one feeling that pain. She knew he felt it, too. Besides, she needed him. She needed him to listen when she said how sorry she was for letting her out there in that street. She needed him because she just did.

She looked into his eyes and wanted to somehow convey, transplant, all that she was feeling at that moment to him. Austin blinked, once, twice, then again, and a single tear fell from his eye, and Trace knew he understood. He stood there, head shamefully turned down, looking as though he didn't deserve sympathy, or love, or anything else. Trace quickly grabbed him, and she felt his arms go around her.

"I'm sorry, Trace," Austin cried. "I'm so sorry."

Just before they left the hospital, tears falling down her face, Trace told Austin everything that happened. How their daughter was waiting for him and ran out into the street, thinking she was running to her father. Austin didn't try to defend himself, said nothing in his behalf, said nothing at all.

On the way home, still not a word was spoken. Trace held Troy in her lap, caressing him, as if she felt she might also lose this child to some horrible fate. Once there, Trace carried him to bed, then took the stairs back down to the living room to find Austin standing at the mantel, looking at the family photos that sat atop of it. Trace stood there on the stairs, just watching him for a moment, wondering what he was thinking, hoping that he was regretting leaving her, them, hoping he could be as happy as he was in those photos, but realizing that would never be, because he'd killed that possibility forever.

Trace took the rest of the stairs down, pounded the boards beneath her, drawing Austin's attention away from the pictures. He turned, the same sorry expression on his face as when he walked into their daughter's hospital room. He looked as though he needed to be comforted more, almost as if he was expecting it, but Trace was past that stage. Past the point of wanting to make him feel better about what happened, because she realized that what had happened wouldn't have if his ass had been where it was supposed to be.

The hell with the comforting, she thought, as she walked up to him, stood in front of him. She was angry, and she needed nothing more than for him to know that.

"What?" Austin said softly, as if he had no clue to what she was feeling, what was going on in her head.

"Where were you?!"

Austin didn't answer, just stood there, guilt written all over his face.

"I said, where the fuck were you?" And this time, she threw her hands on him, swatting at his face, hitting him on his chest. Austin grabbed her, tried to hold her arms, but she continued to fight him until he took her, wrapped her up, and contained her in a hug.

"What are you doing?" he yelled. "Can't you see I'm just as hurt as you are?"

She fought him some more till she tired, then stopped, huffing, breathing heavily now, wishing she had the strength to break his hold, but she didn't.

"I didn't ask if you were hurt. I asked you where the fuck you were. And I want to know, Austin," she said from behind clenched teeth.

"I'll tell you, if you don't go crazy and start swinging at me again."

Trace didn't answer.

"Promise, or I won't let you go."

"I promise," Trace spat.

Austin lowered his arms and Trace jumped away from him, as if he were a man attempting to rape her.

"Now tell me."

Austin turned his back, ran a hand over his head, blew a deep sigh, then turned back to her. "Something happened at the office. A very important client came late. It's a case I've been working on some time now, an important case, and when he came in, I just . . . I just forgot about picking up the kids. When I finally got home, it dawned on me. I tried calling you immediately, but you weren't home, and when I checked my messages, that's when I heard about Bethany. I rushed right down, Trace."

Trace shook her head, for it was all she could do. "And you wonder why," she said, still shaking her head with disgust, looking away from him, because she couldn't stomach the sight of him at that moment. "You wonder why I won't allow you to see the kids, why I try to keep them from you."

"Yes, I do wonder," Austin said, trying to sound as much like the victim as possible.

"Because you're a damn liar. I tried calling your office, and they said you weren't there."

"That's because I took the client out," Austin said quickly. "We discussed the case over dinner because we were tired of sitting around the office, and we were hungry. We were hungry, Trace," Austin said emotionally. "I'm sorry, but I just forgot." He had walked away from her again, turned his back to her. Trace stood there staring at the man, seething, wishing she could know if he was telling the truth or not. Either way, it didn't matter, she thought, because if he was, he was irresponsible, and if he wasn't, he was a damn liar.

"Just get out of my house," Trace said, massaging her tired face with both her hands. "I don't want to hear any more of your lies or excuses, or whatever they are." And she expected to feel Austin walk past her, but when she brought her hands down, he was still standing there in front of her, facing her.

"Did you hear what I said? I want you out of my house."

"I can't do that, Trace," Austin said. "Our daughter's hurt in that hospital, partially because I wasn't there for her when I should have been. From now on, I'm going to be there. That means when she comes back from the hospital, I'll be here," he said, pointing to the floor. "In this house. So if you don't mind, I'll be sleeping on the sofa for a little while."

I do mind, Trace thought. But she didn't feel like fighting the man anymore, especially when he was really trying to be there for his daughter. And she knew it would have a huge impact on Beth, seeing her dad for more than just a few hours at a time.

"Whatever," Trace said, as if it made no difference to her either way. She turned to climb the stairs, then said without looking back, "You can get your own damn sheets. You know where they are."

32

Upon waking, Julius felt a little better, but what difference did that make, now that he knew he was dying for sure. He didn't want to get out of bed, didn't want to go home just yet. He was brimming with anger, still filled with so many questions that he felt no one could answer. He got in his car and resorted to just driving around. The morning was beautiful, too beautiful for him to have to deal with news so bleak. He was heading home, even though he didn't want to go. He needed something more, a better understanding. He wanted to feel more settled with what was happening with him before he broke the news to Cathy, and he had no idea of how that was going to happen, until something caught his eye.

Julius slammed on the brakes, the car skidding to a halt, the church Cathy had dragged him to a while ago in his driver's-side window. He pulled the car over to the curb, parked, and got out. He stood just outside his car, looking up at the beautiful old church, its steeple stretching toward the heavens. The feeling within him was odd, for he didn't want to go inside now any more than he'd wanted to when Cathy had brought him the first time, but something was pulling him, compelling him, to go in.

He forced himself away from the car, in the direction of the church. He didn't even know if the place would be open, but Cathy said it was always open, and Julius found himself hoping that she was right. He wrapped his fingers around the iron handle and pulled. The door did not open, and Julius's heart sank.

This wasn't for him to have, he told himself, turning to walk away, when the door to the right was pushed open from inside, allowing someone to walk out. A young woman walked passed him, smiling. "Good morning," she called, waving a hand at Julius as she passed, as if she was a good distance away from him, instead of right there in front of him.

He smiled briefly, the expression dropping from his face the moment he turned his head to the door.

He tugged at the door. It opened, to his surprise, and he knew now that the cancer wasn't just affecting him physically, but mentally as well. Instead of just trying the other door, he assumed that it couldn't have been open, that he wasn't worthy of it being open, because he was condemned, and nothing would ever go right for him again in the short life he had remaining. He shook his head, clearing it of all the babble, the negative self-talk, for he had enough going against him without self-created obstacles.

Again the church was dark, quiet, and it seemed to swallow him in its peacefulness, as if stealing him away, just a little, from the outside world he'd entered from. He stood just behind the inner doors, not knowing if he was intruding, not knowing if there was someone with whom he should have cleared his being there. The last time he was here seemed a lifetime ago, when he had a lifetime to live. Everything appeared different now, and he looked about the huge room, quietly, like a big-eyed frightened child, as if seeing it for the first time. He would have to walk in there, he told himself. He was behaving like a child, but found it within him to scold himself, telling himself that nothing worse could happen to him than what was already happening. He walked toward the front of the church, stopped, and stood before the altar. He looked up at the statue of Jesus staring down at him, and he knew this was supposed to be where he knelt again, where he prayed, but something wouldn't let him fall to his knees. He wouldn't let himself, and it was because he was angry. Angry at God for one day giving him what he thought was a clean bill of health, and now suddenly snatching it away without any warning or any time to prepare. It wasn't fair. He has no right, Julius thought, slowly, angrily, stepping away from the altar, backing up, and sitting down in one of the pews.

He leaned his body forward, thrusting his face in his hands, pushing the heels of his palms into his eyes, trying to hold in his tears. It just wasn't fair. There was so much he still had to do, so much he had yet to make up for. And his son Caleb had just returned to him, and now, all of a sudden, it was time for his father to die.

The tears came, pushed past his hands, and slid down his face. He wept silently at first, sniffling, trying to hide his crying. Then his body started to jerk from his emotion, and Julius's crying could be heard aloud, echoing off the walls of the cathedral. It wasn't fair, he thought, becoming even more emotional, wondering why it had to happen now, why he was being taken now. It wasn't fair, he cried again in his mind, and then he said it aloud. Yelled it out loud. "It's not fair. It's just not fair!" he yelled, striking the wooden bench with the flat of his fist. The paths of tears, shiny, wet, and wide, were covering his cheeks as he looked at the statue of Jesus again. Julius looked into his eyes, tried to find something there, anything, that would explain this to him.

"I've waited all these years to be here for my son," Julius said, his voice low, trembling. "And he's waited five years to be with me. He went through five years of hell being locked up, and now that he's finally out, now that we've had a chance to finally be with one another, you go and . . ." Julius stopped, still looking into the face of Jesus. His mouth stopped moving, but his brain, his heart, were working, as if he was receiving a message and silently processing it. And it took him a moment, but he thought about the words he'd just uttered. He thought about the fact that he was supposed to have been dead five years ago. But Julius knew that he had to stay alive for Caleb's little boy. He was the only father that Jahlil had then, and when Sonya left and took him, deciding that she never wanted to see or hear from Caleb again, Julius knew he had to be there for his son. He had to be there at least long enough to get him through the hell he was in, because he felt partially responsible for it. He told himself one day that he was going to be there to greet his son when he walked off that plane, and he was. They spent time together, got to know each other, value each other, and, although it was just for a short time, it was more than Julius could ever ask for.

The fact was, Julius had been given time, time that he wasn't supposed to have. Suddenly the anger that was on Julius's face lifted, his features softening, his lips parting, his mouth falling open as if in awe. He was enlightened. He knew now that he had truly been blessed. The moment he and his son were driving down that highway, the top down, the wind blowing in their faces, the sun warming their bodies, came into mind. And he remembered saying to himself that he had everything he wanted at that moment, and if he had to be taken right then, he would go a happy man. Well, he would go, for it was time, and he now knew that.

Julius got up from the bench, walked back over to the altar, and kneeled before it. He said a silent prayer, thanking God for the time that was given him, for the blessing that had been bestowed upon him, and asked forgiveness for all the wrongs he had done. Then he lifted himself, turned toward the door, and headed for home.

Julius lowered his head, standing there just outside the front door of his house. He didn't want to go in. He wanted to turn back around and run, never come back, because something in him made him think that if he never confronted Cathy or his son with this, they would never have to suffer through his dying. They could go on with their lives, and he could find some dark, lonely corner to die in, and they would never have another memory or worry of him again. But Julius knew it wasn't that simple, knew that his wife would want to be there by his bedside to care for him while he died. Julius quickly shut his eyes against the terrible image that found its way into his head, the image of him shriveled up to nothing but a gaunt, skin-covered skeleton, with barely enough strength to expel a breath out of his lungs or lift his own eyelids. He didn't want to think about that, and forced himself not to, knowing that time would come soon enough. Now he had to deal with letting his family know the awful news.

Julius slid his key in the door and, gently, as quietly as he could, opened it and backed into the house, softly fitting the door back into its frame, without making the slightest sound. He didn't know why he was trying to be so cautious, trying to sneak in unnoticed as if it were three in the morning, when it was actually approaching noon. After closing the door, he turned, and was shocked to find Cathy sitting right there in the living room chair. She was angry. He knew that by the fact that she had nothing to say to him upon his entering the room. She was dressed, but something told Julius that those were not clothes she put on early this morning after waking and showering, but the same clothes she'd had on the day before. Something told Julius, by the sleepless look in her eyes, by the way her hair was mussed about her head, and the wrinkles that creased her shirt in a million places, that she had been sitting in that chair all night, waiting for him to come home.

Julius walked farther into the room and just stood before her, like a child appealing to his mother not to punish him for coming in way past curfew. She looked up at him sadly, shaking her head, and he knew she knew something was wrong, terribly wrong.

"What's going on?" Cathy asked gravely.

"I . . . I . . ." Julius tried to say. He tried to tell her, but realized that she wasn't the only person that he had to break this news to. "Has Caleb left yet?"

"No. I don't think so. But what does he . . ."

"Just wait one moment, please," Julius said, gesturing with a raised finger for her to stay put. He left through the back door and went up to the guest house. He knocked, and when Caleb opened the door, he was smiling, buttoning a shirt. "How's it going, Dad?"

"Come with me, son," Julius said, pulling him by the hand.

"Well, I was just about to head down to the store."

"I know. But this won't take a minute."

Judging by the way the smile Caleb was wearing slowly disappeared from his face, Julius saw that his son must have realized how grave this matter was. Caleb followed his father silently into the house and into the living room, where Cathy was still sitting.

"Sit down, Caleb," Julius said, gesturing to the sofa.

"I think I want to stand," Caleb said, and his expression suddenly seemed as solemn as Cathy's.

Julius paced a slow, short line before the two of them, wringing his hands together, looking down at the carpet beneath him, then stopping and throwing his head back toward the ceiling. There he stood for a moment, as if praying, Cathy and Caleb looking on, worried expressions on their faces. They glanced briefly at each other, as if wondering if one of them should do or say something, but turned back to Julius when he began to speak.

"There's no way I can put this mildly," he said, his head still lifted, eyes still closed, and then he turned to them, looked at them. "So I'm going to just tell you. The reason I didn't come home yesterday, Cathy, is because I went to see Dr. Phillips. I went to get the results of some tests I took," Julius said, and he noticed worry starting to filter more into his wife's expression with the mention of the doctor's name. She leaned back into the chair a bit, wrapping her arms around herself, as if bracing for what was to come. He looked away from her, from them both, when he spoke the words. "The tests were positive. The cancer is back."

A sharp cry came from Cathy as Julius stared at the wall in front of him. He didn't want to see his wife suffering, because seeing that would make him break down, and right now he had to be strong. He had to be strong to even say the words, strong enough to know that one day soon he would be leaving her, leaving his son, and there was just nothing in the world he could do about it. No matter how much he loved her, loved Caleb, he would be taken. And how unfair Julius still felt that was.

He looked over to his son, and his boy was standing there strong, taking the news as if he knew that this day would come. He stood there with a look almost of acceptance on his face, as if he was just thankful for what he and Julius had had till that day. But how could he be so accepting, Julius wondered, when Julius had taken so much from him, and given so little back? Julius still owed him so much, but now would never be able to repay him.

Caleb walked over to Julius, raised his arms, lowered them around him and, as if reading his father's mind, said, "It's okay, Dad. Because whatever happens, I'm going to be here for you, just like you were there for me."

"But I wasn't," Julius said, only able to look in his child's eyes for a moment, then shamefully looking down. "I wasn't there for you, and now that you're here, I can't . . . I want to, but I can't. I'm so sorry that I'm leaving you."

Caleb pulled away from his father some, bent down, and looked into his father's downturned face. Caleb wore a slight smile, something that could not be touched by worry. "You were there for me. You saved my life, Dad, and I'll never forget you for that."

Julius and Caleb embraced again, and then he felt his son's arms falling away from him at the sound of Cathy's weeping. Caleb was aware that Julius would have to console her far more than him.

"I'll let you two be alone," Caleb said, and as he left the room, he laid a consoling hand upon Cathy's shoulder.

Julius waited till he heard the back door close, then he turned to his wife. She was folded over in the chair, her arms roped around herself, rocking, tears streaming down her cheeks as if she was in great physical pain. Julius walked over to Cathy, kneeled down in front of her, and took her face in his hands, kissing her wet cheeks.

"I'm sorry," he whispered over and over again to her, both apologizing and trying to soothe her with his calming voice. Her crying slowed some, as did her rocking, enough for her to ask, "How long did he say you have?"

"Cathy, it's bad. It's all over my body."

"How long did he say you have, Julius?" Cathy repeated.

"A couple of weeks to a month."

And Cathy gasped sharply, but managed to hold on to herself. She started to smooth her tears away from her face with both hands, trying to pull herself together.

"Then we'll just beat it again. How is he going to treat it?" Cathy said, sounding confident that a plan of action had already been laid out.

"Cathy, he's not going to treat it," Julius said. "There is no treatment. I told you, it's bad. It's gone too far. This time I think he's right."

"So that's it?" Cathy said, her desire to fight taking over the compulsion to wallow in pity. "So you're just going to listen to him? He was wrong last time, and he can be wrong again. In fact, I know he is," Cathy said, sounding more confident of the doctor's incompetence. "Julius, you did it once, you can do it again. You can fight this thing."

"No, I can't," Julius said loudly. "Cathy, he's right, and I'm not saying that because I'm blindly trusting him, but because I feel it. I feel it inside me and I just know."

"No. Don't say that, Julius. Don't," Cathy said, shaking her head from side to side.

"It's true. I know now I was given that time because there was something I had to do, and that was to be here for my son. I was given the chance to redeem myself for leaving him, and that has happened. Now it's time for me to go, and we both have to accept that."

"No. I won't accept it."

Julius grabbed her arms, urging her to look into his eyes. "Cathy," Julius said softly, slowly. "I'm going to die. I need for you to accept this."

"No," she said, the tears starting to fall again from her eyes.

Julius pulled her closer to him, tightening his grip on her arms.

"Please, Cathy, you must. I'm not strong enough to go through this with you looking at me, expecting me to fight this when I know I can't. I'm going to die, and there's nothing that either one of us can do about it."

"We can. I know we . . ."

"Now, I want you to say it with me," Julius said, cutting her off.

Cathy looked at Julius, her eyes wide with disbelief, a breath stuck in her throat.

"I am going to die," Julius said, slowly, pausing briefly between each word. "Please. Say it with me."

"No!" Cathy screamed, and whipped her head wildly about, trying to break free of Julius's hold. "Why are you asking me to do this? I won't. I won't, Julius. I love you, and I won't!"

But Julius shook her, shook her hard, some of his force motivated by the anger he felt for having to be in this agonizing position.

"You will!" he urged. "You will, because I need you, and I can't do this alone," he said, lowering his voice. "Don't you understand? I don't want to leave you. I love you so much, but I have no choice. I'm going to die, and I'm scared, scared of the pain I know is coming, scared of never seeing you again, but, most of all, scared of feeling that after I'm gone, you're thinking I gave up on you, that I didn't do all I could to remain with you. So I need to know that you accept that I've done all that I can, and regardless of that, I'm going to die."

Cathy looked at him, not saying a word, breathing heavily.

"Now say it with me," Julius said, prompting her by squeezing her arms again.

"I," he began, and waited till he heard her follow him, which she did reluctantly.

"You are going to die," she said with him, and Julius could tell that there was nothing that she wanted to do less, but she did it for him, for her love for him.

Cathy looked blazingly into his eyes, as if she hated him that moment for forcing her do this, then she spoke the words one final time. "You are going to die."

"Thank you," Julius said, opening his arms to hug her. Before he could say another word, Cathy pulled herself from the chair and angrily walked out of the room, leaving Julius there on the floor. He watched her go, and he understood. What he'd done was harsh, and he realized that. But she would realize that she needed to let go of whatever false hope she had that he would beat this, because now Julius was certain his time was coming.

33

Marcus rang Trace's doorbell with one hand, while trying to hold on to the huge stuffed polar bear with the other. It was big enough to obscure his entire upper half. It was so big it blocked his view. When he heard the door open, Marcus said, smiling, "She's going to love this. What do you—" but he didn't finish his sentence, for when he lowered the huge stuffed animal, standing there in front of him was his brother Austin, and not Trace, as he had expected.

He swallowed hard, wondering what to do, then said bravely, "I came to give this to Bethany. I am going in there to see her, regardless of what you say, and if you want to throw another punch at me, you'll have to do it after I give this to her."

"C'mon in," Austin said, tugging him by his elbow. "I'm not going to hit you again."

"Are you sure about that?" Marcus asked.

"Yeah, I'm sure," Austin replied, as if he couldn't possibly fathom ever taking a swing at his brother.

"And I can go upstairs and see her? Give her this?"

"Yeah, but for only a few minutes. She really needs her sleep. Besides, I got to talk to you."

Marcus climbed the stairs, maneuvering the huge bear in front of him. When he got to Bethany's door, he set the bear down, turned her doorknob, picked up the animal again, and backed himself in the door, the bear coming through after him.

Marcus sat the giant stuffed polar bear down on the floor just beside Bethany's bed. It was so big that its head rose over the bed. Its eyes would have been staring Bethany straight in the face were she awake. Marcus grinned at the surprise she'd get when she woke up, then lowered himself in the chair that sat at her bedside.

He looked compassionately over at her, her arm in a cast, the hardened bandages already scribbled on with markers and pens in a zillion different colors by a number of her friends.

He searched for a clean spot on the graffiti-riddled cast. He got up from his chair and leaned over her, examining the cast closely to find a space. There it was, almost on the very underside of her arm. Marcus scanned her nightstand, and saw a marker sitting on top of it. He picked it up, stuck it in his teeth, then carefully took Bethany's arm with both hands and turned it gently, till the clear spot was facing up. He pulled the marker from his mouth, leaving the cap still in his teeth. He quickly doodled a funny-faced cartoon character on her arm, then wrote beside it, "Keep smiling. Uncle Marcus loves you!"

He looked up to see if he had woken her, but she was still sleeping soundly. He leaned over and kissed her on the cheek. "Sweet dreams."

So here they were again, Marcus thought, the only difference being that they were in Austin's driveway, as opposed to his. After Marcus had come down from visiting his niece, Austin had insisted on their going out into the backyard.

"I don't want to go back there," Marcus said, trying to make his way to the front door.

"You're going, regardless," Austin said, pushing him through the house and out the back door. Now that he was standing out there, staring at Austin, all Marcus could think to say was, "So what? You're going to hit me again?"

"No. I want you to hit me," Austin said, tapping himself lightly on the chin, and Marcus thought to himself that if he was to hit his brother, it sure as hell wouldn't be a tap on the chin with his finger like that.

"I'm not hitting you, Austin."

"C'mon. I was wrong about trying to keep you from my kids like that, when all you were doing was trying to help. Now, come on, hit me," Austin said, walking closer to Marcus, extending his chin up and out.

"I told you, I ain't going to hit you, now just forget it."

"Why not? I was wrong. Even when I was going through my divorce and you were coming around and I was avoiding you. I could've made time for you then. I know that now. So what do you say? A little payback?"

"I said no, okay?" Marcus said, perturbed that it took that much to make Austin understand.

"All right. But I just wanted to bring you out here and apologize for hitting you. I shouldn't have done that," Austin said, sticking out his open hand. "And I was just hoping that we could start over fresh. What do you think?"

Marcus looked at Austin, down at his open palm, then up at his brother again. Without any warning to himself or to his brother, he punched Austin across the jaw, so that Austin bent over, his hands on his knees.

Austin didn't get up right away, but looked up at Marcus first, his eyes appearing just a little cloudy. Marcus bent down, grabbing Austin's arm, and helped him up.

"I thought you said you didn't want to hit me," Austin said, his hand around his jaw, opening and closing his mouth, as if to check if it still functioned properly.

"I didn't at first, but I thought about everything you said, and you're right. You were wrong for hitting me," Marcus said, his arm around Austin, holding him up.

"So now we're even? We can start fresh?"

"No," Marcus said. "My turn to apologize. I had a long talk with someone, and they made me realize how foolish I've been acting. You're my brother, and I can't go disowning you because you do something I don't like. Truth is, man, my feelings were just a little hurt, and I guess I was trying to make you feel some of that. I'm sorry."

"Now are we even?" Austin asked.

"We're even," Marcus said, taking his brother in a hug. "Now all I got to do is tell Caleb the same thing. Do you know where he is?"

"He went to California to stay with a friend."

"Why?" Marcus asked. "Where in California?"

"Don't know. He hasn't called me yet. But he has all my numbers, and knowing our little brother," Austin chuckled, "he'll be calling soon for something."

"You got that right," Marcus said, smiling.

34

Caleb worked outside behind the store, cleaning up trash. There wasn't a lot to clean up, but he just didn't feel like talking to Mr. Olin today about sports or the weather.

He was in a funk because he hadn't done anything, hadn't told anyone about what had happened at Sonya's place three days ago. He hadn't tried going back over there, because he hadn't yet figured out just whom she wanted to be with.

When he'd held Sonya in his arms, he'd felt that she had missed him, could feel that she still loved him, but the actions she exhibited said something altogether different.

Caleb swept the last of the trash into a shovel, and dumped it into one of the cans, lowering the lid on it. When he turned around, Thomas stood in front of him, looking haggard and worried, as if he had not slept in days.

"So did you go over there?" Thomas said. "Was it your family over there?"

"I don't really want to talk about it right now, all right?" Caleb said, stacking the broom and shovel.

"I'm sorry, I just wanted to know how things went. If you got back together with them, or not," Thomas asked, and he seemed genuinely concerned, but at that moment, Caleb didn't care.

Thomas had called over to Caleb's house a number of times over the past few days, but Caleb didn't pick up the phone, not wanting to talk to anyone.

"I've been trying to call you," Thomas said. "I've been wanting to hang out."

"Did you tell that man that you wouldn't be selling his drugs for him anymore?"

"No," Thomas said, nervously sticking his hands in his pockets.

"Then we don't need to be hanging out," Caleb said, grabbing the doorknob, moving to go back inside.

"But that's what I've been wanting to talk to you about. I'm going to call him today, but I don't know how to do it, what I should say. I'm kinda scared. Can you help me?"

Caleb turned back to look at the boy, and indeed, he did look pretty frightened. Caleb felt for him, wanted to help him, but at the time, there were just too many problems of his own that he had to work out.

"Just go to him and tell him you want out, that you're not doing it anymore. All right?"

The boy nodded his head, even though everything didn't look all right with him. He stood there, as if there was something more Caleb might want to say to him.

Caleb grabbed the door. "I'll see you around," he said, without turning to even look back at Thomas, and walked into the store.

35

Curtis pulled into an alley, throwing the gear in park, turning up the R&B music louder on his stereo, in hopes that it would help calm him. He reached over and opened his glove box, pulling out a small plastic bag which held a small amount of marijuana, a lighter, and a book of Tops rolling papers. He took the time to roll a thin joint, light it, put it in his mouth, and take a deep toke of the powerful herb. He was in need, definitely in need, after having to deal with this bullshit with Caleb Harris.

After Curtis dragged Sonya into the house the night before, they'd had a huge argument, yelling and screaming, with him having to hold himself back on at least two occasions from wanting to knock her fucking block off.

"You told me you would never see him again," he yelled at Sonya.

"And I thought I wouldn't, but I don't own him. I can't control where he goes."

"And how you think that makes me feel?" Curtis said, walking about the kitchen in his shorts and T-shirt.

"Makes you feel?" Sonya questioned.

"I love you," Curtis said. "I ain't never once cheated on you, never wanted to. All I wanted was what I got right here. I invested in this shit, because you made me think it would be safe to. And that boy in there," he said, pointing toward Jahlil's door. "For three years, I treated him like a son."

"I never told you to do that," Sonya cut in.

"Like I said, I treated him like a son," Curtis said, ignoring her. "And now what happens? His father comes back in the picture, and you telling me he ain't gonna want him back. Want you back."

"It won't matter if he wants him back or not, because I told you, I'm done with him."

"You can guarantee that?"

Sonya didn't answer. She couldn't, Curtis thought, because he knew the bond they probably had as a family. He knew that every time Sonya looked down at Jahlil, she saw that man's face in their child.

It was one thing Curtis's mother had told him never to do, to get involved with a woman who had a child from another man, because that child would always come before him, as would the father of that child.

But Curtis had no choice. He really wanted a son, but he couldn't have children of his own, at least that's what the doctor had told him. Something about low sperm count or some shit. He didn't sit around to listen to the doctor continue telling him how many ways he wasn't a man. He really didn't believe him anyway, but Curtis had busted enough nuts in women to fill a small lake, and still no son.

He didn't know where the intense desire to have a son came from. It couldn't have been because he wanted to be a great dad like his father was to him, because he didn't even know his father, never even saw him. It was just him, his mother, and his little brother, Paul, who was the best thing about his life. Paul was his best friend, who Curtis lived for. He was seven years younger than Curtis, but he was smart, and handsome, and everything his older brother wasn't, and Curtis realized that his life was made better just trying to improve the life of his younger brother.

So Curtis quit high school at sixteen to support his mother, who wasn't making much money as a waitress, and his little brother, who got straight A's. Curtis knew Paul had a bright future, had a way out of the dismal confines of the projects, as long as he had someone to protect him and help him out.

It was selling drugs that put money in Curtis's pockets, and he told himself he would do it only as long as it took to get his brother to college and off the streets of the projects.

He sold for an old dude named Ping. Super-thin brotha, had to be past fifty, and the brown, shiny skin of his face had already started to wrinkle. He was too old for the game, Curtis thought, but his game was tight. He was well respected and no one fucked with him, because he was known to kill anyone on the spot who tried to mess around with him or what was his.

Curtis respected that, and did what he was told. He got paid for slinging the drugs to the kids on the streets and outside the schools, till one day, while he was sitting in the house watching TV, the police knocked on his door. He looked out the window, saw the squad cars out front, heard the police radio squawking outside his front door, and didn't want to open it. He thought they were there for him. Turned out, they were there to tell him that his little brother had been killed, caught by a stray bullet in the temple on the way home from school.

That was the day Curtis's life changed, the day he stopped giving a fuck. The plans he had made to get out of the drug game changed to wanting to take it over. The little bit of money he was paid to sell drugs was no longer enough for him, so he started skimming, telling himself Ping wouldn't find out. But somehow he did, and word got back to Curtis that his number was up, that Ping was going to do him in next time he saw him. So instead, he went looking for Ping, in the waist of his jeans the .32 he had bought with some of the money he had skimmed.

He knew where Ping would be. At the prostitute's house he always visited late on Thursday nights, and that's where Curtis waited sweating for three hours, in the dark shadows of an alley, until Ping came down the back stairs. Curtis moved under them, holding the gun in both his trembling hands, telling himself he could kill this man. When Ping descended the last stair, Curtis jumped out in front of him, the gun extended, pointing in Ping's face.

"You don't want to do this, boy," Ping said, as if he had no concern that Curtis would shoot him. "Give me that gun," Ping said, extending his hand. "You ain't gonna shoot me," and he smiled, noticing the shaking of the gun in Curtis's hands. Curtis tried to hold it steady, knew that he was looking timid by not doing that. He focused his attention on steadying his arms, when Ping lunged for the gun.

"I said . . ." But before he could finish his sentence, Curtis found himself firing the gun, shooting Ping five times in the face and upper chest, the gun bucking in his hand, spitting out orange flame as if it were on fire. It was the first time Curtis ever killed someone, ever shot a gun for that matter, but in his mind, he'd had to do it. He was justified.

He stood over him, looking down, knowing that he'd had to do it, knowing that Ping would've killed him, if he hadn't killed Ping first. The man had to protect his reputation, and Curtis could understand that.

That was twenty years ago, and since then, Curtis had been trying to gain control of his life, trying to slow things down. He was looking for something to make him a more responsible man, something that would give his life some value, something to live for, other than just the money he was making, and all the nameless, faceless women he used to screw. With a family, with a son, he thought he would be safer, not risking as much as he would if he had nothing or no one to be responsible for. He needed someone who truly cared for him, not just the money, or his status as a baller, and he had found that with Sonya and Jahlil.

She gave him hell on occasions, and on those times, he would go out and find some fine-ass chicken head to slide up in. The woman would fall all over him, do whatever the fuck he wanted, realizing who he was, the power he had in this hood. He would fuck the shit out of her, or let her suck him off, and then he would toss her a fifty or a C-note and watch her damn near throw herself to the ground, trying to catch it before it hit the floor.

Those hoes had no class, no respect for themselves, couldn't compare to what he had in Sonya, so he didn't see it as cheating. It was one of the reasons why he loved Sonya, and why he hadn't replaced her ass, even when she did get crazy. She had his back. All those other little skanks on the street were just worried about coming up, and would use anyone to do it.

But now his family, his happiness, was being threatened. Sonya had assured him that that there was nothing to worry about, and at this moment, he wanted to believe her. Violence was what he was trying to get away from, so he wouldn't harm Caleb, at least not yet.

Curtis brought the shrinking joint back to his lips and pulled from it again, holding the smoke in his throat, trying to push it into his brain, in an attempt to maximize its effects. A moment later, he let the gray plumes of smoke float out of his nostrils, and through his slightly parted lips.

No, he wouldn't mess with Caleb, but Caleb had asked him if he knew Thomas, and that presented a problem. The boy had told Caleb that he was selling for him, and that was a grave mistake. Curtis knew he should've never taken him on from the beginning. He lacked something, a hardness, a street sense, but he played the pity story about needing to support his mother, and Curtis knew a little something about that, so he agreed to take him on.

But Thomas thought he was smart, too smart for his boss, and Curtis knew something about that, too. He didn't think anything of it at first, but after Caleb mentioned Thomas's name, Curtis decided to check his records, and something was up. But to give the boy the benefit of the doubt, Curtis doubled-checked, even triple-checked the money that Thomas had been recently giving him, against the amount of drugs he gave to Thomas, and sure as shit, the boy had been skimming, and that was something that Curtis could not let slip by him.

He knew from experience that when a boy skimmed it was because he'd lost respect for the boss, and if word got out about that, all the boss's respect would be gone. The entire neighborhood would be trying to get over on him, and he could not allow that either.

Curtis took the last drag from the joint, smoking it down to the tiny roach, the orange glow almost touching his already lightly charred thumb and forefinger. He pulled it from his lips and mashed it out in the ashtray. His head was light, cottony now, all his extremities feeling slightly numb, partly disconnected, as he bent back over toward the glove box, popped it open, reached in, and pulled out the Glock that rested in there. He held it in his hand, just before his face, turning it slowly, marveling at its beauty and fierceness. Thomas had just called him on his cell phone, told him there was something they needed to talk about. Curtis couldn't agree more.

36

Austin held himself up over his wife, kissing her passionately, his head spinning, his arms weakening, as he slowly lowered himself onto her, feeling his chest mash against her soft, full breasts.

He didn't know how they had gotten there. One moment, they were downstairs, sitting on the sofa, flipping through old family photo albums, and the next, they were upstairs rolling around in her dark bedroom, clawing at each other's clothes, trying to strip them free, so they could get at one another.

Austin had been staying there at the house, sleeping on the sofa for two nights now, and he couldn't help but notice how nice it was to be back among his family. He realized that Trace noticed it, too. At first, she seemed reluctant to even say a word to him, ignoring him, as if he were some homeless person from off the street that she allowed to claim her couch for a few days and nothing more.

The first morning Austin had woken up there, he walked into the kitchen to find Trace and Troy sitting down, eating breakfast. Austin walked through the kitchen, not saying a word, over to the stove, where he saw a pot and a pan sitting. He lifted the covers of both of them to find nothing but the dried film of what was once scrambled eggs coating the pan, and the last few inflated granules of grits clinging to the sides of the pot.

"Where's mine?" he said, turning to Trace.

"At the store," she said around a mouthful of food, not even raising her head to acknowledge him.

That Saturday afternoon they went to pick up Bethany from the hospital, and for the rest of that day, she wanted nothing more than to be beside her father. So she sat there on the sofa with him, watching sports, her leg hiked up on pillows stacked on the coffee table. If Trace wanted to spend time with her daughter, she had to spend time with her ex-husband as well, and so she sat on the same couch. The only thing between her and Austin was their daughter.

At one point, they simultaneously lifted their arms to place them around Bethany's shoulder. When they brought them down, they touched each other's hands, and, in reaction to that, they both snatched their hands away from each other, scooting over some, extending the distance between the two of them.

How ridiculous that was, Austin thought to himself, sitting there cutting his eyes at her, for he knew she was doing the same thing to him. They were sitting there behaving like third graders who couldn't get along. It made no sense, so he told himself then; if Trace wanted to act like a child, he would let her. But this was the first time in far too long that he was able to just spend time with his children and not have to worry about rushing them back to meet the curfew that his wife had set. He would enjoy it.

Austin wasn't sure, but it seemed that Trace had made the same resolution herself, for when she was done putting the kids to bed, she appeared in the living room with a blanket folded over her arms.

Austin was watching some comedy show on TV, his back to her, not realizing she was behind him till she cleared her throat. He jumped and spun around on the sofa, twisting his body to look at her.

"Hey," he said.

"I just thought you might want a blanket tonight," Trace said shyly. "I know it gets pretty cold down here." She set it down on the sofa beside him, then turned and headed for the stairs.

"Thanks," Austin said, grabbing the blanket, setting it atop his lap, and resting his arms on it. Then he turned back to the TV, thinking how thoughtful the gesture was. A moment later, he felt a presence behind him, and turned to see his ex-wife still there.

"What is it, Trace?" Austin asked, concerned.

"No. Nothing important," she said, stepping back over toward him. "I just wanted you to know how much fun Bethany had spending today with you. She couldn't stop talking about it when I was putting her to bed, and felt she wouldn't be able to sleep because she was so excited about seeing you tomorrow."

"Well, I'm excited about seeing the kids tomorrow, too. It'll be two days in a row, and I don't know when the last time that happened was." Austin realized he shouldn't have said that last part, right after it left his lips. Trace was trying to be kind, and his remark made him seem spiteful.

"Well, anyway, I just wanted to tell you that." She paused for a long second, dragging a finger against the spine of the couch, then said, "Good night then."

"Hold it," Austin said, standing, gesturing toward the TV. "Um, 'Saturday Night Live' is on. Remember how we used to always stay up and watch that?"

"Yeah," Trace said, smiling, staring glassy-eyed at the television, as if not seeing the version that played at that moment, but the one they used to watch years ago.

"So you wanna sit down and watch with me?" Austin asked, and before she could answer, he noticed a hint of indecision in her eyes, so he said, "C'mon. I won't bite. Promise."

Trace smiled a little wider at that remark.

"Okay," she said, sitting down next to him.

The next day, everyone was in the living room again, on the sofa, except Troy, who was pushed up entirely too close to the TV, watching the Cartoon Network. It was a carbon copy of the day before, but without the attitude, without the silence, without the anger. At one point, while they were playing a board game, Bethany held her piece in her hand, taking longer than she needed to move.

"What's wrong, honey?" Trace asked.

Bethany looked around the room at everybody, then said, smiling, "It's like we're a family again."

There was an awkward moment, a silent stare passing between Austin and Trace, but then he broke the tension, saying, "That's right. It is like we're a family again."

Trace smiled, looking away. But Austin didn't agree with his daughter just to appease her or end the uncomfortable silence. She was right. They were like a family again. He felt it, and he was sure Trace did as well, even if she didn't want to acknowledge it.

That night, Austin didn't have to ask Trace to sit and watch TV with him. After putting the kids to bed, she came right down and sat there beside him. They talked and laughed, and somehow the mention of old pictures came up. Then they were thumbing through old photos of them, Trace puffy-cheeked and pregnant, and snapshots of the two of them during their honeymoon. They were howling as they turned the last page of the final book. They closed the album, and both grabbed opposite ends of it to put it away, but because of the force the other exerted on the book, they were caught there staring into each other's faces.

They held each other's glance for a second that seemed forever, then they turned away laughing, Austin grabbing the book again, saying, "I'll put it away."

He took the album, turned to put it on the table beside the sofa, and when he turned back, he was met with Trace's lips against his. He was shocked at first, not knowing what to do with his hands, with his lips, but then, feeling her mouth on his, her tongue sensually, playfully, probing inside of him, he softened, his arms wrapping around her, his hands curving to the shape of her hips, her waist.

They kissed there on the couch, the television droning on before them for fifteen minutes. Then Trace pulled away from him, staring him seductively in the eyes.

"You don't have to sleep down here tonight," she said suggestively. Austin didn't know what to say, so he said nothing, and when Trace stood and lowered her hand to him, he took it. Not a word was said as they climbed the stairs, her leading the way, Austin following obediently behind her. It was as if they both feared that if a sound was made, it might break the spell that was cast over both of them, and make them realize that what they were about to do was possibly very wrong.

But that thought was never fully out of Austin's mind, and as he now continued kissing his wife, enjoying every minute of it, he couldn't help but feel guilty about the lie he had told to her regarding their daughter. She believed him when he lied right there to her face. She seemed to have forgiven what she thought was his irresponsibility, and accepted him back in her home, even after knowing that, regardless of what the excuse was, he was still to blame for their daughter being injured.

Now she even seemed willing to give herself to him. And, although Austin wanted nothing more than to take what was so easily being offered up to him, and although he knew that informing his wife of the lie he told would probably end his possibility of having her now—or ever again, for that matter—he had to be honest with her.

So he continued kissing her, raising his arms over his head, allowing her to pull off his shirt. And he even helped her when she groped for the buttons of her blouse, and took that off. And when she popped the clasps at the front of her bra, he did not object, because Austin was still trying to make all this come out right in his head. Trying to tell himself that, yes, it was the right thing to do, to tell her the truth first, and then, if she still wanted to make love, then so be it.

But it was hard. Not just the decision, but him as well, and Trace could barely slide his boxers off, because his rock-hard piece was stopping her. And then, all of a sudden, he was over her, and he was leaning in closer to make that connection, and she was pulling him, too, her hands clasped around his ass. And all Austin had to do was tell himself that it didn't make a difference that she didn't know the truth, she had already forgotten about it, and everything would be fine.

So that's what he told himself, and he allowed Trace to pull him farther down, and allowed himself to fall flatly on her body. He slid himself right up to the point where he felt the heat and moisture from within her graze his tip, then he closed his eyes and said, out of the blue, "I did it on purpose."

"You did what on purpose?" Trace said, her hands still around Austin's butt, but no longer urging him forward.

"I didn't show up to pick up Bethany on purpose," Austin said, softly.

It took a minute for Trace to erupt, but when she did, she did it by heaving Austin off her. He lost his balance and tumbled onto the floor, landing on his back.

"You did what?!" Trace yelled, standing now, stark naked, clicking on the lamp.

Austin pulled himself from the floor, reluctant to rise above the protective barrier of the bed, but he stood anyway.

"Our child could've been killed. She was run over by a damn car, because you chose not to be there to pick her up. Why did you do it, Austin? Why?" she asked, standing on the opposite side of the bed, trembling so much it appeared she was on the brink of exploding.

"To teach you a lesson," Austin said bravely, still supportive of him-self regarding the decision he'd made.

Before he knew it, he was ducking the heavy metal Big Ben alarm clock Trace slung at his head. It just missed and struck the wall behind him, cracking in half and falling to the floor.

"To teach me a fucking lesson?!" Trace yelled. "Your child could've died!"

"What the fuck else was I supposed to do?!" Austin yelled loudly, and immediately he caught her attention, stunned her. He didn't know if it was because, in all the years they had known each other, he had never yelled like that at her before, or if it was just the full volume, the frus-tration for all that she had done to him, that came out in that yell. Either way, she was standing there, seeming ready to hear him, if only for a moment.

"You wouldn't allow me to see my own kids, Trace. Do you know what that was doing to me? It was tearing me up inside. There were things I could've done to see them, though. Hateful things that would've dragged you into question as a mother," Austin said, pacing slowly across the room, his body as naked as Trace's. "But I wouldn't do that, because I love my kids too much for that, and I respect you too much."

"But did it have to be like that? You told Bethany you'd be there, and you just didn't show. You lied to her, to me. Why?"

"Do you remember what you told me the day of Troy's party?" Austin said, stopping now, staring at her from across the bed. "You said that it didn't make a difference to those kids if I was here or not. That if I stopped coming around, that they'd just forget me. Did you mean that?" Austin asked, walking around the bed, putting himself face to face with her.

Trace didn't respond to him, just looked away angrily.

"I said, did you mean it?" Austin repeated, raising his voice.

"Of course not!"

"Then why did you say it?"

"Because I was hurt. That's why," Trace said, crossing her arms over her breasts. "You left me, Austin. Twice," she said, holding up two fin-gers. "And the last time, the way you told me—on our son's birthday. Do you know how that made me feel?" Trace said, her voice wavering some with her emotion.

"The anniversary of the end of our marriage is the same day as our son's birthday. You walked out on me, on us, for the second time, and I hated you for that. Still do. But I also hate myself, because the day you left me, I still loved you, and I think I still do," Trace said, dropping her face into her hands.

"You couldn't," Austin said, softly.

Trace looked up at him, a questioning look in her eyes.

"Because if you did, you wouldn't have tried to keep our children from me like you have."

"I guess I was trying to teach you a lesson," Trace said, smoothing a tear from the corner of her eye.

"And I guess I was trying to teach you a lesson, and look where it got us."

Trace lowered her head, ashamed of both their behaviors.

"Trace," Austin said, placing his body very close to hers. "I think you know that we'll never be together again like we were, but can we stop all this now? Can we stop trying to hurt each other, because it seems the only ones we're hurting are our children."

Trace turned her face, wiping the tears from her cheeks, and when she looked back at Austin, she was wearing a slight smile.

"Yeah. I think we can do that."

37

Marcus stood beside his bed, his arms crossed, searching his memory to see if he had forgotten anything. He had just moved out of the closet, after making sure that Reecie's hospital bag had been packed properly and was sitting just inside the door. He had done that so when the moment came, all they had to do was snatch it, throw it in the car, and be off to have their baby delivered.

Marcus marched back and forth through the room, rubbing his chin, trying to make sure he had everything covered beyond the obvious, which was keeping the gas tanks in both their cars topped off, parking both cars in the driveway facing toward the street, so he wouldn't have to worry about backing up in a hurry, and setting out a pair of jeans and a T-shirt for him. He also set out a pair of sweatpants and a T-shirt for her, so they wouldn't have to wonder what to throw on while they were playing beat the clock with their unborn baby. He'd run drills, three of them. One from the living room, if they happened to be watching TV when the time came, the other from the kitchen. And now Marcus was preparing to fire the old starting gun on the drill from the bedroom.

They would put on their emergency clothes, for they were in their pajamas now, grab the bag from the closet, head downstairs (not too quickly), and then jump in the car. At that point Marcus would look down at his watch, as he had done when they completed the first two drills.

So now, stopping in the middle of the room, he asked Reecie, "Am I forgetting something? It seems as though I'm forgetting something."

"No, Marcus. You're not forgetting a single thing. If there were something more to do, we'd end up too busy preparing to go to the hospital to actually go to the hospital."

"That's not very funny," Marcus said, looking over at his wife, who was under the blankets. "You ready for this last run?"

"Can't we wait until the baby comes to do the last run?" Reecie whined.

The phone rang, and Marcus walked over to catch it. "No, we can't," he said, grabbing the receiver and pressing it against his chest. "We should get this down so we can do it in our sleep. Hello," he said, now speaking into the phone.

"Marcus?" the raspy voice asked.

"Yeah. Who is this?"

There was a pause, and then, "This is your father, Marcus. I was just calling . . ."

But Marcus didn't hear what else was said, because he slammed the phone down into its cradle.

"So you ready, Reecie?" Marcus said, turning to his wife, as if nothing had just happened, as if he was not bothered in the least by hearing his father's voice.

"Hold it. Who was that?" Reecie said, throwing the blankets from her, and gingerly getting out of bed. She was in front of him now, looking in his face as if she knew something was wrong.

"It was nobody," he said, turning away from her, trying not to let her read the emotion on his face. "Get back in bed so we can do this right."

"Don't play this off," Reecie said, bobbing around in front of him, trying to look Marcus straight in the eyes. "Something's wrong. Is it Austin again?"

"Me and Austin are fine."

"Then who?" Reecie asked impatiently.

"That person said he was my father," Marcus said, and the phone started ringing again. "Let it ring."

"Pick it up, Marcus."

"No."

"You can't just let it ring."

"Why can't I?"

The phone rang three more times, then Reecie picked it up and handed it to Marcus. He just stood there, his arms crossed, staring evilly at it. Reecie jerked the phone at him, mouthing something that looked like, "Take the damn phone!"

Marcus finally snatched the phone from her hand.

"Hello."

"Marcus, don't hang up," Julius blurted.

Marcus didn't respond, but didn't hang up either. And that was only because he was looking at Reecie standing before him, watching her mouth "Be nice."

"I haven't spoken to you in a while, and I just wanted to call and see how you're doing."

"I don't have nothing to say to you. I thought I was perfectly clear about that five years ago."

"Yeah, yeah. You were, but I guess I'm just hardheaded."

"Yeah, I guess you just are," Marcus said, attitude thick in his voice.

"So, um, what's going on? Is there anything new in your life?"

That question threw Marcus, because he was surprised to see how he was reacting to it. He hated the man on the other end of the phone, but for some reason, he wanted to tell him about the child he and his wife were expecting. He didn't know if it was just because he was so excited about the birth, being a father, or if this was just the type of news that a son waits all his life to tell his old man, but he definitely felt the urge. He wouldn't let himself succumb to it, though. He struggled to suppress it a moment, telling himself the man didn't deserve to feel any of his joy, then said, "No. Nothing new."

"So, how's your girlfriend. What's her name . . ."

"Would you just get on with it?" Marcus pushed. "Why the hell are you calling me?"

"I was just wondering," Julius spoke slowly, softly, "if maybe you had forgiven me since the last time we talked. I was thinking that, maybe, you could fly out here so we could, I don't know, spend a little time together. My treat."

Marcus almost didn't hear the last thing he said because he had started laughing. It wasn't a happy, hilarious laugh, but a hurtful, hateful one, and Marcus made no effort to cover it up, or lower the volume at which it came out. He wanted his father to hear it, wanted to let him know how ridiculous even the thought of Marcus forgiving him, or seeing him, was.

"I guess you *are* just hardheaded. You don't get it, do you? I'll never forgive you for what you did. I hate you," and with that remark, Reecie was grabbing for the phone, trying to take it from him.

"No," Marcus said, yanking it away from Reecie, staring her in the face. "He needs to hear this once and for all. . . . You made the decision for us not to be father and son anymore, not me. I didn't do this, you did," Marcus said, his voice starting to tremble. "There is no going back. It's done. It's over. And I don't ever want to hear from you, or see you, again. Do you hear me? Ever!"

Marcus wanted to hang up the phone, but something wouldn't let him, so he held it there, a firm grip on it, pushing it into his ear.

Moments passed with nothing but silence on the line, then Julius spoke.

"Marcus, I just want to tell you something."

Marcus didn't respond, but still held the phone close to his head, his jaws locked, his heart raging in his chest and hot anger swelling within him.

"I always have, and always will, love you, son," Julius said.

Marcus thought about responding to that, or asking all the questions that went unanswered during his father's absence. But instead, he just said, "Go to hell," and hung up the phone.

"I'm sorry, Reecie," Marcus said, looking at her, knowing that she'd be angry at him. "This is just too big to forgive."

She took him in her arms, holding him tight. "It's okay, baby."

"Don't just say that to make me feel better, and then go turning on me, leaving me again," he said, starting to draw away from her.

"I won't do that," she said, pulling him back in. "I understand."

"Because I can't take losing you and our baby. You two are the most important things in my life. I love you so much," Marcus said, grabbing his wife, holding her tighter. "I don't want to lose you two."

"Don't worry, baby. You could never do that."

38

Over the past four days, things had been different around the house, Caleb thought, sitting at the kitchen table, the room mostly dark, save for the small fluorescent lamp that hung over the sink area. He sat there, his hands crossed, in a somber mood. It was the mood the entire house had been in since the news his father delivered to him and Cathy, and there was no way avoiding getting infected by that mood and succumbing to it, as his father had succumbed to his cancer. And it didn't help Caleb's attitude toward life, considering how things were going with his attempt to get his family back. Many times, he thought of talking to his father to let him know what was going on, get his opinion, but Caleb would stop himself, realizing Julius had enough to contend with.

Caleb didn't know if it was because the disease was just so aggressive, or if it was because his father had finally accepted his fate, making it easier for the cancer to ravage his body, but Julius was declining quickly. Over the short period of time since Caleb had found out that his father would soon die, less and less he would see him out of the house, then, fewer times, he would see him out of his room, and now the man rarely left his bed.

He was sick, truly, deathly, and there was no denying it. From the moment his bedroom door was pushed open, the smell of sickness was thick in the small dark space. It was like it was growing in there, and each time that Caleb went in, it got bigger and bigger, and it would keep growing, Caleb knew, till it was large enough to eat his father whole.

Caleb paused before the door each time he was about to go in, resting a hand there, placing his ear to it. Why, he didn't know. Then he lightly knocked on the door, even though it was always left cracked open. Julius answered with a grunt or a groan, or sometimes, when he was feeling better, he would tell him to come in.

Caleb would grab the chair near his bed, noticing all the tiny orange-brown bottles crowding his nightstand—pain medicine that Julius never wanted to take, because it took him out of it. It made him seem sicker than he was, he said. But Cathy made him take it anyway, saying that it would make his pain, if not go away, at least tolerable. And then Caleb would sit, trying not to pay mind to the weary look on his father's face, the hopeless look in his eyes, the way his body lay under those blankets, never seeming to move, like something made out of stone.

It was eerie to Caleb, seeing his father there like that, his body so quiet, as if not even breathing. It was more as if air was escaping from his body like a slow leak in a bicycle tire when he exhaled; the rise in his chest was undetectable when he breathed in. It was how his mother breathed so many years ago when she was dying of the same disease, and Caleb decided not to ask himself if this was fitting or not, his father lying there.

Caleb was sitting in the kitchen, and was pulled out of his thoughts when he heard Cathy enter and go to the stove to check the soup that was simmering over a low flame.

"Do you need any help?" Caleb said, beginning to stand from his chair.

"No, I'm fine," she said, not turning around, her voice low, preoccupied.

Caleb watched her turn off the burner and move the pot to the back of the stove. She took a bowl, poured the soup into it, set it on a plate. She went to the cabinet where the spices and herbs were kept. Seeing this, Caleb quickly raised from his seat, and went for the cabinet, which was a little easier for him to reach.

"Let me get that for you," he said, opening the cabinet. "Which one do you want?"

"I told you, Caleb, I don't need your help," she said, annoyed, still not looking in his face, but purposely away from him.

"I'm sorry," Caleb replied, sitting back in his chair, watching as Cathy snatched the bottle of seasoning she wanted, then closed the cabinet. And then she just stood there, her hands braced against the counter. Caleb sat watching her, not wanting to interfere again, even though he knew something was wrong. She was unscrewing the top of the small plastic bottle, sprinkling seasoning over the soup, gently at first, then with more force, and then to the point where it seemed she was being driven by nothing but anger and frustration, the tiny leaves being sprayed all over the counter and floor.

Caleb walked up behind her and took her arm.

"Are you okay?" he asked her, and he felt her entire body trembling violently beneath his touch, felt her trying to control her rage, but barely able to. He grabbed the tiny plastic bottle and had to pry the thing from her hand, she was holding it so tightly. He stepped back from her, giving her space. She stood for a moment longer, composing herself before turning around, facing Caleb, her face more calm than her body suggested.

"Are you mad at my father?" Caleb asked.

Cathy clamped her eyes down tight at the question, wincing as if in pain, then said, "No. I'm mad at myself. Mad at myself for loving him so much and not being able to let him go. I don't want him to try and struggle to live for me, when I know he's being called home. I just have to work harder at not being so weak," she said, dropping a fist against the counter.

"You're not weak. You just love him. That's what it is, you just love him, is all."

Cathy looked at him, as though grateful for his words, then gave him a hug.

"You were the best thing that happened to him. You know that, don't you?" Caleb said over her shoulder. "Dad told me that, but he didn't have to for me to see it."

Cathy squeezed him tighter, then pulled away from him some.

"Thank you, Caleb, for everything."

"You're welcome," he said, releasing her. "Now let me take care of this. You've been working like crazy, okay?"

"Okay."

When Caleb backed into his father's room with the fresh bowl of soup atop the serving tray, he was surprised to turn around and see Julius sitting up, looking relatively bright-eyed and responsive.

"How's it going, Dad? Gotcha some soup." He set it down across his father's knees. "Hope you're hungry."

Julius looked down at the soup, then up at Caleb, not moving to touch anything on the tray.

"She's mad at me, isn't she?" Julius said, looking as if he already knew the answer.

"About what?"

"Don't act like you don't know. I know she is. She's short with me, doesn't want to sit and talk to me. And when I force her to, all she does is just stare at the wall."

Caleb sat down beside him. "She's not mad at you. She's just trying to accept the fact that you're dying. Doesn't that make sense?"

"Yeah," Julius said, nodding his head. "I just want her to go back to being herself."

"She will. And I was thinking that maybe that would happen sooner, if I quit working, helped her out around here."

"Don't you even think about it," Julius said, lowering his spoon into the bowl. "I don't need you here. I'm fine, I'm telling you," and then, as if to prove he was lying, all of a sudden he started coughing, long and hard. Caleb stood, leaned him forward some, and patted him on the back till he stopped hacking. He laid Julius back softly against the pillows behind him, placing the cup of water from the tray in his hand. Julius took a sip of the water, paused a moment, then smiled as if to let his son know he was okay.

"You're still going tomorrow, all right?"

"Okay."

"Now get out of here, so I can eat my soup in peace."

"All right," Caleb said, walking to the door. He stopped short, then walked back over slowly and sat down beside his father again.

Julius was just about to bring a spoonful of his soup into his mouth, but lowered it gently into the bowl, careful not to make a splash.

"There's something else?"

"I want to know if you want me to call your other sons."

By the look on Julius's face, the question seemed to catch him off-guard, but, after only a second of thought, he answered, "No. I don't want you to do that."

"Why?"

"Because you know they don't want to hear from me."

"I know Marcus doesn't, but I know Austin would want to see you. And who gives a damn what Marcus thinks, we should call him anyway," Caleb said.

"No," Julius said, grabbing his son's wrist, as if Caleb were trying to break from the room to try to call them that moment. "Don't call Marcus, and don't call Austin. I don't want them coming to see me just because I'm dying. I don't want pity to bring them out here, when they otherwise wouldn't come."

"Dad . . ." Caleb said, moving to stand.

"Don't!" Julius said firmly, tightening his grip on his son's arm. "Do you hear me? Don't. Promise me."

"I won't call them," Caleb promised.

Caleb left the room, closed the door gently behind him. He went straight downstairs and into the living room where the TV was playing, the volume down low. Cathy must've left it on, Caleb thought.

Caleb pulled out a slip of paper with all of Austin's numbers jotted down on it, and looked it over. He wasn't about to let his father die without seeing his other sons, especially when Caleb knew it was what Julius truly wanted, even though he said otherwise. Caleb picked up the phone, and dialed Austin's number.

The phone rang several times, but there was no answer, so Caleb hung up. He looked up briefly at the television screen, noticing the picture of an exploding gun behind the speaking anchorwoman, the words, "Shooting Deaths" above it. Caleb shook his head with pity, then picked up the phone again, looking down at the paper in his hand, and punched in Austin's cell phone number. Three rings and Austin was on the phone.

"Austin, it's Caleb."

"I was wondering if you just took off to Hollywood, became a star, and didn't tell anyone," Austin said playfully.

"I wish," Caleb said, getting to the point. "The real reason I'm calling is . . ." and Caleb felt his next few words hanging up in his throat, unable to dislodge them. He casually looked up to the television again, and now he saw a black-and-white photo of his friend Thomas on the screen.

"Caleb, you there?" Austin said.

"Hold on, Austin," Caleb said, reaching for the remote, frantically thumbing the button till the volume of the anchorwoman's voice was almost deafening.

"The body of fifteen-year-old Thomas James was found late last night in an alley near Ventura Street. He had been shot several times in the chest. The killing is believed to be drug-related," the anchorwoman said.

39

The tiny funeral home was packed tight with brown weeping faces. People filled the pews, filled the folding chairs lining the back and side walls, and stood wherever they could. Sonya had sat the entire time, her arm tightly around her son, thanking God that it wasn't him in that coffin at the front of the room.

"We got to go to a funeral," Curtis had said the day before, walking into their bedroom, his head held low. He grabbed her hands, and said, a huge lump in his throat, "Thomas, the boy who used to work for me. They found him dead. He was shot."

To Sonya, Curtis looked as though he was on the verge of tears, she could feel his hands trembling in hers, but still there was this overwhelming suspicion that he had something to do with it.

Curtis lowered his bald head into her lap, and she just looked down at him, still holding his hands, but barely, the question on the tip of her tongue. And for a moment she thought she wouldn't ask him. She told herself that there was no way that he would be involved with something like that, even though he did sell drugs, and even though this was the exact type of thing that happened in this business. But before she realized it, the words were coming out of her mouth.

"You didn't have anything to do with that, did you?" she said very timidly.

Curtis looked saddened, astonished, as if he couldn't believe that she would ask such a thing of him. A tear fell from his eye, and Sonya was sorry that she'd ever questioned him.

"I'm sorry, I shouldn't have . . ."

"No. You want to know?" Curtis said, lifting his head, staring very seriously into Sonya's face. "Then I'll tell you."

"Curtis, no," Sonya said, trying to stop him, already convinced, or at least, telling herself she was.

"I had nothing to do with this," Curtis said, pausing thoughtfully between each word. Do you understand?"

"Yeah, I understand, and I believe you, baby." And she did, and that would be the end of it.

The morning of the funeral, Curtis walked into their bedroom and told Sonya he was going to drop Jahlil off at a friend's house.

"For what?

"What, you forgot? The funeral I told you about is today," Curtis said.

"I know it is. That's why you aren't taking him to his friend's house. He's going," Sonya said with authority.

"No, he's not. He don't need to be seeing some boy not that much older than him lying dead in a casket."

"That's exactly what he needs to see. He needs to know that life out there ain't all fun and games. He needs to know that there are consequences that people face for everything they do, and sometimes those consequences are being killed. So you might as well go back and tell Jahlil he needs to start getting dressed."

Sonya looked down at Jahlil sitting beside her now, dressed in his little black suit. He looked out, with little interest, toward the front of the room as the preacher spoke. She knew it was because he was only ten years old, and at that age, kids thought they were invincible, thought death could not touch them, that they would live forever. He probably felt he had no business there, this had nothing to do with him. But Sonya was hoping somehow, a memory, some tiny lesson, would stick in this boy's head. It would be something, so in the future, if he was ever in a situation where he was about to make a move that could threaten his life, he would think about this day. He would think about the little boy lying in the casket, his body like stone, his eyes closed, never to open up again. She hoped he would remember that image, and something told her he would, for when they stood over the casket to view the boy's body, Jahlil stared down at him for quite some time. And when she took his hand and pulled him away so the line could continue, her son yanked on her arm, getting her attention, then whispered up to her, "Is he really dead?"

Sonya stopped right there, knelt down to him, gripping him by both shoulders, looking directly into his eyes, and said, "Yes, baby. He's really dead, and he'll never come back again. Never."

Afterward, everyone was filing out the doors, standing in front of the building, shaking their heads at what a tragedy this all was. Some of the people were dabbing the drying tears in the corners of their eyes with handkerchiefs, others talking, moving toward their cars, most waiting to pay their respects to the boy's mother, a beautiful woman in a wheelchair.

"This is all so sad," Sonya said to Curtis, who was standing on the other side of Jahlil, holding one of his hands, as she held the other.

"I know. I know it is," he said, somewhat disconnected, looking over the crowd of people. "I need to go and pay my respects to his mother. I'll be right back." He left, pushing past a few people, and then he was swallowed into the crowd, disappearing from Sonya's sight.

She turned back around and jumped at the sight of the man who was standing right near her, his face pushed near her ear.

"He killed him, Sonya," the man said, and it took her a second to realize that this man was Caleb, because he looked so frantic, so paranoid, like someone was after him, trying to kill him.

"What are you doing here?" she asked, shocked, pulling Jahlil behind her back.

"He killed that boy, Sonya," he said, grabbing her by the arm. "He was the one I told you about the other day, the one that sold drugs, Thomas James. He killed him," Caleb said, more anxiety in his voice now, pulling on her arms, as if trying to get her out of there.

"Hold it," Sonya said, yanking away from him. "Who killed him?"

"The man you're with," Caleb whispered loudly, angrily, as if she knew this all along, but refused to accept it. "I need to get you and Jahlil out of here."

"No," Sonya said, shaking her head. "He didn't do it. He told me."

"But he did, Sonya," Caleb said, trying to again convince her to follow him out of there.

"Mommy, what's going on?" Jahlil asked, looking up at Caleb, and then at her.

"Nothing, baby."

"C'mon. We gotta go," and now Caleb was looking this way and that, over his shoulder, as if planning to plot a route for their getaway.

"Caleb, we aren't going nowhere!" she said, wrestling with him.

"Mommy, where are we going?" Jahlil said, looking up nervously into her eyes. But before she could answer another question was posed to her.

"Yeah, where are you going?" Curtis said, standing just behind them. He looked Caleb up and down, a menacing glare on his face. Caleb turned and regarded him the same way.

"Why did you do it?" Caleb asked.

"Do what?" Curtis said.

"You could've let him go. You could've just asked him to give you the money back he took from you, and you could've let him go. Why did you have to do it?"

"Do what?" Curtis said, laughing casually now, as if the entire line of questioning was ridiculous.

"Kill him!" Caleb whispered harshly, keeping his voice as low as he could, so as not to inform the people standing and passing by them that the killer was there among them.

"What?!" Curtis said. Then he looked to Sonya and said, "Do you believe this? Do you hear what he's saying?"

At that moment, no, she didn't believe it, but she looked at Curtis long and hard, trying to see if he would give anything away that would let her know for sure.

"That boy worked for me. I paid for this funeral. Why would I do something like that?" Curtis said, pressing his fingers into his chest, sounding as if he were the victim. "I wouldn't have killed that boy, because now I have to replace him."

When Caleb heard this, he exploded at Curtis, whipping a fist into his face, sending Curtis stumbling backward into a group of people. Sonya couldn't believe any of this, and when the fighting started, she had pushed Jahlil, hoping he would not get in any of it, or get hurt. The people around them reacted, some moving away from the incident, some rushing over to get a better look. It took Curtis only a moment to recover. He threw a hand to his eye and examined his palm for blood.

Then he set his fury-filled sights on Caleb. He had changed pretty fast, Sonya noticed, from the innocent man who laughed at Caleb's accusations, to the man who was about to charge Caleb, looking as though he wanted to . . . kill him.

He lunged at Caleb, snatching him, rearing back, but his fist was caught from behind by somebody before he could let it fly. He was held and dragged away by three other men, two men wrestling Caleb away as well.

"All right, all right!" Curtis said, insisting that he was calm, demanding release from the men who held him. When they let him go, he looked at Sonya. "Come on. We're leaving," he ordered.

But Sonya didn't move, just looked over at Caleb, seeing the cautionary look on his face.

"I said, come on!" Curtis yelled this time, popping out an arm, urging her to take his hand.

"I'll be home later," Sonya said softly, pulling Jahlil closer to her side.

"What?" Curtis said, a look of disbelief on his face. "You believing that fool. You think that I . . ."

"I didn't say that. I just said that I'll be home later."

"Fine," Curtis blew. "If you want to believe that man, fine. I don't care no more."

He turned, pushed his way back through the crowd, and headed for his car.

40

Because Curtis had to get to the funeral early, Sonya had driven her car as well. Now she offered to give Caleb a ride home. He told her that he didn't need a ride, but wanted to know if they could go somewhere and talk.

"No, we shouldn't do this, Caleb," Sonya said.

"Please, just a few minutes. This is important."

They ended up at a park, the three of them, sitting awkwardly at a picnic table. How odd it seemed to Caleb. This was his family, his child, the woman he loved, yet they sat across from him, their arms crossed, their eyes directed everywhere but at him.

"Mommy, why are we here?" Jahlil leaned near his mother and whispered, but Caleb still heard. Caleb gave Sonya a look, as though he was waiting for her to tell their son the reason.

"Jahlil, go over there for a while, will you? We'll be leaving in just a little bit," Sonya said, placing a hand on Jahlil's shoulder, and directing him toward the swings. Sonya watched as he walked, and when he was out of earshot, she turned to Caleb and said, "I don't want to hear anymore about Curtis killing that boy."

"He did it, Sonya. I know he did it," Caleb said.

"Then where's your proof?" If he did it, why isn't he being carted off by the police right now?"

And that was a good question. After Caleb found out that Thomas had been shot, he had gone to the police to tell them it was Curtis who'd killed him. A huge, white officer stood in front of him, listening intently, seeming ready to spring into action.

"How do you know this, sir?" he asked Caleb. The officer had opened up a pad, and was ready to jot down the information Caleb told him with the pen he was holding in his other hand.

"I just know it. Thomas was skimming money from him, and he was going to tell Curtis that he was going to quit selling for him, and that's why he's dead," Caleb said, trying to sound as convincing as possible.

"Is that all you have?" the officer said, looking at Caleb as though he was wasting his time.

Caleb didn't say anything, while he was trying his best to think of anything more to incriminate Curtis, but that was it.

"I said, is that all you have?"

Caleb nodded his head. "Yeah," he said, disappointed, knowing that it wouldn't be enough.

The officer closed his pad, slipped it into his back pocket. "Call the station when you have more."

Caleb looked at Sonya, and told himself that if she didn't want to believe it, he couldn't make her, but he knew the truth, and somehow, he would make sure that Curtis paid for what he did.

Caleb slid himself around on the bench, turning to look at his son playing on the swings.

"This can't go on much longer," Caleb said to Sonya, still looking at Jahlil.

"What can't?"

"Me living without my son. I want him back, Sonya."

"It's not that easy, Caleb."

Caleb spun back around to face Sonya. "And why not? Because you'd rather have that man raise him, that killer?" Caleb said, shaking his head.

"Why do you say that? Why do you think he killed that boy? He paid for his funeral. He used to work for Curtis, like he said."

"That's right. Used to work for him selling drugs, Sonya. The boy told me," Caleb said, getting up from his side of the table and sitting very close to Sonya. "But that's not all he told me. He told me he was skimming, stealing money from him. Thomas didn't think he knew, but how could he not? I know that's why he killed him."

"You don't know nothing," Sonya said, getting up and stepping away from the table. "With all the shit going on in South Central, I hate to say it, but black boys get gunned down every day, for a million different reasons. And what, you think Curtis has shot them all?"

"No," Caleb said softly, looking at the ground. "Just this one."

"You're crazy. You don't have no proof."

"Okay, so I could be wrong," Caleb said. "But what if I'm not? What if he did shoot that boy, kill him for taking a little money from him? What then? You go back to him like nothing has happened? Let him continue raising our son? What happens when he wants to bring him into the business?"

"That's not going to happen," Sonya said.

"How do you know?"

"I just know it won't."

"Does Jahlil know he sells drugs?" Caleb asked.

"No one ever said he does but you," Sonya said, looking in Caleb's eyes, then quickly looking away.

Caleb paused before speaking again. "Don't play me for a fool. You and I both know that he does. Now answer the damn question. Does Jahlil know?"

"No, he doesn't," Sonya said, giving Caleb a resentful look, as if she would never have known Curtis sold drugs if Caleb hadn't made her admit it.

"And what happens when he finds out?"

"He won't."

"He will. It's just a matter of time. And then what happens when he starts to admire him for all the money he's making, for the respect he gets around the hood, when he wants to be just like him, just like every little boy wants to be like his father?" That last part hurt him to say. He paused for a moment, looking over Sonya's shoulder at his son, realizing the boy didn't know his true father from a stranger.

"And what happens when he's old enough to say that he doesn't give a damn what you think and decides to sell drugs anyway? What happens when he looks into your eyes and says that they can't be that bad because his own mother let one raise him, his own mother lived with one and allowed one to fuck her every night?" Caleb said, and wasn't surprised to feel the hot sting of Sonya's hand as she slapped him across his face.

"You act like you have no faults," Sonya said. "You act like what you did wasn't illegal. You're a criminal just like he is, but worse, you're a convicted criminal." She sighed heavily, shaking her head from side to side, as if this helped her control her emotion. Her face started to fall apart, and she put a hand to it, covering it. "What was I supposed to do? You left me, us, Caleb. I was alone."

"You had my father."

"Your father!" Sonya said loudly. "The only reason he was allowing me to stay there was because of you, and I couldn't accept that."

"So living with this Curtis, this drug dealer, is better?"

Sonya looked up to the sky, then lowered her body back onto the bench. "I don't know," she said, exasperated.

"And what are you going to do now?" Caleb asked. "Because even if you don't want to admit it, I think you know he killed Thomas. You know that, don't you?" Caleb said, lowering himself next to her.

Sonya turned to look at him, looked deep into his eyes, and he knew she was hurting, knew she was lost. He wanted to save her, take her away from all this, but he could not do that, not until she allowed him to, allowed herself to just let go and let him be what he once was to her, what he should be now. Just let go, Sonya, he tried to will her, looking back deeply into her eyes. Just let go. And he moved still closer to her, not touching her, not placing an arm around her, but trying to reach her on another level, the level they once shared. And then she seemed to relax, the tension falling away from her body, the expression on her face softening, and Caleb felt himself being drawn to her. He slowly leaned forward, his eyelids dropping at the same rate at which he advanced toward her, and then felt his lips lightly touching hers. They were trembling, as he felt her body doing, when he placed his hands on her shoulders. He pressed his lips harder against hers, and she did not resist, but seemed to welcome him, her lips softening under his pressure, the trembling and nervousness draining away. Caleb slid his hands from her shoulders, wrapping his arms around her, pulling her in, and still she did not pull away. He continued kissing her, their lips pressed together, and something in her body was telling him that she was comfortable with this, that this is where she wanted to be, where she belonged. He parted his lips, extended his tongue into her mouth, tasted the sweetness that was inside of her, but it was brief, for a moment after that, she was pushing away from Caleb, turning her back, wiping the kiss from her lips with her hand.

"What's wrong?"

Sonya shook her head, turning even more away from him, trying not to let him see her face. "I shouldn't be doing this. There's too much going on right now. Too much that has to be sorted out."

"Then what are you going to do?" he said softly.

"I don't know, she said, looking as though she was about to cry, and then she quickly moved her body around to face the other way, toward Jahlil. She stared at him, love in her eyes, as did Caleb. They shared that moment, admiring their son together, and then Caleb said, "I'm going to go over there now and talk to him about some things."

Sonya looked at Caleb sadly, and he knew she knew what he meant by his statement. But this time, she conceded, nodded her head, and simply said, "Okay."

When Caleb approached his son, the boy immediately started to pump his legs and push forward on the chains of the swing, getting himself going, back and forth, higher and higher. Before he saw his father walking in his direction, he had just been sitting idle in the swing.

Caleb paused just beside him, waited till his son was swinging backward, then crossed in front of him and took the swing next to him. When his son blew by Caleb on the swing, Caleb called out at him.

"How you doin', Jahlil?"

Jahlil whooshed by him again in the opposite direction, not speaking a word, not turning to acknowledge the fact that Caleb had spoken.

Caleb waited till the boy swung by him again. "I want to talk."

"I don't," Caleb heard coming from the blur that streaked past him.

"It's important."

"No."

"Please, Jahlil. Just five minutes. Please."

Jahlil continued swinging, paying Caleb no mind. Caleb sat there for another full minute, hoping he would stop, but he didn't. He has no words for me, Caleb thought, and why would he? In Jahlil's eyes, Caleb was more a stranger than his father, and what could be so important coming from him. Too much had gone on today that Jahlil wasn't clear about. Caleb would approach him another time, when his mind was calmer, and he was more open to what he had to say.

Caleb got up from the swing and started to walk away, but stopped when he heard the sound of feet dragging against the ground. Caleb turned around to see that Jahlil was slowing himself down on the swing, bringing himself to a stop, amid a cloud of gravel dust kicked up by his feet. Then he sat there, looking at Caleb, not inviting him back over, but not looking like he would get up and walk away if Caleb approached him again.

Caleb walked back over and sat down. "Thanks for stopping."

Jahlil didn't say anything, just looked out in front of him, his hands still high on the chains of the swing.

"I got something to tell you. Now you probably already heard something about this, but that's not the way I wanted it to come out. I wanted to be the one to tell you, so I'm going to do that now. Jahlil, I'm your father. You might not remember, because I've been away, and that man Curtis has been there pretending to be your father. But he's not. I am. You know that, don't you?"

Caleb expected his son to jump from the swing, to look shocked, surprised, upset, angry, astonished—something—by the news, but his demeanor did not change a bit. He continued sitting there, as if he had been deaf and hadn't heard a single word Caleb said.

"Did you hear me, Jahlil? I'm your father," Caleb said again.

"Yeah, I know that," Jahlil said plainly.

"I'm sorry. You shouldn't have found out that way," Caleb said sadly, moving closer to his son, trying to rest a hand on his shoulder.

Jahlil abruptly moved away from his father's touch. "I heard it when you and Curtis were fighting, but that's not the way I know. A long time ago Mommy had a picture, and sometimes when she looked at it, she'd cry. She never would show it to me, so I sneaked into her purse and found it. It was you in the picture."

Caleb didn't know what to say. There were words that he felt he should have been speaking at that moment, but they hung in his throat, refusing to come out.

"I've always loved you, son."

"You left me," Jahlil said, disappointment in his eyes.

"I was in prison. I had no choice," Caleb defended.

"I don't care."

"I went there for you, for your mother. I tried to steal money so I could take care of you. It was wrong. I know that now, knew it then, but it was because of how much I loved you that I was taken away from you, do you understand?" But Jahlil was looking away from him now, turning sideways in the swing, trying to distance himself as much as he could from his father.

"Jahlil, I love you," Caleb said, but Jahlil did not respond. Caleb got up from his swing, placed himself in front of his son, knelt down to his eye level, and said it again. "Jahlil, I love you."

"I don't care."

"And while I was away, I only thought of you. I couldn't wait till I was able to see you again. You got to believe me," Caleb said, reaching out and taking his son in an embrace. But Jahlil fought him, pushed his hands into Caleb's chest, tried forcing him away, but Caleb held him even tighter.

"Let me go," Jahlil cried, squirming, trying to push his way out of the swing and away from his father.

"No, Jahlil, don't," Caleb said, looking into his son's face, seeing how distraught he was, how terrified he seemed of his own father. He rocked his son, trying to calm him, calm himself, because hearing Jahlil wanting nothing more than to get away from his own father was breaking Caleb's heart.

"Let me go, please. Let me go," Jahlil cried. And then he started calling for Sonya.

"Mommy! Help! Mommy!"

And Caleb quickly turned his and Jahlil's bodies so his son could not see his mother. Caleb whipped his head around to Sonya, knowing that by now she was probably standing, probably racing toward them in full strides. Caleb was still holding his son tight, and when he looked to Sonya, he threw up one of his hands, waving her off, stopping her at half the distance to them. He shook his head at her, giving her a look he knew she could understand the meaning of. Let this happen, the look meant. It has to, for both of our sakes. Sonya backed off, holding her position there.

Jahlil was still screaming for his mother, still fighting to free himself.

"Shhhhhhhh! Shhh! Shh! Jahlil, Jahlil." Caleb spoke over his son's ranting. "I'll let you go if you just calm down, if you'll just listen to me, okay?"

But Jahlil kept yelling, kept resisting, till Caleb had to take him by the shoulders and gently shake him. "Jahlil, now stop it! Stop it, okay!" he said, looking sternly into the boy's eyes. Jahlil went silent, and Caleb didn't know if it was in response to what he'd told the boy, or because he was finally out of his father's embrace.

"Now, I just want to let you know that I love you. I always have, and I always will. I would do anything for you. I'd kill for you. Do you know that?" Caleb asked, serious about the statement, looking for Jahlil to answer his question, but no answer came.

"And just let me tell you one more thing, son," Caleb said, scooting a little closer to Jahlil. "No man will ever love you as much as I do. Because, no matter what, I am your real father, and I always will be. I was there when you were a little baby, and I know it's hard to remember now, but when you're in your room at night, and it's dark, just try to think back, okay, son? Try to think back, and I know you will remember us. Will you do that for me?" Caleb said, laying a hand against the back of the boy's neck, just under the curve of his skull. "Will you?"

A long moment passed before Jahlil nodded his head, the fear, the uncertainty, that was present in his face before was still there, but he seemed to be coping with it just a little better.

"Will you do that for me, son? Please," Caleb asked again.

Jahlil looked into his father's eyes, and swallowed hard.

"Yes," he said. "I guess."

41

There was nothing resolved during the exchange he'd had with his son, but the boy at least knew who he was now, Caleb thought as he drove away from the park. He knew who he was, and that meant there was at least a chance that he could still win Jahlil back.

He was happy at this moment, happier, it seemed, than any time since he'd been out of prison, when all of a sudden, a car raced in front of him, then skidded to a stop. It wasn't a car, actually, but a jeep, the black Range Rover, and the door quickly popped open and out jumped Curtis, looking singed with fury. He sped over toward Caleb. Caleb saw the man coming for him, tried to reach for the button to trigger the electric locks, but before he could reach it, Curtis was already swinging the door open. He snatched Caleb out by his shirt, and dragged him around to the vacant parking lot behind an abandoned store. Immediately, he hit him across the jaw with a hard shot that sent him back-pedaling, his arms whirling into a stack of garbage cans. Caleb fell in between them, the cans falling on top of him.

"Motherfucker, fucking around in my business," he heard Curtis growling, as he wrestled with the cans, trying to recover. When he'd cleared them from himself, he saw the huge man bearing down on him, and before Caleb could get up, he was snatched up again, and, this time, hit in the gut with two punches, knocking him to his knees. But he was only allowed to remain there for a second, because Curtis had ahold of him again, forcing him backward against the brick wall of the building.

"You wanna mess around with my family when you ain't got no place there, hunh?!" he spat, slamming Caleb into the bricks of the building, where pain was sent radiating through his entire body. He steadied Caleb there, reared back, as if he intended on punching Caleb's head through the wall, but when he threw his shot, Caleb dodged the blow. Curtis's fist struck the wall with a dull thud. He screamed out in agony, shaking the limp hand wildly. Caleb quickly seized the opportunity, ramming a knee into the big man's crotch.

Curtis doubled over, grabbing himself with his good hand, the other shoved into his armpit. Caleb then pulled back, punching him across the chin with everything he had. The blow knocked Curtis to the ground, where he rolled on his stomach, both his arms disappearing under him. Caleb bounded over to him, grabbed him by the back of his shirt, ready to finish him off, but when he flipped him over, Caleb was met with the barrel of a Glock to his face. He immediately froze, throwing his hands open, raising them a little to his sides.

"Yeah, motherfucker. What you got to say now?" Curtis said, pulling himself up from the ground, the gun steady on Caleb's head. "Tough man now?" he said, on his feet, walking Caleb backward, till there was nowhere else to go. Caleb's body was plastered against the wall behind him.

Curtis rested the cold tip of the barrel against the soft space between Caleb's eyes, which crossed as they focused on the tool that could take his life.

"No. Look at me, motherfucker," Curtis ordered. "'Cause it's me that's gonna kill you. The gun is just what I'll use to do it."

Caleb refocused on Curtis, saw his menacing face there behind the huge weapon, looking as if he wanted nothing more than to pull the trigger.

"You fucked things up for me," he said, his face twitching with anger. "All I wanted to do was be good to Sonya and Jahlil, to my family, but you come fucking shit up for me."

"They're my family," Caleb corrected defiantly, the gun still pressed to his head.

"Not no more, motherfucker. And I'm gonna see to it," Curtis said. Then he pulled back, striking Caleb hard across the head with the gun, knocking him unconscious, sending his body falling to the cold hard ground below.

42

Austin's plane landed a full twenty minutes before it was scheduled, so he stood at the airline gate, his carry-on bag in one hand, his
trench coat draped over the other arm, waiting to spot Cathy. She insisted on coming to pick him up, even though he'd told her he'd take a
cab, and now as he stood there, looking down the long corridor, his
mind drifted back to Caleb's phone call.

"You have to come to California," Caleb had said, and he sounded as
if something was tragically wrong.

"Come to California for what?" Austin said.

"It's Dad."

"What are you talking about?" Austin said, frustrated at his brother's
vagueness.

"Dad. Our father. You have to come here."

And Austin couldn't believe what he was hearing. He hadn't seen or
heard mention of his father in five years, the day that Austin had
brought Julius over to Marcus's house so the two of them could talk
things out, patch things up, so they could all be a family again. At least,
that's what Austin wanted. But after their talk, his father came back and
told him that it wasn't going to happen after all. He said it wasn't time
yet, maybe sometime in the future, "Maybe in five years." So this was
the phone call, Austin thought. They would finally reunite now, and
Austin could feel excitement and happiness growing within him.

"Are you telling me that you're staying with Dad? He was the friend you grew close to in prison?"

"Yeah," Caleb said sullenly.

"And now he wants me to fly out there," Austin said. But Caleb must have heard the excitement in his voice, because his next words to Austin were, "It's not for what you think. He's sick, Austin. He's gonna die soon."

Caleb told Austin that their father had had cancer for some time now, had it even when he came to Chicago that time five years ago.

"Then why didn't he tell me? Why the fuck are you just telling me?!" Austin yelled into the phone.

"Because he didn't want you to come out here just because you felt sorry for him. He doesn't even know that I'm calling you. But I know he wants to see you before he . . ." Caleb paused for a moment, " . . . before he dies."

So Austin had to fly to California, he'd told Bethany.

"I want to come and live with you when you get back, Daddy," Bethany had said. She had been out of the hospital for a few days now, and she was getting back to herself again. The only signs that something had ever happened were the casts on her arm and opposite leg, but they didn't seem to slow her down much anymore, for she was up hobbling about, oftentimes making a game of it, calling herself a one-legged pirate.

"Why do you want to live with me?" Austin had asked his daughter. She wasn't looking up at him, but nervously painting a deep, dark blue circle on her cast with a Magic Marker.

"Because Mommy never lets me see you. She's always mad at you, and whenever I ask to see you, she always says she'll think about it, and she never does."

"Baby," Austin had said, laying a hand on his daughter's, stopping the circular motion of the fat marker. He politely took it from her, placed the cap on it, and set it aside.

"It's not your mommy's fault. She really wants us to see each other all the time. She wants nothing more than that. The only reason she says she has to think about it is because she knows how busy I am. And the reason we never actually saw each other is because I was just too busy."

"But you're here now," Bethany said, looking at her father with big sorrowful eyes.

"That's right, sweetheart," he'd said, brightening some. "And when I get back, we're gonna see each other as much as we want to. Mommy says it's okay. We talked about it, and I'll make as much time as you want me to."

Bethany had leaned forward as far as the cast on her leg would allow, and wrapped her arms around her father's neck.

"Do you promise?" she'd asked.

"I do," he'd said, thinking, as long as Trace comes to her senses like she said she would.

After that, Austin had stepped into his son's room to tell him the news. Troy was sitting cross-legged in front of his TV, playing a video game. He was able to pull himself away from the space monsters long enough to give Austin a hug, and say, "Love you, Dad. See ya when you come back." Then he'd picked back up his controller, took the game off pause, and went back to the annihilation on the screen.

Austin saw Cathy from at least fifty yards away, and was surprised that her face had remained that firmly implanted in his memory. It was five years ago, when he'd first and last seen her.

Now she was standing in front of him, smiling widely. She threw her arms around his neck and gave him a huge hug.

"It's so good to see you again, Austin."

"His room is right there," Cathy said, pointing down the hall.

"And you said you didn't tell him that I was coming?"

"No. If we had, he would've fought us all the way on it. It's better to do it this way," Cathy said, pressing a hand against his arm, gently taking it away, then leaving him there in the hallway to deal with the flood of emotions he was experiencing by himself.

Austin wished Marcus was there with him, but even after all of his attempts to convince him, Marcus wouldn't budge.

"Fuck that!" he yelled angrily, pacing quickly across his living room carpet. "Fuck him. I'm not going."

"I thought you had a talk with Reecie. What about the things you said to me?"

"That's regarding you and Caleb. He's entirely different," Marcus said, pacing by him again. "No way."

"Marcus, he's dying."

Marcus halted in his tracks, looked over at his brother. "What did you say?"

"I said he has cancer, and he's going to die soon. You should see him," Austin said, and he could tell by the way Marcus seemed to have drifted off momentarily that the news affected him. But then he snapped out of it, and started pacing again.

"I don't care. Doesn't change things."

"Just forgive him, Marcus," Austin said. "What harm would that be doing to you?"

"It wouldn't be doing me any harm now, but it would clear him of all the harm that he did to us in the past, and I want him to take that with him to his grave. And if it's at all possible, I want him to suffer with that for eternity."

Austin looked at his brother sadly, shaking his head in pity. "You shouldn't feel that way. You have to let that go and forgive him, just like you did with us, because his misery is almost over. If you continue on like you're doing, you and only you will be the one that'll be suffering."

"Then I'll be the one that has to deal with that."

His father's door was there in front of him, four or five steps away. Austin took two of them, stopping, unable to take the last two just yet. It's been five years, he told himself. Five years since his father showed up at his door, after disappearing twenty-five years before that, to ask to be Austin's father again. Five years since he'd lost his father for the second time, and now to find out he was dying. He would have taken him back though, for he still loved the man. Always loved him, regardless how Marcus felt. His father could have done no wrong that was bad enough to make Austin never want to see him again.

But standing there now, just outside his door, Austin didn't know how he would feel on seeing him. Would he have sympathy for the man, or would Austin's heart be cold, unmoved by what lay before his eyes? There would only be one way to tell, he thought, forcing one leg in front of the other, and that was to finally see him.

At the door, Austin softly knocked, moving his ear very near the door, listening closely for his father's response.

"Come in," the raspy voice said from behind the door.

Austin pushed the door open and stood there within the frame, staring at his father. Julius had his head turned in the opposite direction. Blankets were pulled up to just below his chin, and all Austin could see was the back of his head and the imprint of his sickened, shrinking body under the covers.

"Cathy, could you . . ." Julius started, slowly turning his head toward the person he obviously thought to be his wife. He stopped, the next word caught in his throat, a stunned look on his face when he saw it was his son Austin standing there, looking just as stunned as his father.

"Hello, Dad," Austin said, not knowing what else in the world to say.

Julius didn't respond at first, just lay there, looking at his son, with sunken, tired eyes, his chest heaving, his mouth open, in attempt to pull as much air in as possible.

"Austin," Julius said. He said it with a finality, as if he'd known this day would come.

Austin saw his arms moving under the blanket, saw Julius trying to raise up to his elbows, sit up some in bed, but he was too weak and he struggled, breathing even harder after the effort. Austin moved quickly over to him, grabbed a pillow from the chair beside Julius's bed, lifted his father's head, then placed the pillow behind it.

"How's that?" Austin said, holding a smile on his face, although he wanted to do nothing but cry at the sight of his father.

"Better," Julius said, smiling slightly, too. "Sit down."

Austin pulled the chair as close as it would come to the bed, and sat down, leaning over to his father.

"I guess you know everything. I'm sure Cathy told you."

"Yes, I do," Austin said solemnly.

"I didn't tell you about this myself because . . ."

"No, no," Austin said, placing a hand low on the blanket, feeling for Julius's hand through the cover, finding it, then holding and squeezing it. "Caleb told me everything, and I understand, Dad. I just hope you don't mind me being here now."

Julius moved his head slowly back and forth on the pillow. "No," he said, smiling wider now. "I'm so happy, son."

"Good. Because I'm going to be here by your side every minute from now on."

43

When Caleb finally came to, he felt pain throughout his entire body, and when he moved, the dull throbbing intensified into sharp jolts of pain attacking his back, his midsection, his jaw. He lay on his stomach, his arms stretched out in front of him, his face pressed against the hard pavement. When his eyes opened slowly, darkness lay outside of them, and he could not place where he was at first, didn't know why he was outside, behind some building, lying amid a pile of scattered garbage cans.

He gently pushed himself up on trembling arms, found his way to his knees, then looked around some more, as he searched his mind, his memory, telling himself that he had to remember. He got to his feet, his legs shaky, his head spinning, heavy with an unshakable pain. He raised a hand, placed it gently on the side of his skull, and felt a huge lump protruding there. How did that happen, Caleb asked himself, and then, all of a sudden, it came back: Curtis standing over him, the words that Curtis last said. "Not no more, motherfucker. And I'm gonna see to it." And then the blow to the head.

Curtis would see to it that Sonya and Jahlil would not be Caleb's family anymore, but what the hell did he mean by that? Caleb asked himself, starting to worry, starting to wonder how long he had been stretched out, unconscious, on the ground. He wondered, as he climbed back in Cathy's car, what Curtis could have done in that time, what he was capable of doing, period. He had to find out. He had to get to Sonya's house to warn her, if it wasn't already too late.

There was no sign of the black Range Rover when Caleb pulled up to Sonya's house, but he wished there was, for even though it would have meant Caleb would have had to tussle with the big man again, at least he'd be there, and not racing off with Sonya and Caleb's son.

Caleb quickly ran to the door, ringing the doorbell, then pounding on the door with the side of his fist. He anxiously spun a nervous circle when no one came immediately after he knocked. Then he raised his fist again, but the door opened, halting him with his fist raised over his head.

It was Sonya, and a sense of relief fell over him, but it lasted only a moment, till he saw the expression of fear she wore. Something was wrong, but they could talk about that after he had them in the car, and on their way away from there.

"Caleb," Sonya said, looking shocked to see him.

"Is he here?" Caleb said, looking past Sonya, into the house.

"Caleb . . ." Sonya tried to speak, but Caleb cut her off.

"Is Curtis here?" he said, his tone more pressing than before.

"No, but . . ."

"Sonya, just grab Jahlil, and come with me. Don't say nothing. Just grab him and come on," Caleb said, inside the house now, looking around for his son.

"He's not here, Caleb," Sonya said, sounding on the verge of crying.

Caleb spun, looking at her with wide eyes. "What?"

"That's what I've been trying to tell you. Jahlil's not here, and I think Curtis took him."

He couldn't believe it. He couldn't believe she'd allowed some drug-dealing killer to take their son. If she never had hooked up with this man in the first place, none of this would have ever happened, he thought.

He rushed toward her, grabbing her by the shoulders, shaking her, his fury starting to get the best of him. "How do you know this? How do you know?"

Because his stuff is gone out of his drawers, and so is Curtis's. He's gone, Caleb," Sonya sobbed, feeling weak now in his hands.

He wanted to strike her, wanted to hurt her for being responsible for hurting him, but he just snatched his hands off her, ran to the phone, and started dialing.

"I'm calling the police," he said to Sonya, punching in the last number one.

"I already did that," Sonya said from somewhere behind him. "They said they couldn't do nothing until after twenty-four hours."

Caleb turned to her, the phone to his ear, no one picking up yet. "Did you tell them that you know he took him? Did you tell them that our son is in danger?"

"They said I couldn't know that for sure, because Curtis was my boyfriend, because he's been living with me, raising Jahlil. They said I had no proof they weren't just out doing something." Sonya lowered her face into her hands, shaking her head, seeming to know that some of this was her fault.

Caleb slammed the phone into the cradle. "Goddammit!" he yelled. "Do you know where they are, where they could have gone?"

"I don't know, Caleb. He never told me where he went, where he worked. I thought and thought," Sonya said, pushing away the quickly falling tears. "But I don't know."

"Shit!" Caleb yelled, storming over to her, rage in his eyes. "This is all your fault. I told you. I told you this could happen," he hollered, Sonya cringing as he hovered over her.

"Don't say that, Caleb. Don't. I didn't want this to happen, you know I didn't. If something happens to him, if something . . ." and then she trailed off, her words becoming cries of pain and anguish. She held herself, looking as though she was trying to retreat within herself to a place where none of this was happening. And Caleb knew he was wrong for chastising her like that, knew it did no good but to relieve some of his frustration, and it did very little of that. He wrapped his arms around Sonya, held her tight.

"Nothing will happen to Jahlil. Don't worry," he said. "Because I'm going to get him back, if it's the last thing I do."

44

It was no longer his body, Julius thought, as he lay there in bed, in the dampness of his own sweat. It was cold, heavy, immovable, like a slab of granite. He opened his eyes, something he only did on occasion now, and looked down in front of him, seeing what was once so familiar to him, his body, stretched out beneath the blanket. It would no longer respond, and when it did, it was only by doing things that hurt him, that made him miserable. His body was nothing more than a nursery for pain and disease.

These thoughts were occurring in his head, just as he was coming out of his sleep. Sleep was the place where he was most of the time now. Cathy dropped drugs into his mouth these days as if they were nothing more than colorful, candy-coated goodies, and he was thankful for them, for when he was conscious, his body stayed alive with pain, torturing him unbearably, many times making him wish for . . .

Julius shut his eyes and concentrated on his breathing, which was no longer his either. It was no longer smooth and fluid, but heavy and choppy, and when he tried to take a deep breath in, he could hear things moving around in his chest, things that were never there in the past, that weren't supposed to be there now, and he knew it was the disease. An image of a thick black-and-brown goo growing in his chest, crusting his heart and lungs, often came into his head. It was the cancer, and he didn't know if his picture was accurate or not, but he knew it was there, and it was growing, swallowing him up. It was moving faster than he'd ever thought it could. But then, this was a good thing, he told himself, tried to persuade himself.

It was a good thing, because how many more times did he want his wife to have to come in here, rolling him like a log to clean the plastic-covered mattress of the fresh brown liquid shit that had just seeped from him. How many more times did he want to come to from his drug-induced sleep and see the faces of his two sons too slowly come into focus, looking down pitifully at him, and not able to say any more than a grunt or a groan to them.

How many more times did he want to feel like a burden, feel like the chore that had to be done, but that no one wanted to do? Feel like the strange thing upstairs, behind that closed door, lying, dying, in that bed of this disease, breathing out contaminated breath that stunk up the entire room, and part of the hallway that led from the room. And how long did he want to exist in a life where there was no more pleasure, but only pain, where he could no longer do for himself, but had to be done for? How long did he want to continue to live, when he knew that while he was alive, what he would most be remembered for was the pain he brought the family who was now watching him die? He wouldn't think about it anymore, Julius told himself, for his head was starting to hurt from the questions, but then again, had it already been hurting? The sickness was so overwhelming now that he had forgotten how it felt to be well.

A soft knock came at the door, but before Julius could respond to it, the door was being pushed open, and a second later, Caleb was standing over him, looking frightened.

"Dad," he said, taking one of Julius's hands in his own and squeezing it. His son bent over and kissed him lightly on the forehead. "You're not that hot today," Caleb said, and Julius stretched a smile across his face.

"Are you okay? Do you need to be changed?" Caleb asked, moving to reach for the draw sheet that hung over the edge of Julius's bed, to turn him and check.

"No. No," Julius said, surprised to hear his own voice so clearly, and he realized that today must have been one of the occasional days when the disease momentarily forgot about him. He didn't need to be changed, and even if he were sitting in a small lake of crap and piss, he wouldn't have wanted to be touched. He had already caused them enough trouble.

"Okay, okay," Caleb said, backing off. He grabbed the chair, placed it near the bed, and sat. He looked at his father, in his eyes, and Julius could tell something was bothering him, something pressing so hard on his son's heart that he needed to speak about it.

"What?" Julius said, his voice heavy and somewhat groggy.

"Nothing," Caleb said, shaking his head. "I just came to see you. See how you doin' today." Caleb looked away, as though afraid his father would read his thoughts if he had access to his eyes.

"Caleb that's—" and then Julius was hit by a short coughing fit. Caleb immediately stood from his seat, was looking about the room, about the small table beside the bed. "Can I get you something, Dad?" he said frantically.

Julius found the strength to point in the direction of the water, which Caleb picked up. He cupped the back of his father's head and fed him some of the water.

"Now what were you saying, Dad?"

"I was saying that's bullshit," Julius said, his head still elevated in his son's hand. Caleb lowered him, put down the glass, then sat again.

"Tell me," Julius said.

Caleb looked up at the ceiling, shook his head helplessly.

"There's nothing to tell. Everything is fine, and I don't want to burden you with any more than what you're dealing with."

"Tell me!" Julius ordered, in as loud a voice as he could summon.

Caleb shook his head, truly not wanting to bother his father with this, knowing that it would only worry him, but he, Caleb, could not hold it in.

"He's got Jahlil, Dad. And I don't know where they are. Sonya don't know."

"Caleb, Caleb. What are you talking about? Who's got Jahlil?" Julius said, trying to calm his son down.

"The man killed a boy who was selling drugs for him, Dad," Caleb said, ignoring his father's questions. "And now he's got Jahlil. He's got Jahlil, and I came to let you know that I'm going to get him, and just in case something happens . . . I just wanted to let you know that . . ."

Julius saw the anguish on his son's face, the unbearable pain that he must be feeling. If only he could have gotten out of that bed, if only he wasn't struck down by that illness.

"Did you call the police?" Julius said.

"We did that, he hasn't been missing long enough. I'm going to find him, but I spoke to Jahlil a few days ago, and . . ." Caleb trailed off.

"And what?" Julius said.

"And I think he looks at that man as his father. I don't know if he wants me to even come and get him." Caleb lowered his head and gripped his father's arm, and Julius knew he was trying to draw some strength from him.

"I left him. I wasn't there for him, and this man was. And now, just out of the blue, I expect to get him back. What if he doesn't want me to be his father again?"

Caleb dropped his head upon his hands, which rested on his father's arm. Julius raised his other hand and placed it on his son's head. Why did this have to be happening to him? He wasn't the one who had wronged his son, I was, Julius thought. It just wasn't right.

"Go get your son," Julius said, his voice low.

He felt his son stir under his palm. Caleb lifted his face. "But what if . . ."

"It doesn't matter, son. You didn't want me when I came for you, but I didn't hear it. Whatever it took, I was going to get you back. You are my son, and I am your father, as Jahlil is your son, and you his father. It doesn't matter if right now he doesn't want you back. You show him that you love him, do whatever it takes to get him back, and he'll see that with you is where he belongs."

Caleb leaned over and hugged Julius. "Thanks, Dad," he said.

"No, thank you, son," Julius said, releasing his son from the hug. "And don't worry. Everything will be the way it's supposed to be."

Caleb stood from the chair, placing it back against the wall. He walked out the door, and was shocked to find Austin standing there in the hallway, looking as though he had been there some time. Caleb pulled the door gently closed, then tried walking around Austin, as if he weren't even there.

"Hold it," Austin said, grabbing him by the arm. "Where you going?"

"Out to grab something to eat," Caleb lied, not looking into his brother's face.

"You're a damn liar, little brother. I heard everything that went on in there. You're going to try to find Jahlil, and I'm going with you."

"No, you're not," Caleb said, pulling away from Austin's grasp. "You don't know what's going on. You don't know this guy. He sells drugs, he's killed someone."

"That's all the more reason why you shouldn't go alone."

Caleb shook his head. "No. Hell no. This is my business. This has nothing to do with you."

"This has enough to do with me. Jahlil's my nephew, don't forget, and you're my brother." Austin rested a heavy hand on Caleb's shoulder. "I told you, if there was anything you needed help with, I'd be there for you. Well, I'm keeping my promise."

Caleb nodded his head, looking as though he realized it was foolish to fight his big brother any longer. "Are you sure?"

"Yeah," Austin said. "I know what it feels like to be deprived of your children."

45

Caleb pulled Cathy's Volvo wagon to a stop in front of a small house.

"Why are we stopping here?" Austin asked, looking through his window at the run-down house.

"The boy that Curtis killed lived here," Caleb said, looking at Austin, then toward the house. "He used to work for Curtis, and hopefully his mother knows where that is. This is the only place I know to come to. If she doesn't know nothing," Caleb said desperately, opening the door, stepping one foot out, "then I won't know what to do."

Caleb stood in front of the door, Austin by his side, praying that the boy's mother had the information he needed. He raised a trembling finger, pushed the doorbell, and waited. The door opened and Thomas's mother stood gravely behind the screen, not saying a word, just looking up at Caleb and his brother. Then, after a moment, she said, as if she had been pulled out of sleep, "It's late."

"I'm sorry. I'm Thomas's friend, Caleb. Remember me?" Caleb said, reaching for the handle of the door. "There's something very important we have to talk to you about. Can we come in?" Caleb asked, his hand still on the door, but waiting for permission to open it.

The woman didn't respond right away, as if giving herself time to think it over. Then she looked into Caleb's face, and even through the screen mesh, she obviously saw the urgency in his eyes, and said as she slowly stepped backward away from the door, "Come in."

"I'm sorry for your loss," Caleb said, once inside. "Thomas was a good young man. I liked him a lot."

She spoke a barely audible and insincere, "Thank you," looking away from him uncomfortably.

"This is my brother Austin," Caleb said, breaking the tension. Paula James gave Austin a quick look, then directed her attention back to Caleb.

"Can you just tell me why you're here?" she said impatiently.

"The man your son worked for, do you know who that was?"

The woman looked bewildered, perturbed, for even being asked such a question, so late at night, regarding her son, who wasn't even alive anymore. Caleb could understand that. Her son had been slain, she'd made peace with that fact, and had seen him lowered into the ground. And now, here was Caleb showing up at her door, as if carrying a shovel, wanting to dig him up again, reawaken those painful feelings.

"No. I don't know who he is, never met him, and what does that have to do with anything?"

"Do you know where Thomas worked?" Caleb asked, ignoring her.

"He worked in some warehouse stacking boxes. I told you that before," she said, anger building in her voice, on her face. "What does that have to do with you being here?"

"What warehouse?" Caleb said, becoming impatient himself, and he was stepping nearer to her now, bending some, bringing his face closer to hers, so she could see how important his need to know was.

"I don't know. I was always sick. It's not like I was picking him up after work," she snapped.

"Well, you're his damn mother, you'd think you'd at least know where your own son worked," Caleb barked back.

Paula gasped, rearing back, as if she had actually felt a physical strike by the insult.

"I'm sorry," Austin said, grabbing Caleb's arm. "He didn't mean that. He's just upset."

"I don't care what his excuse is," Paula said, turning toward the door. "I want you out of my house."

"No. We can't do that," Caleb said, quickly rushing around her to block the door. "We can't leave until you tell me where that ware-house is."

"I told you, I don't fucking know!" Paula screamed, seeming to be coming unraveled. "And why is knowing for who or where my dead son used to work so damn important?!"

"Because the man your son used to work for killed him!" Caleb yelled down at her. "And he has my son now." After the words flew from his mouth, he regretted them. It wasn't what he wanted to say, but had to say. She hadn't known that Curtis had killed her child, and he was never going to tell her, because what good would it have done her. But it was out now, and it hit her like a strong blow to her abdomen, pushing the wind out of her, making her slump over some.

"I'm sorry," Caleb said, moving to touch her, but stopped when she moved away from him. "I'm sorry you had to find out that . . . "

"How do you know?" Thomas's mother said all of sudden, raising her head, and looking into Caleb's eyes. "How do you know it was him that killed my boy?"

"I don't have any proof. But the day Thomas told me he was going to tell Curtis he was going to quit was the same day the police found him. Something just tells me that it was him."

Paula looked up toward the ceiling, as if trying to find her son up above her, searching for some sort of verification of what the man stand-ing before her was saying. She looked back into Caleb's eyes, then said, "And now this man, he has your son?"

"Yes. That's why I need to know. If you have any idea, if you ever heard Thomas mention where he used to work, I need for you to tell me," Caleb pleaded, looking desperately into her eyes.

The woman didn't speak, just let her lids fall heavy over her eyes. Caleb had no idea what was going on. He turned to Austin to see if he had more of an idea of what was happening, but by the look on his face, he was just as clueless as Caleb. Caleb turned back, looked into Thomas's mother's face again, saw the faint movement of her eyes un-der the thin skin of her lids. He waited a moment longer, and then she opened them.

"Crenshaw and Helms, or Hines Street. Something like that," she said, as though the names had not been recovered from her memory, but given to her by some spirit. "I think I remember Tom saying something like that."

"Is that all you can remember?" Caleb asked.

"That's all I remember, and I don't even know if that's right. I'm sorry," Paula said, her apology sincere.

"No. Thank you. That's more than we have," Caleb said. He took her hand, held it in his for a moment, then moved toward the door. Austin shook her hand as well, thanked her, and turned to leave.

"If it was him," the woman said, halting Caleb and Austin just as they were about to walk out the door, "if that's the man that killed my boy, please find him so he can pay for what he did to my son."

Caleb looked back at the woman, standing there saddened, trying to remain strong, fighting to stop the tears that he knew would come after they were gone. Her son was all she had. He was killed for a reason that could never justify the action, and now she had nothing but her pain and memories.

"We'll find him," Caleb said softly, closing the door.

They took the stairs quickly to the car. "So you think you know where this place is?"

Caleb didn't answer, his eyes focused on something far away, his mind somewhere else.

"Caleb," Austin said, taking his brother by the arm, stopping them in the walkway just outside the house. "Do you think you know where this place is?" he repeated, pausing between each word, as if he were speaking to someone with a learning disability.

"Oh, yeah," Caleb said, snapping out of whatever trance he was in, but still looking somewhat distant.

"You all right?"

"Yeah, I'm fine. C'mon. We gotta go."

Caleb unlocked his door and jumped in the car, while Austin walked around. Caleb started the car. Austin tapped on the window, catching Caleb's attention, pointing down to the lock, motioning him to unlock it. But Caleb didn't move, just shook his head slowly.

"Unlock the door, Caleb," Austin said firmly.

"I can't do that, Austin." Caleb spoke loudly enough for his brother to hear him through the car's windows. "This is my business, and you don't need to be involved."

"Open the fucking door, Caleb! Don't be a fool," Austin yelled, now banging on the hood of the car.

"Sorry. But don't worry," Caleb said, throwing the car in gear. "Everything will be all right," he said, stepping on the gas and pulling away from the street. He focused again on finding the warehouse and finding his son. He didn't look back in the rearview, for if he had, he would have seen Austin still running after him, waving his fist, yelling words he couldn't hear, an expression on his face that suggested he thought Caleb may have been driving to meet his death.

But Austin will be all right, Caleb thought, as he turned a corner. He had his cell phone with him, so he could call a cab to take him back to Julius's house. And that's where he needed to be, not out with Caleb, because if Caleb's life was in danger, he didn't want to bring his brother into it, and risk getting him hurt as well. If someone's life had to be sacrificed for Jahlil's life, it would be Jahlil's father's and no one else's.

46

Marcus feverishly tossed the papers about his drawing table, looking for the doctor's number. But it wasn't there, and he was condemning himself for not having it at his bedside like every other little thing, waiting in preparation for the moment that happened just three minutes or so ago.

Marcus thought it was a dream, for dreams like this came a lot now, considering how close his wife was.

"Marcus," he heard Reecie say in his dream. She was very large now, her middle protruding out, hanging round and low, her arms swinging slow and wide around her huge belly as she walked like a very fat man. They were outside, strolling along a gravel path, alongside a small blue pond, Marcus's attention on a large white bird perched in a tree some distance away from him.

"Marcus," Reecie called again. Marcus only grunted a response, still eyeing the big white bird, as he continued sleeping on his back.

Then Reecie grabbed his arm, shook him. "Marcus. Marcus," she called, trying to get him to look out on the pond, but he had no interest. He pulled away from her in the dream, and turned away from her in real life, rolling over onto his side, scooting away from her on the bed.

But she wouldn't let him watch the bird—wouldn't let him sleep, and she tugged at him again, trying to get him to look at the water, trying to pull him over to it. And then, in his dream, with his head still turned up toward the bird he had now recognized as a stork, Reecie was saying something, going on about the water. Saying something about that she wanted him to look at the water because it wasn't working, or that it stopped. It was nonsense, Marcus thought, as he tried to comprehend why there was a stork high up in the tree above him, looking down at him like it was actually about to speak to him.

But Reecie wouldn't let Marcus alone, and she continued to tug at him, dragging him over to the water, and, outside of his dream, he was rolling over, turning to face his wife, slowly coming out of his sleep, but still seeing the gravel walk, the pond, and the stork.

Then she said it again, obviously realizing her husband didn't understand her the first time. "Marcus, my water broke. It's time." Now there was no misunderstanding. Marcus's eyes shot open, he bolted upright in bed, yanking his hand away from the warm wetness that had soaked Reecie's side of the mattress.

He jumped out of bed, landed on his feet, his arms spread out, his head whipping back and forth across the room, looking as though he expected them to be attacked.

"Okay, okay," he said nervously, turning around in two frantic circles, not knowing what to do first. "We're ready for this."

"Marcus, calm down," Reecie said, scooting over to the edge of the bed. "We are ready for this. You made sure of it."

"Okay, okay, that's right," Marcus said, rushing over to Reecie's side, placing a hand behind her, helping her off the bed. "Are you okay, can you make it?"

"I'm fine," Reecie said, wincing slightly against a mild labor pain. "Let's just get to the hospital."

Marcus helped her stand, and was ready to grab his jeans and shirt and get dressed, but when he pulled away from her, Reecie's knees buckled and he felt her stumble, almost fall to the floor. Marcus wrapped both his arms around her, catching her, lowering her back to the bed.

"Whoa. Are you okay?" he said, looking directly in her eyes.

"Yeah. I'm fine," Reecie said, her breathing slightly more forced than normal. "I'm just a little dizzy."

"Your pressure is low, Reecie," Marcus said, concerned, placing a palm to her forehead to see if she was warm.

"No, it's not. I'm fine. I just got up too fast. Now help me up, before I have this baby on our bedroom floor."

Marcus helped her up to her feet and stood beside her, clinging to her like a father trying to teach his infant daughter to take her first steps.

"Marcus, let go. I'm fine," Reecie said, pulling away from him. "Just get dressed."

Marcus got dressed in less than thirty seconds, sliding into his jeans, whipping on his shirt, and jumping into his socks and shoes. He grabbed Reecie's "pregnant bag" out of the closet; it was packed and waiting for just this moment. He shouldered it, grabbed the keys to the car off the nightstand, threw on his jacket, then started toward Reecie, because it looked as if it would take her forever to pull on that pair of sweatpants.

"No, don't you dare. I can do it." Reecie looked up at him, baring her teeth like a wild animal whose food was being threatened. "Are you ready?"

"Yes. Everything is ready. I got your bag, got the keys to the car. All I need is you."

"Did you call the doctor to let her know we're coming, so she'll be there by the time we get there?" Reecie said, pulling the huge wide waist of the pants high on her belly and loosely tying the drawstring.

"Damn! I almost forgot that. What's the number?"

"I have it in my purse somewhere," Reecie said, walking over to the purse, which looked more like a duffel bag.

"That's okay, because I know how long that'll take. I have it written downstairs on my drawing table. Just stay right here, and I'll be back for you."

"Marcus, I'll just come down. I'm almost ready," Reecie said, sliding her purse strap over her shoulder.

"No," Marcus said, shooting a finger at her. "Just stay right here, and I'll come back up for you.

So now Marcus was attacking his desk, throwing papers that once covered his table into the air. They fell to his feet, but not one of them had the doctor's number on it. Just the other day, he had used the number to call the doctor. He had placed it back on the table, just where he knew he could find it, but now it was gone.

Reecie, Marcus thought to himself, and he couldn't help but smile, because he had told her a thousand times not to come in there and organize his work space. But she'd do it anyway.

"A cluttered desk is the sign of a cluttered mind, and you shouldn't have anything on your mind but me," she'd say.

Marcus pulled open the drawer to the side of the table, shifted some of the stray pages and envelopes about, and there it was, the doctor's number, jotted across a blank page in black marker. He snatched the phone from its cradle and punched in the number. Marcus looked at the clock on his desk, and it was a few minutes past 1 A.M. The phone rang once, then twice, and Marcus thought to himself that Reecie's doctor would be pissed being awakened at this time of night. But she was just going to have to be pissed, he thought, because his wife was about to pop out his little baby boy. Marcus caught himself smiling again, when he heard Reecie calling.

"You find the number?" she yelled from the top of the stairs.

"I found it. I'm calling her now," Marcus yelled back, walking as far out of the room as the phone cord would allow him. He was just outside the door, unable to see her.

"Well, I'm coming down."

"No, Reecie. I said don't move," Marcus instructed, and he was about to put the phone down, rush out to her, and help her down, when a groggy voice came on the line.

"Hello."

"Did you hear me, Reecie?" Marcus called, ignoring the doctor's voice.

"Yeah," he heard his wife pout.

"Doctor, it's Marcus Harris, Reecie's husband. It's time," he said, filled with a nervous, excited energy.

"Are you sure?"

"Oh yeah. Her water broke, and I practically drowned in my sleep."

"How far apart are her contractions?"

"Marcus," and that was Reecie calling again from the top of the stairs.

Marcus pulled the phone away from his ear, pressed it against his chest, and hollered out to his wife. "Hold on. I'm on the phone with your doctor. I'll be up in a second."

"I'm sorry. What did you ask me?" Marcus said, bringing the phone back up to his face.

"How far apart are the contractions?"

"I don't know, but . . ."

"Marcus," Reecie yelled again, but Marcus cut her off before she could say another word.

"Reecie!" he yelled, and with some force this time, making sure that she understood him. "I told you I'm on the phone with your doctor and I'll be up in a second."

"I'm sorry again," Marcus said into the phone.

"Don't worry about it," the doctor said. "Just bring her in and I'll meet you there."

"Great, so we'll . . ." and before Marcus could say another word, he heard a loud, heavy tumbling, so forceful that he not only heard it but felt it. And with each bump and thud, as though it was crashing closer to him, it got louder, heavier. He felt it in his feet, for the vibrations trembled the walls of the room he was standing in, traveled through the floor and into his body, shaking every inch of him with the realization of what was happening. After it had finally stopped, after the last heavy thud had dropped, Marcus listened, but there was nothing but silence.

"Oh, my God!" Marcus breathed. His heart dropped from his chest into his stomach and ceased to beat. He could not breathe, and he just stood there in a shock-induced trance, clutching the phone to his head, because he knew very well what had happened.

"What was that?" the doctor asked, startled. The noise was so loud that she must've heard it, too.

"It's Reecie," Marcus's words funneled out strangely slow and composed, even though complete horror was racing through his body. "I think she just fell down the stairs."

"What!" the doctor screamed into the phone. "See if she's okay!"

Marcus threw the phone down and ran out the room in the direction of the stairs, but stopped just before turning the corner that would put him directly in front of the stairway. He stopped there because he didn't have to turn to know what happened, because he could feel a presence just around that corner, the way you can feel if someone is behind you even if you didn't hear them place themselves there. He felt her weight lying there on that floor, could feel her being there, and he was so frightened, because if she was . . . if their baby was . . .

He ripped the thoughts from his mind, and tried to strengthen himself as much as he could for what he was about to face, and then he turned the corner.

It was as he knew it would be, as he saw it in his mind, his wife's body there at the foot of the stairs, her body, flipped, turned over, her back to him, her right arm slung out behind her back, then disappearing somewhere in front of her. Marcus threw himself down to her, calling her name, then he saw the other arm. It was wrapped around her belly, loosely cradling their baby, as if in a final attempt to protect it.

47

Caleb was not as lost in the dark maze of giant, metal-sheeted buildings as he thought he was going to be. After finding the intersecting streets he was looking for, the building jumped right out at him, prompting him to slow his car, cut off the headlamps, park some distance away, and turn off the engine.

The warehouse before him was the place, wasn't really even a warehouse, but a small shack, something like a large garage. He knew it was the place, for it was the only building on the large lot. The lights were on inside, the double doors of the place were swung open, and there, just outside the door, was Curtis's truck, the back hatch open, the brake lights glowing red.

Caleb knew what was taking place. The man was packing up, he was leaving, most likely planning on taking Caleb's son with him. He was relatively sure of this, but it was confirmed for him when he saw the big man come out carrying a box, which he slid into the back of the Range Rover. Then he saw Jahlil run out the door and hand something else to Curtis to put back there as well.

What did he tell my son? Caleb thought, sitting behind the wheel of the Volvo, crouching some now, so as not to be seen. Caleb knew he hadn't told Jahlil the truth; I'm stealing you away from your mother, and you'll never see her again, or he would have never gone along. Caleb had to stop them before they finished packing and Curtis whisked his son away forever.

He dug his hand into one of the baggy pockets of his jeans and brought out the bundled hand towel. He unfolded it, revealing the butcher's knife that was inside, the knife he had slid into his pocket before leaving Julius's house. But how foolish he felt, sitting there with this knife in his hand. What did he expect to accomplish, wielding nothing more than a sharpened piece of metal when he knew that Curtis had a gun?

Caleb focused on Curtis and his son. They had brought some more boxes out, Curtis slipping them into the back of the truck, then he said something to Jahlil. Jahlil said something back, causing Curtis to laugh and rub Jahlil on his head as they walked back into the building.

He acts as though Jahlil is his son, Caleb thought, feeling jealousy creeping into his body, as he looked on through narrowing eyes. He waited until they were inside for a moment, then he popped the door of the car and crept out, and was about to make his way toward the building, when he saw the interior dome light of the car was still on. He quickly scrambled back inside the car, reached up and switched the light off, looking over his shoulder, out the front window, his hand still raised and on the light switch, making sure that Curtis hadn't seen him and wasn't racing after him with guns drawn.

As Caleb made his way to the building, he heard their voices from inside, heard Curtis talking about how much fun they would have once they were gone.

"And when is Mommy coming?" Caleb heard Jahlil ask.

"In a week. I left her a ticket, and she knows exactly where we'll be. She's coming in a week," Curtis lied. Caleb wrapped his hand around the handle of the long, wide knife, calling on what courage he had, preparing to face this man and take back his son.

"So why isn't she coming with us now?" Jahlil asked.

"Because . . ." Curtis started to answer, but swung his head around when he heard Caleb now standing behind him say, "Because she doesn't know that you're leaving, son."

"Dad," Jahlil said, shocked, turning to see his father.

Caleb stood there in the center of the small warehouse, the knife still in his hand, large boxes around him pushed off into corners and against the walls. But what caught his attention were the scores of large, square plastic bags, filled fat with the white powder Caleb knew could only be cocaine. They were stacked in front of Curtis in layers, one atop the other, like sandbags in preparation for a tremendous flood. He had one of them in his hand, about to drop it into a deep box, when Caleb came in.

But what was even worse were the guns. Six of them, neatly laid out, their barrels all turned in the same direction, each gun equal distance from the next, as if on exhibit. They sat on the table just beside Jahlil. It was from there that Curtis grabbed one of the guns and pointed it at Caleb.

"What you doing here, motherfucker?" he said, his arm extended, the gun held firmly in his hand. He looked Caleb over, then let his eyes fall quickly to the knife he was wielding. "And what you gonna do with that knife? Carve you a turkey?"

Caleb ignored the question put to him and raised his arm, extending a hand out to Jahlil. "Come here, son. Let's leave."

Jahlil didn't move, didn't show signs that he was about to. Curtis moved over beside him, placed what he was trying to make appear like a fatherly embrace around Jahlil, but Caleb knew it was more of a head-lock to keep his son from leaving.

"I don't think so. He don't want to come with you."

"Look," Caleb said cautiously, taking a step toward them. "I don't want any trouble. I'll even put down the knife," and he stooped down and set it on the floor.

"Oooh, I'm so relieved you did that," Curtis said sarcastically.

"I just want my son back," Caleb said, his hand now in front of him, his palms open.

"He ain't your son no more," Curtis said, raising his voice, tightening his grip on Caleb's son. Jahlil didn't react at all. He just stood there and let himself be held, looking blankly at Caleb.

"This here is my boy. I raised his ass for the last three years. I took his ass in when you went off to prison and couldn't do shit for him. I be-came his father then. Isn't that right, Jahlil?"

Jahlil didn't answer Curtis, just continued staring blankly at Caleb.

"That's right," Curtis continued, as if Jahlil had answered him. "I gave him years of my life, invested in him, and I'm not giving all that back just because you pop up out of the blue and want to play Daddy again."

"I'm not playing Daddy," Caleb said, still taking slow, tiny steps forward. "I am his daddy, and it didn't just happen in three years. I gave that boy life. And we talked about why I went away to prison," Caleb said, directing his attention to Jahlil. "I explained that to you, didn't I?"

"Don't look at him," Curtis directed.

"I told you that I still love you, that I always loved you, didn't I say that, son?"

"I said, don't fucking look at him, motherfucker," Curtis yelled, raising the gun again, jabbing it at Caleb, as if he were firing imaginary bullets into him.

But Caleb couldn't do that, because he felt as though he was making a connection to his son. His son was staring straight into his eyes, as if in a trance, and Caleb knew his words were affecting him, so he continued talking, not paying any mind to Curtis's ranting, or the threat of the gun being pointed at him.

"Son, look what's in front of you. Those are drugs. That's what this man does, don't let him tell you any different. He sells that death to people, to kids like you, and doesn't care that it makes them sick."

Jahlil looked down at the bags of white powder in front of them, his eyebrows furrowing some, as he was regarding them in a way he never had before, looking at them in the light that Caleb cast upon them.

"I said shut the fuck up!" Caleb heard Curtis yelling again, but the voice seemed far off in the distance, because he wasn't listening to it, because he was looking into his son's eyes, and nothing could tear him from that.

"And this man is lying to you. When he said your mother was going to meet you out . . ." and then Caleb was ripped from that bond, regardless of how strong it was, for Curtis had rushed over to him, and slammed him over the head with the butt of his gun, dropping Caleb to his knees. He threw his hands over the place on his head where he'd been struck.

"I told you to shut the fuck up. He ain't going back with you. He ain't going nowhere but with me." Caleb heard Curtis speaking, and again he sounded far off, but not because he was focusing on his son, but because the blow to Caleb's head sent him somewhere very close to blacking out, and he was finding his way back now. Still on his knees, his upper body folded over them, his hands still gripping his skull, he opened his eyes, feeling the dizziness subside. There before him, he saw red circles of his own blood, plopping down to the cement, and he felt the warm trail oozing between his fingers. But it wouldn't stop him from letting his son know all that was going on.

"Your mom's not coming with you, Jahlil. She doesn't even know where you are," Caleb said, raising his head, a thin line of blood extending from his hairline, stretching down the center of his face.

"Don't listen to him, Jahlil," Curtis said, now looking over at Jahlil, running to him, as if he could distract the boy, physically stop him from hearing Caleb's words.

"She's worried sick. She was crying, wanting to know what happened to you, that's why I came. I came to bring you back, son. Just come with me," Caleb said, extending a blood-covered hand.

Jahlil looked confused, as though thoughts and loyalties crashed about in his head, but he stirred at Caleb's last request, taking a step from the place where he had been standing.

When Curtis saw that, he yelled at Jahlil. "You stay your ass right there!" Then he rushed over to Caleb, and again swung the weapon down upon Caleb's head, collapsing him to the floor. After he had fallen on his belly, Curtis pulled back and kicked him in the ribs, flipping Caleb's beaten body over, whereas Jahlil cried out, "Curtis, don't," cringed, and shed a tear after seeing Caleb's bloodied face.

"I'll kill you!" Curtis yelled, standing over Caleb, pointing the gun straight down at him. "I'll kill you right here, motherfucker, you say another word to him."

Caleb rolled over onto his belly, then weakly pushed himself to his knees, wobbling some, his head throbbing, blood running into his eye, stinging him there. He composed himself as best he could and said, "I know you'll kill me." Then he looked past Curtis, to his son, and said, "He will kill me, Jahlil. I know he will, because he killed Thomas James."

Then Caleb felt the cold pointed barrel of Curtis's gun dig into his skull.

"That's it, motherfucker," Curtis said, and he wasn't yelling anymore, but speaking calmly, as though he had changed into a different person, from a man who shouted threats to a man who carried out promises. "You say one more word and you're dead."

And Caleb halted for a moment, knowing that Curtis wasn't lying, feeling that the man would not hesitate to pull the trigger and blow his brains out all over the floor in front of his son. Caleb saw the explosion, the blast of red and white flash from his torn head, saw his body slowly fall to the ground, and he was snatched back to when Ray Ray was hit with those shotgun slugs, peeling through him, ripping his life away, sending him to the ground, where he cried, bled, and pleaded for the last moments of his life. Caleb was snatched back into prison where he was held as those men mercilessly drilled themselves into him until he blacked out on that cold cement floor, bleeding profusely from his anus. And then he was pulled back to when he saw Thomas's body in his mind, lying there dead, after being pelted with countless gunshots.

Caleb thought about all of this death, this pain, as he sat there on his knees, feeling the barrel of that gun continue to bore into his head, and he could not deny that, in one way or the other, he'd caused those deaths, and the punishment he received while in jail, although excruciating, now seemed as if it wasn't enough. He thought back to the faces of Ray Ray's parents. The torment that was on his mother's face as she pulled at his shirt with her fist, telling him that it was his fault that her son was dead. And then the promise she had Caleb make. That he would repent, that he would do something to make up for her son's death, but he had fallen short, failed, and a child was dead because of it.

So now, as Caleb looked up at Curtis standing behind the huge gun, intent to kill him written all over his face, Caleb thought of his options, and the repercussions of those options. He could not say another word, pull himself up off his knees, walk away, and save his own life. But what would happen after that? Curtis would take his son, and somehow, Caleb knew that years from now, his son would be selling drugs, dealing with guns, and ultimately, he knew Jahlil would be lying dead in some alley, or on some curbside, his insides seeping out into the gutter, and Caleb couldn't allow that. He would do anything to prevent that, including giving his own life to save his son's. Caleb could take the bullet, he thought, allow his son to witness his own father's death, and that would truly reveal the man that Curtis was. It would send Jahlil fleeing from him, having nothing ever to do with that man, drugs, or guns. Caleb would be giving his life to save that of his son's, and it would be worth it. He would be saving Jahlil's life, but not only that, repaying his debt to Ray's parents.

So when Caleb opened his mouth to speak again, he was not scared, wasn't even feeling the barrel of that gun pressed into his temple. Caleb looked out, trying to see his son, but he could see nothing, for all that was before him was a bright whiteness, and faint images of him as a child, his mother smiling down at his face, his mother and his father chatting over coffee. And then said words, words that he didn't even hear because of how loud his heart was beating, but knew the words were about Curtis killing that boy again, words that somehow he knew Jahlil would hear, even though they did not reach his ears.

But what Caleb did hear, loud and clear, was the cocking of the weapon just beside his head, heard as the bullet slipped into the chamber, heard Jahlil's voice scream out, "Daddy!" and seemed to echo forever all around him. And then he heard the huge explosion, blotting out all other sounds, and then all went black.

48

"This is the place, right here," Austin told the cabdriver, after seeing the shack and the truck parked out front. He threw a twenty-dollar bill at the man and jumped out of the cab, ready to run in, hoping it was not too late. But just when he slammed the door, he heard an explosion coming from the building.

Austin froze, questioning himself as to if it was the slamming of the door that had made that noise. Praying that it was, but knowing that it wasn't, he ran toward the double doors of the shack, only able to hope that his brother had not been hurt too badly, because he knew, just knew, he had been the one the bullet had been directed toward. Unable to shake the image of his brother's dead body lying out before him, all Austin could think was, I wasn't able to tell him that I loved him. I told him that would never happen again, but it has. I didn't tell him I loved him. I broke my promise to him.

When he finally entered the building, his worst fears had been confirmed. Caleb's body was stretched out across the cement floor, blood dripping down his face. Austin, in shock, took a slow step toward him, for some reason only now taking in the entire picture, and seeing the other man's body, lying almost on top of Caleb. Jahlil was standing just a short distance behind him, a smoking gun in his hand, a look of extreme shock on his face.

"Jahlil," Austin said, softly. "What happened?"

"He was going to kill Daddy," Jahlil said, his hands and arms trembling under both the weight of the gun and the reality of his action. "So I shot him."

"You shot who, Jahlil?" Austin asked nervously. "You shot who?"

"Curtis," he whimpered, allowing the gun to drop from his hands, where it fell heavily to the ground.

Austin looked back over to the man named Curtis, then quickly over to Caleb, whom he saw slowly start to move. Austin raced over to him, pulled him by his arms, trying to drag him up to his feet.

"You aren't shot? You aren't dead?" Austin said, still fearful, but excited that his brother was even moving.

Caleb looked up at Austin, his face a mess, smeared with blood, and shook his head. "Un huh," he breathed. "I thought I was, but . . ." and he paused a moment, as if trying to recall. Then, with the recollection, he quickly looked over the place, trying to find his son. "Jahlil," he said, after finding him, opening his arms for the boy to run into them.

"What are we going to do?" Caleb said, holding Jahlil in a tight embrace, looking down at Curtis's dead body. "How are we going to explain this?"

Austin looked around, saw the table loaded with drugs, the guns on the table just beside that. He walked over to Caleb, gently pried Jahlil from his father, and looked down into the boy's face.

"You said this man . . ." Austin said, looking in Jahlil's face, but pointing a finger in the general direction of Curtis's body, " . . . was going to kill your father. Correct?"

Jahlil nodded his head, still looking slightly frightened by all that just happened.

"So you killed him to save your father?"

Jahlil nodded again, this time a small, "Un, hunh," coming from him.

"And are you okay with that? Do you know that you didn't do anything wrong, but kept something wrong from being done? Do you know that, Jahlil? You know that you're not a killer, but a hero for saving your father's life?"

Jahlil swallowed hard, as if trying to accept the burden of now being a hero. He nodded his head again.

"Good," Austin said.

"You still haven't said how we're going to explain this," Caleb said, sounding worried.

"After we take you to the emergency room, we'll call the police, and we'll tell them the truth. That's how we'll explain it. Nothing illegal has been done on our part. Everything will be fine."

Caleb reached for Jahlil, placed both hands on his shoulders.

"Son, you saved my life," Caleb said, feeling a lump grow in his throat. "There was a time when I thought I'd never see you again, when I thought you'd never want to see me, and I guess I could've understood that, because I left you. But now, here you are in my arms, and you saved my life, son. I'll never do anything that'll have me taken away from you again," Caleb said, a single tear rushing down his cheek. He pulled his son into his arms, and held him as if he would never let go.

"I love you so much, son. Don't you ever forget that. I love you."

"And I love you, too, Dad," Jahlil said, holding his father just as tight.

On the way home, Austin pulled out his cell phone. "I'm going to call Dad and Cathy and tell them that everything is all right, and that we'll be home soon." He looked up into the rearview to see Caleb holding his son in his arms.

Austin pressed in the number and waited for someone to pick up. After so many rings the machine answered. He immediately hung up the phone, telling himself that that was odd, and punched redial. When the same thing happened, he told himself to go ahead and speak to the machine, thinking that Cathy must have been busy doing something for his father, and she would call him right back.

"Cathy, Dad, it's us. Everything is fine, but give me a call as soon as you get this." He disconnected the call, still feeling as if there was something not right.

"What's up?" Caleb said, leaning forward from the backseat, obviously seeing the perplexed look on his brother's face in the rearview mirror.

"Oh, nothing." Austin shook it off, setting the phone on the passenger seat. "No one picked up. Cathy must be busy. But she'll call right back."

As if prompted by Austin's words, the phone rang.

"Told you," Austin said, reaching for the phone. "Cathy?" he said, a slight smile on his face. Then, all of a sudden, the smile was gone, and Austin was pressing the phone against his ear, as if trying harder to hear the words Cathy was saying.

"Okay. All right. Don't worry," Austin said, making a wild U-turn in the Volvo that tossed Caleb and Jahlil a bit in the backseat. "We'll be right there."

"What? What's going on?" Caleb asked, again leaning forward on the seat.

"It's Dad. They're at the hospital, and she doesn't think he'll make it through the night."

49

It was all his fault, Marcus kept telling himself, as he sat alone in the hospital's waiting room. He had been there two hours now, and had heard no word on what was going on, and even though he did not like not knowing, something about that comforted him. If the doctors were still in there, feverishly working on his wife, on his child, that meant they couldn't be out here telling him that they had both died.

The thought stung Marcus with a sharp pain. It had been a thought that he had been denying for the two hours that he had been sitting there. It was something that he kept trying to tell himself, convince himself, was not a possibility, but he had to accept that it was. It had entered his mind when the paramedics rushed Reecie, still unresponsive, out of the ambulance, toward the double doors of the emergency room, still hollering instructions to one another, one working on Reecie, the other trying to do what he could to make sure the baby was still all right.

During the entire trip from Marcus's house to the hospital, Marcus yelled out, trying to get answers, as the truck dodged in and out of traffic, its sirens blaring overhead, Marcus, the paramedics, and everything in the truck being tossed back and forth.

"What's wrong with her?! Will my child be all right?!" Marcus shouted, grabbing either of the two men, both of whom batted his hand away, trying to continue working. They seemed not to want to answer him, and Marcus wasn't sure if it was because they were too busy trying to save his wife and child, or if it was because they didn't want to tell him that his wife was dying even as they frantically worked on her.

Once inside the hospital, they rushed her to surgery, on the order of the first doctor that the paramedics relayed all of Reecie's information and vital statistics to. Marcus couldn't understand what was being said, couldn't decipher all the medical jargon, but he could tell by the tone of the paramedic's voice, the grim look on his face, that it wasn't good. The doctor's expression darkened as he looked down at Reecie's unresponsive body. He spread open her eyelids with his hands, flashing a light in both of them. He quickly popped his stethoscope into his ears, pressed the listening end to Reecie's chest, then to several areas on her belly. The concern seemed to grow on his face as he moved the instrument around some more, almost frantically, across her belly, looking for something, listening hard to something that it seemed he couldn't find.

"Get this woman to surgery. Stat!" he yelled, as he raised up, jumped behind the stretcher, and started pushing, two nurses rushing to the sides of the gurney, directing the stretcher through the patient-filled hallways of the ER.

"What's going on!" Marcus shouted, running over to them. "What's happening? Is she going to be all right? Is my wife going to be all right?" Marcus asked desperately of the doctor, while running beside them, heading toward a waiting elevator.

"Sir, we're doing everything we can. But right now, we need to get your wife to surgery." And that was all that was said before they rolled his wife into the elevator, leaving him there, not knowing what had happened or what was going to happen.

That was two hours ago, and Marcus couldn't help believing that it was because of him they were there, Marcus sitting in this waiting room, his wife lying there in that operating room, God knows what being done to her, to her child. He could not deny the fact that this was all his fault. If he had just run to her when she'd called. If he'd just helped her down when she'd asked him to, instead of going down to look for that number. And why did he even have to go down there in the first place? The stupid number was in her purse, wasn't it? Didn't she hand him the purse and say that it was there? Didn't he only have to stick his hand in and search a little for it? If he had done that, they would not be here, and his wife would not be going through what she was.

He threw his face down into his hands. What if for some reason the baby wasn't turned the right way, or if the umbilical cord was wrapped around the poor child's neck, or if, regardless how much the doctor tried, he just couldn't pull the baby free from Reecie's body. What if, when he finally did deliver the child, it was just a limp, lifeless body, eyes shut, chest still, its skin a deep shade of blue.

Marcus shut his eyes tight, but couldn't stop his thoughts from running wild. After the baby was stillborn, Reecie would stop breathing. All the machines that monitored his wife's vital signs would blare and scream, informing the doctors and nurses that Reecie was dying. The doctor would race around to Reecie's chest. The nurse would tell him that they were losing her, that her blood pressure was dropping, that there was no pulse. The doctor would call for the defibrillators. They would be thrown into his hands. The nurse would yell that they were charged. "Clear!" the doctor would yell, shocking Reecie, her body jumping in retaliation to the volts her body was given. She would land back on the table. No change. "Clear!" the doctor would cry again. He'd shock her again, Reecie's body flying off the table again, her arms flailing, legs snapping, her back popping, then flopping back onto the table. The doctor would look at one of the monitors, and the line would still be flat.

"Go again," the doctor would say, and he'd zap Reecie three more times, all ending in the same result. Nothing. In Marcus's mind, he saw his child, discarded, lying dead on a cold silver counter in that operating room. He saw his wife's face, her eyes closed, the peaceful expression she wore, just before someone raised the sheet over it, never allowing Marcus to see her alive again.

A ringing jolted Marcus out of his thoughts. He looked down, realizing it was his cell phone. He pulled it out of his pocket, flipped it open, and was about to push the talk button, when he saw just how much his hand was trembling. Get ahold of yourself, he said softly in his mind, then took the call.

"Hello."

"Marcus. It's Austin."

"Austin, this is a bad time right now. I'll have to . . ."

"It's Dad, Marcus," Austin interrupted. "Everyone's at the hospital. He might not make it to the morning. I know it's late, but we were hoping you could catch a flight out. See him before he passes."

Marcus had to fight back the urge to explode at Austin. How dare he ask that of him, considering all that was going on? His wife, his child, were in there fighting for their lives, and Austin had the nerve to ask him to abandon them to fly out to see a father who never cared a thing about him. Julius had only once, in Marcus's memory, even told him that he loved him. How dare Austin ask him such a thing when all this was going on. But he didn't know.

"I can't," was all Marcus said.

"Why not? He really wants to see you, Marcus. Can't you just put all that aside and . . . ?"

"No. I can't," Marcus said, raising his voice somewhat angrily, then settling. He thought of telling Austin why, but they had grown apart so much that telling his brother would be like telling a stranger. He was probably wrong, but something told Marcus that Austin wouldn't care about what he said, wouldn't try to offer to do anything about it, and even if he did, Marcus was pretty sure he wouldn't have wanted the help from him.

"This is just a bad time now," Marcus said calmly, masking his anger.

There was a long moment of silence on the phone. Austin was searching his brain, Marcus thought, trying to find a way to convince him. But there is nothing at all in the world he can say. Nothing at all.

"Well, I called the airlines. There's one flight left tonight, if you change your mind."

"I won't be doing that."

Austin gave Marcus the flight number, its time, and the hospital that they were all at, just in case, he said.

It was a waste of his breath, because Marcus couldn't have cared less whether the old man lived or died, actually hoping that he would die. It would be deserving, considering all that he had done, leaving Marcus's mother, leaving him and his brothers. He deserved to die, Marcus thought bitterly, as a surgeon walked into the waiting room, pulling his paper hat from his head, wiping his sweat-covered brow with it.

Marcus sat there, overcome with fear of what the man might say, his heart pounding wildly in his chest, feeling like a criminal awaiting sentencing.

The doctor came up very close to him and said nothing but, "You can see your wife now."

Marcus stuck his head into his wife's hospital room, and he saw her body lying under the covers, her head turned away from him. He slowly walked in, not wanting to wake her if she was sleeping, not knowing all that she had been through. He took two steps in, placing him just past the narrow hall that led into the room. He stopped there, trying to look over to the other side of his wife, wanting, needing, to know that she was turned over that way because she had their child in her arms, was cradling him or her, and wanted it to be a surprise when Marcus walked in. That had to be what was going on, because he didn't know what he would do if that wasn't the case, didn't know if he could go on living.

He walked closer to her, and she turned over slowly toward him, exhaustion and tears on her bruised and scratched face. There was no baby. Their child was dead, something screamed within Marcus's head, and he wanted to collapse right there. He wanted to fall to his knees, sobbing, beg God, curse God. Why would he take his child like that, when there was nothing more that Marcus wanted, when this was all the family that he had? Why would he do that to him? And then the anger and the hate started to fill his body. The hate for those who had what he so desperately wanted, but didn't know how to appreciate it. Austin, who had two beautiful children he couldn't seem to find the time for. Caleb, who couldn't stay out of prison long enough to raise his child. And Marcus's own father, who just chose not to be there for them. But Marcus was the one who was penalized, the one who had to pay with the life of his child.

He lowered his head, took another step toward his wife, and took her outstretched hand. He looked in her eyes, saw the tears there, saw a look that he couldn't describe—but why should he expect to be able to, considering what she had gone through. How he wanted to tell her that he still loved her more than anything in life. How he wanted to tell her that it didn't matter that they'd lost this child, that they would have another, and everything would be all right. But he just couldn't find the words.

He looked down at her again, and saw a slight smile begin to lengthen across her face. She squeezed his hand, the smile growing wider, as she looked past Marcus to someone behind him. Marcus quickly turned around to see a nurse walking around him, holding a beautiful brown baby girl. She lowered the child into Reecie's arms, then, without saying anything more than a soft, "Congratulations" to Marcus, she left the room.

"Congratulations, Daddy," Reecie said, smiling brightly at Marcus, then at their daughter. "You have yourself a little girl."

50

It would come soon, Julius told himself, because there was no denying it now. He lay weakly in the hospital bed, his eyes closed, letting the drugs make his pain as tolerable as possible. But there seems to be no more pain, he thought, and something told him that it wasn't the drugs that were relieving it, but that this was just what happens to people some hours before they die. They felt no more pain, they became accepting of what lay before them, almost looking forward to what was ahead.

He was resting now, his family all around him. They had been there for hours, because they knew his time had come as well. He was given his opportunity to say good-bye to all of them, to tell them how much they meant to him, how much he loved them.

"I'm so glad . . . you came back to me, son," Julius remembered saying to Austin not an hour ago. He was holding his hand, looking up at him through weary eyes, admiring what a good-looking man he had become. "I just wish I had been . . ."

"Shhhhhh," Austin said, placing a finger before him. "That's done. It's over. We're together now," he said, "And that's all that matters. Okay, Dad," Austin said, trying to smile, but the quivering of his lip, the blinking of his eyes, let Julius know he was near breaking down.

"I love you, son."

"I love you, too, Dad," Austin said, wrapping his arms around his father, burrowing his face into his chest.

His eyes still closed now, Julius thought about his son Caleb, remembered him stepping up to his bed after Austin walked away. He was smiling, looking down at his father as if they were more old friends than father and son.

"Dad," he said, extending a hand down to him. "I got my son back."

Julius nodded his head. "I knew you would," he breathed, trying to stretch a smile across his face as well.

"And Sonya's back. She's right here."

Julius could feel someone reach around and hug him, and then he saw Sonya's face smiling sadly over him.

"It's good to see you again, Mr. Harris."

"You, too," was all Julius could push out, for he was feeling out of breath again. Sonya kissed him on the cheek, then disappeared.

"We've been through it all, hunh, Dad?" And that was Caleb again, and Julius had to refocus on his face. Julius nodded at what his son said.

"We've been there for each other. We saved each other's lives. And to think, there was a time when I never wanted to see you again," Caleb said, looking wistfully into his father's eyes.

"You weren't wrong for that," Julius said softly. "I was a bad father."

Caleb's expression went from reflective to serious. "No, Dad. Don't you say that. You made a mistake is all, and that happens. But when you realized that, you came back. You were there for me as much as you could've been." He squeezed his father's hand tighter, spoke only loud enough for the two of them to hear. "You beat death for me, fought it off until I got out of prison. A bad father wouldn't do that, Dad. A bad father couldn't do that."

They embraced, said that they loved each other. Then Julius said, turning his head slowly, looking about the room, "Where is my wife?"

"I'm right here, Jay," Cathy said, walking up, taking Caleb's place at the side of the bed, taking her husband's hand.

Julius looked up at Cathy and just smiled at her weakly, his eyes barely open.

"You okay?" he asked.

"I'm not going to cry. I love you, but I'm not going to cry," Cathy said, moving her face every which way she possibly could to keep her promise.

"And why not, baby?"

"Because I'm going to be strong for you. Because you prepared me for this, and I'm going to be strong," she said, quickly brushing away tears that welled up in the corner of her eye.

"That's all you've ever been for me. You are the best thing about me."

"I love . . . you know . . ."

"And I love you, too," Julius said, cutting her off, doing his best to raise his heavy arms. He could do no more than open his palms, but Cathy understood, moving into him and giving him a hug. He painfully wrapped his arms around her, remembering that she'd promised him she wouldn't cry, and she didn't. But he knew it wasn't a promise he himself could keep, as he felt the tears start to roll down the sides of his face.

That was a while ago. Just how long, Julius couldn't tell, for time seemed almost beyond understanding now. There were periods when he was awake, cognizant, times when he was asleep, and periods where he felt he was somewhere in between, and he didn't know how long any of those periods lasted.

What he was doing now was just resting, listening to his family move around him, speak softly about him, about themselves. He was trying to conserve his energy, waiting, because just before he closed his eyes, he called Austin over again.

"You said you called him, right?" Julius asked his son.

"Yeah. I called him and told him that there was still a flight out tonight."

"And what did he say?"

Austin paused, looked away from his father a moment, then looked back at him. "He said, he'd be on the flight, Dad. He said he'd get here to say good-bye."

"Good, son," Julius said, smiling up at Austin, but Austin just drew away.

His son was lying to him, Julius knew that, and he kind of chuckled to himself, thinking, why would Austin think he could get away with that? He couldn't when he was five years old, and he couldn't now. But he knew why he was doing it. He wanted his father to think that all of his sons, not just the two who were there, had forgiven him for the horrible thing he had done so many years ago. He wanted his father to go to his grave thinking that there was no more to regret, even if it meant lying to him. But Julius was not upset, because he knew, even though Austin thought he was lying, he wasn't. Marcus would come, Julius told himself, and he didn't know how he knew, didn't know what chain of events would occur that would put his middle son on a plane, but Julius knew it would happen, and he told himself, he would hang on until he was able to tell Marcus good-bye.

51

Not five hours later, Marcus was speeding in a cab away from LAX airport, toward the hospital his father was in. It all struck him when Reecie handed his daughter to him, and he gingerly took her in his arms. He looked down in her little innocent face, and something changed in him, just that fast, something changed, and he felt a weight slip from his shoulders. How beautiful life was, how amazing, how blessed he was to be given this gift, and again he was asking God why him, for at that moment he felt as undeserving as any man could. He was not worthy of holding such a miracle for all the hate that had lived in his heart for as many years as he could remember.

And then he realized how foolish he had been to hold a grudge against his brothers, his father. They hadn't been around for him at one time or another, but that was because they had problems of their own. And even if they didn't, what kind of sense did it make to disown your own brothers when they were all that he had, and when he had worked so hard to keep them together in the first place? It made no sense. And now, and only now, did he truly understand this. Yes, his father had left him, walked out on his brothers, their mother, left them to fend for themselves, but he'd come back to them, remorseful, and trying to reconcile. Marcus could have forgiven him, but he didn't. Marcus held on to his hate for the man, held on to those memories of misery, knowing they would do nothing but keep the flames of hate burning within him. But really, what did the harboring of hate do? How did he truly benefit by continuing to hate this man? He gained nothing.

So as he looked down at his daughter in his arms, beautiful, perfect, she triggered a response in him, jiggled the key in the lock that held his heart closed, ripped the blindfold from his eyes. But now it was so clear to him, now he felt nothing but love, and now he had to share it, he had to let his father know, had to see him, touch him, embrace him, let him know the past meant nothing now.

He brought his daughter up to his face and kissed her softly on the cheek, then lowered her back into his wife's arms.

"I'm sorry, sweetheart, but I have to go."

"Where?"

"To see my father. Austin called and said he might not make it through the night. I don't want to leave you, Reecie, but I have to see him before . . ."

"Go, baby," Reecie said, seeming as if she truly wanted him to go, and he knew she did. "Your daughter and I will be here waiting when you get back."

As the cab raced Marcus closer to the hospital, he wanted to tell someone so badly of his enlightenment that he pulled out his cell phone, and phoned the hospital. He wanted to speak to his brothers, but tell them not to tell his father that he was on his way, because he wanted it to be a surprise. Marcus called directory assistance, got the number, then called the hospital. He got the operator, had him ring Julius Harris's room, but after several rings, no one picked up.

"Try again," Marcus said, but still no one picked up.

Marcus wondered what was wrong, disconnecting the hospital and calling Austin's cell phone. After several rings and then being switched to Austin's answering service, Marcus decided that something was definitely wrong.

"No," Marcus said, shaking his head, smiling some, making a failing attempt to tell himself everything was all right.

When the cab finally made it to the hospital, Marcus paid the driver, then bolted out the door and into the hospital lobby. He stopped at the information desk.

"Julius Harris. Room 305. Which way is it?" Marcus said anxiously to the aging woman behind the desk. She was slowly fingering through a box of cards when Marcus said, "Can you hurry up, please! This is an emergency."

"Catch the north elevators up to three, and make a left," the woman said, ignoring Marcus's rudeness. Marcus turned and ran down the hall, jumped into the waiting elevator, and kept stabbing the number-three button till the door slid closed.

"It's okay," Marcus said to himself, jetting out of the elevator. "Everything's okay." He was sprinting now, and he thought to himself, ten more feet, maybe, around the corner, first door on the left probably. His mind put him there before his body. Moments later, his face covered with sweat, his heart banging in his chest, Marcus stood frozen in the doorway of his father's hospital room.

He looked around, saw Caleb holding Sonya, her head buried in his shoulder, weeping. Austin stood beside them, his face in his hands, his body shaking with emotion. And Cathy, poor Cathy, was on her knees at Julius's bedside, holding on to one of his hands, pulled from out of the bed like the rope of life. She cried aloud, her body rocking back and forth with her anguish.

"No, Jay. No," and Marcus knew, and it felt as if all of the life was racing from him. Marcus ran across the room. "No!" he said, stooping over his father, reaching down to grip his shoulders and shaking him. Julius's eyes were closed, his face shrunken, his head rolling limply across the pillows.

"No! Wake up!" Marcus commanded.

A hand was placed on Marcus's shoulder. Austin or Caleb, he didn't know, and then a voice, "Marcus . . . he's gone."

"No, goddammit! He's not gone. I have to tell him I forgive him. I have to tell him that none of it matters anymore. That I still love him, that I always have, but that I was just too angry to tell him."

And then he felt the hand tugging at him again, a slight squeeze, as if trying to pull him away. But Marcus would not be taken away. After all those years, he finally realized what mattered, and now . . .

"Dad! Dad!" Marcus shook him again, but still there was no response from his father.

"No, motherfucker," Marcus yelled angrily. "You have to hear this. I know now, but you're gone, and you can't hear it. You've left me, just like before. You could stay alive for Caleb, but not for me," Marcus cried. "You've left me again, and now what am I to do? What?!"

Marcus fell to his father's chest, pulling, groping at Julius's body, digging his hands under his father's heavy frame, trying to wrap his arms around him, hug him as tightly as he could.

"Marcus," he heard behind him, and this time it was both Austin and Caleb, trying to pull him away, or trying to comfort him, which he didn't know. But he wrestled them off him, telling them, "He's not dead. He can't be. He has to know that I still love him. He has to know," Marcus said, looking into his father's face, tears dropping freely to the thin shirt that covered Julius's chest. He stared at him for a long moment, how long he didn't know, wishing him, needing him, to still be alive, so he could know that he was forgiven, that he could die with his conscience clear.

And then it happened. It was shallow, faint, but he felt something, something light, like a tap from within his father's chest. There was another one, and then another, and Marcus saw his father's eyes slowly open. They fully opened, and he stared directly into Marcus's eyes.

Although he could feel his father's heart beating, it felt as though Marcus's had completely stopped. "Dad, I love you, and I forgive you," was all he was able to say, was all he feared he had time to say, because he knew that his father had come back only to allow Marcus to say those words.

"I love you, son," he heard Julius say, his lips turning slightly to a smile, and then there was nothing more. His eyes closed, his face went slack, and the tapping within his chest fell silent. But he knew. He knew that Marcus forgave him, and although Marcus had spent so much of his life, so much of his energy, hating this man, he felt as though somehow, he had taken all that away, in just those few words.

Marcus stood and turned to his family excitedly. "Did you see that? You said he was dead, but he wasn't. He waited for me."

Caleb and Austin looked at each other strangely. Cathy looked at Marcus as though she had no idea of what he was saying.

"What are you talking about, Marcus?" Austin said, taking a step toward him.

"Dad. Didn't you see him? Didn't you hear him? He opened his eyes, he said he loved me."

"Marcus, Dad died at least fifteen minutes before you walked in," Caleb said. "He couldn't have . . . you know."

Marcus thought about what his brother said, then about what had just happened between him and his father, and told himself no one else had seen it, because it was just meant for him. This was something that he and his father had shared alone.

"It doesn't really matter," Marcus said for their benefit, moving toward Cathy, Sonya, Caleb, and Austin, opening his arms to embrace them. "It just feels good to be with my family again."

About the Author

RM Johnson is the author of two previous novels, *The Harris Men* and *Father Found*. He lives in Chicago.